CONCEALED

The Book of Joshua

A NOVEL

F. R. "Fritz" Nordengren

ISBN: 0615765912
ISBN-13: 978-0615765914

CONCEALED

To you, the reader.

PART ONE

FALL SEMESTER

Chapter 1

The attack

THREE FLOORS ABOVE THE NORTHWEST parking lot at Grant's Hill College, Professor Joshua Stone glanced around his office and skimmed over the papers on his desk before turning off the lights. It was a few minutes after 6 p.m. and he had just finished teaching his last class of the week. On his way out the door, he flipped the brim of a bobble head doll near his computer and then closed the door behind him. The other offices in the building were dark, as typical for a November Friday on campus.

Just as the faculty offices in the Quad were known for their predictably quiet Friday nights, Professor Stone was known around campus for his predictably classic, if not cliché, wardrobe. His common uniform included a simple knit tie with a blue oxford weave shirt and a muted tone corduroy jacket. He dressed the part of a college professor. While his students' clothes would go out of style, along with their music, a college yearbook photograph of Professor Stone from 1998 and 2008 and today would look remarkably similar and yet, never unfashionable.

Even though his wardrobe was predictable, there were changes this term. He had struggled that morning as he fastened the grey flannel trousers in his bedroom. He had difficulty making the button meet in the center. He drew in a breath and tried a second time, and buttoned them around his waist. As he wrapped the belt through the loops, he realized it fastened one notch farther out to the end than last season. With a look in the mirror he had sighed, hoping the rest of the clothes in the winter garment bag would be more forgiving.

As Joshua continued down the stairs, he paused on the second floor. Liv Olsson's office was on this floor. She was the Director of Academic Counseling. Just last week, she had been taking a walk and told him it was only coincidence that she walked by his house. Neither of them believed it was just that, but he made them both some fresh coffee and they sat on his front steps.

That day was the closest they had come to a kiss. As awkward moments go, neither of them felt awkward; it was just a kiss that didn't happen. One in a continuing series of missed moments.

As he reached the first floor, and made his way outside, he passed the Skeppshult Swedish touring bicycle he rode to campus each day. He began to cross the mostly vacant parking lot to the West.

Then he noticed the smell. At first, just a whiff and then a powerful, disgusting, strange odor. He had never smelled anything like it. He walked towards the source, the space between the parking lot and the church next door to campus. That was when he saw the smoldering pile at the end of the median along the edge of the parking lot. It didn't look like much of a fire; it seemed more like the remnants of a Halloween prank.

Halfway across the parking lot, he passed the emergency beacon. The automatic alarm was one of a series of solar-powered call boxes placed around the campus. Each had a distinctive bright blue pole with a small canopy light and stenciled word EMERGENCY. The idea was like a fire alarm: breaking the glass in the alarm box, and then pressing a button the size of a silver dollar generated an emergency alarm in the Grant's Hill Sheriff's dispatch center.

As he approached a car parked on the church side of the parking lot, he felt as if he was wholly surrounded by evil and fear. It wasn't a ghost-stories-around-the-summer-campfire fear. It wasn't the kind of fictional fear he had shared with his students as they explored the novels of the twentieth century. This was an overpowering, guttural, end-of-life fear. The air turned to ice; he was unable to catch his breath. The hair stood on the back of his neck. The professor had written that phrase in a few of his novels, but had never experienced the feeling first hand. Then his head pounded as if he had smacked it into an overhead beam and in his last conscious thought, he realized that something big had hit him.

His beating was severe. After the initial incapacitating blow, his face was slammed twice into the trunk lid of the parked car. He hit with enough force to dent and deform the sheet steel. As his body slumped to the ground, he was repeatedly kicked in the chest, kicked in the head and kicked in the back and pelvis.

Joshua, unconscious, dreaming. He was falling, faster and farther, deeper and darker. In his unconsciousness, he didn't feel his wallet being taken from his jacket pocket. He didn't feel his feet slip out of his shoes. He didn't see the face of his attacker.

In between the skull linings protecting Joshua's brain, a very tiny blood vessel was leaking. His body's initial response was to get more oxygen to his brain and other organs. His heart rate sped up, his breathing sped up. His heart and lungs could only do so much, the trauma was too severe. He would not recover without help.

He wasn't conscious to see his attacker turn the red can over his fetal-positioned body. The tiny bit of gasoline in the can dribbled onto his blood stained jacket. He wasn't able to watch him strike a match, smile and toss it onto the jacket where it slowly burned itself out before it had a chance to ignite the fabric.

Professor Joshua Stone was left there to die. Given the time of night and the day of week, it would be hours before he would be discovered.

CHAPTER 2

CLASSES START

SEVERAL WEEKS EARLIER IN THE term, Mrs. Thorn had greeted Professor Stone on a Tuesday morning when he reached the top of the stairs, after taking them two at a time. She nodded at him as she always did, before he walked to his office. She complimented his necktie as he passed her desk and he, in turn, thanked her for the work she had done getting ready for the new semester.

This was the first semester using the new online course management system. It was one of the few changes to his course during the last 15 years. What used to take half a day of Mrs. Thorn's time, photocopying and stapling syllabuses, Joshua Stone now did via remote control from his office in the college Quad. As he worked, the computer cursor hovered over the link on the screen that read "Course Access" and with the click of a mouse, the status line changed from "Hidden" to "Visible" and the students in his class could now log in and see their syllabus, their readings and their assignments. As he waited for the computer to update, he flicked the cap brim of the bobble head mascot given to him by one of his students.

The syllabus he uploaded was for one of his two courses, and his most favorite to teach: *The American Story in Modern Fiction.* Professor Stone kept the syllabus unchanged since he first brought it to campus, not out of laziness, but out of belief that there are few new stories. In his classroom, he used popular movies and books to unlock the idea of the story archetype. His goal was to broaden his students' minds and reading habits, to lead them to see how a story is built.

This was Tuesday, the day after Labor Day. His fifteenth Labor Day on campus, his fifteenth start of classes for fall semester. It was also the fifteenth year he would lead his other class, Freshman Composition. Freshman Comp is one of three required courses for all Grant's Hill students and his first section would meet this term on Tuesdays and Thursdays for 90 minutes each session.

Depending on the number of students, and the availability of contract adjunct faculty to teach extra sections of the course, Stone usually taught two sections of Freshman Comp each semester. His three total course sections, grading, his own writing, and work on college committees filled his week. While science professors conducted research experiments, fiction professors were expected to write fiction and write scholarly reviews and critiques of other writer's work.

Just before 10 a.m. he picked up his soft-sided leather briefcase and left his office. He passed Mrs. Thorn, who was on the phone with a student's parent, and started down the stairs to the classrooms on the first floor. Halfway there, he met Alan Neal from Mathematics and stopped a few stairs above his taller colleague. Neal, who was six foot four and played high school and college basketball, was the organizer of the campus 3-on-3 league that teamed faculty and students in basketball games during December and January.

"Doctor Stone, you're looking rather tall today, ready for some B-Ball?" Neal spoke with a deep voice that resonated in the stairwell like a broadcast booth announcer. At five foot eight,

Stone was used to looking up to Neal, the height advantage of the stairs made him feel cocky.

Stone goaded his taller colleague, "Dr. Neal, I'm thinking maybe this year I should just play on a mobile stair case."

"Shoot, you averaged 13 points a game last season; you are Grant's Hill's own Nate Robinson."

"Really?" Stone asked.

"No way! I'm kidding. You're more, let me think... Spud Webb. I just wanted to make you feel taller."

"I'll take the inch any way I can get it."

Neal laughed with a broad smile, exposing the small gap between his front teeth.

"Didn't you used to play for Borah High in Boise?"

Neal smiled and nodded his head, "Borah Lions. Man, how do you remember stuff like that?"

"No, hear me out! I've got this kid in Freshman Comp. He was center at Borah High. I'm headed to the class now. Maybe he remembers you?"

Neal grinned, "I'm a name on a dusty trophy in a glass case in the lunch room. The glory days are long gone."

"Your glory days were over the day I took you down... how many points?"

"Let me see, Dr. Stone, you averaged 13 points a game and, wait? What's this?" Neal pretended to look at a records sheet, "Alan Neal averaged 14 points?"

Stone laughed, "You're dreaming Neal, we're on today, 2 p.m. Don't wuss out."

With that Joshua continued to the classroom. Students were standing in the halls and chatting in small groups as he walked into the room. He set the leather brief case on the desk and turned to write on the white board in the room:

Dr. Joshua Stone - Freshman Composition

The last few students filed in and sat around the room.

"All right, let's get started. Hopefully all of you have been able to log into our course management system and download all our paperwork." He scanned he room and received some nods in response. "You should have the course syllabus and I will take a break in a bit to answer any questions, but let's get started with introducing ourselves to each other. What I want you to tell us is this: your name — and the name you want us to use in class, and your hometown and then finally, the last book you read."

He leaned back against the table at the front of the room, and then slid up on the surface and casually sat as he turned his attention to the student in the second row and the class shifted its attention as well. As the student drew a breath to speak, Joshua began speaking instead.

"Oh, I forgot. There is a rule in my class." He paused and looked at the four young men sitting in the back row of the classroom.

Speaking in a fake loud voice, as if they were in the far distance, Joshua said, "There is a fee for sitting in the back row."

The students looked at each other.

"I said. There is a fee. A fee... For sitting... For sitting in the back row. It costs a quarter!"

The rest of the class snickered.

Joshua walked back and extended his hand with his open palm up.

"Is this a joke?" The first student asked.

"Let me think. No. Twenty-five cents." He took a quarter and turned to the tallest freshman in the middle.

"You're Troy Waterman, aren't you?" The freshman looked up, surprised. "You were center for the Borah Lions, right?" the student grinned.

"You averaged something like 13 points a game?"

The center's grin grew bigger, enjoying the praise of his professor.

"It still costs a quarter to sit in my back row."

One of the students muttered something about complaining to the administration.

"Oh I understand, a quarter is a lot... Frankly, I encourage you to complain. But whatever you do, do not complain to President Rose, word on the campus is..." Joshua changed his voice to a stage whisper, "word is, he charges $1.75."

Stone set the stack of four quarters on the lectern and returned his attention to the original student in the second row.

One by one the students introduced themselves, told of their hometowns; and by the end of the introductions, Joshua had identified the high school and team name for almost all of them, just as he had for the last decade and a half at Grant's Hill.

Some people follow baseball, or the stock market, or music. Joshua Stone was a fan of high school basketball. With the rise of the Internet and online stats, following the weekly games and players of the far-away Warriors of Cedar Rapids Washington, the Lions of Boise Borah or the DeSmet Jesuit Spartans was just as easy as following the Grant's Hill Surveyors. Stone's credenza held mascots, bobble heads and souvenirs from the high school teams of his students. He had relics and mementoes for 347 high schools. His high school knowledge helped establish a bond with students, some of whom were away from home for the first time in their lives. The mascot knowledgeable professor created a casual atmosphere that also helped students bond with each other. Whenever a student had the team name Eagles, the other students in the rooms whose hometown pride was also named the Eagles gave a cheer, even if their Eagles were from different hometowns.

Introductions and questions took half of the allotted class time, and then the serious work of Freshman Composition began.

"We're going to start with something current and our assignment is to tell me who you are. How many of you have read *Twelve* by Nick McDonell?"

Three hands rose timidly.

"Who can tell me about it?"

"It's about a drug dealer."

"It's about messed up families, man."

Joshua nodded. "Okay, yes. Do any of you remember how it begins?"

The room filled with an empty silence. Joshua picked up his notes and began to read aloud.

He read only the first paragraph that introduces the main character, White Mike, and includes some slang. Whispers and giggles filled the room when he read "doobie."

"What do we know about White Mike?"

"Dude is rich."

"He's close to his cousin."

"He's a hypocrite."

"Great, yes. What can you tell me about the author?"

Another awkward silence filled the classroom. A warm breeze blew in the open window and fluttered a few papers on desks. Joshua smiled to encourage the three who had read the book. None of them replied.

"Folks, this is the good stuff. Nick McDonell...was 17 years old when this was published."

The class responded with surprise mixed with freshman wonder.

"You all can do this. You all have a story to tell, it's inside you. So here's what I want you to do: For our next class, turn into our course management system a one-paragraph introduction of yourself. Tell me as much about your emotions, your relationships, your motivations, your habits, your secrets, let me know you...In a paragraph. You can do this."

He looked around the room, as normal for this opening assignment, about a third of the class was smiling, another third failing to make eye contact, a final third was deep in thought. The middle third, the students not making eye contact, were the ones who would get low grades unless he could motivate them. They were his challenge and the reason he enjoyed teaching.

He let the silence linger and then took the stack of quarters from the lectern.

"Look at this: four quarters. Here's my trick. Show of hands? I'm going to flip these quarters all at once, all four in the air, above my head. Then I'm going to catch each one: one, two, three, four. Before they hit the ground. Show of hands, how many think I can do it?"

About half the class raised their hands, the other half laughed and nudged each other.

Joshua stacked the quarters carefully on his thumb, which was resting at the top of his closed fist, the tip of his thumb pressed against the flesh of the first knuckle on his index finger. With a flick, he flipped the quarters and they went soaring up to an arc just in front of his body. With his left hand, one by one, he plucked each quarter out of the air until he had all four in his fist.

The class took it all in, paused and then cheered the trick.

"Anything is possible, if you believe in yourself. See you on Thursday."

And with that the students gathered their things and left the classroom.

As they filed out of the room they passed Dr. Olivia Olsson, who was standing in the doorway. Her lips were curled at the edges in a light smile as she leaned against the doorjamb and watched Stone. She was wearing a ribbed turtleneck sweater and a long, ankle length skirt with a simple metal belt at the waist. Olsson was three inches taller than Stone, with defined shoulders and wide, curvy hips and a striking face that was accented by her long, straight, shoulder-length blonde hair. Her nose had the distinctive upturn shape of a Swede, and her blue eyes were set high on her clear skinned face.

She waited to say anything until Joshua saw her standing in the door. He turned and noticed her after he closed the open window in the middle of the classroom wall.

She said, "I was watching your lecture, and the trick." Her English conversation was colored by her slight Swedish accent and was sprinkled with a few scrambled idioms that became her vocal trademark. "You will show me how to do it some yesterday, won't you?"

"What, the trick? Yes, I will — *some yesterday*," he mimicked. "It's easy, you just have to practice."

She fiddled with the bracelet on her left arm.

"I had an uncle in Sweden who could make a kronor coin disappear. Then he would pull it out of his magic wooden box."

Joshua nodded. The two of them met the year he was promoted to full professor. From the beginning, he called her "Liv." After five years, he still had not asked her on a date. On the small campus, they should have found a way to spend time together, it never seemed to happen. Alan Neal was both jealous and honest when he went so far as to call them "beauty and the beast."

"What are you saying?" Joshua asked him on the court, "She's Julia Roberts and I'm Lyle Lovett?"

"No, Joshua, I am so sorry, I don't mean it like that," Neal said, then added with a playful smirk, "I mean, I've heard you sing. You are no Lyle Lovett."

Joshua chest butted Neal and stole the ball, making a basket. But Joshua was comfortable in his own skin and knew that he was as ordinary in looks as Liv was pretty.

Joshua stepped towards Liv with a slight hesitation, realizing this was the first time she had come to one of his classes. He took it as a sign of mutual interest and moved closer to her. He didn't know if she was here as Director of Academic Counseling or something more personal. Was she curious to know him as Joshua, and not just Professor Stone? The moment between them lingered until she broke the silence.

"Joshua, I came to ask you about one of your students, Emily Owen."

Joshua paused for a moment, trying not to react to her use of his first name. "Emily... Emily, oh from Mission Hills?"

Liv looked surprised, "First day and you know where she is from? I'm impressed Professor Stone. Yes, Emily. She has good transcripts from high school, and is asking to have additional time for any in-class quizzes or tests."

Joshua took out a pen and made a note on the file folder Mrs. Thorn gave him before class.

"Not a problem. They take their tests all online, I can be sure she has as much time as she needs."

Liv nodded and said, "Thank you," and began to turn away. He tried to read her face; she had called him Joshua and Professor Stone. He saw this was going to become another opportunity that slipped away from them, so he called her name, "Liv?"

She turned and looked at him expectantly, their eyes lingered until Troy Waterman, walking past them both as he breezed into the room heading to his former seat, broke the silence.

"Sorry, Dr. Stone, I think my wallet fell out of my pocket."

Stone turned to follow the student across the room as he bent down next to his seat. "Here it is. Thanks, Dr. Stone."

Joshua's eyes followed the freshman as he left and then turned back to Liv. But she was no longer in the doorway. He could smell a slight hint of perfume. He wondered if it belonged to her or one of the women in his class. He stepped into the hall, and she was gone. As he walked up the stairs, he debated stopping on the second floor and looking in her office. However, as he reached the landing, he second-guessed her intentions, continued up the stairs, missing one more chance to invite her to dinner.

JOSHUA RETURNED TO HIS OFFICE and peered out the window overlooking the campus Quad and the many gardens of Grant's Hill. Under the window, his black Labrador mix dog, Rex, was sleeping.

The college takes its name from the most obvious geographical landmark in the county: Grant's Hill. The town and the college were named for the cartographer who accompanied a party of American soldiers as they mapped out part of the Louisiana Purchase. Percy Grant, who was otherwise unknown in history, named the hill; and, as the town grew and settlers came, the name stuck.

The campus is an oasis, settled in an otherwise nondescript town in rural America. A place where the grain elevator and the railroad grew together.

For the last few decades, the townspeople had watched the defection of their young people to the nearby bigger towns. Jefferson, the county seat 20 miles down the road, offered jobs in the county hospital, a couple of small assembly factories, and a long term care center for the elderly. Some of the town's children ventured farther to cities like St Louis, Columbus, and Nashville. Those who remained took the jobs that remained: the county road crew, stocking shelves and check-out at Royal's grocery and hourly wage jobs in the small businesses that farmers relied upon to service their equipment and care for their livestock. Very few worked at the college; most of Joshua Stone's colleagues at Grant's Hill were transplants to the town.

Mrs. Thorn was one of the few townies who worked at Grant's Hill College, and had worked there the longest. She had gone away to secretarial school in the early 1970s and had returned after nine months away to take a job in the mailroom of the college. She progressed into the secretarial pool and was one of the first secretaries to use an IBM Selectric — a typewriter with the typeface mounted on an interchangeable ball rather than individual typebars for each letter. It was an innovation in the desktop world: swapping out one ball of characters for another could change the type font.

A few years later, in the mid 1980s, she began to work with a memory typewriter, and standard letters sent to all students could be stored on a memory card. As her skill progressed, she earned a desk outside the office of the college president. And when President Rose was hired in 1997, she was moved to be the program secretary for the English and Literary Studies department. It was the same year Joshua arrived on campus. Her first official duties were arranging his travels and time schedule for his job interview when he applied to join the faculty.

Stone had come to Grant's Hill as a 28 year old PhD. He had a dissertation on the *Role of Narrative Immediacy in American Storytelling* in one hand, and a small down payment for a home in his briefcase. He had won a $15,000 prize for fiction writing and during his final on-campus interview, he managed to win over the other members of the faculty and the Program Chair Thomas Moore. His presentation lecture, a kind of audition of his ability to speak in a classroom, was sparsely attended and the other faculty, sitting in the student chairs, out of sympathy or apathy, lobbed only softball questions at him. He was hoping to receive the official job offer during the informal dinner with the department on his last night of the visit.

It was there, sitting near the back at a small table in the Corner Booth diner, that he began to know the two other faculty members of the department and his potential boss. The Corner Booth was the kind of place that served honest food, wine from a box, and two choices of beer: cans or bottles.

Annette Demming was the matriarch of the department and later became Joshua's most trusted friend and advisor. He didn't know her age, but guessed she was 25 years his elder. She had a plump, robust figure and stood five and half feet tall. She dressed in subtle colors and bright lipstick. Annette had come to Grant's Hill the fall of 1970 after she opted out of her contract at her first university. She had remained at Grant's Hill since.

"But that is what we need, Joshua, we need that new vision of lit-ra-ture," she began with a cooing voice as she stared at the other tenured professor, David Adams, sitting to Joshua's left. "Lit-ra-ture... to spark the minds of young learners." She stopped, took a sip of the red wine from her glass, and continued, "Or at least let them see the difference between Chaucer and Cheever."

Annette liked to play with people's impression of her as much as she liked to play with words and pronunciation. She taught the department's courses in semantics and linguistics, recognizing students who were north or south of the so-called "greazy - greasy" line of dialect in the US. She would often chose a word and make it an affectation. "Lit-ra-ture" was that night's play on words, the mood struck her and it seemed to make everyone laugh, which only encouraged her. She enjoyed teasing students, in a playful way. She would give them challenges, forcing them to think and reconsider. When the church next door to campus was renamed The First Apostolic Church, she convinced several student's they had misread the sign and it was truly named the First Apologetic Church.

"Annette," began David Adams, pulling down his wire frames and looking over the top of his glasses, "if they knew the difference, we would be out of work." He let out a comical, make-believe sigh, "and go back to our other lives of toil and despair and quiet desperation... And that, frankly, is why I got into academia. It's all inside work and no heavy lifting." He ended with a resounding laugh. It rose above the din of the other tables and caused a few heads to turn.

"Joshua what do you think? I mean, when Arthur retired last year we knew we could finally breathe some fresh air into a very old department and maybe replace some Chaucer with some Cheever. You write well, you'd be a great artist in residence...But are you really sure you want to *teach*..." she looked around the room, "*here*?"

Stone heard the change in her tone of voice. She was testing him. The softball questions were gone and the wine had taken any restraint off the table. But he liked what he saw of the campus and he liked these people and town life seemed approachable and affordable. He made it a point to make eye contact with each of them. He paused and took in Annette's rosy cheeks and bright lips, David's wire frame glasses and salt and pepper mustache, and Moore's bright, florid complexion and endless smile.

"Well, why not?" he asked. There was a long silence.

"Yes, why not?" answered Adams with another loud, overpowering laugh.

Later, as they stood outside, the grain trucks lumbered past the diner, which sat near the edge of town. To Joshua's back was Town and Country Vet clinic with the feed store on one side and Royal's grocery on the other. This was the main highway in and out of town, "Town" was further north and the campus sat at the north edge of town. Thomas Moore turned to Joshua.

"Joshua, listen, I shouldn't tell you this, but you'll find out soon enough. The faculty like you. HR likes you. I like you. You'll receive an offer tomorrow morning. It will be a fair offer."

Stone tried to hide his surprise.

"Don't take it," Moore continued.

Stone's jaw dropped but he kept his lips closed. He thought he had just received a job offer and lost it in the turn of a sentence.

Moore smiled, "Ask for $5000 more. You'll get it. You just didn't hear it from me."

And with that, Dr. Joshua Stone came to Grant's Hill, bought a modest Tudor style house, and put down roots at the quiet school in a quiet town. He made it home, alongside its 1200 students and 75 faculty.

CHAPTER 4

GRANT'S HILL

THE PRIVATE, LIBERAL ARTS COLLEGE at the crest of the hill had a rural setting, beautiful topography, and classic architecture. It was the picturesque beauty that made college catalog designers and photographers love their jobs. And every photographer who visited the school insisted on photographing two buildings: the Quad and Eastford Chapel.

The Quad is a collection of four three-story rectangular buildings, with their narrow ends adjoining at right angles and forming an open courtyard. In the beginning, the academic programs were divided by building: Humanities, Sciences, Education, and Home Economics. The gender bias of earlier times also lead to the common description of the buildings as the "girl's side" and the "men's side" of campus. Beginning in the 1960s, the Grant's Hill Board of Trustee's perception of gender differences began to erode and the Home Economics program dissolved. Their wing of the Quad became home to the political science and world studies programs, although the inscription above the archway was never updated to reflect the changing focus and still reads Home Economics.

If architectural design is made up of solids and spaces, it is the spaces between the solid buildings that make the Quad so photogenic. The central courtyard of the Quad is where students gather, parents take photos, and faculty hold impromptu discussions. The centerpiece is a large fountain, modeled after the many fountains of Italy, with a colorful tile mosaic of the seven liberal arts. From the South, you can see the tile and stone depictions of the *Trivium* of grammar, logic and rhetoric and the *Quadrivium* of arithmetic, geometry, music and astronomy. The Grant's Hill motto *Scientia Tranquillitate Fidelitate* — Knowledge, Tranquility, Fidelity — surrounds the tile edge.

The other most photographed campus landmark is Eastford Chapel. Eastford Chapel was inspired by Boston's Old North Church, and built with local, Midwestern building materials, mixing limestone with hardwoods and plaster. Originally built by Methodists, it has been home to Presbyterian, Lutheran and Anglican congregations and included a 5 year run as a Unitarian church before the Board of Trustees voted to make the chapel non denominational, suspending all formal prayer services and affiliations. Eastford Chapel hosts 20 – 30 weddings each spring and early summer and the college choir performs a mixture of spiritual and contemporary holiday music there each Christmas.

The spire of the chapel is 101 feet tall and lighted so that it can be seen for miles. Most visitors to campus remark that the first hint of Grant's Hill is the bright white painted chapel spire. During the great depression, in the thick of the March fog of 1931, a United States Postal airplane pilot was lost and disoriented, several hundred miles off course. College folklore maintains that it was the beacon light atop of the spire that the pilot spotted as his engines died from a lack of fuel. He was able to glide the plane to a successful, non-powered landing on the grassy field north of the Quad. The sound of the sputtering engine in the fog attracted everyone's attention. Students left their seats and began looking out windows. When the engine gave out, the hopes of several students faded with it and then, once the craft had come to a stop, word quickly spread of the safe landing and classrooms were abandoned. Cheering young men and women mobbed the plane and its pilot. The pilot, Arlen Rooney, was hoisted to the shoulders of several of the largest men on campus and was paraded back to the center of the Quad. By then, every classroom and office had been abandoned and the fog began lifting.

His safe landing became a student tradition called "Pilot's Day" a day when classes are cancelled and everyone skips work and plays games in the lawns. Pilot's Day never falls on the same date any year, rather it is declared at the whim of the college president. The current college president, Matthew Rose, typically declares it before spring break, on a day when the temperatures climb into the 60s.

Eastford Chapel has served as a lecture hall, a performance hall, a town meeting room, and had once hosted a Governor's debate. The visibility from the televised debate brought a spike of applications to the college from around the state. The subsequent enrollment surge encouraged the Board of Trustees to build a new dormitory in 2000. Looking today, a newcomer would have a difficult time identifying which buildings were built first, and which were built recently.

The paint, trim, masonry and window design is consistent across the entire campus, so much so that the dormitory built in 2000 looks as old as the Quad. Inside, as well, the hallways, classrooms, offices and meeting areas are neat, tidy and in meticulous repair.

During his first year on campus, Joshua admired two things about the grounds crew and maintenance workers who supported the college. First, the grounds were impeccable. Dead trees were quickly uprooted and replaced with new ones, the lawns were mowed, the gardens edged, the sidewalks clear and level.

But what was missing, or never seen, was the work and the workers. It was only when Joshua worked late, or arrived on campus very early, that he saw the white haired, round bellied maintenance worker scooting across the Quad lawn on a zero-turn radius mower, his path lighted only by the mower's headlamps.

Later on, Joshua came to know and respect the man who looked like Santa Claus in the off-season, riding the green mower. Bob Thornton had the reputation of being a hard drinking, skirt chasing, former combat soldier. In reality, Thornton was a decorated Gulf War veteran who hadn't had a drink since 1994. But he did little to silence the rumors about himself.

The window washers visited the school each spring, the week before graduation ceremonies. But the upkeep was mostly invisible. The place was always just right.

It was a student's shout across the courtyard through the open window that returned Joshua's attention to the present day. Rex, the black dog, rolled over and lifted his head as Stone's thoughts of his hiring dinner mingled with thoughts of now. Remembering Annette made him smile. He missed her friendship and inspiration. She made fun of him just enough to remind him to never take himself too seriously.

Thomas Moore stuck his head in Joshua's office and smiled broadly. Moore always smiled. He had a happy smile, a silly grin, a serious smile, an 'I understand' smile…but always a smile. Joshua tried to read the meaning of this smile. "Got time for a quick sit down?"

Joshua nodded. Moore's idea of intra-department communication was chats over a meal, chats at the faculty club, and "quick sit downs."

He plopped down in the visitor's chair and gave a sigh, still smiling. Rex rolled over and echoed with a matching sigh. The two shared a smug similarity. They both resembled self-satisfied pups after a large meal. Joshua noticed a small spot on Moore's tie, probably from lunch. As Moore began speaking, he moved a bit in the chair and Joshua almost started following the spot as if he were following a bouncing ball to sing karaoke. He shifted his gaze back to Moore's face.

"I want to ask you about something. I've run this past David and I want to make sure I don't step on your toes. But I was chatting with the folks over in the sciences wing and they've got a bit of a rising star over there. Just published a nice paper and has been awarded some outside research funding. A National Academy Grant." Moore leaned in and lowered his voice. "Six figures." He gave an exclamatory whistle.

Joshua leaned forward and nodded. "Wow, that's great! We ought to have a little get together, maybe some cake or hors d'oeuvres?"

Moore's smile grew for a moment. "What I'd like to ask is, how do you feel about someone *outside* of our department chairing the search committee for Annette's replacement? I mean, the job is yours, you've earned it." He watched Joshua's eyes for a reaction. Seeing none, he continued. "You'll still play a large role, but the folks over in basic sciences don't anticipate anyone leaving and don't anticipate having a search committee for a long time. They'd like this rising star to get tenure and being the chair of this search committee would help."

Joshua's poker face didn't flicker. He wanted to stand up, and run around the room, high five slapping invisible teammates of his 3-on-3 tournament team. As much as he wanted to influence the choice of his new coworker, the idea of working with HR and their countless regulations and rules was annoying. And then there would be the aggravation of scheduling telephone interviews with the entire committee, each with their own egos. He maintained his poker face a bit longer.

"Well, I was kind of looking forward to it." He peeked down to see Rex. In the moment, he watched the dog roll his eyes. The dog's internal lie detector was sounding loudly.

"Sure, Tom, lets do that, it'll buy us some points with those basic science guys. What's the harm?"

Moore stood up, smiling of success. He reached to shake Joshua's hand, and as he did, he caught sight of the spot on his tie.

"Oh look. Dang it," and he began rubbing the spot with the tie's narrow end. "Dang it," he looked back at Joshua smiling sheepishly. "Lunch, I guess" and wandered back to his office.

Joshua called over at Rex. "Rex? High five!" and held his hand at dog height. The dog got up and scampered over and sat, then raised his left paw and batted at Joshua's hand.

"Good dog."

It was common to see Rex on campus with Joshua. He would often slumber in the corner of the office, or sniff around the lower drawer of Mrs. Thorn's desk for the dog biscuits she denied were there. It was only once Joshua saw her reach down and silently hand Rex a biscuit.

A few years back, on "Pilot's day," Stone initiated the tradition of bringing dogs to campus. That holiday was the first time Rex ran alongside the man's bicycle as he rode the short ride from home to campus. Since that first day, Rex was a campus regular with the perpetual energy and naïveté of a freshman.

Joshua stood up, grabbed the leash that was hanging behind his door, and latched it to the dog's collar. The two of them walked to the stairs and then down to the main level of the Quad and out into the fall afternoon.

As he opened the door, two students greeted him, "Hi, Dr. Stone."

Joshua smiled and held the door for both of them, Shelly Lewry and Jack Reading. He knew them both from last spring in

Freshman Comp. Rex walked at a trot as they passed the interior bicycle racks. On the sidewalk, he noticed a student carrying an overflowing backpack. She stopped and smiled when she saw her professor.

"Hello, Dr. Stone."

"Hi, Barbara. How is your dad?" Barbara Wilkinson's father had been in a car accident during the summer. Joshua had seen an article in the newspaper and sent her a short note. Barbara, a senior English major was probably headed to meet Alex — rather, *Alexander* Foreman. Alex Foreman began Joshua's Freshman Comp class and by the end of the term, said he wished to be addressed as Alexander. Joshua enjoyed being a witness to young men and women coming of age. He didn't remember when Alexander and Barbara first started walking across campus together, but as a couple, he was certain theirs would be one of the marriages this spring in Eastford Chapel.

Joshua watched the two of them walk to the Quad sciences wing and as they did, he felt like fall was the beginning of a great year on campus, and he never grew tired of the feelings and sights of the new school year.

A group of students cheered as Rex took one of his occasional swims in the fountain in the middle of the Quad. His post-swim shaking created screams of delight and surprise from the young women as they sat and sipped drinks and sunbathed between classes. Rex had been a part of campus for five years.

PART TWO

THE BLACK DOG

CHAPTER 5

SIDE OF THE ROAD

FIVE YEARS AGO, THE CELEBRATION for Joshua's promotion to full professor was hosted at the president's compound on the edge of town. A realtor might describe the property as a lovely sprawling acreage, with tennis courts, riding stables, and indoor and outdoor swimming pools. White, three-rail fences surrounded it. Flowering crab trees shaded the half-mile long driveway. Cherry trees and magnolias were all in bloom and the reception for the year's promoted faculty took place in the garden and later in the large gathering room. The stately, two story home was one of five large buildings on the compound.

The president's job at Grant's Hill pays well, but not well enough to afford a home like this. The compound had been given to Grant's Hill by a local tycoon who fell on hard times following the stock market crash of 1929. The Grant's Hill trustees voted to use part of its endowment to pay overdue property taxes and a small lien in the exchange. About a decade later, a wealthy donor bequeathed a large gift with the contingency the funds would be exclusively for the preservation and restoration of the land.

Sometime in the 1940s, some wags on the faculty began referring to the house and grounds as "Xanadu," after the mansion from *Citizen Kane,* and the name stuck.

As post-war prosperity returned to the country and the campus, the faculty promotion celebration grew in size and social status and became known as the Soiree. By the time Joshua was promoted to full professor, he had attended only one of these gatherings, when he moved from assistant to associate professor. Now as full professor, he would be attending them all at the invitation of President Rose and Dean Eggars. The surprise of the night was receiving the $5000 check from President Rose; the customary bonus awarded all full professors. In reality, it was only $500 a year for each of his ten years, but just the same, $5000 was $5000.

Near the end of the evening, Moore said his goodbyes to the group and slowly worked around the room towards the door. When he got to Joshua, he was smiling a proud smile. It was clear he enjoyed bragging to other chairs about his faculty.

"Are you heading out?" Joshua asked.

Moore nodded and smiled.

"Would you give me a lift? I rode here with Annette, but I think she is going to be a while."

Annette was sitting next to Olivia Olsson, the new Director of Academic Counseling who arrived on campus just that spring. The two of them were debating half a dozen colleagues about feminism and the role of Geraldine Ferraro after the democratic presidential convention of 1984.

It was dusk as the two men walked out together and climbed into Moore's sedan. Moore turned the car around and they took off down the drive and turned south back into town.

"Joshua, we're all very proud of you. You know that, right?"

Joshua stared down the country road in front of them and smiled. "I think I made the right choice, coming here."

"Right!" Moore laughed, "It's a great choice. It's really a great gig. We're right in the middle of the country. The cost of living is affordable. We get to go to great parties and don't have to pay the bills."

"Or clean up," interjected Joshua.

Moore ticked off the accomplishments of the department. "We've had a good year. Your promotion, two books and a play published. That doesn't happen everywhere."

"You're right." Joshua agreed.

It had been a very good year. Joshua's novel, *One Good Bread Pudding*, was one of the department's publication triumphs. Joshua crafted the story of a line-cook in a cafeteria who worked each night developing a winning dessert for a regional culinary competition. Wilson, Adams, Annette and even Mrs. Thorn loved his project at first. To understand his character, Joshua made each dessert as background research. By the end of 12 weeks, they were all 5 pounds heavier and demanded he stop bringing his research to the office.

Moore smiled and then clicked on the hi-beam headlights. By the side of the road, a dark lump lay motionless. As they got closer, Moore slowed just a bit, and both men recognized the lump as a dog that had been struck by a car. Moore, hesitated for a split second, and then continued driving.

Joshua, in the passenger seat, looked at the dog as they passed by. Its hip was deformed and there were traces of blood around its mouth. The dog opened its eyes and Joshua and the dog regarded each other and Joshua turned his body as the car passed. Neither man nor dog broke the stare.

"Stop the car."

Moore's right foot jumped from the gas to the brake and he pulled the car to a halt.

"That dog is alive."

As if he were an oarsman responding to the order of the coxswain, Moore put the car in reverse and backed slowly. Joshua opened the car door and began walking toward the crippled mass on the edge of the road.

"Joshua, just be smart, it's hurt — it could bite you."

Joshua had seen wounded animals in the past: angry, confused, and self-protective. He slowly approached and kept looking into the dog's eyes.

"Take me home."

"What did you say?" He turned to Moore who was standing on the far side of the car in the space of the opened driver's door.

"I didn't say anything...Sad day. Shall we go?"

Moore smiled his concerned smile and made a sympathetic face. He glanced up and down the road to check for any oncoming traffic.

"Help me load him in the back seat. " Joshua took off his suit coat and laid it next to the dog's body.

"Aww. I just had the car detailed." Moore stood motionless and then consented. "All right."

And the two men knelt next to the dog and moved it onto the suit coat. Using the jacket as an impromptu sling they shuttled the dog towards the car. Moore opened the back passenger side door and the two of them slid the dog and jacket onto the upholstery.

"There's a vet in town, right?"

Moore got in the driver's seat and started down the road.

"Now you ask? Yeah, it's by the feed store. I doubt anyone is there on a Saturday night. But we can check. Maybe they post an emergency number."

Joshua stroked the dog with careful, purposeful strokes, first to gain trust, and second to feel for injuries. He had no idea what a broken bone felt like, but figured between his touch and the dog's reaction, he would learn. There was blood on the dog's nose and mouth, and a long cut on the left rear leg. The hips were deformed and the dog, laying on its right side, was panting. The dog's mouth was dry, and it stared into Joshua's eyes as both their faces glowed as the car passed under a streetlight and then fade back to darkness.

It was just after 8 p.m. when Moore cut across the parking lot of the Grant's Hill Feed Store and came to a stop near the doors of the Town and Country Veterinary Clinic. There were no cars in the parking lot and no lights inside.

Moore got out and walked to the door while Joshua stayed in the back of the car. Moore pounded on the glass door and looked around.

The second time he pounded, an employee from the feed store was walking across the parking lot.

"Hey, do you need the vet?"

Moore turned, "Yeah, a dog's been hit by a car. We wanted to drop it off."

"I'll get Sissy. She's inside." And the woman disappeared into the feed store.

Inside the car, Joshua was holding the dog's front paw. He had no idea why. The two continued looking at each other when he heard it again.

"Take me home."

"Where is home? Who do you belong to?" Joshua felt around the dog's neck There were no tags and no collar.

The back door opened and standing there was Moore, the woman from the parking lot, and Sissy. Sissy was the part time receptionist at the vet clinic and part time cashier at the feed store.

She said, "Oh dear God, look at you."

Joshua wondered what was wrong and looked down at his clothes.

"Not you, silly, the dog. Okay, let me open up and I'll call Dr. Cynthia."

As Sissy opened the front door of the clinic, the other three guided the dog out of the car, still using the suit coat as a make shift stretcher. They carried the dog inside and Sissy led them to an exam room. Joshua had never been in a vet clinic and assumed it would smell like a hospital, but it had a very different smell: sterile and redolent of animal fur, with a hint of cat and dog foods.

"Thanks y'all for bringing him in. We'll see what we can do to fix him up and find his owner. Someone is worried sick about this pup."

Moore and Joshua walked outside. "I am really sorry for messing up your car."

"No, don't worry about it. It'll be fine." They inspected the back seat and it was surprisingly clean.

Moore opened the door and dropped into the driver's seat. Joshua opened his door and sat down, looked one more time at the vet clinic, and then closed his door. They drove in silence. When they pulled to the front of Joshua's house, Moore said, "You did the right thing, someone is going to be very glad they can take their dog back home."

The two looked at each other.

"Thanks."

"What a night, what a story. Congratulations, professor."

Chapter 6

Vet hospital

THE NEXT MORNING, THE SUN shining through the window created a rectangular shape of light and shadow on the floor of his second bedroom-turned office. It reminded him of a Mondrian painting as he walked across it holding a cup of coffee in one hand and a printed copy of a student essay in another. Reading and grading were his favorite Sunday morning, after-church activities. Today's grading gave him a welcome distraction from the night before. He wondered if the dog had indeed survived. It occurred to him that someone would need to pay the bill and since he was the guy who dropped him off, he should be the one.

He laid the student's paper on the desk. His desk had far fewer trinkets than his office on campus. A small polished piece of granite was engraved with the phrase:

Be Strong and Very Courageous — Joshua 1:7

The stone placard was a gift from his mother when he graduated from high school and he carried it with him to this day. He ran his finger over the letters, a habit that, from the wear and patina, he had done many times and then picked up the phone. He dialed 4-1-1 and got the recorded prompts:

"What city please?"

"Grant's Hill"

"What listing?"

"Town and Country Animal Clinic."

"The number is 989-9979. Stay on the line and be connected for forty additional cents."

He waited for the phone to ring and it rang 8 times before he received a recorded message. He waited for the beep.

"Hello, hi, good morning, this is Dr. Stone. I brought a dog by last night that was struck by a car and I didn't get a chance to leave my name and number. I suppose you will find the owner, but if you don't, I wanted to say that I would pay for his care. That is, if he is still alive. So please call me, Dr. Joshua Stone, 989-4240."

Joshua hung up the phone and focused his attention back to his grading.

The assignment was from the Freshman Composition course. Out of 20 students in the class, Joshua could count on some predictable writing.

How I Overcame Adversity, which given the demographics of the student body meant not being named homecoming/prom/pep-club king, queen or president.

The Person I Admire Most, which given the social circle of the student body meant mom or dad or grandma or grandpa.

And,

The Person I Would Most Like to be is _____, which given the star struck nature of the student body meant a sports figure, rock star, or actor.

The paper Joshua was reading was different, the title was *This one time, at band camp, I almost...* and it shared a series of vignettes about choices. More precisely, about not making the wrong choice. It played with ideas like peer pressure, social norms, and fitting in.

It was at the same time, funny and sad, reflective and descriptive. It was a solid "A" paper.

The prior paper was a cross between head banging rock lyrics and a parody of Alan Ginsberg's *Howl*. *Howl* was one of the required readings for the class and the student put together a collection of words that created a sense of noise and silence. This was fresh and Joshua decided the student was either very lucky or very talented. If it was talent, grad school was the future and if it was luck, well, it was still a great effort. He wrote in the margin near the last paragraph, commenting on the student's borrowing from Ginsberg's "angel headed hipsters" and making it contemporary.

Howl made him think of the dog again.

He picked up the phone and pressed REDIAL on the receiver. The phone rang and the message played again.

"Hello, hi, this is Dr. Stone again. I left a message earlier. And I was thinking, if you don't find the dog's owner, well I would adopt it. I, ah, I don't know much about dogs, but I've always felt like it would be great to have one. And so, thanks again and my number is 989-4240."

Around noon, Joshua looked out the window and saw his neighbors, the Jenkins family, playing fetch with their dog. The dog sat expectantly at their feet, watching their hands and the moment they tossed the ball, the dog sprang into action and raced down the yard in pursuit. After skidding through the grass, he grabbed the ball with its mouth and came prancing proudly back to drop it at their feet. As they repeated the game a dozen more times, Joshua watched out the window. He reached over into the chair where he had propped the book of dog breeds from a shelf in his office. He picked it up and leafed through the pages until he landed on a page about Labradors and saw a photo of a St. John's

Water Dog, an extinct breed, often called the predecessor to modern retrievers.

He stared at the photographs. Black dog, with some small white markings on its chest and paws.

He scrutinized the photo and tried to picture the injured dog in the back seat of Moore's car. With that, he closed the book and got up and walked outside to the garage. He opened the door and walked over to the touring bicycle leaning against the side wall. The green bike was a Skeppshult Nature. A high end, Swedish touring bicycle with fenders and guard that kept his clothes clean, a pedal generated headlamp, and a spring clamp rack for his briefcase and balancing groceries. He clipped a cuff clip to each ankle, and then hopped on the bike and rode down the driveway. He turned south towards town and away from campus. He crossed Main Street and turned back east towards the feed store and the vet's office. He made a mental note to stop at Royal's grocery on the return trip, thinking of the list he had written and put in his wallet earlier in the day.

When he arrived at Town and Country, there were two cars in the parking lot. He slowed the Skeppshult and came to a stop just beyond the entrance. He rested the bike and removed his clips and then opened the glass door. The lights were on and the reception area was empty. He called out, "Hello?"

A voice answered from the back, "Be right with you."

A woman in her late 50s greeted Joshua from the hallway, wearing an old denim shirt and blue jeans.

"I'm Dr. Kanzen, can I help you?"

"Hi, I'm Dr. Stone."

"Ahh yes, from the phone messages, we just called you, but you were out. Come on back, let's talk."

Kanzen led Joshua back to the far examining room and in the center, on the table, laid the dog from the night before. Sissy was standing along side and nodded. The dog and the rescuer made eye contact and the dog moved its tail.

"Well, looks like he remembers you."

"Yes. It's a he is it? I guess I never bothered to check."

Joshua gently stroked the dog's short black fur. He looked him over and confirmed he had the markings and head shape of the dog from the book.

"He's a cross breed, some Labrador mostly, but his tuxedo coat is different. He has sort of a St John's marking to him. Do you know dogs?"

"No, not really, but he does look a bit like a St John's Waterdog, from the photos I've seen."

"It's an old breed, but long gone. The pure strain died out in the 1980s but there are so many crosses and variants. This one's a mix. I haven't seen him before and I see almost all the dogs in the county. I'm guessing a stray? Or maybe lost from someone traveling?"

Joshua scratched the dog behind the ears and it shifted and then yelped in pain as it moved the hind leg. Joshua snapped his hand back fearing he had caused the pain and looked over at Kanzen.

"Yes, about that," she continued. "Well, we have some options. I know you said you would pay for care, but I need to be honest about what that means. As a vet, I have three options for coxofemoral hip luxation — hip dislocation. To begin with, we can euthanize him. That sounds harsh, but it is painless and I won't charge you to do it. I respect that you were being the Good Samaritan and I appreciate compassion," she looked to see any signal from Joshua.

"Is it that bad?"

"Well, no. There are two other options, but they are much more expensive. You must understand that time is of the essence in hip dislocations. Getting this pup whole again, what I mean by this is, where the hip joint is restored to like-new condition, only works if done right away. We can do surgery and reset and relocate the hip but I need to do it today or tomorrow morning at the latest. Brace yourself, that's $3000. I don't mean to be heartless, but this is my business and I have to pay the bills and keep my employees. And there are no dog HMO's"

Joshua shuffled his feet slightly, shifting his weight. The $5000 bonus from last night was shrinking in the light of day and this news. "And the other option?"

"The other option is amputation."

Joshua cringed at the sound. "Amputation?"

"It sounds harsh, but three legged dogs do quite well. Your dog can enjoy a long life. He won't have every day pain."

"What if we just wait and see?" Joshua asked, looking back and forth between the dog and the vet.

"Dr. Stone, 'wait and see' is easiest on you and hardest on the dog. The dog may walk and make it around the house OK, but he'll never be without significant pain. Just like now, his silence doesn't mean he's pain free."

The hum of a refrigerator holding medicines was all that could be heard as the veterinarian paused.

"Eventually, a fibrous connection may form between bones that will allow your dog to hobble on the leg... but without care," she gently stroked the dog's fur, "this dog will live in pain, always."

Joshua looked back at the dog.

"Take me home."

Joshua turned to her, "I'm sorry did you say something?"

She looked blankly at Joshua, "Um no, would you like me to? I can give you some more time to — "

Joshua interrupted. "I don't need any time, thank you. Please do the surgery. I'll write you a check today. What's his recovery like?"

"Well, all things being equal, the dog will be off his feet for a couple of weeks, limited use for four to six weeks and I would say in a couple of months, be as close to normal as we will get."

She touched Joshua's arm, gave a reassuring squeeze, and showed Joshua out of the room and he and Sissy walked to the reception area.

"You are very kind to pick up that dog, most folks around here would let him be, or would have run over him."

Joshua nodded and reached in his jacket pocket for his checkbook.

"I need to fill out information in our computer screen for billing. Have you given him a name?"

Joshua recalled the last paper he graded, the rock and roll lyric influenced version of *Howl* and briefly considered Ginsberg, but instead, chose Ginsberg's mentor. "Put down Rex? — Short for Rexroth."

Sissy typed R E X R O T H into the computer, "Sounds kinda fancy, is that a poet's name?"

"Yes, he was a poet, and a pacifist. We need more of both in this world."

Chapter 7

First day home

THE FOLLOWING DAY, JOSHUA AGAIN rode his bicycle
out of his driveway and again turned south towards town, rather
than north towards the college. In a few minutes, he was at the
door of the Town and Country Veterinary clinic. He walked inside
and looked expectantly down the hall for either Sissy or Cynthia
Kanzen.

Sissy came out of a back room and motioned a come-hither
finger gesture to Joshua. When he reached the end of the hall, he
saw Rex, lying on his side with a dressing on his hip. He was
sleeping.

"He did great in surgery, Dr. Cynthia has him sedated; he
might be awake this afternoon if you want to come by then?"

Joshua reached down to the dog to stroke his face and ears.
The dog raised its head and then set it back down and sighed.

"Sure, I have class late tonight, but I can be here around 7:00.
Is that too late?"

"I'll be here, just finishing up the dinner shift...I'll leave the
lights on for you"

And with that, Joshua went back to his bicycle and rode off to
campus. It was the final week of classes on campus before summer
break. He parked the bicycle in the rack and took his briefcase

from the spring clamp carrier on the back. He wiped it off and then headed to his third floor office.

Adams stuck his head in the door, pushing his glasses a bit higher on his nose. "It's not enough to be full professor, now you want the Nobel Prize for animal rescue, too?"

Joshua looked up from his book and then nodded at the collection of high school sports memorabilia on the credenza, "And basketball player of the year!"

"You know, I had a coworker at the publishing house who found a dog like that on the side of the road and rescued it. It lived 15 years."

Joshua stood up and the two men moved toward the open window. From outside, the smell of warming earth and blooming flowers filled the air and the old stale air of closed up offices was leaving.

"David, your book is amazing," he gestured to a copy of Adams' book he was reading when the senior tenured professor came in the room. In the dust jacket photo, Adams was wearing a fly-fishing vest — a shorter version of the photojournalist style travel vest that David was prone to wear around campus.

"Thank you, thank you. It was a great project. I learned a lot."

Adams' book, *Flies that Bind* was the autobiographical story of his life in his twenties. A kind of coming of age with his father and how he and his father took up fly fishing together when the older Adams contracted prostate cancer. It was the English department's other publication triumph of the year.

"Dr. Adams!" Came a loud accusatory shriek from Annette across the hall followed by footsteps as she paraded into Joshua's office.

"How could you possibly share…*this*?"

The two men turned to see Annette holding a copy of *Flies That Bind* with her fingers about two-thirds of the way through the printed pages.

Joshua turned to Adams and said, "Yes, I was wondering about that, too." He looked at Annette, "I'm guessing you read the..."

"The sex scene? Yes! Does Ellen have any idea that you put this in here?"

Joshua felt himself blushing. Blushing felt odd, it wasn't really an erotic sex scene, and it wasn't so revealing that he would have concerns about sharing it with his students, but this wasn't just another sex scene, this was David and his wife, Ellen, having sex on the floor of a fishing shack.

"What are you doing?" Annette berated him. "Boasting to your publishing buddies? Joshua, help me here. What place does..." her voice trailed off as she pulled her half frame reader glasses from the chain around her neck and placed them on her nose, reading through the frames, she began to quote:

"Ellen looked at me with the fire and hunger of passion. She took me, hard. She pulled me to the floor, undressing me, holding me close to her body, biting my neck as we joined in a rocking rhythm on the plank floors."

Joshua eyes shifted between the two of them. Annette's face was red, half in anger and half in embarrassment for Ellen.

Adams now looked embarrassed, too. He fumbled for the words he was about to say. "I, uh. Well. The thing is. I didn't. I didn't write that passage."

Joshua laughed, "What?"

"Ellen did. I wrote something else, well, lots of something else — about a dozen times. That was a very awkward period for me and my dad's disease. So finally, after seeing the umpteenth draft, Ellen took a pad and paper and wrote that section for me."

Joshua opened the book and found the pages that continued with more specific details. "Even the parts about..." his voice trailed off.

Adams nodded his head, "Ellen wrote that whole section."

Annette smiled up at the two of them "Really? Well," she winked, "that's a whole new twist on things, isn't it?"

She took the glasses off and nodded to them both as she retreated to her office. She paused at the door, turned to face Adams, and mocked a bite with her mouth.

Joshua's evening classes ended at 6 p.m. He returned to his office and after he finished returning phone messages, he made his way to his bicycle in the rack in the Quad.

By the time he rolled into the parking lot of Town and Country, it was exactly 7:00. Sissy met him at the door and walked him back.

"I'm kinda surprised he isn't eating yet." Sissy shared. "Hasn't pooped, either"

Joshua glanced around the room and found the bowl of dog kibble and water dish. Instead of being in a kennel cage, the room was divided with padded divider barriers 3 feet high. He looked at Sissy and then unbuttoned his blazer and slid it off his shoulders. He folded it in half lengthwise and then draped it over the back of the chair across the hall and returned to the room.

He rolled up each of his sleeves and then bent down to pick up the dog kibble.

He approached Rex who wagged his tail briskly. He sat down next to the dog and the two remained motionless for a moment. Joshua picked a kibble and placed it near the dog's face and it opened its mouth and took the food.

Joshua picked another, and another, and for the next hour, fed the black dog one bite at a time. Near the end, Joshua moved the water bowl and the dog rolled on its belly enough to take a drink.

When it rolled back, it lay its head on Joshua's lap and fell asleep. Joshua sat there, listening to the dog breathe in and out, and recited a line from Jack London, "He was beaten (he knew that); but he was not broken."

It continued like that for two weeks. Each morning and again each evening, Joshua met Sissy or Cynthia Kanzen and then spent an hour or more with Rex.

When it was time to bring the dog home, it took a bribe of fresh brewed, Kenyan coffee, made with fresh ground beans sent by a former student, to persuade Moore to give the dog another ride in the back of his car. Joshua finally made good on Rex's plea to "take me home" and brought him to the house just south of campus.

When Joshua opened the door, Rex walked in, taking a few steps at a time exploring the new smells. In the kitchen was a pair of new stainless steel bowls, one filled with water the other filled with dog kibble. Rex passed them both and went to explore the living room and then the second bedroom office. He sniffed at the closets and wandered the perimeter of each room.

Rex's black coat was shiny and shorthaired. His face had the classic shape of a lab and his tuxedo markings on his chest were the size of a dime. Moore slapped Joshua on the back. "You did good, Josh. Well done."

"Me? I'm thinking you should be in the side business: pet ambulance."

Moore laughed, "Seriously, we must have been drunk to stop and pick up that dog on the side of the road."

"We were sober as I recall."

"Yes, yes, we were."

Joshua reached onto the top of the bookcase and retrieved a blue woven dog collar he had ordered from the feed store. REX was embroidered into the fabric and Joshua secured the plastic clasp around the dog's neck. Both men stared as the dog stood proud, as if he wanted to be wearing the collar. "I think he wants to belong."

"You've got to taste this coffee. James Thomas sent it to me from Kenya. It's very rich. Do you like dark coffee?"

Moore nodded and the three made their way to the kitchen.

Joshua poured two mugs, handed one to Moore, and the two sat down. Moore brushed a few strands of his white hair off his forehead and swept his hand over the top of his head.

"Joshua, I know this has been a big year for you, the promotion portfolio, and the whole full professor interviews and review committees. I was going to bring this up earlier, but with the dog and all, I didn't know when to say this...but..." Moore's smile turned huge and child-like. Joshua watched his eyes twinkle in a way that peeled away years of wisdom and maturity and replaced them with the impish expression of a crazy uncle.

"Oh no, wait, please don't tell me, not the Joke?"

Moore pulled a small photo album out of his jacket pocket. Joshua recognized it from the first time he saw it years ago. It was the photo album that accompanied the assignment for telling the Joke.

Moore smiled like a schoolboy who had pulled a prank on his second grade teacher. "I did it last year, so now it's your turn."

The two men finished their coffee, Joshua poured each of them a second mug, and they sat in his kitchen, watching the dog's antics and laughing about faculty member's larks. Joshua didn't know if it was the promotion, the dog, or time, but he felt as if he and Moore shared more in common than in earlier years. As the golden light of late afternoon began to light up the room, both men looked at empty coffee cups and nodded with mutual friendship.

Joshua took the album in his hand, walked Moore to the door, and prepared to tell the Joke for the second time in his career at Grant's Hill.

PART THREE

MIDTERM EXAMS

JUST AS HE OBSERVED THE Grant's Hill rituals and the English Department rituals during his tenure on campus, Professor Joshua Stone had personal rituals, too. Every September, November, April, and June, he opened the closet doors in the second bedroom of his home. Inside were four hanging garment bags, each with a hand printed label: fall, winter, spring, and summer. One of the bags was empty, its contents in the main closet in his bedroom to be worn for that season.

Stacked neatly on the floor were four plastic, under-bed tubs, also labeled spring, summer, and winter. The fourth, marked fall, was empty. Along the right side wall were shelves with a few pairs of shoes.

It was November, and just like every November, Joshua took the empty garment bag and the heaviest garment bag marked winter and carried them into the bedroom and placed them both across the bed.

As he laid the empty bag across the opposite end of the bed, he unzipped and opened it to accept clothing. From the closet, he removed several long sleeve dress shirts and placed them in the bag. From a shelf in the closet, he took a stack of khaki pants, refolded each one, and arranged them in a neat stack on the bed. His last retrieval from the closet was a collection of fall weight jackets. Still on their hangers, he placed them in the bag and zipped it up. Taking care to be sure the fall label was in clear view.

He carried the now full fall bag to the office closet and returned to the bedroom to open the winter bag. He reversed the procedure and the empty closet was filled with other long sleeve dress and casual shirts, a corduroy jacket and two black wool suits. On his last trip from office to bedroom, he brought the two plastic tubs: winter and fall. He filled the fall box with some sweaters along with a few rugby shirts and neckties, and, then moved the clothing from the winter tub onto the shelves of the closet.

He closed the closets in both rooms and sat down at the desk in his home office with a file folder given to him by Mrs. Thorn. Throughout the afternoon, he switched his attention between the folder contents, the telephone calls from friends and former students, and Rex. The dog was initially content to chase his toy around the hardwood floors of the house.

By the end of the seventh phone call of the afternoon, Rex was showing a clear lack of patience, so man and dog went out to the back yard. Joshua tossed the rope toy to the far edge of the lawn and Rex chased after it and returned it to the praise of the master. The days of fall were shortening and the sun faded late in the afternoon. Joshua was like the dog; he never tired of the same game. He loved throwing the toy to Rex. He looked over the north sky towards the spire of Eastford Chapel on campus. He saw the lights switch on for the evening and reluctantly called to the dog, "Come on Rex. Let's call it a night."

It was unseasonably warm on Friday morning, shirtsleeve weather in November. Rex got off his dog-bed pad and performed the only yoga move a dog knows how to do: downward facing dog. The dog explored every corner of the room with his nose for any thing unusual before coming to the side of Joshua's bed and sitting down. He stared at the form under the covers for several minutes before making a small grunt-like yip. Joshua knew the routine.

It began with the grunt, and progressed to a more vocal bark, and then, only then, would Rexroth attempt to break the rules buy placing one foot on the edge of the mattress.

"Good morning, where's my handsome dog?" The man covered his own face with the sheets. "Where are you? I'm so happy to see you." Joshua said aloud. Rex wagged his tail and barked at Joshua's sheet covered head. Joshua quickly pulled the sheet down and the dog scampered in a circle to the other side of the bed and then back. Joshua got up, walked with Rex to the kitchen, and opened the cupboard door. He opened the plastic storage container filled with kibble, measured out two level cups, and poured it into Rex's bowl.

Rex waited for the series of commands with anticipation. Joshua worked with the dog in their very early years together and developed a regular routine. "Sit" and the dog sat. "Down" and the dog dropped to the floor, prone. "Up" and the dog jumped to its feet. "Sit." Again the dog sat, never breaking eye contact. "Wave" and the dog raised his right paw.

"Good boy, eat" and Rex walked to his dish and began breakfast, as he had every morning since they both rode home from Town and Country together in Moore's car.

Joshua turned on public radio and headed for the shower. The commentators were discussing off-year elections as Joshua splashed the hot water over his body, hearing only bits and pieces of the on-air conversation.

The host had two guests, both discussing the recent statewide referendum about some gun issue. Joshua neither cared about nor understood the points, but gathered it was something to do with carrying guns and how the state issued permits. By the time he was out of the shower and within earshot, they had moved the conversation on to flooding in India and a new wing at the State History Museum.

Friday also meant Joshua had late class, 4:30 – 6:00 p.m., Freshman Composition. He loved this class, his students were academically sound, but he had to question their practical intelligence: what bright student takes a freshman year class, on a Friday, that ends at 6:00? He was never sure if he should give them all A's for effort or all F's for a lack of common sense. But no one at Grant's Hill ever got a grade lower than a B-, so perhaps, they all deserved a C.

If Joshua was having dinner at the F Club, the unspoken rule between dog and man was the dog got to spend the day on campus. Otherwise, Rex's stay home routine was to enjoy his toy and a series of naps. Friday night reunions meant a long walk and then popcorn for dinner. Joshua set the popcorn maker on the stove as a reminder and finished dressing in his bedroom.

He opened the door, let Rex out into the back yard for his morning constitutional, and looked around the neighborhood. The leaves were falling from the trees, which gave him a clear view of the Eastford Chapel steeple on campus. On days he rode without Rex, he could count on his usual brisk 10-minute ride to campus. He joked with his students that it was "up hill, both ways."

One year he made the mistake of adding "in cardboard shoes" to his story about riding his bike and on the last day of the semester, the students gave him a pair of shoes made from cardboard and paper maché. They were not only ugly saddle shoes, but larger than the shoes worn by clowns in the circus. Rex destroyed one of them and the other sits as a reminder to avoid hyperbole in Joshua's office.

Joshua called Rex to come in and when he began to close the door, the dog moved to place himself in the frame, looking first at Joshua and then back towards the hook where his leash was clipped. Joshua shooed the dog in and began to close the door a second time. Again, the dog pressed himself in between the frame and the door. On his third attempt, Joshua shook his head and returned to the kitchen through the door. He grabbed Rex's leash and Rex sat down and waited for it to be clipped to his collar.

Joshua clipped his cuff clips around the cuffs of his grey flannel trousers and the two walked to the bicycle. The man climbed onto the bicycle seat and the pair of them headed to campus. His estimated 10-minute ride became 20 with Rex trotting along side, but man and dog had worked out the ballet that was their ride together quite well. Rex rode on an extendable leash, giving them up to 30 feet of separation. Joshua watched to be sure the dog's sudden stops didn't yank the bicycle careening into a curb and most of the time, Rex jogged at his side.

As they made it to mid-block, Tom Steves shouted as he walked out to his mailbox, "Hey Stone, it looks more like that dog is walking you."

Joshua smiled and waved.

When they got to campus, Joshua parked the Skeppshult in the bike rack at the entrance to the Quad and nearest the stairway to his office. Rex looked around and then followed Joshua up the stairs. Near the top, Joshua took him off the leash and walked down the hall. This morning, Rex stayed close to his heels, avoiding the normal check-ins with other open doors and when Joshua unlocked the door to his office and paused, Rex sat at his heels. He didn't walk over to Mrs. Thorn's desk as usual. As the two crossed the threshold and Joshua sat down in his chair. Rex lay down under his desk with one paw over the man's shoe.

David Adams stuck his head in the door, "Big weekend plans?"

Joshua and Rex looked up "I dunno. A couple of good games on Saturday, might listen to them as I finish my yard work. If it rains, I'll be addressing Christmas cards."

Adams grinned, stroking his black and silver mustache as he looked around the office. "If you want to come to the State Championships, you're welcome to ride along with me. I'm thinking I can win and take the trifecta."

Joshua remembered the collection of trophies and pictures of shotguns in David's office, "Remind me again, is this trap or skeet?"

Adams leaned forward, arms extended to the trigger and stock of an imaginary shotgun "Pull! It's skeet, my friend, skeet!"

Adams was an avid fly fisherman and a competitive shotgun shooter, winning several state and regional trophies, medals and assorted trinkets. On his office wall, above the standard issue credenza for full professors, hung half a dozen color 8 x 10s of him shooting or receiving awards. He toured for three seasons with an exhibition team sponsored by a regional sporting goods clothing and bag company. Even though the company was long out of business, the photo of David and his teammates was the center of the wall. The cover of each of his books was framed and hung on the same wall.

Joshua had seen skeet in movies and listened enough to Adams to know it was harder than it looked. Although, he imagined Adams made it look easy as he had won dozens of contests and tournaments. "When is it?"

"I leave at zero dark thirty to drive to the club, I could pick you up along the way."

"Sure, sounds great. Should I pack a lunch? Or how awful are the hotdogs in the concession trailer?"

"Either way, Ellen usually sends along some treats for the road. I'll get you around 5:45?"

"Great, I can have the neighbors let out Rex. Hey, did you hear public radio this morning? What's the deal about the gun referendum?"

Adams rolled his eyes, "Ahh, the precious Second Amendment folks. It depends on whom you believe. The law in this state used to be that the county sheriff could decide if you can have a permit to carry a concealed weapon...or not."

Joshua interrupted, "You mean like for security guards and private eyes?"

"No, anyone. And that's what they wanted. They wanted to change the law so anyone who applies and gets training can have a permit to carry a pistol."

"Serious? Hmm...Who knew anyone can carry a gun?"

"Yep, even Mrs. Thorn if she wanted one." Mrs. Thorn had just walked within earshot when she heard her name.

"Whatever you say Dr. Adams, whatever you say." She mimicked him politely. Joshua tried to imagine Mrs. Thorn with a pistol, as a James Bond 007 Bond Girl. He looked at her again. Perhaps a Bond Girl's mother.

"So you would get one of these, right, since you do all this shooting?" Joshua asked.

"Me? Ha! No, what would I do with a pistol? Who needs to carry a pistol in this day and age? But, I suppose I support this indirectly since a portion of my dues at the club goes to pay for the gun lobbyist at the statehouse. Besides, it's against school policy to carry a gun on campus, and we don't live in the Wild West anymore. That's why we have cops. Grant's Hill's finest."

Joshua thought about the Grant's Hill Sheriff. He had seen them in parades. That was the only time he remembered hearing sirens the entire time he lived in Grant's Hill.

A student knocked on the door and looked expectantly at the two of them. Joshua looked up and recognized her from his Friday afternoon class: Courtney Maddocks-Martin. She was doing well in class, finished her assignments on time and was eager to discuss the readings. She hadn't caught his attention as a gifted writer, but most of the Freshman Comp students were still in search of their voice.

"Hi, come on in, Dr. Adams and I were just finishing." He looked over at Adams. "See you tomorrow morning then?" Adams walked out the door, waving as he left.

Rex looked up at the student and then back at Joshua and remained at his feet, with one paw still across his shoe.

"Please, sit down, Courtney. How can I help?" Joshua looked across the desk. "How is your assignment coming?"

"My assignment is okay, but I came to ask you a favor. I know I am only a freshman, but there is an essay contest sponsored by the National Animal Welfare Conservancy. The first prize is $5000." She said it in an odd way that caught Joshua's attention. He couldn't understand her lack of enthusiasm for $5000. She continued with building excitement.

"But second prize is a summer fellowship in their Alaska wildlife refuge. So, I know it sounds funny, but I'm hoping to win second prize because I really, really, really want to work there..."

She paused, realizing how immature her sentence sounded. "I was hoping you might read my essay and give me your critique."

Joshua was well aware that writing involved both risk taking and rejection. He found that freshmen usually lack the depth to be successful and early rejections often did more to discourage than motivate promising writers.

He felt he had to hear her out, so he asked what her idea was, before giving her an answer.

"I'm comparing Jack London's *Call of the Wild* with John Krakauer's *Into the Wild*."

Joshua maintained his poker face but inside felt a candle-size fire warming his heart.

Courtney continued, "I am exploring the archetype of the wild as portrayed in both books, even though they were written 93 years apart."

Joshua thought to himself, "'Archetype'? Did a freshman just walk into my office and say 'archetype'? Without me prompting her?"

Courtney looked down and she chose the next words in her mind before saying them. "I want to show how characters Buck and Chris McCandless are representative of the archetype of the wild. They both leave their former homes to answer the call of the wild."

Joshua listened to her words. About every five years, a student like this walked into his office and reminded him of the gift of being a teacher. She had the potential to be brilliant. And she was only a freshman.

"It's really a contrast of intimacy and fear, and I think the synthesis of these ideas is what drives both story lines, but in opposite directions."

Joshua looked her in the eye. "I'll be happy to read it," he agreed as he extended his hand to take it from her.

He set the paper in his leather briefcase. "When is the deadline?"

"It's December 31, but I'd like to send it off to them by mid-December."

The impressed professor nodded at the student and she excused herself and left his office.

Joshua looked at the dog and Rex looked up. "Buck. Maybe I should have named you Buck?" The dog sighed and lay its head back down on his paws.

Throughout the rest of the day, Rex followed him as he moved from meeting to meeting and office to office. Ordinarily, Mrs. Thorn and her secret biscuit stash kept Rex near her desk. The students and the staff were so accustomed to Rex's wandering that no one commented or noticed.

By a quarter after four, the third floor was nearly vacant and Mrs. Thorn stuck her head into Joshua's office.

"Good night, Dr. Stone, have a good class this evening. I made copies of your reading assignments and left them in your basket for tonight's class"

"Thank you, Mrs. Thorn, good night." He smiled, thinking old habits die hard. Neither of them considered posting this in the new course management system.

Joshua turned his attention back to his computer. His current work was a novel. He struggled with short stories, never knowing exactly when to quit. Novels took longer, and were harder to publish, but he felt at home with the process. This was a comedy. A story of a single mom and her teenage daughter who, after a series of comedic exchanges that usually occur in stage plays, jump to the wrong conclusion that the other is pregnant.

He pictured the mother and daughter at a summer cottage, maybe on Chincoteague Island or Kennebunkport. It was his second attempt at writing from a woman's point of view, and it still eluded him. The first time was his still unfinished book, *Ladies for Tea*. He loved the idea: a senile woman in a brownstone who made weekly tea for ladies who never came. A quirky high school girl learns of the teas and talks her anime club into dressing up and going to tea. His dialogue was stilted, the characters one dimensional, and the whole project lacked rhythm. Adams had coached him, suggesting he go to a couple of Tupperware parties and just listen. Stone considered Adams a good editor, but wondered if Tupperware existed anymore. When Adams had made the suggestion, Joshua had gone online to search and according to the Internet, the parties were alive and well. He even found one in Grant's Hill and telephoned the hostess to tell her he was coming. His courage lasted until he got to her street, and when he saw a group of women laughing and chatting in her driveway, he rode his bicycle right on past the house and returned home.

Adams had also suggested listening to female students on their cell phones.

"That way, you only hear the woman. Listen to how they speak, how they phrase, how they link ideas. You'll find your character's voice." This current book wasn't going much better than *Ladies for Tea*.

At 4:25, he looked over at Rex and called the dog. He noticed his collar was loose and adjusted it for a better fit and finished by stroking the dog's fur and scratching behind his ears. Joshua and Rex walked down the stairs and to the end of the hallway, where he closed the door to the classroom on the ground floor. Rex found a corner near the front of the room and lay down in a tight ball.

"Good afternoon."

"Good afternoon," responded the class and Joshua quickly skimmed the room to see who had opted to do something else on a Friday afternoon. Everyone was there, and seemed in a good mood. When he had walked in, there was some music playing and the groups were talking and laughing and looking over each other's shoulders and computer screens. Not long ago it was magazines, Joshua mused, and they began the class.

As he did, he noticed four of the freshmen were sitting in the back row. He paused.

"Guys, what's my rule about sitting in the back row?"

They grumbled as he approached them and each dug in their pocket for 25 cents.

"Last day, we were discussing irony and sarcasm. Who can remind us what we found?"

Several hands went up and Joshua pointed to one of the first hands. It was Zack Bowes, and as he answered, something about Rex caught Joshua's eye. Rex was not napping, but was watching his movement as he crossed the room and coaxed the students to dig deeper. He realized Rex's leash was still clipped to his collar and considered walking over to unhook the clasp, but he was focusing back on the student response. As they explored irony in some of the required reading, Joshua continued to watch Rex and Rex watched the professor with his head resting on his paws.

"Give me an example of irony?"

Bowes continued, "It's like that bit in the student handbook about death."

Joshua felt he was being set up for a joke, and debated moving on, but took a chance to let the student continue.

"It says in there, 'In the event of the death of a student, contact the Office of Student Life.'"

Snickers followed the brief pause and a few groans.

"Brilliant!" Joshua replied, "Irony. Who knew? Great stuff!"

Joshua moved towards the right side of the room, near a reluctant student who wrote great essays and seldom contributed in the classroom. He stood close to her and when he caught her eye, his facial expression encouraged her to raise her hand.

"Dana, can you give us an example?"

Dana looked at the professor and began, "I was thinking Jane Austen and *Pride and Prejudice*."

"Okay, and what gives us a clue Austen is using irony?"

She looked at him like he was the dumbest person in the room, and then answered, "Well all you have to do is read the opening line," and from memory she recited, "It is a truth universally acknowledged, that a single man in possession of a good fortune must be in want of a wife."

Some of the young men got the joke.

Joshua smiled, in one line she had just demonstrated what the others were trying to grasp.

She continued, "And what you just did was irony, Socratic irony."

Joshua looked back and she continued, "Like Socrates, you pretend to not know Jane Austen or *Pride and Prejudice* so that you would make us think."

He nodded at Dana and then glanced at Rex who seemed to nod with approval as well. Just as they were getting to a deeper understanding of the content, the 90-minute class came to an end and Joshua looked up at the clock. 5:59.

"Alright, we're done for the day and the week, remember on Monday we'll be picking up metaphors. Be sure to read the assignments from our syllabus."

Joshua stepped to the side and opened the classroom door. Rex looked out the door, unsure if he should get up or remain. He glanced back at Joshua; his leash still clipped to his collar.

"The trick," came shouts from the back of the class. Joshua now figured out why the freshmen, who knew his rule, opted to sit at the back. They had bet each other on the outcome of the toss. Just the same, he was game to entertain their ruse. They had worked hard in the class. He took the stack of four quarters and placed them on his thumb at the top of his outstretched fist. The class counted down "three — two — one" and he flipped the coins. Rex watched as the four quarters rose, hit their arc, and Joshua, as he had done countless times, reached out and caught each one in mid flight.

Except.

He missed.

He caught three of the four quarters in mid air and somehow managed only to bat the fourth quarter sideways. It hit the linoleum floor with a resounding ping and then rolled on edge across the room and out the door.

Rex went out, slowly following the quarter. The class, with mixes of "boos" and "awws," gathered their things and left the room.

"Professor Stone?"

Joshua looked up to see Dana Wilkinson. "Dana, nice work on your last essay." He smiled warmly, and then added, "I'd like to hear you speak up more in class. You did very well today. Socratic irony. Nice"

"I just wanted to be sure you weren't mad at me. I don't talk back to teachers."

"You did fine, Dana. I hope you'll consider *The American Story in Modern Fiction* class next term. I think you'll find some challenging content."

The student left the room. Joshua gathered his papers, and began to close the door when he searched around for Rex. The dog was not in the classroom or the hall, so Joshua gave one more look, and decided to walk upstairs to his office to see if the dog was hunting for biscuits in Mrs. Thorn's desk.

REX FOLLOWED THE ROLLING COIN out the classroom door and into the hallway. The outer door that led to the parking lot was propped open. Rex sniffed the night air. It was still warm for fall and Rex could hear the scurried habits of squirrels and rabbits. He walked out the door and looked across the parking lot and then looked back to the hallway. Rex smelled a predator and, following his instinct, began crossing the paved parking lot, moving slowly as he approached the end of the pavement near the tree line. When the dog reached the grass, he stopped. He let out a growl as the fur on his neck and back began to stand up aggressively.

Rex understood evil and was prepared to face it. DNA and the animal memory of battles connected a long string of ancestral learning to his mind from prior generations.

His leash yanked tight and the dog spun on his loins to turn to face who ever had taken control of the loose end. It was a dark figure with a smell of evil and Rex sensed rage as he struggled to avoid the man's boot.

The man was focused. He had been hiding in the trees, hoping to snare a rabbit or squirrel as he had the other nights. This dog was a trophy, a new conquest. The dog fought back more than his other prey, so he dropped his foot back and slammed it forward into the dog.

Hampered by the leash, the contact was unavoidable as the boot kicked his side and left shoulder. Rex tumbled, rolled over and twisted his neck as far as he could to the left, trying to loosen the collar and square off against his attacker. Feeling no relief, the dog twisted to the right, almost as far, turning his head away from his attacker and hoping to break free of the restraint. A second and third kick came, hard enough to shatter his leg as the boot smashed against him. His yelps of pain echoed in the November night. He bared his teeth and growled and felt the boot kicking again and again at his body until his other front leg was shattered too.

The dog's yelps brought more rage from the man in the boots. The sound of the breaking bones encouraged him to kick harder.

Rex tasted blood and vomited some of Mrs. Thorn's biscuits. As he did, he struggled, kicking with his hind legs to pull away from the leash. The attacker stepped closer and trapped the end of the leash between the sole of his boot and the ground, pressing the leash into the soft earth and limiting the dog's escape to a just a few feet. Rex remembered the pain of being struck by the car and then felt the pain for real as the attacker closed the distance and the boot smashed against his hind quarter, dislocating the hip socket put back in place by Dr. Kanzen at Town and Country.

The man's face was shaped into a chilling partial smirk, partial grin. This was the time to do it. With a rabbit or squirrel, this was when he would take the knife and slide it between their fur and their muscles, skinning them. Exposing them as he stared into their eyes and watched them wriggle to escape the torture. But the man had new plans tonight.

Rex's nose recognized the next smell, but didn't know what it was. The dog first smelled it from the cars he would pass in the parking lot, and knew it was a smell unconnected to Joshua. He had smelled the smell on Adams, Mrs. Thorn, Moore, and most of the students, but never on Joshua.

The boot kicked the dog's head and Rex struggled to see out of his eyes. Through blurred vision he saw a red can and then a sudden whoosh of air and heat as the wetness poured on his fur turned to heat and fire. The flames were taller than Rex and the dog yelped in pain, unable to escape as the world around him burned and his attacker stepped back.

Rex lost control of his body, and the remaining vomit, feces and urine leached from their cavities as his hair was matted, then burned, then ash. The dog's left leg dug into the soft ground, trying to gain traction against an unbreakable strangle hold of the collar on its neck.

The inferno died and the smoldering continued.

The boot that had done so much damage gave a final kick to the charred dog that was known to everyone on campus. What remained was unrecognizable. The man was breathing fast, his heart was pounding, and he wanted to do it again. The flames were much bigger than he expected, almost burning his own clothes before he jumped out of their way. Now he reached down, loosened the charred collar from the dog's neck and unclipped it from the leash. This was his keepsake. But it wasn't enough. The man with the boots looked around for something else to kill and set ablaze. He had power. He had control. Kneeling down next to the car, he tried to catch his breath, and waited.

This was the night Joshua was three stories above the parking lot and at the opposite end of the building, This was the night he turned off the lights in his office, scanned around one more time, and then turned down the stairway, past Liv Olsson's dark office and moved towards the first floor and the door to the parking lot. As Joshua stepped out, he called Rex's name.

This was the night he noticed the smell. He had never smelled anything like it, and walked towards the church. It was then he saw the smoldering pile at the end of the median along the edge of the parking lot. It didn't look like much of a fire; it seemed more like the remnants of a Halloween prank.

As he walked, he glanced around to see if he could spot his dog, and about half way across the parking lot, he passed the blue emergency beacon.

Joshua mused that the dog wasn't able to press the warning button that would bring help, so searching for him was his only hope. It was as he approached a car parked on the church side of the parking lot, Joshua felt as if he was wholly surrounded by evil and fear. The air turned to ice, he was unable to catch his breath, he felt the hair stand on the back of his neck, even though he had never experienced the feeling. Then his head pounded as if he had smacked into an overhead beam and in his last conscious thought, realized that something big had hit him.

The boots kicked their next victim: the hunter's ultimate trophy. When he was finished with the beating and ready to burn the unconscious man, he patted the man's corduroy jacket and retrieved his wallet. Two keepsakes in one night. Double score. When he struck the match, he watched and waited. And when the match didn't set the man on fire, the boots kicked him one last time, and walked away.

This was the night Professor Joshua Stone was beaten and left to die. Given the time of night and the day of week, it would be hours before either the professor or the dog would be discovered.

This was the night it all changed.

IT WAS JUST AFTER 4 p.m. when Paramedic student Sophie Carr began reviewing the ambulance checklist with her preceptor Eric Gill and his partner Tom Smith. Sophie was younger than most of their students. She was 19 years old and two years out of high school. In that time she had been a waitress, a cashier, and a nurses aide in the county nursing home. It was there she first met Eric and Tom when they responded to a call for a woman who had fallen in the hallway. Sophie had helped and walked with them out to their ambulance. As they raised the ambulance cot to the lip of the ambulance, Sophie took a look inside at the lights and the gear. It was love at first sight. She knew this was her calling. Everything so orderly, so active. She could picture herself sitting in the back jump seat, tending to a dying patient. She knew it was her future.

Sophie Carr couldn't afford tuition and was earning minimum wage feeding patients and cleaning them after they soiled their beds, unable to use the toilet on their own. So she reached out to her grandfather and asked for a loan. He agreed and the following year she applied to community college. This was her final rotation as a student.

Eric and Tom both felt she was skilled. What she lacked in years of maturity, she made up in initiative and concentration. During their down time, if she was ever missing, they could find her in the skills room, practicing on one of the life-like training manikins, or rooting through one of the many bags that held their gear, exploring how all the tools of the trade went together. The ambulance was a portable emergency room, so everything either was carried by a handle or stored in a bag. Most of the bags were special purpose collections of equipment: pediatric splints for fractures, a special bag for childbirth, supplies for intravenous fluids with catheters and tubing, and medication bags with security seals and locks.

Sophie's intensity had led her to suggest they unpack their main equipment bag — the "first out" bag that went with them on every call — and re-organize it so that they could get the things they needed faster. She also lightened it by seven pounds by helping them see things they didn't need in those first few minutes of a call. Even though they fought her on every item she wanted to delete, and their supervisor made them write a 3-page memo to justify their actions, both preceptors agreed that she had made the bag better.

If there was a bag Sophie most wanted to use, it was the specialized bag that contained all the gear to manage a patient's airway by intubation. She had done it countless times on a manikin, but never in the field.

"Hell yeah," Tom would often say, "let's see those frat-boy-docs try it in the snow and mud at 2:30 in the morning on a puking drunk."

The paramedics often boasted of their own skill by putting down the relative ease of intubating a surgical patient in a temperature-controlled, well-lit operating room with a height-adjustable operating table. Sophie had done that during her rotations in Jefferson County Hospital.

"Frat-boy-docs" is a clue to the college — townie relationship. Or more accurately, the lack of relationship. Most of the local doctors and even those at Jefferson County Hospital did their undergraduate work at Grant's Hill. There was never any animosity expressed in the decades the town had been home to the college, but the two worlds rarely overlapped and they never socialized together. The small group of shops that catered to college students had the most contact across town and gown lines. The Campus Book Store, the Varsity theater, Myron's drug store and a few clothing and gift stores that seemed to come and go as often as the graduating class. Murphy Z's pizza and the Corner Booth kept a college crowd during the school year and a townie crowd in the summers. To a visitor, there was no visible segregation, but if you lived in town, you got your hair cut at the Curl Up and Dye, if you were a student or faculty, you got it cut at Cutting Class.

By 5 p.m., Sophie had already re-inventoried their medications and had cleaned the drug locker shelves. Eric and Tom enjoyed the extra help and knew that within the week, the drudgery of chores would fall back on just the two of them.

At 6:02 they were having a quick dinner at the Corner Booth.

At 6:57 they were headed back to the station, ready to watch some TV before the night's calls began to pick up in frequency.

At 7:19 their pagers sounded. The dispatcher relayed the call: an emergency beacon alarm at the North parking lot of Grant's Hill College.

In the event of activation of the emergency beacon alarm box, Standard Operating Procedure was for the dispatcher to send both an ambulance and a sheriff's car to the college. The alarm was activated 2 or 3 times each year, almost always as a false alarm or the occasional drunk student who had puked, but was otherwise stable.

The ambulance radio crackled as Sophie, in the passenger seat of the cab, flipped on the overhead light-bar and other emergency lights.

On the opposite side of Grant's Hill, Deputy Bill Simmons had just pulled into his driveway at home to take a supper break before finishing his shift. The only thing between Simmons and his supper was this FIDO call.

FIDO was department slang for the kinds of nuisance calls that deputies never want to take. It stood for "Fuck It Drive On." A typical FIDO call was a trash can that had blown in the street, a pre-teen child smoking a cigarette behind a garage, or a dispute between two neighbors over who should shovel the occasional snow from their shared sidewalk. Simmons radio call sign was car 6-30.

"Dispatch from 6-30. I'm just going 10-7 for supper, does the squad need me on this?"

Sophie looked over at Eric for some guidance.

"This is your trip — your call. You decide."

Sophie considered what she knew about the call. An unknown problem from an alarm box on the campus. In town, she might have been more concerned, but campus was always safe. She picked up the microphone and keyed the switch.

"Dispatch from Squad, do you have any other caller's from this incident or other information on this?"

Eric smiled to himself, thinking it was a good question for his student to ask.

"Squad and 6-30, this is a drop alarm, I have no callers or witnesses at this time."

Sophie decided to let Bill eat his supper.

"Dispatch from Squad, you can advise the deputy to 10-22, we'll call if we need assistance."

Eric looked at Tom and back to Sophie. He tapped the siren as they crossed the intersection and then continued on their emergent drive to the campus.

As they rolled into the parking lot, the blue strobe light was blinking at the top of the emergency beacon. There were two cars parked several spaces from each other. The first impression, shared by all three responders, was the lack of a crowd. Even more curious was the absence of someone waiving them down near the alarm box. The parking lot had the signs of a typical Grant's Hill College false alarm. Eric slowed the ambulance and Sophie took hold of the spot light mounted in the door pillar and started sweeping the edges with its beam.

They spotted a man slumped behind a parked car on the grass between the college parking lot and the First Apostolic Church next door.

"There" said Sophie and all three looked around for any other people.

Sophie drew a breath, and said, "Probably a drunk, but I'm gonna do this by the numbers." And with that, she began to recite a checklist.

"Scene safe?" She looked around the parking lot, "At this time, yes."

"Number of patients? Equals one."

"Problem? Unknown."

She began to take command and give instructions.

"Eric, will you secure the truck and light our scene? Tom, you get the first out bag and long back board."

The ambulance came to a stop and Eric flipped the alley lights on the cube of the ambulance body. The entire area was flooded with light. The shape on the ground was a man, facing away from them.

"Be sharp," Sophie commanded, "we can't see if he's holding anything."

Tom and Eric exchanged smirks. Sophie was doing this like the textbook, yes, but a bit much for the little ol' Grant's Hill College's passed out drunk. Sophie opened the squad door and called to the fallen man.

"Sir, did you call 9-1-1? Can you hear me?"

The body did not move or respond.

"Let's go" Sophie said, and the three medics stepped into the parking lot. The first thing they noticed was the stench. It was gut wrenching, and almost forced Sophie to vomit.

It smelled like a cross between blood and feces and burning hair, it was like nothing any of them had smelled before.

"What the fuck is that?"

Eric did one more overview of the area and seeing nothing, knelt at the head of the crumpled man. Sophie began giving instructions, "Eric, take c-spine, Tom, lets you and I roll him over."

She did a quick visual inspection of his back and lower extremities and then the three of them gently rolled the patient onto his back on their long backboard. They would secure him to this as soon as they were ready to get off scene. For now, there was immediate care to be done.

His face was grotesque, battered, and bloody, already beginning to swell. Eric held the patient's head and neck, a move they called managing c-spine, short for cervical spine. As he did, he manipulated the man's jaw and thrust it forward, which stopped the snoring sound in the man's throat and he began to breathe. He estimated respirations to be about 30 times a minute. The breathing still sounded like gurgles. Sophie quickly checked for a radial pulse and felt nothing.

"Shit, no pulse."

She moved to the carotid artery and found a weak carotid pulse.

Sophie's voiced quickened and her breathing increased as she reported what she was finding. "I've got a carotid. Um, let's get the monitor on him Eric and I'm going to intubate."

"Sophie?" Eric's voice said in a calm manner. "Slow down. Do you want me on c-spine and airway? Or the monitor?"

"Why? What did I say?" Sophie looked around, flustered as she took in the events, and then regained her focus. "Okay. Tom, get the monitor, Eric you're right. You stay where you are, like we started. Can I do the intubation?"

With Eric holding manual c-spine stabilization, there was little room for Sophie to work at the man's head to see what she was doing. She retrieved the endotracheal kit from the left pocket of the first out bag and while Tom cut the top of Joshua's shirt open to apply the cardiac electrodes, Sophie began to open Joshua's airway. To her surprise, his mouth was filled with blood and visible chunks of something white.

"What is that? Did he puke?" Sophie asked.

Eric peaked in the man's mouth. "Teeth... It looks like pieces of his teeth."

Sophie first suctioned his mouth using the portable suction machine and then visualized with the laryngoscope. She advanced the endotracheal tube past the epiglottis and watched as the tube passed between the white vocal cords. She inflated the balloon on the end of the tube and then began to ventilate her patient.

The cardiac monitor showed a tachycardic rhythm around 110 beats per minute. Sophie knew with the absence of a radial pulse, his blood pressure was under 60 systolic. In the calm quiet of a doctor's office, or in a routine call for medical help, Sophie would have taken the time to wrap a blood pressure cuff around his arm and listen to both the systolic and diastolic sounds that would tell her a blood pressure reading. Her training told her this was a critical trauma patient. So instead, she used the shortcut and by estimate, his blood pressure was less than half of a healthy person's. This was not time to "stay and play" as they used to say in school. This was time to "load and go."

"I'm not sure I want to risk starting an IV rolling down the road, I want to start it here. Then we need to haul ass." Sophie said. Eric and Tom nodded in agreement.

As they did, Deputy Bill Simmons rolled up in car 6-30.

He rolled down his window, "You guys okay? Is he drunk?"

Eric shot a look at Deputy Simmons and flipped his chin up in a gesture to suggest Simmons get out of his car. Simmons concluded this wasn't a FIDO call.

"I thought I would stop by before I went to chow. What's up?"

"Looks like this guy has been beaten pretty bad and what the hell is that smell?"

Simmons got out with the flashlight from his belt and began to systematically search around the vehicle. When he got to the far side of the car, he stopped. He shined the beam down the length of the median between the college and the church parking lot. The grass was uneven height at the demarcation between where the church employees mowed and Bob Thornton mowed. The median was only 4 mower passes wide, yet Thornton's boss insisted that Thornton only mow the half that belonged to the college. Simmons turned back to the medics and their patient. Joshua's body lay on the long-grass, church side of the median. He looked one more time, very quickly, at the two cars, the ground, the grass and the parking lot before grasping the microphone on his shirt lapel. His bright tactical flashlight lit up the burned area near the edge of the tree line and the end of the mown grass. The sheriff's deputy recognized foul play beyond a prank.

"Dispatch from 6-30, I need a second car here."

Sophie's IV start was in the patient's right antecubital space. Tom started one in the comatose man's left arm. They loaded the unconscious Professor Stone onto the stretcher and into the ambulance. Simmons secured his crime scene by looking in the windows and underneath both cars. Confident that the assailant was not still on the scene, he began stringing yellow tape all around the car and into the church parking lot, creating a wedge shaped crime scene. The words on the tape were upside down, and read POLICE LINE DO NOT CROSS. The ambulance siren broke the silence of the campus.

CHAPTER 11

SERGEANT JESSICA ADDISON

SERGEANT JESSICA ADDISON HAD BEEN on her way home when she heard the radio dispatch request for a second car at the college. Addison had been Sergeant for five years and now worked three days a week as a School Resource Officer in Grant's Hill Consolidated High School. Normally on a fall Friday night, she was on the sidelines of the football field, with an ear listening to the walkie-talkies of the other officers and her eyes on the stands of both the home and visiting teams.

It was good duty for the farm girl who grew up here and married her high school sweetheart. Grant's Hill was her school, her team, her life. Back then, she was Jessica Nystrom, the third of the Nystrom girls to go to Grant's Hill High. She started attending the Friday night games as a freshman, and as near as anyone could remember, she'd never missed a home game. This Friday night, the Grant's Hill Surveyors football team wasn't playing. After suffering a double overtime defeat the week before in the quarter finals of the state football championship, the season was over and instead of Friday night lights, she was doing Friday night paperwork and then headed home.

Once there, she would make a quick dinner for herself and then pack a large cooler with sandwiches, chips, and snacks, with a thermos of coffee. If she timed it right, and none of the farm equipment had broken down that day, she could meet her husband on the combine about the time he finished the back 120 acres. She tried to remember if she heard him come in last night or leave this morning. The radio call for a second car at the college meant his dinner might not make it and tonight, she would be the one coming in late.

She rolled up in time to see Bill Simmons finish securing the yellow POLICE LINE DO NOT CROSS tape around the perimeter. She giggled because he looked so out of place doing it, until she saw his clenched teeth and the intensity of his gaze. She put the car in park and stepped out into the warm night air.

"Ugh, what is that smell?" she asked as she ducked under the yellow tape and around the left side of the car.

She followed the beam of light from Simmons' hand. Further down the median, at the tree line, Rex's remains smoldered. The haze rose like a ghost in the beam of Bill's flashlight. From the look of the ground and the condition of the remains, the dog had been alive when it was set on fire, but unable to run from the inferno. A charred leash lay in a footprint from a man's boot. The dog had been held there as the fire ravaged around him.

"Oh dear God."

Simmons and Addison both wrote reports at the scene of the attack. Simmons took photographs of the dog, the boot print, and the leash. With each photo, he placed a bright yellow, numbered, a-frame marking tent. The deputies would use the numbers to identify evidence in each photo.

As Simmons approached the back of the car, he saw the trunk. The damage was from Joshua's head repeatedly being smacked into the metal lid. He took close ups of the blood spatter and the area just behind the car. He also took some wide-angle photos that included the parking lot at the college and the emergency beacon.

It was half past midnight when they finished working the crime scene and began putting what they had seen on paper. As they wrote, the talked over what they saw and possible theories.

"So did this guy set the dog on fire? And someone else stopped him and kicked him to hell?" Simmons asked.

"Could be, did you see his shoes?"

"Yeah our vic had penny loafers, like those college profs wear." He pointed to the trunk of his squad car. He had picked up Stone's shoes and placed them on the car after he took the photos. They shined their lights and found no footprints other than the boot print over the dog leash.

"Look at the size of those gun boats, that must be like a size 13 boot?" Simmons exclaimed.

The deputy changed his theory, "So if this guy didn't attack the dog, who did? Some guy whacks our vic and then torches the dog? Why didn't the dog fight back? Or maybe that's why the dog was attacked? Robbery?"

Addison asked Simmons, "What about personal effects, watch? ID? Wallet? Cash?"

"Don't know. The squad was in a hurry to get him going. I don't think he's going to live." Simmons paused, and then asked, "Do you remember the postman?"

Addison flashed back to one of the first calls she attended as a sheriff's deputy. A postal worker had parked against traffic and stepped out of his truck to put mail in a rural box. As he did, he was struck by a mini van driving at highway speed. It was the first time Addison had seen a dead human being before the mortuary clean up.

"I remember the postman."

Simmons nodded, "Yeah, this guy?" Simmons paused looking around, "This guy looked like the postman."

"Okay, I'll take the ER report and grab the evidence for chain of custody. You finish up here and I'll see you back?"

Simmons and Addison were thinking the same thing: murder in Grant's Hill? The last murder had been sometime in the early 2000s. But local thugs were getting more aggressive and both knew it was just a matter of time. The highway had become a major drug route into the capital and further on to Chicago, St Louis, Columbus, Omaha, and all the little towns in between. With the transient drug runners came more guns and a more aggressive disrespect for all authority. Simmons and Addison wanted to keep this case and not turn it over to the state police. Their cop pride wanted to work this to its conclusion. Simmons turned the flashlight on the dog's remains and turned back to Addison.

"This is a sick mother fucker."

Addison shivered as she zipped up her blue windbreaker, "You know what they say, torturing animals is the beginning to torturing people. Looks like our perp reached his graduation. Welcome to college," she pointed at the spire on Eastford Chapel.

PART FOUR

THE HOSPITAL

CHAPTER 12

LUCID

JOSHUA WAS LOST BETWEEN REALITY and confusion.

He was in bed, he faintly remembered falling down a hole into darkness, and his memories were jumbled. He was riding his bicycle, faster than ever, the wind in his hair. Rex was chasing him. Or he was chasing Rex. Rex was running farther away and Joshua was writing something on a chalkboard. And he was holding a piece of chalk in his mouth. The images in the dream were difficult to grasp, except the chalk was getting bigger and longer. The dry chalky tube grew as it snaked down and now was caught in Joshua's throat.

He opened his eyes to hear sounds of several people walking and see the face of Sophie Carr hovering above him. He could tell he was rolling on a cart, his eyes darted left, then right.

"Don't move, you've been in an accident. You're in the hospital and there is a tube in your throat to help you breathe. If you understand, nod your head."

Joshua nodded and his entire head pounded with pain.

A second face appeared in his field of vision. It was blurry and out of focus, he strained to recognize it. It was a young man in his late 20s looking down and walking alongside him.

"I'm Dr. Madow. You're at Jefferson County Hospital. You had an accident. The paramedics brought you here by ambulance. Blink your eyes if you understand?"

Joshua tried to speak but could not talk because of the endotracheal tube. He blinked and nodded, and again his head pounded with pain.

When they arrived at the trauma bed, just adjacent from the main nurse's station, several people grabbed the long backboard Joshua was strapped to. He heard a voice count to three and then he was moved from ambulance cot to the bed. A group of people began moving IV tubes, oxygen lines, and adjusting monitoring equipment. Madow shined his penlight into each of Joshua's eyes and then performed a quick assessment of his overall body. A nurse was drawing blood and Sophie Carr, with Eric at her side, was giving the rundown.

"Elderly male, 50 years old, unresponsive in the church parking lot near the college, obvious signs of head trauma and multiple contusions and abrasions to the face and chest. Coma score of 3, gurgling respirations, no radial pulse, carotid pulse at 110."

Joshua was confused, "50 years old? I'm not that old." he silently objected.

Dr. Madow nodded. "How long was he out?"

"He woke up right as we pulled in the garage, he seems pretty with it, was able to follow commands," Carr continued.

Madow placed his fingers near each of Joshua's hands. "Squeeze my hands." Joshua obeyed and gave equal squeezes with his fists.

"Close your right eye." Again Joshua obeyed.

"Left Eye?" And again, Joshua followed the command.

"Can you smile?" The damage to Joshua's face and mouth were severe but he managed to move his lips around the endotracheal tube in his mouth and airway.

The doctor moved to the foot of the bed and clasped Joshua's feet, "Move your right toes." Once more, Joshua complied.

"Your left?"

Joshua's eyes closed and he did not move.

"Sir? Sir! Sir?" Madow returned to Joshua's head and asked the team, "Current vitals?"

"BP is now 160 over 100, heart rate is 62"

Madow, used to being in the larger hospital where he was shadowed by medical students and first year residents, challenged the room with a pop quiz, "Lets see what we're up against. Paramedic?"

Sophie and Eric turned, "What were your initial vitals?"

Sophie reviewed her notes, "Heart rate was 110, pressure was estimated at 60 and respiratory rate was 30."

"And now? What do you see?"

She scanned the monitors and back at the doctor.

"Based on what you see what do you suspect?"

Eric saw Madow's motive, this is when the insecure students doubt their initial findings and second-guess themselves. This was a difficult patient. Rather than speak, he let Sophie work it out for herself.

"Male patient with severe head trauma, initially unconscious, brief lucid period followed by non-responsive state. Shift in vital signs suggests potential for increased ICP — inter-cranial pressure." She should have stopped there. That was the extent of her protocols. But she added this last bit, "He needs a head scan to rule out a hemorrhage."

Everyone in the room stopped at stared at the 19-year-old paramedic student.

Madow clapped and grinned, "Good work. You all heard the lady; let's get this man a head CT... I just happened to bring one with me."

Madow was in Jefferson County Emergency on that Friday as a good-natured favor. He was working with the large hospital system in the state capital, and traveling with a semi-trailer truck that held a portable CT scanner to do some outreach education with rural doctors. Ordinarily, a patient with Joshua's injuries would be flown by helicopter to the trauma center in the capital. Madow, who tended to live outside the rules, agreed to cover a dinner break for the attending doctor in the ER. It was all against policy, but by the time the ambulance rolled up to the front doors, it was too late to set everything straight.

Having accepted the patient, Madow was now committed to his care and reluctant to either fly him out by medical helicopter or overextend the capabilities of the small county hospital. He was now the ironic contradiction to a brash statement he made in a meeting, claiming, "tiny, understaffed county hospitals are places where patients go either to fly or to die." Now, Madow's pride was determined to let his patient do neither.

The head CT on Stone revealed a minor epidural hematoma, about 6 mm in diameter. Madow decided to keep Joshua chemically in a coma — to medically sedate him — and not do an invasive drainage of the blood. The hospital staff had already shaved half of Joshua's head before Madow decided on the more conservative therapy. It was very conservative — in the trauma center, his colleagues would take him to surgery and drill a hole.

But he decided to wait and see the progress of the blood trapped between the inner and outer layers protecting the brain. His patience proved wise. The hematoma did not grow and reduced nearly 2 mm over the next few days.

CHAPTER 13

WAKING UP

WHEN JOSHUA OPENED HIS EYES again, he was in a quieter room, and the pain was dull. He was lying on his back, staring at the ceiling and when he turned his head to the side, he caught the eyes of a nurse. She walked over to see him,

"Good afternoon, I'm Connie. Don't try and talk. Do you know where you are?"

Joshua nodded his head with only a small bit of pain. His jaw throbbed, his throat was dry.

"You've been asleep for a while, but you are very stable. You're doing well. If you can stay awake for a few hours, we can get that tube out of your mouth."

Around 6 p.m., Madow and Connie came back to the room.

"We're going to remove the breathing tube from your throat. It's not going to hurt, but I need you to do exactly as I say. Do you understand?"

Joshua nodded.

"Okay, the tube is held in your trachea with a small balloon I'm going to deflate the balloon and then I'm going to ask you to cough. When you do, I'll take out the tube." He turned and addressed the nurse, "Connie, have some suction ready and a basin."

Madow took a pair of trauma shears and snipped the small thin tubing that controlled the balloon at the end of the ET tube. Joshua could feel the pressure release in his trachea and began to cough.

"That's it: cough — cough-cough," Madow instructed as the tube slid up and into the doctor's gloved hands.

Joshua caught his breath and looked around.

"Take it slow, can you tell me where you are?"

"Hospital," Joshua said coarsely. "County."

"Can you tell me your name?"

"Dr. Joshua Stone."

'Do you know what day it is?'

"Friday."

"Close, nice try. It's Tuesday, we kept you asleep for a while." Madow made some notes and looked back up at the professor. "Can you tell me what happened?"

"I was in class," Joshua tried to remember; he remembered teaching class and then falling down the big hole. Or at least that's what he thought happened. In his brain, his words sounded like nonsense.

"I taught tonight. And then I woke up here. Did I pass out?"

Madow looked at him. "You were assaulted. You were beat up pretty bad. The sheriff wants to talk to you." Joshua looked at Connie, then back at the doctor. He couldn't imagine what he had done that got him in trouble with the sheriff,

"Did I break the law?"

Madow shook his head, "No...No...but someone else did."

"Wait, what about Rex?" Stone asked.

Madow looked at Connie, "Who is Rex?"

"My dog," Joshua interrupted, "where is my dog, was he with me? I was looking for him. He had wandered off. Did someone find him?"

The doctor stopped and turned back to face Joshua.

"Dr. Stone. It looks like your dog was... The Sheriff found a dog at the scene."

"Oh that is a relief. Is he at the pound?"

The doctor hesitated. "No, I'm not sure I know the whole story."

Connie turned away and the doctor looked straight at Joshua.

"When you are ready, the Sheriff is here and wants to talk with you."

Joshua swallowed and nodded his head. "I can talk with him."

He sat alone in the room for several minutes, trying to remember what happened. He could picture the classroom. He remembered tossing the four quarters and missing the fourth quarter. He could hear it falling on the tile floor of the classroom. He could picture Rex walking ahead of him somewhere. He searched his mind for the rest of the memory, but it was blank, like the blinking cursor of his word processor when he had writer's block.

The door to his room opened and a woman walked in. She had short dark brown hair, styled in a pixie cut and parted on the side with bangs swept to the opposite side. She was wearing a blue lined windbreaker with an embroidered badge on the left front. Joshua noticed the windbreaker gave her a squared shape. Her torso was slightly longer than her legs. Joshua guessed her to be in her late 20s. She walked with strong, assertive posture.

"Are you," the woman paused, looking at her notes, "Dr. Joshua Stone?"

Stone answered, "Yes."

"Okay, I'm Sergeant Addison. They tell me you just woke up."

"A couple of hours ago, can you tell me what happened to me?"

"Dr. Stone, I was hoping you could tell me. Can you tell me what you were doing at the church?"

"I — I wasn't at the church. Was I? I was teaching, on campus, is that where they found me?"

"You were in the parking lot of the church. Were you meeting someone?" Addison skimmed her notes.

Parts of Joshua's memory came back.

"No, no, I was teaching, we finished class at one minute to six. My dog Rex wandered off and I was looking for him in the parking lot. I ride my bike and he runs alongside."

She had seen the man on the bike, with his dog along side, regularly as she patrolled Grant's Hill. Addison looked again at the professor's face. His bruised face looked nothing like she remembered.

"But we," Joshua continued, "I don't know, Rex saw something or ...I walked over to the median between the college and the church. Yes, I remember I walked up to the median and then I was falling..." Joshua stopped; his distorted memory remembered falling down a hole.

Addison stepped closer to the side of the bed.

"Dr. Stone, do you normally carry a wallet?"

Out of habit, Joshua felt for his jacket pocket but found only a hospital gown where his jacket and wallet would be.

"Yes, I do. Wallet, checkbook, all in one. I keep it in my coat pocket. It will fall out if I put it in my trousers."

"Dr. Stone, what I have to tell you is not easy to hear," She paused. "Dr. Stone, you were the victim of a very serious beating, when the paramedics found you, you were barely alive. You had no wallet, no ID."

Joshua shook his head, "What happened? Where is Rex, can I see him? The doctor said you found my dog there."

Addison stopped, she had delivered the "I regret to inform you" speech only twice in her career, but somehow, delivering the news of a dead dog seemed harder. She looked at him and Joshua noticed the change in her expression. Her russet brown eyes shifted up as if they were searching for words on a script. Her mouth tensed, ever so slightly. Her nostrils flared.

"Doctor Stone, the dog we found at the scene was killed... right there... on the scene." Joshua turned away from her face.

"Whoever did this," Addison kept her eyes focused on Joshua as he turned away and she saw the fresh cut hair and visible scalp, "is a brutal killer."

Addison wasn't ready to tell him the whole story. She didn't say anything about the leash, the visible struggle, and the burned remains. Addison tried to close the smell out of her memory.

Stone looked back in disbelief. "No. No one would do such a thing. It couldn't have happened. Where's Rex?"

Addison continued. "Doctor Stone, I am very sorry. There are things that go on in this world that I see that no one should ever see. But they happen, and this time, it happened to you...and you have no idea how sorry I am for your loss."

A long silence filled the room.

Addison began again. "Okay, Doctor Stone? I am conducting an investigation and have to explore lots of possibilities. I need to ask you some personal questions. The best thing you can do to help yourself is to be 100 percent honest with me. If you try and hide something, I can't help you and I can't get this person off the street. If I don't stop this guy, he'll hurt you or someone else again." She looked to see if Stone broke eye contact, but he returned her look, anticipating what she may ask him.

"So let's start with the obvious, do you have any idea who might have done this?"

Stone shook his head.

"Do you have any enemies?"

Stone shook his head again, "En-mes? Me-no. Not." The scrambled syllables were his attempt to make the sentence in his head come out as words from his mouth.

"Any students who got poor marks who want you to change their grade or want revenge?"

Stone smirked. He wondered what she would say if he told her the lowest grade any student got at Grant's Hill was a B-. Hardly worth fighting over.

Again, he shook his head

Addison looked at Joshua's left hand and saw neither a ring nor a white patch of skin where a ring had been.

"Doctor, are you married? Do you have an angry girlfriend?"

He shook his head about the girlfriend question. He and Trish Stevens had stopped seeing each other six months ago. He'd gone upstate to spend time with her after spring classes ended. One morning at breakfast, both of them realized neither was quitting their job to be with the other. They didn't have a fight, and she was never the angry type.

Again he shook his head.

The Sergeant pressed on, "Maybe an angry boyfriend? Are you sleeping with someone you shouldn't be?"

Joshua again shook his head.

Addison reviewed her notes, "There is no evidence of a sexual assault."

She spoke the phrase with a perfunctory tone; he heard it with shock and revulsion. He had not considered it as a possibility. He asked her again, "Can I see Rex? Can I see my dog?"

Addison looked down at her notes. "No, I'm sorry, no. It was brutal. After he was beaten, Doctor Stone, your dog was set on fire. In my duty, I see the worst of the worst things that people do to each other and to animals. I have to say this has hit most of us in the department very hard. This isn't something we see a lot... And

I really don't want you to see it. For both of us, remember your dog as he was."

Joshua began to tear up again. He felt dizzy. The room began to spin, he closed his eyes, trying to make it stop. "How does someone do that? How is that even possible? I don't understand."

"We're looking for the witness. Someone became concerned enough and activated the emergency beacon, but they were in the wind when the ambulance and my deputy arrived. It's possible they saw something that can help us find this person, but we won't know until we talk to him or her. We would very much like to talk with them, but..."

She paused and thought for a moment, then added, "Maybe they just came by after it was all over and hit the alarm and then drove off. According to the paramedics, who ever hit that alarm saved your life."

Joshua wondered what he would have done in that situation. He put himself in the shoes of a parking lot onlooker. If he had seen someone being attacked, watched the killing of a dog, or even just saw someone unconscious on the ground. Would he have intervened? Would he press the alarm? He wondered if his students abandoned him. Did someone see it all happen? He was grateful and angry with the witness at the same time; grateful to be alive and angry they didn't stop the attack. He and Rex had suffered alone. He knew Grant's Hill students; they could never just look away. He wondered what stopped them from helping him.

"If you think of anything, I'll leave my card on your table here. Call me."

Her cop gut told her this was not a local. They hadn't seen or heard of animal mutilation or missing family pets in the last few years. This was most likely, one of the transient drug mules that traveled along the highway corridor. If they didn't find this guy today or tomorrow, he would move on.

Addison's other nagging thought was the feeling of premeditation. The gasoline smell on the dog's remains and Stone's jacket confirmed it as the fire accelerant even without a lab analysis. But there was no gas can or source anywhere near the scene. Whoever did this brought the gasoline with them and took the container when they were done. That meant pre-planning in her book. She looked at her notes again, robbery might have been the motive, Stone's wallet and ID were missing, but robbery is a crime of opportunity. Most robbers don't hang around to torture and burn animals. Her hunch was the wallet was taken as a trophy.

It was just as she was opening her car door outside the hospital that her cell phone rang. The phone display read BILL SIMMONS.

"Jessica, it's Bill. I'm at Royal's. Do you wanna swing by here and take a look at someone?"

"Hi, Bill. What do you have? I'm over at County. I'm at least 25 minutes away."

"I have a Hispanic male, big guy, over 6 foot, early 20s using our vic's credit card at the store. He doesn't speak much English and has our vic's wallet, checkbook. I think we've got our man."

"Yes!" exclaimed the Sergeant and she slid into the seat, cradling the cell phone against her left shoulder and sliding the car keys into the ignition with her right hand.

"Great work!"

"Tina figured it out. She knows our vic and recognized his name on the credit card at the checkout. He smells like he's been around a fire. Why don't I take him to booking and then you can meet me there?"

"Okay, see you in a bit." Addison hung up and pressed speed dial.

The phone rang several times before she heard the hum of the muffled combine on the other end. "Hello, baby."

"Hi hon. How many acres today?" Larry Addison on the other end of the phone scanned the ground around him. "Almost done. I think maybe another 30 or 40 tonight and we're finished for the year."

"Great! Awesome. Look, I need to do some stuff at the station, meet you for a late dinner. Late — late — late?"

Larry Addison looked at his watch and the gauges on the combine and then at the distance back to his pickup truck. "I'm guessing 3 hours — maybe 4, back at the barn?"

"See you then," she said, and both Addisons disconnected.

PUTTING ALL THE PIECES TOGETHER was no easy task for the Sheriff or the campus.

The only person who had seen Joshua's body, and witnessed the attack, activated the emergency beacon and disappeared. Joshua's students had long left the building and campus was quiet.

Joshua's five or six regular Friday night callers assumed he was out for the night and didn't suspect he was missing. No one was looking for him. It was David Adams who ultimately helped the sheriff's deputies and the college community make the connections to identify Joshua as the dying man in the grass.

On campus, the Wednesday after the attack, President Rose called a Town Hall meeting to talk about the event with students and faculty. The group of about 100 students and twenty faculty members gathered in the Eastford Chapel hall. Thomas Moore was sitting in the pew next to David Adams, eager to hear what had happened. Moore was smiling and acknowledging others in the room, and listening to Adams.

"So, I'm sitting in his driveway, too early to honk the horn. I mean, it's pitch black dark, right? But there are no lights on in his house and he's not answering his phone. I rolled down my car window and I could hear his phone ringing inside the house as I dialed. And keep in mind, we're talking about Joshua 'I'm always on time' Stone, right? I mean the German's could set their train schedules by him."

Both men smiled.

Adam stroked his mustache and pointed his finger in the air. "So I assumed he just forgot. Then I think, maybe we were confused and he's waiting for me at the office? His bike is nowhere near the house. So I decide to drive to campus and literally...I'm on the phone with Ellen, we're talking about Joshua and I roll into the parking lot and this glimmer catches my eye and I look over at the bike rack and there is his damn bicycle. Right? So I hang up with Ellen — she says, 'hi' by the way, and wants to know if you want her to send you more of that spinach dip from the other night?"

"That would be nice, tell her thanks."

"So, I walk up to the office and it's dark. No Joshua. So, I walk back down the stairs and that's when I see the yellow tape across the church parking lot. I walk up and it says POLICE LINE DO NOT CROSS. No joke, just like in the movies. Right?"

Moore turned, "Really? Police Line? Wow. So what did you do?"

"What do you think I did? I called Ellen."

"And what did she say?"

"She said, 'Call 9-1-1.'"

"So you did?"

Adams reached into his photojournalist vest and pulled out his cell phone as if to make his point.

"No. That's not what 9-1-1 is for, 9-1-1 is for emergencies. So I dialed directory assistance, got the number of the sheriff's department and dialed it. And they sent a car out, and I'm talking with this cop and telling him my friend is missing and his bike and the crime scene and..."

Dean Eggars, who was standing in the aisle next to Moore and Adams, interrupted Adams' story. "Dr. Moore, we were so sorry to hear about Joshua, any news on when he'll be returning?"

"Dr. Evans, hello. No. No word, Dr. Adams was just telling me about — "

The dean had already moved on and was speaking with two faculty members in the row ahead of them.

"So this cop — did you know they have laptop computers in their cars? I mean, it has maps and GPS and anyway, this cop types in my name and I describe Joshua and tell him he's missing. That's when he tells me someone was assaulted and the description matches Joshua."

Moore nodded, "David, that must have been so hard on you. Thank you for doing that, for all of us in the department."

Following Adams' identification, news of Joshua's assault and Rex's death began to spread. The local newspaper covered the story in their once a week edition on Monday afternoon saying how Joshua had been beaten and Rex had been killed. The story did not tell of the grisly fire and mutilation of the dog. Addison had omitted that wanting to keep some facts concealed, partially not to alarm town residents and partially to help in their quest for the assailant. Only someone close to the crime would know that detail.

At the front of the chapel, a single podium sat in the middle of the aisle and as President Rose began his remarks, a student from the school newspaper sat next to the town reporter. They both pulled out pens and took notes as he began to speak.

"While we are all shocked and saddened at the tragedy that struck Professor Stone," he paused, avoiding a discussion of Rex, "I hope to give everyone a chance to share their feelings together in the spirit of healing and openness that is the hallmark of our great college." He worked the room with his expressions as he spoke.

"It is a time of reflection, a time of uncertainty, but also a time of resolve. We are an oasis of knowledge — of tranquility — of purpose. And while often, unfortunate events generate even more unfortunate rumors, we are an oasis of truth. I open the floor to you."

A sophomore woman stood up holding a yellow ribbon, "I'm Cynthia and I just want you to know that our sorority is putting these yellow ribbons all around campus to remind us all how happy we will be when Professor Stone returns."

The audience applauded.

Jerry Coogan stood up beaming at the president and the dean. "I'd also like to say that we are fortunate to have such attention to security on our campus — the warning beacons in the parking lots are amazing and without that beacon, who knows what might have happened, so kudos to you, President Rose, for your leadership and wisdom."

Again, applause from the crowd.

The dean stood, nodding, "Yes we are proud to be good community members and while this awful incident took place off our campus and totally outside our control, if our warning system in any way assisted, we're pleased to be a part of the Grant's Hill community."

Both reporters scribbled notes.

One of the senior athletes stood at the back of the room. "I'd just like to say that the athletic squad is having a fundraiser and you can pledge for each pushup we can do in a 24 hour period, and the proceeds will go to a fund to support crime victims in town."

Again, applause from the crowd.

The reporter from the town newspaper raised his hand, "President Rose, I'm just curious, do you have parking lot security cameras and if so, did you share the contents of those recordings with the Grant's Hill Sheriff's Department?"

The president stood up, "What an excellent question and yes we do have cameras," he glanced at the dean who was gesturing a subtle thumbs down with his fist, out of view of the audience.

"And at this time, I cannot comment on what the cameras may or may not show, because this is an ongoing investigation, but I assure you," he looked directly at the two reporters realizing the student reporter was taking a photo. Eggars moved slightly to the side to be certain he was included in the frame of the photo.

"We will do everything possible to assist the community in this time of need and we look forward to a day when we can take down the yellow ribbons because we are welcoming Professor Stone back to campus."

From behind the dean and the president, maintenance foreman Bob Thornton, stepped forward. "I want to remind all students and faculty that we continue to work to keep you safe while on campus." The dean beamed at the words 'on campus' and looked around at the faces in the room.

"We've installed mirrors in the corners of the parking lots for visibility and we've sent flyers out with safety tips. I hope you all will read them, and if you have any concerns, please call my office between 9 and 5 any work day."

The meeting broke up and the city reporter turned to the school reporter. "Ahh, yes, let's protect Miss Jeanne Clery."

"Who's Jeanne Clery?"

The city reporter pulled the college reporter aside. "Jeanne Clery was a freshman at a university when she was raped and murdered in a campus residence hall. The law passed in her name requires colleges and universities that receive financial aid to report and disclose crime on campus, in non-campus buildings and on public property."

The student thought for a moment, "But not next door?"

The city reporter nodded and rolled her eyes.

Near the back of the room stood Sergeants Wiggans and Addison, both working the room with their eyes, looking for something or someone out of the ordinary and, at the same time, listening to the words and ideas from the speakers.

"Okay, I'll tell you, it was quite pusillanimous of the dean parading out the Jeanne Clery stats and saying that we are supportive of you on one hand and yet it happened 'off campus and is out of our control' on the other hand."

Wiggans realized he'd never heard the word pusillanimous but it didn't sound like it was a good thing.

"What? We have one case up here and already you are starting to talk like them? Pusillanimous?"

Addison shook her head, "No, just the word-of-the-day calendar. Larry bought it for me for Christmas. It wouldn't hurt you to read something now and then."

Wiggans shrugged.

Addison moved towards Thornton and caught him as he was walking towards the rear door of Eastford Chapel.

"Hi, I'm Sergeant Addison, this is Sergeant Wiggans. Would we talk to you about viewing the video tapes?" Thornton looked up and appeared ready to say, "Yes," when Dean Eggars stepped forward.

"On behalf of President Rose, I want to thank you and your entire department for the work you do and particularly in working with this case and the tragic assault on our colleague. If there is anything we can do to assist you, please feel free to let me know, I'm the college dean, Brian Eggars."

"Yes, actually, I was just asking about the cameras, can we look at the recordings?"

Eggars looked at Thornton and then back at the deputies. "Yes, but I need a commitment from the two of you that they cannot be made public. I appreciate the need for a police investigation, but the privacy of our students cannot be violated."

The four of them walked to the administration building and Thornton unlocked the door to a room that contained digital recording devices connected to on-campus cameras. He typed a few commands on a keyboard and several monitors filled with the same image recorded just before sunset the previous Friday.

The cameras showed the entire northwest parking lot, with the exception of the emergency beacon and the back row parking and the median between the church and the college parking lot.

"Let's see your other view," Wiggans said, "this one is blocked by trees."

Thornton rolled his eyes and then spoke diplomatically, "Yes, the cameras were placed before the trees were planted and as they grew, they obstructed the view of the parking lot."

Addison, trying not to sound agitated, "So fast forward, please?"

He moved the dial and the tape played at a minute per second. Just after 7:20, the screen shows the ambulance rolling into frame and then out of view as it stops to work on Joshua. No person, animal or vehicle crossed into camera view during the entire time.

Addison, Wiggans and Thornton exchanged rolled eyes with each other and turned to look at Eggars, who seemed relieved the video omitted the attack.

"Keep this video, don't erase it, in case we decide we need to see it again, but otherwise, it's not much help."

"We're pleased to be whatever help we can to the community," Eggars said.

By the end of the day, Bob Thornton had a work order to remove the trees blocking the cameras, and by the weekend, they were a memory. As with most projects on campus, no one saw or heard the chainsaws and chippers.

CHAPTER 15

REFLECTION

JOSHUA WAS ABLE TO STAND and look at himself in the mirror for the first time. He wasn't sure what to think. He looked for several minutes. The body he remembered was average height and in reasonable athletic shape for an amateur ball player. His long black hair swept back from his face and over the top, fine and straight and ended just below his shirt collar in back. His complexion was dark from the sun, and his skin showed the beginnings of too much of life without sunscreen. He was five foot eight and according to his hospital chart, 179 pounds. The numbers quantified his own perception that his clothes were all tighter. It was the heaviest weight of his life. The hospital had trimmed and shaved his black hair, and it needed a good shampoo. He decided it would have to be cut off to make it grow back even. What was left still had crusty black matted blood stuck to the strands. His forehead was high and broad, and his chin was covered with uncharacteristic stubble. In years past, it was all black, now it was highlighted with some grey. Women gave him very few compliments about his looks, but always told him he had a nice smile.

He knew his injuries left two lines of stitches, but first, he opened his mouth and saw the damage to his upper teeth. What was left of his smile was a jagged mess. He expected the teeth to hurt more than they did. Still, overall, his body ached. The pain medicines numbed the sharpness, but it was ever present.

The first new line of stitches was across his forehead, in a neat row that would fade in the coming years as his face grew more lines. His left cheek had a jagged row. A beard wouldn't hide it. This was the second time his face had been sewn together. The first was after he charged Alan Neal on the court on a January night and missed the play as Neal turned. Neal's elbow collided with Joshua's nose and tore the skin. It was seven stitches that further enflamed their friendly competitiveness. The two continued to brag over who felt worse about the incident. Joshua captured the spirit of the events and turned it into what a handful of critics called his breakout novel. He called it, *The Fist Fight,* and it told the story of two 8 year old boys, and a long hot summer that lead to a broken nose in a one-punch fist fight. He dedicated the book to "A.N. and other eight year old boys everywhere."

Neal returned the favor the following year in a mathematics publication on set theory, naming the set in his discussion as the "Joshua Set" and describing it has having a null value.

Joshua turned to the side. His arms and hands dangled below his hips. He doubted he'd be playing in the campus 3-on-3-basketball tournament this year. Remembering the nose stitches made him think about calling Alan Neal to tell him to look for another member for their team. He searched the room for a clock and the time. It was 1:16 and Joshua decided that Neal was in class.

Joshua leaned into the mirror and saw the swelling under his eyes and around his nose. His skin was a mix of colors, some red, some purple, some blue. The white of his right eye had a small pool of red blood. "Hyphema," the nurse had said. His vision in that eye was a bit distorted, but not distracting. He wondered how long it would take to reabsorb.

He remembered Sergeant Addison's words, "If I don't stop this guy, he'll hurt you or someone else again." The idea of reliving the ordeal made him twitch. He felt odd, he remembered nothing of what happened, but felt its aftermath. He made a mental note to ask about amnesia, and then quickly forgot it.

His ribs were wrapped in elastic bandage. It hurt when he took deep breaths, or coughed. He then shifted his gaze to take in his whole body. In his own clothes, he thought, he looked the same as last year or even five years ago. Now standing in the hospital gown and wounded, he saw an older stranger looking back. The last time he was in a hospital was his father's care center. He was glad his parents couldn't see him now. He would be ashamed to tell his father, the soldier, he didn't fight back. And to tell his mother he hadn't been strong.

A wave of dizziness swept over his head and body, he hobbled to the toilet and vomited. He hated throwing up. Even as a child, he taught himself not to. He could count on one hand the number of times he had thrown up as an adult. He couldn't imagine what it was like to have a serious food illness, puking day and night. A chill shivered down his back as he flushed the toilet and ran some warm water in the sink to wipe his face. In the mirror, his face was paler than before. A knock came from the hallway and he shuffled back to the bed as the door opened.

Thomas Moore walked in first, followed by Eggars and Rose. All three men hesitated when they saw Joshua's face, but then walked the rest of the way into the room. Moore's smile never dimmed. He brushed his hair back across the top of his head two times.

"I didn't know I had a meeting. I would have worn a tie," Joshua said to the trio.

"Joshua, we have a sabbatical policy. There are easier ways to get time off." Moore joked, hoping to lighten the opening of the conversation.

Joshua laughed and winced in pain. "Don't make me laugh."

Eggars and Rose look around the room, eyeing the monitors and supplies. Joshua wondered if either had ever been in a hospital room before.

"Joshua," President Rose began, "if there is anything you need, we want you to know that Grant's Hill is ready to help in every possible way."

Joshua nodded as a thank you.

Rose continued, "I've spoken with the HR people and the trustees, and you can take as much time as you need to recuperate. Our insurance carriers will provide the coverage and any medical assistance you need."

Dean Eggars nodded.

Moore spoke up, "So it looks like I come off the bench and into the classroom, first time in years. I'll be taking over your courses."

Joshua reflected on the news. It struck him odd that he had forced this on Moore. Grant's Hill Program Chairs never taught in the classroom. He felt bad about letting his colleagues down, especially since they were short one faculty member since Annette's retirement.

"Annette? Did you let Annette know?" Joshua asked as he looked at Moore.

"Yes, we spoke on the phone. She sends her best. She was crushed by the news about Rex." Moore shifted subjects, "Are they saying when you can go home?"

Joshua pointed at the chart on his wall and then out into the hallway, "They think later this week. I guess I'll be black and blue for 4 to 6 weeks. They already have a dental re-constructionist lined up for me."

Rose and Eggars smiled, and then stopped, becoming self-conscious about the subject of teeth and smiles.

Men can't face their own fragility, Stone observed. He wanted to write it down; his author instincts felt it was a line that might work in his novel. He wanted to laugh at the three of them, standing there, not knowing what to say. He wanted to yell at the three of them, for not doing something to save him.

His guests wore stalwart expressions: sincere, compassionate, and honest. And yet Joshua felt abandoned, and unable to trust any of them. The confusion bothered him. He started remembering the taste in his throat when he was dizzy and threw up and that was a mistake. Remembering it made the urge return. He began thinking about anything to take his mind off the sensation in the back of his throat: basketball, Thoreau, David's over amplified laugh, Liv's perfume, but none of it worked. He was able to reach the small basin on the bed table in time as his stomach emptied its final contents. Eggars reached forward and pressed the nurse call button. Rose and Moore looked at each other, unsure what to do.

A nurse Joshua had not yet met came into the room and the three men said their goodbyes and seemed unsure who should leave the room first. They hesitated, and then settled on an order, Moore, then Rose, then Eggars.

The nurse took the basin when Joshua was done and gave him a warm washcloth to clean his face and mouth.

"Not to worry," she said, "this is very common. The doctor has orders for medicine as you need it." She gave him a dose of promethazine and as she was leaving said to him, "It makes some patients drowsy, so stay in bed for a bit to see how you feel and how it affects you."

It was the last thing Joshua remembered that day.

CHAPTER 16

DISCHARGE

DAVID ADAMS MET STONE AT the front door of the hospital just as the nurse was letting him stand up out of the wheel chair. Adams was wearing one of his signature sporting shirts, with a ventilated panel across the back and shoulder epaulets. And a tie.

"Do you believe they actually make me do this?" Joshua said to Adams.

"Sure. From a liability standpoint, they have to. They don't want to put you back together only to have you fall down and hurt yourself. I was writing a story about hospital accidents once. If you knew how many people were injured in hospitals, you would never want to stay in one."

The nurse standing with them frowned defensively.

Adams had done a double take, half of Joshua's hair was long, and the other half looked like it had been caught in a paper cutter.

Joshua stood up and thanked the nurse, and then turned to Adams.

"Thanks for coming. I didn't know who would be out of class that could pick me up."

"Of course I would come. Come on, let's go home." Adams held the car door for Joshua. He was wearing a hospital donated t-shirt and scrub bottoms and his shoes, which had been returned by the sheriff. His blood stained clothing had been cut off. Some was disposed of as a biohazard and some retained as evidence by Addison.

Joshua reached to grab David's shoulder as a wave of dizziness returned. He panicked, thinking he would puke all over his colleague, but the dizziness subsided.

Adams got in and started the car. The pair remained quiet until they were on the county highway heading back to Grant's Hill.

"When do you think you can come back?"

Joshua looked over. "Soon I hope. I have to meet a re-constructionist" he opened his mouth and revealed a jagged smile with missing and broken teeth.

"Yikes," Adams exclaimed

"They considered about putting a hole in my head."

"Ah a burr hole. Did you have an epidural hematoma?"

"Yes, that's what they said, but a very small one. So they watched it and it resolved. But I feel like I lost days of my life."

Adams shifted in the car seat. "I knew a guy, a rock climber actually, we climbed in the Rockies together for a few summers. He fell and had a bleed like yours, but much larger." Adams thought for a moment, and then turned the conversation back to Joshua, "What other follow up?"

"The portable CT machine comes back in two weeks, so I have another scan and if the headaches stay away, they will release me in time for the Christmas Gala at Xanadu. Until then, limited activities and rest."

They were quiet again and Joshua began looking at the telephone poles and fence posts out of the corner of his eye. It was a poor choice, the dizziness returned and he was only able to say to Adams, "Stop the car," moments before he pushed open the door and spewed what was left of his breakfast on the side of the road.

Adams didn't react. He looked ahead out the windshield and when Joshua was back in the car, he shifted into gear and the pair continued back to Grant's Hill.

As they turned on Joshua's street, Joshua saw the Eastford Chapel spire and then looked in the foreground to see his house. Adams parked the car and Joshua opened the door, and then reached for the back door out of habit to let Rex out. He stopped himself and walked up the driveway to the side door.

Adams pointed to the garage. "Your garage was unlocked, so I brought your bike home and rolled it inside. The rest of the house was locked up tight. But you know, someday, you really need to buy some blinds for your windows. You can see right in!"

Joshua smiled. "Is that your new book, *Home Decorating with David Adams*?"

He took out his keys and said his goodbyes to Adams.

Adams' phone rang and he motioned to Joshua to wait.

"Joshua, it's Ellen." Adams handed the phone to Joshua.

"Hi, Ellen."

"Joshua, I just wanted to tell you that if you need anything, please call us, please dear?"

"Ellen, thank you, I hope to see you at the Christmas Gala, I think you owe me a dance from last year."

"Oh, I remember. If you need anything, call us."

Joshua handed the phone to Adams and he smiled on the way to the door, turned the key and pushed it open. Adams returned to the car and drove off. Joshua walked inside the kitchen. It felt empty. Like he was visiting a replica of his home. He turned and saw Rex's leash on the hook by the doorframe and took it down. He doubled it on itself and then doubled it again and placed it in the kitchen cabinet that held the dog food. The popcorn maker was still on the stove, ready to be put into service for their Friday night dinner.

He walked across the kitchen and into the hall and then into the bathroom. He turned on the shower, undressed, and stepped inside and thoroughly washed what was left of his hair. He looked in the mirror. The bruises on his torso and face were a multi-hue rainbow of yellows and browns and blues. The facial stitches were smaller than he had imagined at first. A couple of scars for stories to tell later.

He dressed and picked up the phone to call Cutting Class for a hair cut. He looked on the note pad where he jotted the number and became confused. He thought there were too many numbers for a telephone. He counted the digits. It still didn't look right, so he opened the phonebook a second time and jotted the number again. The numbers didn't match, so he looked again and wrote it down a third time. The third phone number matched the second number, so he dialed it, and was greeted by a woman's voice that answered, "Cutting Class."

When he finished making the appointment, he hung up, and the phone rang back. It was Alan Neal, and they talked about Rex and about Joshua's not playing 3-on-3 this year.

Joshua tried to find words to tell Neal what had happened beyond the basic facts, but also wanted to spare his friend from living his pain.

After Neal, came calls from Dana Wilkinson and Courtney Maddocks-Martin. Courtney told him that she appreciated his help, and not to worry about reading her paper, that she would send it on and to hurry in his recovery.

He walked into the bedroom and was numb. He felt tired and violated. When he cleaned out his parents' house after they died, it was a mechanical, emotionless undertaking. He felt just as mechanical and emotionless now. Like a checklist to work through as part of the grieving process. Rex was gone, time to clean up.

Check.

Joshua rolled up the dog bed mat that Rex slept on, gathered his toys, found his braided rope toy near the front door, and put them all in a box and carried it out to the garage. Into the night, the calls from current and former students came. By the time he went to bed, he had heard from 13 of them. The last call was from Sergeant Jessica Addison, asking him to meet her at their offices in the morning and apologizing for calling so late. Joshua agreed to come and when he hung up, he turned out the light.

The house was quiet and felt cold. He looked around the room and got out of bed, moving a chair to the spot where Rex's bed had been. He got back in bed and closed his eyes, beginning to shiver. He waited for it to pass, but it continued for nearly an hour. He got up, found an extra blanket in the closet, spread it across the bed and hurried under the covers. He continued to shiver, so he got out of bed again, and walked to the thermostat in the front of the house. He dialed it up to 74 degrees. He felt his own head, unable to tell if he had a fever. He stood, shaking in the bathroom with the thermometer under his tongue, waiting for the beep, signaling time was up. When it signaled, he read the display — 98.6 degrees.

He shuffled to the warmth of the covers and began panting as he shivered. His head and ribs throbbed with each breath. Somewhere after 3:30, he fell asleep.

PART FIVE

RECOVERY

CHAPTER 17

THE SHERIFF

JOSHUA PARKED HIS BICYCLE IN the public rack in front of the former courthouse, an older two-story brick building with a wide stairway and a metal rail down the middle. It was the place the skateboarders in his classes all bragged they would love to glide across, if, of course, it wasn't the sheriff's department, which probably made the temptation all the greater. The building had been the county courthouse, county administration offices, sheriff's department and jail until a voter referendum 10 years ago merged county government with the city government in Jefferson. The taxpayers agreed to float a bond referendum to build a new joint administration building and library next door to the Jefferson County Hospital. As a result, most county workers left Grant's Hill and the building was vacant except for the sheriff's deputies and dispatchers who used it as their field base and the clerks and courtroom staff for weekly small claims and traffic court.

As he passed through the entry doors, a security guard in an oversized polyester blazer greeted him. The guard asked Joshua to empty his pockets into a plastic bin. Joshua removed his keys, and some cash, but still had not replaced his wallet or ID. The guard took the basket and set it on the far side of the metal detector. Joshua walked through and when he picked up the few items he had in the basket, the guard handed him an ID badge with the word VISITOR in block letters on a plain white background. He motioned to an old wood reception desk that looked more like it belonged in a train depot than a courthouse. The hum of radios and computer fans filled the lobby. Joshua looked before approaching the desk.

He took the sheriff deputy's card out of the breast pocket of his jacket and read her name.

"I'm here to see Sergeant Jessica Addison?"

The desk deputy didn't make eye contact and shouted over the top of his papers, "Addison! Front desk."

For several minutes nothing happened and Joshua rocked back and forth from foot to foot looking behind and around the desk deputy to see an indication of anyone coming to greet him. From his back, through two swinging doors, a voice called his name.

"Professor Stone?" Joshua turned to see a man in his mid 30s with huge biceps greeting him. A badge hung from a chain around the man's neck. His t-shirt had a drawing of a stick figure, in a muscle man pose, with stick-figure biceps and a caption that read, "Welcome to the Gun Show."

"Yes?"

"I'm Sergeant Wiggans. I work with Sergeant Addison. She's on the phone. C'mon back."

The two of them walked through the double doors into a room of desks, cubicles, paper and noise. It resembled the squad rooms in television shows and looked a little like civil servant hell. Most of the desks were within a few inches of each other and it appeared that 8 to 10 people worked in a room that Joshua estimated to be the same size as Thomas Moore's office in the Quad.

Sergeant Addison was standing at her desk, reaching across to the desk opposite her, trying to pick up a file folder. Joshua stopped and gaped. She was wearing tight pants, made of some synthetic fabric, which hugged the curved outline of her hips. Her sweater top was riding up, revealing a flash of skin above her belt line and it inched higher as she reached farther. Wiggans, who had walked up behind the professor, whispered in his ear "Easy there, Doc, she's married. Don't get any ideas."

Joshua grinned, but he was getting all the ideas he needed. Yes, he saw the woman's shape, and yes, he saw the swatch of skin, but what caught his eye was just behind her hip.

Under the waistband of her pants, was a semi-automatic pistol. He had seen her in the hospital, and even standing this close, it was impossible to tell she was carrying a gun. A sheriff's gun. He angled his head and tried to make out the words on the butt of the pistol. "40 S&W." Joshua had no idea what it meant or what it stood for, but if it was good enough for the Sheriff, it must have been a good gun.

Addison hung up the phone and extended her hand to Joshua.

"Dr. Stone, good to see you. You are looking great. Much better than our last conversation."

Joshua nodded and said something about getting better.

"New haircut? You're looking like one of us."

Joshua ran his palm over the top of his crew cut hair. He hadn't had hair this short since he was six years old.

"I've got good news. We caught him. We have the man who killed your dog and attacked you. Right after you and I spoke at the hospital one of our deputies arrested him."

Joshua felt his stomach tighten. He wanted to feel relief, but all he felt was fear and rage. He didn't want to show it so he merely nodded.

Wiggans cut in, "Here's the deal Doc, this guy is an illegal. From either Nicaragua or El Salvador." Wiggans shrugged his shoulders, "we don't know yet. He's probably a drug mule, scum of the earth type. He has no papers, so he's here illegally. He also seems to be… I don't know… odd or something. He doesn't speak right."

Joshua took offense to what sounded like a racial slur, until Wiggans continued.

"He speaks no English. But he talks with too many gaps in his words, it's not quite a stutter, but it's not like flowing phrases. Kind of a stutter mutter thing. Even our translator had trouble following him. I'll tell you this: he's not normal in any language. All he says is 'feed the dog' over and over."

Wiggans paused as if he was trying to make sense of it.

"Oh yeah, and that he lives 'under the castle to hide from the enforcers'." Simmons rolled his eyes.

"He's a big guy. He was wearing work boots and his boots are the same size and have that work boot tread like we found at the scene," Wiggans continued. "We looked them over; they look like they had been around a fire. A little singed."

Addison picked up the story, "The legal situation is this: we can hold him and try him. I'd love nothing more than to see him spend some time in our jail. We've got some real animal lovers over there."

She gestured with her thumb towards what Joshua took to be the county jail.

"They may be thieves and psychopaths, but the jail has a code of its own. Kids and dogs — strictly taboo." She stood tall and looked straight at him, "But the thing is — "

Joshua felt bile in his throat. His heart was racing. *They are going to let him out. They are going to let him kill me.* Instinctively his body tried to self-protect. His fists clenched and his head started to nod down as a protective reflex. He didn't realize his posture changed, but both Wiggans and Addison saw the movement and responded. Wiggans unfolded his arms, and Addison, with a nod towards Wiggans, stepped back and softened her stance, ever so slightly. As she did, they both noticed Joshua relax.

Addison continued, "We understand how irritating this is. You need to understand this is irritating to us too. The thing is, both DEA and Immigration have offered to take him into custody and then deport him. And as much as we'd like to keep him, we are a small town and our boss knows how much it will cost us to do this. We can send his boots to the state crime lab for some analysis, do some interviewing... Or we can lock him up now, today, without any of that."

"So what are you telling me?"

Addison shook her head. "If we give him to the Feds, he'll be locked up for 12 – 18 months and then deported. The Feds never work quickly. If we keep him, the best we could do is a charge for animal cruelty and assault. That's only a sentence of six months to two years. But likely the lower end. If we try to convict him on attempted murder, it's a trial that could be delayed a year or two from now."

Addison paused, looking at her victim to gauge his reaction.

"So one of the things to ask yourself, Dr. Stone, is do you want this over today? Or, do you want to relive this again and again for the next year?"

Joshua didn't know what to say. He wanted them to give Rex back and say it was a mistake, that some other dog was killed.

The three shared blank faces and an uncomfortable silence.

Joshua spoke, "Sure. I understand. So can you tell me his name? Can you tell me anything?"

Wiggans looked at his notes, "Miralies. Iñigo Miralies, as near as we can tell, age 22. Like I said, Nicaragua or El Salvador. He's got some ink — some tattoos — from a drug gang down there. If we were going to keep him, we would get a better translator and tell you more. But if he goes with the Feds, well, what's the point? Right? We got him."

Joshua was uncertain. "Do you know it was him? I mean, you do this all the time. I know when a student is doing well or poorly. Do cops know the good guys from the bad guys?"

Wiggans interjected, "Damn straight, yes."

"But what if he wasn't alone. I mean, I'm no pro athlete, but could one guy alone have hurt me this much?"

Addison looked at Wiggans and then answered, "He had every advantage, Doc. You were distracted, it was dark, he already had a plan, and he blitzed you from behind. Once you were out, you never had a chance."

"But what if he wasn't alone, am I safe?"

Wiggans turned his head. "That's up to you, Doc. I know from experience that your life won't be quite the same. It's normal to be a little more cautious. Use a little more situational awareness. Just be more heads up. Stop looking like a victim."

Joshua thought the deputy was implying it was his fault.

"Wait, what did I do? This isn't my fault. This is your job, to keep these people locked up." The indignity of his voice caught the attention of the other deputies in the room.

Addison turned diplomatic, "You are right. It is our job. And no, this is not your fault. What Sergeant Wiggans is saying is you have a choice, suffer silently, or learn from this. Learn what to do to be more aware. It's not your fault. But now, this is your opportunity."

The three of them stared at each other for longer than either was comfortable. It was awkward.

Addison continued, "O...kay...so the county attorney says the charges will still remain open. Miralies will be transferred into federal custody and he'll spend time in federal lock up until they deport him. No trial for you and hey, the good guys win."

Joshua surveyed Addison's desk. There was a photo of Addison standing next to a man and a John Deere tractor with a Border Collie dog between them. A shot of pain zapped through Joshua's jaw and his eyes met Addison and then Wiggans and then he looked down at the floor. As he looked up, he tried to make out the outline of her gun under her sweater, and he saw nothing but the shape of her body. Amazing, he thought.

"Okay, listen," Addison handed him a card that read RAPE CRISIS CENTER. "I know what you are thinking, but everyone needs someone to talk to. The card says rape crisis, but these folks talk to all kinds of crime victims."

Joshua resented the word. "I'm a professor of English," he asserted to himself, "I am a man, not a victim." His internal bravado faded to resignation. He admitted he was a victim. He was powerless at the violence of another man. He couldn't protect himself or his dog. And he never even saw it coming.

He took the card and said, "Thank you."

"Now I just need you to sign the property receipt and we're done."

"I don't understand, what receipt? I didn't give you anything."

"No, Dr. Stone, we're giving you. Everything: wallet, cards, ID, grocery list, checkbook we got it all back. Everything but your driver's license, Miralies didn't have it on him when we arrested him." She slid a clear envelope with a red top and the word EVIDENCE stenciled on it across to him.

"I don't have one. A driver's license," Joshua said and he opened the Evidence packet. Inside his wallet was his grocery list, written on a Post-it note and stuck to one side, opposite the large and garish faculty ID card issued by the college.

"If the clerk at Royal's hadn't recognized your name, he might have been still hiding; but, she said she knew you and when he gave her your card, she tripped the alarm in the store and the manager called us. Isn't that great?"

Joshua looked at the contents of the envelope.

"You got everything back, big win."

He eyed the photograph on her desk. "Everything...Back... Yeah."

Joshua left the Grant's Hill Sheriff's Department, turning in his Visitor ID badge on the way out the door. When he arrived at home, a delivery was waiting for him on the front steps. He parked his bicycle in the garage, closed it and carried the collection of long boxes inside the house.

Each contained a window blind he had ordered. He spent the rest of the day moving from window to window, room to room, turning brightness into darkness. By the time the late afternoon sun was hitting the west windows, Joshua was lowering the new blinds and twisting the side rod to close out the glare.

He sat down at his desk and picked up a pile of envelopes and Christmas cards. He took an address book from the center drawer, flipped it open to the middle of the alphabet and found where he had left off. He began addressing cards and had finished a short stack when the power blinked and then the lights went out. The smoke detector in the bedroom and the microwave oven in the kitchen both gave out a beep that sounded like a dying gasp to signal the power loss.

Joshua rummaged in the drawer and found a small pocket flashlight and walked into the front room of the house. He opened the blinds and scanned up and down the neighborhood. There were no lights on his street. It looked like the whole town might be without power.

He then walked to the back of the house, opened another newly installed blind and looked north towards campus. Campus had its own power generator and the lights on the spire of Eastford

Chapel shined brightly. Joshua shrugged and closed the blinds. He walked back to his desk and as he sat down, the power returned and the lights came on. The digital clock on the radio in his office blinked 7:19. He told himself he would reset it later.

THE ENGLISH DEPARTMENT IN THE northwest wing of
the Quad was quiet. Each wing of the Quad has faculty and staff
offices on the second and third floors. The English department has
occupied the third floor Quad offices since the building was
constructed.

While many of the floors of the Quad looked similar in layout
and organization, visitors to the Quad noticed that each building
had its own, unique smell. The former Home Economics wing still
had a yeasty smell even though nothing had been baked there for
50 years. The Sciences wing had a blend of acetone, sulfur and
formaldehyde. The English and Literary Studies department
smelled like old books and leather.

In the weeks leading up to Thanksgiving break, Mrs. Thorn
noticed Thomas Moore and David Adams leaving their office as if
they were heading to talk to Joshua. On each occasion, she
pretended not to notice them as they realized mid-walk that he was
at home recovering. The silence made the third floor wing feel
even lonelier.

Late one afternoon, Moore was standing in his corner office,
looking out the window overlooking the courtyard below. After a
few minutes, he walked out and pulled up the guest chair next to
Mrs. Thorn's desk. Moore had held the department chair

appointment for 10 years when Stone arrived on campus. His broad face and thick eyebrows were highlighted by his receding hairline and a bright red complexion. It gave him both the look of an elder advisor and an impish prankster. With his white hair, he could seem to be 60 years old one day and confused for a mid-20s student the next. Ordinarily, he was a jolly man, but the quiet made him more reflective than normal.

Mrs. Thorn told him he was a wonderful program chair. She admired both his personality and his office decor because it was so appropriate to his title. His desk, larger and more ornate than the others in the department, was dark and traditional, and the rest of his office furnishings reflected his longevity on campus.

David Adams walked out of his office, two doors down from Moore. Adams was the adventurer of the program. Despite his claims of wanting to work in academia because "it is all inside work and no heavy lifting," David Adams had made a life and career of doing both. If there was a sport, feat, or achievement, most likely he had done it or written about someone who had. He had spent several years at east coast publishing houses and served as editor of an adventure lifestyle magazine before finishing his PhD in his late 40s and taking the non-fiction slot on the faculty.

Adams had a string of books, a few of which managed to make the *New York Times* nonfiction lists, nothing ever in the top 10, but high enough to warrant a Wikipedia page. Joshua had read all of Adams' books, but found his first book, *Tin Roof Rusted*, to be his favorite character study. It was about Adams' conversion of an old horse stable on his family farm to a writer's cabin. He began the restoration the week Ellen told him she was pregnant with their only child. He finished the conversion the week she delivered their son, Sean. In it, Adams described his idea of self-therapy. That when he became frustrated, he flung his hammer as far as he could throw it. Writing, "By the time I walked, picked it up, and returned, I was calm and ready to solve my problem like a grown man."

Between Adams and Moore's office was the now dark office of Joshua Stone. It had been Annette Demming's office and when she retired, Joshua moved into it. Both men looked at each other and then at Joshua's empty desk. Neither said the words, but both men missed him.

"Do you remember moving all those dang bobble heads?" Moore said to break the silence. "He must have a hundred of them."

"347, Dr. Moore," said Mrs. Thorn as she adjusted her computer monitor and continued typing the project spread across her desk.

"God, what a day. I thought moving books took for ever, he moved every single one," Adams said as he tipped the chair back off the front legs and rocked gently in the space next to Mrs. Thorn's wastebasket.

"Do you think he's doing okay?" Moore asked.

"Sure, I think so. Do you think so?"

Moore thought for a moment and then shared, "Sure, he's Joshua Stone. He'll be back soon. What else would he do, where would he go all day?"

"What's he doing now? It must be driving him crazy." Adams slid a hand into his vest pocket.

"Sure, but at least he has Rex."

The conversation stopped uncomfortably.

The telephone rang and Mrs. Thorn cleared her throat, cleared it a second time, and then answered, "Good afternoon Department of English and Literary Studies."

Adams and Moore looked at each other silently, and Moore turned and walked to his office. Adams set the front legs of the chair back down on the floor, stood up, peered into Stone's office.

From the doorway, he saw what would be every student's first impressions: books, and bobble heads, and a dog bed.

He turned back to Mrs. Thorn and gestured with his hand as if he was unlocking the door. Mrs. Thorn nodded, reached down into her lower desk drawer, all the way to the back, and pulled forward a key with a tag. She handed it to Adams who unlocked the door, walked inside, rolled the dog bed mat into a bundle, and then carried it to his own office. He returned to lock Joshua's office door and handed the key to Mrs. Thorn, who took it, returned it to its hook, and closed the drawer — all the while continuing the conversation with the student on the phone.

"Dr. Moore?" Adams said as he passed the office. "I'm going to the F Club for a drink. Will you join me?"

Moore smiled and took his coat from the coat rack behind his door.

"Sure, I think we could both use a drink."

CHAPTER 19

THE F CLUB

ADAMS AND MOORE CROSSED CAMPUS to the far east
end and walked in to an old bungalow home that was once the
rectory for the Eastford Chapel. It was slated to be demolished in
the 1950s when a few of the faculty got together and offered to
buy the place and renovate it into a faculty club, not unlike the
officer's clubs many of the faculty had enjoyed while serving in the
armed forces during World War II and Korea. They managed to
pool a few dollars and worked a sly scholarship for the daughter of
the local banker in exchange for a very low interest mortgage.
From the outside, the architecture and style matched the decor of
all the buildings on campus; it would be an easy building to
overlook during a tour. Inside, the modest bungalow was
converted to a dining room with 8 tables, a smoking lounge, which
became a game room in the 1980s and a coffee bar in the 2000s.
The kitchen and one of the bedrooms were converted to a small
but efficient commercial kitchen and the faculty pay monthly dues
that support the commissary overhead and the employment of a
chef and two servers. Simple lunches are available each workday,
and a Friday night dinner is served by reservation. No alcohol is
served until 5 p.m. and the bar closes at 10 p.m.

Officially, the name of the faculty club was The Rectory, and
the menus, invoices, matchbooks and linens included the name and

a script letter R embellished by laurels. During the 70s a group of students managed to confiscate all the matchbooks and transform the 'R' into a script 'F' and from that day forward, The Rectory became known as the F Club.

During his first years on campus, Joshua stayed away from the club; it made him feel self-conscious and a bit of a voyeur. In those days, the only function he attended was the annual department dinner, each April on the Friday following spring break.

But about the time he was promoted to associate professor, he began going there each day for lunch and the occasional Friday night for dinner. Later, when Rex came along, he would tie him out back, near the kitchen door, and the chef would often make a plate of scraps for the dog. Joshua was never sure who looked forward to it more, the chef or the dog. On hot evenings, Joshua could look out the side windows of the bungalow and watch the chef, in his white t-shirt and checkered pants, carrying the plate out and talking to Rex in his native Croatian "Vi ste vrlo debeo pas" Which he always told Joshua meant, "you are a very pretty dog."

A few years later, Joshua mentioned this to a student from Croatia who laughed and said, "No, no, he says, 'you are a very *fat* dog,' not pretty." Joshua laughed because the joke was on them both.

The servers were college students, never townies, and often juniors and seniors, who were vetted and hired by the loose group of faculty who agreed to manage the club. Young men and young women seemed equally interested in the job, and they turned over about every third semester. As wait staff jobs went, it was easy. There was never any cash exchanged at meals, each faculty member kept a positive credit balance in their account and charges were debited.

While lunch became a daily habit, it was the department annual dinner that always stood out as a memorable night. They were a funny team and a creative and supportive group of co-workers. But what made the department dinner most memorable was: the Joke.

The Joke is a long-standing tradition of the Grant's Hill English department, it began sometime in the 1920s, although no one remembers how or where or when it began. Each spring, at the annual department dinner, a member of the faculty is required to tell a joke: "the Joke." The same joke is told every year, and each teller brings his or her own originality and style with it. Who ever tells the joke has the responsibility to choose the following year's jokester. When it originated, there were no formal rules, other than the general understanding that the same jokester could not tell the joke in two consecutive years.

However, when Chuck Palahniuk penned *Fight Club* in 1996, the year before Joshua joined the program, the department lampooned the rules of *Fight Club* to become the rules of the Joke:

You don't talk about the joke.
When someone says stop, or goes limp, the joke is over.
Only two characters in the joke.
One joke at a time.
You tell the joke with shirts and shoes.
(A rule later broken by Annette)
The joke goes on as long as it has to.
If this is your first year on the faculty, you have to tell the joke.

The joke itself is straightforward. The basic story line goes like this:

A rancher, sometimes it's a man, sometimes it's a woman, lives on the range — alone, way out west.

The rancher doesn't see another human being for months at a time. One day, a stranger passes by on horseback and the two get to talking.

The stranger invites the rancher to a party on Saturday night.

The rancher agrees.

The stranger says, "Well sometimes, there's some smokin' and drinkin' that goes on at these parties."

The rancher says, "That's okay."

"Sometimes, there is cussin' that goes on at these parties."

The rancher says, "That's okay."

"Sometimes, there's some card playin' that goes on at these parties."

The rancher says, "That's okay."

"Sometimes, there's some fightin' that goes on at these parties."

The rancher says, "That's okay."

"Sometimes there's some sex that goes on at these parties."

The rancher says, "What goes on between two consenting adults is okay. I'll be there, what can I bring?"

And the stranger replies, "You don't need to bring nothin', it's just gonna be the two of us!"

There is a photo album that memorializes pictures of the faculty each year as they tell the joke. The joke changes with the times. Sometimes the two people are both men, or both women, or one of each. In 1969 they were astronauts on the moon. In 1976 they were revolutionary war soldiers. They have been beat poets, and once the Swedish chef from the Muppets. The first time Joshua was tapped, he did a very poor imitation of David Bowie and Mick Jagger.

It passed back and forth among the others several times before Moore gave it to Joshua to tell the second time, the year he found Rex, the black dog.

David Adams had figured out that this spring was Joshua's third time to tell the Joke.

"David, how can you be so sure?" Moore said with a twinkle as he sipped from a beer bottle.

Adams leaned forward in his chair, as if he was about to reveal a mystical secret, then said, "Well, it's not me and it's not you!" His loud laugh rose above the noise of the room and several heads turned.

Moore realized it was true. Annette would only have passed the book on to Joshua. The two men grinned and raised their drinks, toasting, "To Dr. Stone."

CHAPTER 20

ROYAL'S

JOSHUA WAS A TWICE A week shopper at Royal's grocery. He bought only what he could carry on the Skeppshult but could balance more than most people would think. Once a month, he made a trip for dog food. That is, he used to. He stood in line behind a family of travelers. The youngest daughter kept singing "over the river and through the woods" and the older daughter kept rolling her eyes and asking why they had to spend Thanksgiving at Grandmas and why she didn't have satellite TV.

As Joshua skimmed the magazines and tabloids, he realized he didn't recognize any of the women featured on the front covers. It was as if the headlines never changed, but now the photos were of stars he'd never heard of.

When he was a child, he didn't recognize them either. In his late 20s and 30s he felt like he knew them all. Now, they were strange faces. The shopper behind him nudged her cart into his legs and he politely ignored it.

She nudged him again. When she nudged him the third time, he wheeled on his feet and came face to face with Sergeant Addison and another man.

"Hey Doc, Happy Thanksgiving."

"Sergeant. Hi, I feared I was about to ruin some young child's Thanksgiving by scolding them for smashing my leg, and I see it's you instead," Joshua replied.

"I've been accused of being a child," she said with a sly grin as she winked at the man with her. The two men stared at each other expectantly.

"Doc, this is my husband, Larry. Larry, this is Dr. Stone from the college."

They shook hands and Larry smiled, then his expression became concerned.

"Oh say, you're the guy whose dog was killed. Man I'm glad they got that bastard."

By this time the travelers had moved through the check out and the clerk was ringing up Joshua's groceries and joined in the conversation.

Tina acknowledged the shoppers in her checkout, "Yeah, Jessica you did a great job getting that guy. What is it with some of these freaks?"

Joshua nodded and watched the two women as they spoke.

Larry continued, "I've got nothing against those people, if they want to come here legally and work and pay taxes."

Another clerk opened a register and the Addisons moved over to begin checking out.

Joshua and the clerk continued their conversation.

"I knew something wasn't right when he handed me your credit card." She told him proudly.

"What do you mean?"

"The guy, that guy that killed Rex. I'm the one who called the cops while he was here. He was checking out right at this counter and trying to use your card to pay. That's when I pressed the alarm button."

"That was a smart move, Tina, smart move," Addison said from the next checkout stand.

"Hey Jessica, how's your mom and them?"

"Everyone's great. We're headed there for Thanksgiving supper."

Joshua moved to the end of the checkout stand to sack his groceries and the Addisons moved past him and out to the parking lot.

"So he checked out, right here? And you recognized my name on the card? You actually look at those?"

Tina beamed, "I just knew something wasn't right."

"So, what was he buying?"

"Well, that's the damnedest thing if you ask me. He had a 50 pound sack of puppy food. That was it."

The Addison truck drove out of the parking lot as Joshua walked out the store's front door. The roar of the truck's straight pipes kicked in as Larry gunned the gas. Joshua clipped the cuff clips to his pants and straddled his bike, with a canvas grocery sack balanced on each side of the rear wheel. Tucked under the awnings and out of the weather was a pallet of stacked puppy food bags.

Joshua stared at the stack, wondering if Miralies had given Rex some food to calm him down. Wiggans told him Miralies had said, "Feed the dog." He had no idea what that meant. Joshua couldn't imagine Rex not coming to his aid, but he couldn't imagine sweet Rex hurting anyone either. Joshua caught himself staring and then glanced at the flyers of missing cats, cars for sale, and fundraisers, stopping to read an announcement for events at The Grange.

Everything you need to qualify for Concealed Carry.
This class is honored by all county sheriffs and qualifies you for a new shall issue Carry Concealed Weapons (CCW) permit.

Only $85.
Special display by our sponsor, Johnson Sporting Goods
15% off on pistols purchased at the class

Joshua remembered the discussion with Adams about the new state law and Adams saying he didn't need a pistol in Grant's Hill. He rubbed his tongue across his rebuilt front teeth and his hand across his still bruised ribs. Sergeant Addison's words came to him, "You have a choice; suffer silently, or learn from this." And then, "If I don't stop this guy, he'll hurt you or someone else again."

Her words fueled his curiosity about carrying a gun. Miralies may have been arrested, but Joshua didn't feel safe. It wasn't about avenging the past; it was about his preparing for the future. Addison told him it could happen again, and, the image of Addison bending over the desk gave him an idea how to conceal his protection. After a few moments he moved his foot to the top pedal and began his ride home.

LIKE MANY SMALL TOWNS IN the Midwest and West, Grant's Hill had a Grange Hall officially known as the National Grange of the Order of Patrons of Husbandry. What was once a secret agricultural and rural fraternity modeled after Freemasonry had become one of the few places in town where anyone could hold a meeting. Larry Addison was a member and leader of the local Grange and so when Jessica told him a friend was going to hold a class, and she was going to help, Larry offered the Grange meeting room for the town's first concealed weapons class under the state's new "shall issue" regulations.

Joshua arrived at the Grange to find the twenty or so seats nearly full, so he slid into a folding metal chair near the back. The crowd was a mix of townies; there was no one else there from the college. Some were younger men, most were his age and older, and a few women. He was relieved not to know anyone in the room. At 9:00, a man and woman walked up to the front of the room and Joshua recognized them as Sergeants Wiggans and Addison from the Grant's Hill Sheriff's Department. A third man who was talking in the corner walked up to join them.

"Hi everyone. I want to welcome you to our class and thank you for coming" the third man began, "My name is Jack Peers, it rhymes with beers." The men in the room chuckled.

"I'm a firearms instructor, have been teaching firearms safety for 20 years. I teach pistol, self-defense, shotgun, reloading, and rifle classes. As you know, this class meets the requirements for your concealed carry permit. The law changed. And while the local sheriff used to make the decisions about who could and could not carry concealed, the law now says the sheriff "shall issue" a CCW permit. We fought for this for... how long?" He looked at Wiggans and Addison, the two of them shrugged and suggested, "10 – 12 years."

"About a dozen years I guess. This is a very good thing for the community, and our safety. With me are Sergeant Wiggans and Sergeant Addison. They'll work with you on the indoor shooting range in the basement of the old courthouse across the street, for the live fire portion of this course.

"The good news is, you get to listen to my excellent public speaking and lecture skills for the first 3 hours today."

Several of the people who knew Jack booed comically. Addison and Wiggans rolled their eyes.

"And then, you get to show us if you actually know how to shoot. Also, I want to say thank you to our sponsor, Johnson Sporting Goods, they have some pistols on display at the back of the room, and are offering a 15% discount if you purchase or order a pistol today."

Several people turned to look and others applauded.

"Okay, until you get on the range, let me stress, all the firearms in this room are unloaded and there is no live ammunition anywhere in the room," he looked at the deputies, "with the exception of our sheriff friends. I have three guns up here and Johnson's has about a dozen, but they have all been checked, and there is no live ammunition."

"I also have a revolver and a semi automatic pistol that we're going to use in our live fire shooting. These are my personal firearms, so please be kind to them. Any questions?"

A couple of hands went up; one question was about the actual shooting, another question was about reciprocity of weapons permits in other states. Joshua turned around and tried to see a display pistol like Addison's gun on the Johnson's Sporting Goods table. From his chair, they all looked alike.

The lights dimmed and a slide filled the wall at the front of the Grange room. The slide was slightly skewed down and right, but it was in focus and easy to read.

Why are you here?

Peers began speaking, "Being a tough guy is the worst reason in the world to carry a pistol and it will get you killed."

The moment lingered in the room.

"I love pistols. I carry a pistol because I can't fit Sergeant Addison in my pocket. And I sure as hell can't fit Wiggans!"

Again the crowd laughed. Addison punched Wiggans in the shoulder.

"But they do not make me a big man. And as a civilian, it's not a tool of intimidation. Let me tell you what I mean. If you are a sheriff deputy, if you are a spy, if you are a soldier, you need tools of intimidation. You are a professional fighter. Look at the cops: they have the mirrored sunglasses to intimidate you, the baton, the pepper spray, the Taser, the hand gun, the shotgun, the rifle, the SWAT team...Lots of tools. They need to intimidate people and talk them out of violence. If a cop hears a gunshot at the end of an alley, he is running towards the sound.

"If a civilian hears that shot, we're running away. As a civilian, you have lots of tools too. But your tools are for protection, not intimidation."

The room nodded in agreement. Peers' next slide was an agenda for their time together.

Joshua enjoyed Peers' lectures. As they went through the slides, he blended physical demonstration with questions and answers, breaking the room into small groups and giving everyone time to do some hands-on practice. Peers seemed to answer Joshua's internal questions before he started to raise his hand. Some of the people in the room were experienced shooters and hunters; others were like Joshua, learning new phrases like sight picture and magazine — Peers was insistent it never be called a clip.

WIGGANS AND ADDISON HAD SET up two shooting stations in the basement range of the courthouse building. They divided the class into two groups of 10 students, and during an informal question-and-answer period in the lectures, the students came one by one in a predetermined list order to shoot with one of the two sheriff's deputies.

Addison recognized Joshua Stone on the list of names, and had arranged her list so that he was the last person she called into the cold, concrete basement shooting range. It was just after 2 p.m.

"Dr. Stone, I'm a little surprised to see you here, but I think you are making a good choice."

"Sergeant, nice to see you and, well, it was interesting. Tell me what we do here?"

Addison had kept him for last, anticipating the inexperienced college professor would have trouble qualifying. Candidates are required to hit 70% of the shots within the black bull's eye. On the style of targets they were shooting, the bull's eye was 5 inches in diameter, and had a series of concentric circles. The smallest circle, in the center, had the number ten. The next larger circle had the number 9. The final two larger circles were labeled 8 and 7. Already one of the students was told to go home, practice, and to return to another class. Sergeant Addison expected Joshua to be number two.

"So you want to shoot the revolver or semi-auto?"

Joshua reached down and picked up the revolver. "I think this looks easier." And with that, Addison put on her ear protection and slid the box of ammunition across the ledge on the face of the shooting station. About the size of a lunch tray, it supported the two pistols and two boxes of ammunition. Joshua put a neon green, foam earplug in each of his ears and was surprised how much he could hear. He picked up the clear protective eyewear and slid the straight-sided temples over his ears. He loaded the first five cartridges into the revolver and closed the cylinder as they had practiced in the classroom across the street.

He raised the gun with a two-handed grip and found the sight picture they had been show in the slides. He squeezed the trigger.

Bang. The report of the .38 bullet pierced the air and the round penetrated the 10 ring on the target.

Addison reminded him, "Don't forget to breathe."

Joshua shot two more times, each round touching the last, forming a tight group of three holes the diameter of a quarter. Addison watched in disbelief. Joshua shot the final two shots, also in contact, but making the group a bit larger.

"Doc, I am impressed. You're sandbagging, aren't you? Are you former military?"

"No, first time shooting a handgun."

"No shit, not shooting like that it isn't." She handed him the box of ammunition, and he ejected the fired brass cartridges onto the concrete floor. The smell of gunpowder brought back a memory of his first time shooting with his dad along the riverbank. He paused, and then loaded 5 more cartridges into the revolver.

Again he found his sight picture and fired five more shots, one after the other, and at the end, 9 of the 10 shots were touching each other in a group about 2 inches across. One of the rounds was on the line between the 9 and the 10 ring.

Addison knew he was the last shooter, so she was not concerned with monopolizing range time. She slid the semi automatic pistol across the ledge along with an empty magazine. Joshua recognized it as the same gun she carried. He picked the magazine and asked "how many?"

Addison looked at him devilishly, "Top it off. Put all 16 in the mag and one in the pipe."

Joshua loaded the magazine with 16 rounds. He racked the slide as he had seen in class, but kept his hand on the slide as it eased forward.

"Don't ride the slide. Let it slam home," Addison corrected.

He released the magazine by pressing the release button. He caught the magazine in his free hand and added one more cartridge to replace the one he had loaded in the chamber, 'the pipe,' as Addison had called it. He slammed the magazine into the gun.

This pistol was heavier, and had different sights, but he found the target and squeezed the trigger. BAM, the sound of the .40 was different from the .38 revolver. The round hit at the bottom of the black ring.

"Doc, this one isn't like the revolver. Put the sight exactly where you want the bullet to go. Your point of aim is your point of impact on this gun. Remember the difference Beers showed in class?"

Joshua raised his sights to the center of the black dot. He fired a shot. It struck the middle of the 10 ring. He fired again. He fired again. He finished with 5 total shots in the 10 ring and the first shot at the base of the black.

"I've got 10-year deputies who can't shoot like this. Okay, do this for me," Addison pressed a button and a second target traveled down the length of the range on a motorized cable and pulley. There were now two targets side by side.

"I want you to shoot both targets, twice on the far target, and twice on your target. As fast as you can. Bang-bang, bang-bang."

Joshua closed his eyes for a moment and imagined flipping the four quarters in the classroom. This was really no different. He brought the pistol up, shot once, paused, and shot again. Re-aimed to the close target; shot again and again in rapid fire succession. These shots were farther apart, but not out any further than the 8 ring.

Addison sent a fresh target down range. She knew he had seven rounds left in the gun. There were three targets at the end of the range. She turned to Joshua, with a goading grin, "Want to really test yourself?"

Joshua wasn't sure if this was the real test, or she was playing with him, so he played along, "Sure."

"I'm going to call a number, 1, 2, or 3. Number 1 is the first target, 2 is the second, and 3 is the last one. Got it? If I call 3, I want you to shoot target number three. If I call 1, shoot target number one. Got it?"

Joshua nodded. She looked down range and called "3!" Joshua shifted his focus and fired a round, dead center on the 10.

"2!"

He pointed the pistol at the middle target. Again he fired, this time just to the right of the center.

"3!"

He shifted and fired. The shot was slightly above the center.

"1!"

He turned and swiveled to the closest target and fired. He thought it was a miss, but Addison saw that it passed through the hole he had made earlier.

"3-2-1!"

The professor hesitated, then, set himself up. Joshua turned and fired one at each of the three targets, each round, landed in the 9 ring.

They both took off their ear protection. Addison smiled. "Good shoot."

Joshua walked out with his paperwork signed by both Addison and Peers. Wiggans walked into the range. He had been listening outside and knew the number of shots fired was well over the standard 10 round shoot. He figured Addison was giving the college professor a bit more time.

"Addison, good call giving him a chance to figure it out that he's not cut out for this. Some of these guys aren't meant to be shooters. He's a college boy. We gave him a chance and now he can go back to his classroom."

Addison picked up the targets and slid them over to Wiggans. Wiggans ran his fingers over the holes in the center of the black. He looked over at the now closed door where Stone had left.

"Damn, college boy can shoot."

THE JOHNSON'S TABLE WAS TAKEN down and the store employees were gone when Joshua stuck his head back inside The Grange, so he walked with his paperwork down the street to their store. It was just before 3:00 when he walked inside. Stan Johnson, the owner, was handing a customer a shotgun with a camouflage stock. The customer was sliding it into a new shotgun carrying case when Joshua walked up to the counter. Stan greeted him. "Hi, I'm Stan Johnson. Welcome, how can I help you?"

"Hi Stan, I'm Dr. Joshua Stone, I just came from the class over at the Grange. I guess I got done too late."

"Dr. Stone, welcome. We don't get many of you college types down here. Say, do you know David Adams?"

"Yes, David and I work together,"

"He's the man — great guy, great shooter." Stan caught the eye of one of the teenage staff walking down an aisle nearby, "James, will you be sure and restock that sale rack with the thermal glove liners?" Then turning back to Joshua, "Wonderful wife, Ellen. Do you know her?"

Joshua nodded.

"So, are you a skeet shooter Dr. Stone?"

"No, no, first time buyer. Like I said, I just came from the class at the Grange." Joshua looked at the collection of pistols all arranged on glass shelves in a glass case. A shotgun shell in the trigger guard propped up each one. He was staring at a group of very discolored and scratched pistols.

"So what are you looking to find, Dr. Stone?"

"Um, please, call me Josh. I was hoping to get what I shot over there. I think the deputies carry them, too — the semiautomatic 40 S&W?"

"You are just like David. You know your firearms. I figured you for a striker-fired guy."

Joshua had no idea what he was saying, but assumed it was good and replied with, "Yeah, I guess you could say that."

Stan led him to the middle of the store counter and reached inside the case. He pulled out a pistol that matched the gun he fired just a few minutes before.

"I'm new to this, not sure what I can do and can't do in a gun store. Can I hold it?"

Stan ejected the pistol's magazine and locked back the slide.

"Josh, you just earned my respect. Do you know how many idiots walk in here and the first thing they do is grab the gun with their finger on the trigger?"

Joshua shook his head.

Stan continued, "You can point that direction, you won't sweep anyone with the muzzle, and these pistols are safe for dry fire."

Joshua took the firearm, left the magazine out, and he released the slide and let it fall forward, with a resounding metallic snap. He remembered not to ride it forward as Addison had coached. He brought it up to find the sight picture and landed the sights on a stuffed moose head mounted on the far wall. There were no other customers in the store.

"There is a fiber optic green front sight. You can't help but see it," Stan boasted. "It was my idea. Otherwise, she's factory fresh and ready to go."

Joshua looked at the price. "And I get the 15% off today, right?"

"You bet, you can use the discount on a holster, if you like, and I'll take 15% off the price too."

Joshua looked at a display of holsters, some were $20 some were over $100. There was even a shoulder holster.

"Do you remember the TV show *Miami Vice*?" Johnson asked him. "That's the shoulder holster they designed for Don Johnson. I'm the better looking Johnson, by the way." This Johnson had obviously used the line a number of times. "Not that actual holster, but that style."

Joshua turned toward Stan Johnson with an expression that said, "I'm not impressed."

"Yeah, I know what you mean. But we do sell a few."

Joshua walked back to the counter. "I want something that will keep it concealed and be comfortable."

Johnson turned his hip to Joshua and pulled up his vest. Resting inside his pants was a semi automatic pistol. He raised the pistol and holster together as one unit. The holster clipped to the waistband and belt with two metal clips. The rest of the holster was half leather and half hard plastic.

"It's Kydex. This is the one I sell the most of. All the deputies use them." Johnson explained.

Joshua nodded and Stan took one off the display and set it on the back counter.

Stan turned to face Joshua and made a questioning expression. "Doc, I'm not one to pry, but let me ask you a few questions. Are you going to carry your gun when you are at home?"

Joshua paused for a moment, "I hadn't really planned on it."

Stan interrupted him, "The reason I ask is...okay...how about your car? Will you leave this in your car?"

Joshua replied, "I don't have a car, so no and I probably won't wear this around the house."

Stan continued his line of questions and as he did he shifted their attention to a row of gun safes and storage lockers.

"Do you live alone? Or ever have small children come to visit?"

Joshua went through a mental checklist of people who routinely visited him. The phone seemed to ring all day on weekends, but visits were few and mostly, he met his friends on campus for concerts, sports events, and lectures. "No, no kids, and no visiting kids. Yes, I live with my..." He paused, realizing he was used to saying he lived with Rex, "Yes, I, I live alone."

Johnson began again, with more concern than a sales pitch, but it was a sales pitch. "Most guys like you probably wouldn't worry about this then, but you need a gun safe. I have several in my own home, but my thinking on this is simple: anytime your gun is out of your control, it needs to be under lock. Your control means in your hands, on your body, or immediately in front of you — like at a range or when you are cleaning it."

Joshua nodded at the common sense approach.

"Now you don't need one of these..." Johnson rested his arm on a black safe that looked like the love offspring of a side-by-side refrigerator and an ACME safe from cartoons. "Although, David Adams swears by 'em. He owns two, you know?"

Joshua did know. David Adams' monthly poker nights were legend in the faculty. And it was at the beginning of one of the monthly games that Adams insisted the group of card players join him in the garage first, along with his teenage son, Sean. It took the 8 of them nearly an hour to move the heavy gun safe to the basement.

Stan pointed to a thin metal box, the size of a safe deposit box from a bank.

"This is what I sell the most of." He touched a sensor on the top of the box and it opened. Inside was a foam-lined compartment and a blue plastic gun the size of Joshua's pistol.

He closed the safe and handed the box to Joshua. Joshua touched the sensor and nothing happened. He touched the sensor several more times and with a disappointed look, handed it back to the proprietor. "What am I doing wrong?"

"Nothing, that's exactly what it does. Biometric. Latest thing. You program your fingerprints — and anyone else you want to have access, and it opens. Otherwise, it stays locked." Johnson slapped his hands together.

"And you can secure it to your wall or house or furniture. If you do that, even if your house is broken into, they have to steal the wall to take your gun and even then, they can't open the safe. Good place to keep some cash and your passport, too!"

Joshua smiled and nodded. Stan Johnson added a new safe to the counter, along side the holster.

"Ammunition?"

Joshua took in the stacks of boxes on shelves. "Does it matter?"

Stan took Joshua to another counter. "What do you know about ballistics?"

Joshua shook his head.

"Okay, I can make this simple. How often do you plan to shoot — go to the range?"

He had no idea so he repeated what he had heard during breaks at the class a few hours ago. "Not a lot, maybe a 100 or 200 rounds a month."

"Okay, you can spend a lot of money, or less money. I think you probably want to have a couple of boxes of your everyday carry ammunition. This is the stuff I sell to the Sheriff." Stan slid three, 20 round boxes of ammunition across the counter to Joshua.

"It's expensive. I would shoot a box at the range to get a feel for it…and then keep the others for everyday carry. This is your self-defense ammo. Now, for target shooting," Stan pulled a case of cartridges off the shelf. "This is 1000 rounds. It will get you through all or most of the year. It comes in a box of 50 and you'll notice 50 are cheaper than the box of 20 self defense rounds."

Joshua nodded. "So why not carry the cheap stuff?"

Stan looked Joshua in the eye. "This stuff," he slid the self defense ammo boxes down the counter, "goes in, makes a big hole, and for the most part, stays in. Rabid dog, coyote, bad guy."

"This stuff," he held up the practice ammunition, "will go in, make a hole, and maybe go out the other side and make more holes in things you don't want holes in. Your bad guy, your wall, whatever is beyond your wall?"

They finished the transaction and Joshua waited for Stan to hand him the gun as he had done with the shotgun buyer. Stan looked at him, "So, see you Wednesday?"

Joshua did not remember Wednesday and why Stan would be there.

"Three day waiting period, even though your paperwork is dated today, they won't process your permit until Monday, which means, you can pick your gun up Wednesday."

CHAPTER 24

DEREK UNDERWOOD

DEREK UNDERWOOD WAS SHIVERING, EVEN though he had kept his sweatshirt on before lying down on his mattress, his long legs dangling over the edge. He had been asleep, but tonight's dream was more real than before. There was a man, being beaten, severely beaten. There was blood all over his face and hands, but the man wasn't screaming or calling for help. He was quiet and just lay there as he was kicked, over and over again.

Derek knew why he had the dream. It was what he witnessed in early November. He saw the man being kicked. He saw the blood.

He didn't want to tell anyone what had happened, he wanted to walk away, but something compelled him to look one more time at the motionless body by the side of the car. He had hesitated, and then pressed the button on the emergency beacon in the center of the parking lot. The bright blue strobe light began blinking and Derek looked back at the man one last time.

They would come and save him. He would be a hero for alerting them. Everyone would know what he did. Everyone.

He rolled over and from under his mattress pulled a large, spiral bound sketchbook he'd found in the bookstore trash. It was brand new when he found it, it was a great score. He opened the sketchbook to a ribbon-marked page. He began to draw the dream with a pen. First the back of a car, parked at an odd angle. Next a man on the ground, and a giant boot, kicking the man.

He flipped a page and drew the car again, this time with flames dancing all around the edges.

He stared at the images with a mix of wonder and self-satisfaction. He liked the images because they frightened him some. He liked the edgy feeling of fear and art they gave him. As he turned over to go back to sleep, he hoped he would sleep better. And maybe too, the dreams would stop. It had only been a month, but the sleepless nights of the dream felt like years.

IT WAS NO SURPRISE TO anyone on the faculty that Eggars and Rose chose Liv Olsson to lead the campus counseling sessions as a response to Professor Stone's assault. It wasn't their style to bring in an outsider. In Liv's world, academic counseling was long-term work with students and not acute crisis intervention. But Liv made herself available twice a day for drop-in sessions for anyone who wanted to talk. By the end of the fifth session, with no student or faculty takers, she cancelled the remainder of the sessions.

By Thanksgiving, none of the students she was counseling had any remote connection to the assault. By mid December, it was as if the campus had forgotten.

She was looking over end-of-term grade reports for the students she worked with most often when a tall, lanky young man appeared at her door.

Liv turned and was immediately struck by his face and stance. She read the bags under his eyes, his rounded shoulders, and hunched posture as a sign of exhaustion. She scanned his face, listened to his words and tried to catch a whiff of his breath to see if she saw any signs of alcohol or drug use. She saw nothing but a very tired young man who seemed lost and confused.

"Do you help people sleep?"

Liv turned and stood up, "What do you mean, tell me more?"

Underwood looked ahead and slightly above her head. Liv was five foot eleven; Underwood was about 6 inches taller. He drew a breath.

"I can't sleep. I have a secret and I'm not sure who to tell."

Liv nodded, "Why don't you sit down and we can talk? Tell me about you."

Derek took a step back, surprised that she took an immediate interest in him. He began to tell her his story. They both sat down.

"My name is Derek Underwood. I'm from a farm near St Louis, and I'm an undeclared studies student. This is my first year here." He was clutching a red, spiral bound sketchbook with a linen cover and an embossed GH on the front, like many of the art majors carried around campus.

"Are you taking art classes?"

He held the sketchbook closer to his body. "No, I just doodle and sometimes draw."

Liv listened as they continued." And your parents, are they still in St Louis?"

"No, they both died in the summer."

Liv responded, "That must have been difficult for you. How has it been for you being here?"

Underwood smiled and responded with what Liv perceived as a programmed reply, "Oh its great, I like the school and I'm getting along okay."

What Underwood didn't tell, her experience and observation did. He wore an expensive wristwatch. His shoes were the latest sports-star style. His teeth were perfect, though perhaps not brushed recently. His hands were smooth. The haircut, clothes and body odor didn't match the rest of him. He looked as if he had worn the same shirt for several days and slept in it as well. She made a mental note to come back to the topic of his parents later.

He began to reveal his secret. "I'm the one who pressed the alarm. That night, when that professor's dog was burned up. I saw it all."

Liv gasped. It was the first she learned Rex was not just killed, but burned.

Underwood turned away. "I saw it all. I am the one who saved his life. If I hadn't pressed the button, the newspaper said he would have died."

Liv listened to his words.

"Derek, do you want to tell me what you saw?"

Derek talked about the dog being kicked, and then the fire. "I watched the man stand on the leash while the dog burned. I was just going to walk away, it was all over. I didn't need to be there anymore, when the other man came out."

Liv asked him, "What other man, Professor Stone?"

"Yes. And then he was just lying on the ground, being kicked and kicked and kicked. And now, I can't stop the dreams. I keep dreaming it over and over and over and I just want to sleep. Can you do something?" His voice trailed off in a half sigh, half sob.

"I understand," Liv told him, "you did the right thing. Derek, were you attacked, too? Did you get hurt?"

"No, no one ever hurts me. I'm fine."

Liv made another note to come back to the topic later.

Derek pleaded, "I need your help. I thought if you told them, I would be able to sleep. So will you tell them? Will you tell them what I did?"

Liv folded her hands and made studied eye contact, "What we talk about is confidential. I won't share this with anyone you don't want me too. Who do you want me to tell, Professor Stone?"

She noticed a change in his demeanor and body posture. He was fidgeting more and his breathing rate rose slightly. His eyes danced around the room, focusing for brief moments and then moving on. He stood up.

"Thanks, I need to go." He was turned around midway through his sentence and without a goodbye, he walked away.

She watched him hurry out the second door and down the hallway out of her view. Liv made some more notes on a paper, placed it in a file folder, and set the file folder to the side and turned to her computer screen. She logged into the Grant's Hill student database and began a search. She began to type Derek Underwood into the screen when her phone rang.

"Dr. Olsson, this is Dean Eggars. Do you have a moment to meet with President Rose and me? We're reviewing the recommendations in your report for the board meeting and we want to be sure we're saying the right things. Can you come over now?"

Liv answered, "yes," and hung up the phone. She moved Underwood's folder to a stack on her desk and left to attend the meeting.

PART SIX

CHRISTMAS BREAK

Chapter 26

Everyday

THE MONOTONY OF DAYS WAS wearing on Professor Joshua Stone. He didn't feel like a professor. There were a few follow up medical appointments, and the creation of his new smile. It took four visits, sitting in the dentist's chair, mouth open to the point of exhaustion, as the dentist shaped, molded and fixed a combination of bonding and a veneer to create a row of teeth that looked remarkably real. His mouth and bite looked normal, but felt nothing like he remembered his mouth feeling before. It was an odd feeling that led to a new habit of running his tongue over the top row of teeth. It made his tongue raw the first week he did it. But mostly, Joshua Stone sat at home and read, losing hours of his life to waiting. The initial excitement of catching up on reading was replaced with a random switching from book to book and then mostly, just sitting.

Late in the month, Joshua set down his book and stood up from the sofa in the living room. The late afternoon sun cast long shadows across the front yard and the bare trees created patterns all along his street. Before the attack, he would see Rex running among the leaves and rolling on his back. Everyday since, Joshua still looked expectantly out the window, all the time knowing his four-legged companion was not in the yard.

Everyday Joshua hoped the emptiness would get a little less. Everyday it just grew longer — like the afternoon shadows of late fall. The dejected man turned away from the window and walked into his bedroom.

Tonight was the Gala, and the first time Joshua would be with more than one colleague at the same time in six weeks. Individually, some of them had stopped by his home to check on him, offer words of support, and help with daily tasks.

His daily routine was so different from his life before his near death. Joshua Stone was an anchor point in every group he joined. He was rarely the center of attention, but was always in the mix of this or that faculty group. With some, he attended guest lectures. With others, he listened to concerts and then went out for coffee or drinks. He and Alan Neal made it a quest to take new faculty members to Grant's Hill sporting events. Adams often joked it should have been part of the mandatory orientation led by the HR department. Other than Sunday grading and a night or two a week, Joshua neither sought nor had much "Joshua time" as Annette Demming called it.

"My God, are you always with people?" she asked him. "I couldn't stand it. I need my *me time* every day."

"Joshua time" was hopefully about to end. Tonight was a little bit homecoming and a little bit debut. Thomas Moore had agreed to pick him up in about 20 minutes.

He opened the closet door and reached for a black merino wool suit. From his dress shirts, he selected a crisply starched white shirt, and the only holiday tie in his wardrobe. The tie had been handcrafted from an antique Hawaiian shirt, complete with Christmas trees, hula dancers and *Mele Kalikimaka* printed in angular patterns. It was a bit of a joke his first year on campus, and it had become something of a tradition at the president's annual Christmas Gala.

Standing in front of the mirror Joshua dressed in the white shirt, tie and black pants, then, reached over to retrieve the semi-automatic pistol from the pistol safe and the holster that was lying on top of the safe. His holster had two metal clips that fastened to his waistband and over his belt. The holster itself fit between the inside of his waistband and his tucked-in dress shirt. While wearing it, it rested just behind his hip; just like he'd seen Sergeant Addison's pistol the week after his assault. With a slow look in the mirror, he turned to his left and his right and then bent over to see how much the gun grip extended from his body. It was bigger and more noticeable than he expected, but not so much that it made him change his mind. When he slipped his black jacket over the top, the pistol was concealed.

Once again Joshua looked in the mirror, turned left, right and bent over. He switched off the light and returned to the living room.

He sat down and stood up, checking to see if the gun shifted on his belt. It remained in place and while it pressed against his body, it felt more comfortable than he'd anticipated. He sat down again, and shifted back in the sofa, feeling the grip pressed against his kidney. If it were any further around on his belt, it would press against his spine, but as it was, it just rested on the back of his hip, tucked neatly inside his belt.

Joshua sat there, in the silent living room, waiting for Moore and thinking of the friends at the Gala. His perception of the pistol's weight changed, it seemed to grow heavier on his waistband. In his mind it became a 30 or 40-pound burden, as much as a sack of Rex's food. He stood up and it felt as if it was pulling him over to the ground.

"What the hell?" Taking off his jacket, the professor reached to the back of his belt, grabbed the clips of the holster, and slid the gun and holster off and rested it on the coffee table next to his book. His eyes focused on the pistol: the engraved pattern of the grip presented a maze of options and obstacles. It resembled the pattern of a child's game, too complex to figure out. He stood up, picked up the pistol and holster and returned it to the bedroom and set it on top of the dresser. As he stepped back, he shifted his look from the pistol on the dresser, to his reflection in the mirror and then walked back to the living room. He slipped on his jacket and sat down to wait for Moore.

His eyes returned to the clock. Five more minutes. He pictured the pistol in the other room and contrasted the feeling of the pistol's weight on his belt against the memory of waking up in the hospital confused and in pain. He stood back up took off his jacket again, and returned to the bedroom. He replayed Peers' instruction during his concealed weapons permit class.

"Always carry every day."

He looked again at the pistol, took it from the holster, set the holster on the dresser. He pressed the magazine release and removed the magazine from the gun, laying it next to the holster. He took a hold of the pistol's slide with an over-the-top grasp, and with a forceful sweep, racked the slide to the rear ejecting the final live round of ammunition. Just like flipping the quarters in class he managed to catch the flying bullet with his left hand and set that on the dresser as well. His final gesture was to set the pistol on the dresser so all the elements were arranged in a neat row.

Joshua reviewed the line: holster, magazine, cartridge, gun. It reminded him of a memory and cognition test given in psychology courses and mental health assessments. He spoke out loud, "Remember these words: holster, magazine, cartridge, gun. In a few minutes I will ask you some questions about those words."

He sighed heavily, staring at the objects. He reached for the holster, picked it up and then set it back down. He glanced at the clock. Moore was already late and would be knocking on the door at any minute. He looked at himself in the mirror. He smiled, inspecting the changed smile the dentist had created with what was left of his chipped front teeth. He could see the evidence; he wasn't the same as he was.

"Everyday," he said aloud and with that word, Joshua reattached the holster to his belt inside his waistband. He reached for the live round of ammunition on his dresser and instead, knocked it over and watched as it rolled backwards. It reached the gap between the dresser and the wall and fell to the floor. Joshua bent over and looked for the fallen cartridge, but it was all the way back and out of his reach, so he left it to pick up later. He lifted the magazine and pistol with his hands. He seated the magazine in the grip of the pistol and again racked the slide putting a live round into the chamber. He took his time to holster the firearm and stood tall in the mirror. At that moment, Tom Moore knocked on the side door.

Joshua slipped on his suit coat a final time, greeted his colleague at the door, and the two of them walked down the driveway to Moore's car. Moore was telling a story about some students in the hallway the week before.

"So the three of them are talking about *The Man Who Knew Too Much*." Moore turned to make eye contact, "Which I have to say Dr. Stone, Chesterton is a great author for your class. So anyway, the two men, both of whom are in our drama program are arguing about whether Peter Lorre or James Stewart did a better job with their different characters in the older version and remake of the movie. And the girl, I think you've had her in class, her name is Tracy or Stacy, says that it is, of course, nothing to do with the assigned reading, they just have the same title. Now it's all I can do, mind you, not to laugh out loud but I continued to walk just behind so I could listen to the story."

As he was listening, Joshua remembered how long it had been since he was on campus. He missed them all. He interrupted saying, "It's going to be so great to be back, you have no idea."

Moore shrugged his shoulders, "What? Yes, sure." Moore paused. "So anyway. So the girl..."

Joshua interrupted again, "Stacy or Tracy? Oh, you mean Stacy Rutherford. From Ohio. I think she's a poly-sci major."

"Yes, that's her. Stacy says 'no you're both clueless and clearly neither of you read the book. Chesterton's book was never made into a movie, and if you don't believe me, just ask Dr. Moore.' Now at this time, clearly she knows I'm behind them and the men are completely oblivious. So the one man says, 'Dr. Moore thinks he knows so much. He's just the program chair'. So the three of them stop and the girl decides she's had enough of both of them so she turns to me and says, 'What do you think Dr. Moore?'"

"That's Stacy all right. Maybe we should promote her to the honors track?" Moore began to laugh and something about it caused Joshua to begin to laugh, too. It wasn't that funny, but as Moore laughed, Joshua began to double over, slapping his thigh with the palm of his hand. Partially to make fun of the students but mostly remembering their own arrogance of their youth and how at one time or another they were both slapped down by their academic mentors. It was also a cathartic release of emotion. "So what did you say?"

"Well, I took a step closer to the three of them and looked at both men and then I looked at her and said, 'Chesterton's book has nothing to do with either the first or second versions of the movie of the same name, so I guess that makes *me* the man who knew too much.'"

Then Moore laughed and then snorted loudly, which caused Joshua to laugh even louder.

BY THE TIME THEY PARKED the car at the president's compound, they had filled their conversation with details of the campus happenings. Half a century ago, housekeepers and staff might have greeted the two men walking up the steps into the reception hall at the mansion. All that remained of that era was a young college student staffing the coat check rack, taking each of their overcoats and giving them in return a numbered tag. The student was Courtney Maddocks-Martin and she looked expectantly at Stone as he handed her his overcoat. Joshua nodded, not recalling the girl who a month ago he silently praised for using the word "archetype." Just before he turned away, she greeted him by name, "Hello Dr. Stone, nice to see you are feeling better."

Stone turned and smiled out of politeness. He didn't recognize the girl or recall her name. In the moment, he didn't remember talking on the telephone with her after his assault.

As he stepped into the room, the roar of combined voices struck Joshua. After spending so many days in quiet, the room filled with loud party guests was an ear-numbing change. He stopped, took a breath, and then moved to catch up to Moore. It took a moment for people to recognize Joshua with his buzz cut hair, but as they did, they called out to him. A group of the science professors were huddled in a corner and motioned him over with drunken enthusiasm.

"Dr. Stone, welcome back," said Phillip Mareno in a voice that carried across the room. The others were grinning from ear to ear, as if they had been hearing a joke. Stone noticed their wide eyes and the hint of alcohol on most of their breath.

"We were just reliving our students' difficulties this year with December exams." Mareno lamented, "We reuse many of the same exams, but this year, "whoo — we sent a few for a loop."

Stone grinned at Mareno's choice in clothing for parties. He seemed to own one black suit, with pants that were 2 inches too short and a loud paisley bow tie. In the corporate world, Joshua imagined, Mareno would never make the best-dressed list, but in the collection of academics around him, his oddness fit right in.

Jerry Coogan had been tenured for as long as Joshua had worked at Grant's Hill. The students in his *Basic Anatomy* course were juniors and seniors, a few pre-med and a handful of honors students working across the curriculum

"My test is very simple. It's 225 points and the students get 19 points for writing their name on the paper," Coogan told them.

The others looked amused, "Coogan, you're too lenient."

"Au contraire." Coogan offered and he took a sip from his glass.

Joshua smiled. Coogan was the kind of professor who could get away with saying "au contraire." Somehow it worked when he said it.

"The exam has only one question: and you can hear the groans as a each student takes the exam, looks at the question, and passes the remaining papers in the stack back over their head."

Joshua piped up, "Seriously? A one question exam?"

Coogan smiled. "One question: you either know it or you don't. The question is: There are 206 bones in the human body. Name them."

With groans of approval from the other 5 science faculty, Moore and Joshua smirked at each other and instantly began singing "the knee bone's connected to the thigh bone, the thigh bone's connected to the hip bone."

Mareno looked at Coogan and then at Alan Neal from the Mathematics wing.

"I can do you better," Neal said. "I have three questions, but if you can't get the first one, you're lost on the final two. But it's stuff kids understand. I tell them they have a pitcher of beer and a straight sided glass and they are pouring the beer into the glass."

Coogan and Mareno looked at Neal and Moore and chuckled, raising their glasses in a toast.

"So, I tell them, the surface area of the beer in the glass is an ellipse, because the glass is tilted." Several of the men standing around mimic "the glass is tilted" as they tip their glasses.

"As the glass fills, you tip your hand and make the glass upright and when it is full, the surface area of the beer is a circle."

The group nodded with understanding.

"Write the formula that describes the change in the surface area."

Joshua stopped to think, "Okay, area of a circle is Pi-R-Squared."

Alan Neal, who was at least as many glasses of wine into the night as the others, interrupted, "But Dr. Stone, even an English major knows that *pie* are *round*."

And they all groaned.

A woman's voice interrupted their pun fest. "Dr. Stone, here, come tell us what you think." and with that, Anne Strickland took him by the arm and led him to a mixed group of faculty from all four wings of the Quad who were standing next to the piano. As Strickland led Joshua away, the remaining science faculty watched him and then began speaking in lowered voices.

"He looks better than I imagined," Coogan began.

Mareno agreed with a slurred grunt, "Ergh, those scars are ugly now... will they ever heal?"

Neal, thinking back on Joshua's split nose, added, "I remember how he looked that day he split his nose on the b-ball court, I hardly see that scar any more. Maybe these will be like that one?"

Moore smiled, "I'll tell you this, we are glad to have him back. It was kind of odd on our floor without him."

Neal nodded, "He better be at Adams' next poker game, he cleaned me out last month and I'm ready for paybacks."

Coogan quickly asked, "So Tom, what's he saying? What did he do to bring this on? Was he meeting someone? He's not into something we should know about, is he?"

Moore shook his head, "No, I think he was looking for the dog and got blindsided. It could have happened to any of us." Brian Eggars, the dean, walked up to join the group of men.

Mareno looked around the group of men, furled his brow, and cocked his head to the side, "Any of us? Should we do something? I mean, with this nonsense about carrying guns on the news, should we be worried?"

Eggars shook his head confidently, "No, not at all. Grant's Hill is a sanctuary; we're perfectly safe and have been for generations. This happened off campus, and I'm truly sorry it had to happen ... to Dr. Stone of all people. But if college professors start carrying guns, then what does that do to our society? We are the examples in the community."

Strickland led Joshua across the room, where a polite, but slightly frustrated four piece combo was setting up their instruments, trying to work around the standing group of faculty. The two groups moved and dodged to make way for cables and music stands and microphones as the musicians tried to finish their preparations.

"Dr. Stone, welcome back. We were all so sorry to hear about Rex. How are you doing?" The question came from Robert Sutton who worked in the Student Life administrative offices. Sutton was facing both Joshua and Strickland as they joined the group.

Stone smiled and nodded, "He's missed. I can tell you I miss him, but it is good to be back here with everyone." Joshua scanned around the room, looking at the exits, the windows, and who was standing near others and who was standing alone.

Strickland was leading the conversation when his focus returned to their group.

"All I'm suggesting is that we might want to split summer term into two six-week terms instead of one twelve-week term. We could leave a gap in the middle of say — a week. Students who normally take two classes would take one in summer session one and one in summer session two. Faculty could teach one, both or none, and it lets us all have the north facing classrooms in the Quad. What do you think, Dr. Stone?"

Stone shrugged, "I think… I'm glad you are chairing our search committee. I have a hard enough time wrapping my head around my own schedule. You have some great ideas."

The tapping of a wine glass sounded throughout the hall and the guests looked up to see President Rose and his family near the center of the room.

PRESIDENT ROSE BEGAN BY GREETING Joshua and then turned to the room at large and said, "Dr. Stone, we are so pleased to have you back with us. It means so much to the Rose family and our Grant's Hill family that we can all be together to share this holiday season. The season of kindness, the season of trust, the season of values that we express and share with each other every day. Joshua, if you don't mind I wonder if you could share a few words with us. The floor is yours, Dr. Stone."

All eyes in the room turned to Joshua who was standing with his back against the wall. He began to wonder if anyone could see the pistol outline underneath his jacket. This was a moment of deception. From his past, he remembered the pranks of junior high gym class: the famous de-pantsing they would each do to each other. He was just as guilty of de-pantsing the other boys, and in that memory of insecurity he felt naked and exposed in front of his current colleagues. A bead of sweat dripped down his neck behind his shirt collar and down his back. He cleared his throat.

"Dr. Rose, Dr. Eggars," he glanced around the room, looking for his English department colleagues. Until this year, it was always the four of them: Stone, Moore, Adams, and Demming. Now, with Annette Demming retired, it was just the three of them.

"Dr. Moore, friends, colleagues. It is so great to be back with you all and you have no idea what it means to be able to eat food that I don't have to suck in through a straw."

There were nervous glances and a few giggles. Joshua pointed to the hors d'oeuvres table piled high with shrimp, caviar, and cheeses.

"I mean, seriously, have you ever tried to suck a *cocktail* shrimp through a *cocktail* straw?"

The laughter became louder and some of the noticeable tension left the room.

"As a professor, I'm always prepared with a few remarks, so for our lecture tonight, we'll be exploring the antithesis of Greek mythology as it relates to the modern parable in contemporary literature. If I may have the first slide please…"

This comment received the biggest laugh from the room. Rose and Eggars smiled politely, first at each other, then the room. A college photographer, who was mingling in the crowd, stepped up to take a photo of the Rose family and Eggars moved a bit closer to be sure he was included in the frame. Standing next to Rose was his wife, Connie, a stunning platinum-haired woman who had poise and appearance, as if she'd walked from a debutante ball to the president's right arm. Also joining them for the first time was their five-year-old daughter Natalie. She was wearing her "big girl dress" and enjoying the opportunity to be with the grown-ups.

Joshua silently contrasted the Rose family attractiveness and his odd-looking, buzz cut hair and two new facial scars. He made an attempt to lighten the mood.

"On the car ride over, Tom Moore and I were talking about our students and how they discover new authors. We were talking about G.K. Chesterton and it brought to mind this quote. Chesterton, who was often philosophic in his fiction wrote, 'It was one of those cases of a strange face so unmistakable as to feel familiar. We feel, somehow, that we ought to recognize it, even though we do not.'"

In his mind this quote was fitting for the night. But as the words left his mouth, Joshua realized he was taking the festive mood in a very different direction.

The silence in the room hung like a thick fog. Eggars looked at Rose; Rose looked at Eggars. Most of the women looked down at the food or drink in their hand. The men shifted their weight from side to side. Only five-year-old Natalie continued to make eye contact with Joshua, her warm, innocent smile beaming at him and in the quiet, she reached over, pulled her father's hand and in a voice that was as loud as the silence was awkward asked, "Daddy? Why does that man have naked ladies on his tie?"

Everyone immediately recognized the famous Mele Kalikimaka tie, with the hula dancer in the center of Joshua's chest.

Rose looked around the room, smiled, and nodded at Joshua and said, "Because it's a party!" and with that everyone smiled and applauded.

Rose, the experienced politician, made it a point to walk across the room and embrace Joshua. It was a gesture to show that all wrongs are forgiven and for the guests to treat the wronging guest as welcome. Over Rose's shoulder, Joshua saw the tall figure of a woman in a black dress with long blonde hair.

THE WOMAN IN THE BLACK dress was Liv Olsson. Joshua looked a second time to be sure it was her and then stood a little taller and sucked in his waist. She looked like this twice a year. That's not to say she was unattractive or dowdy the rest of the year, but as a psychologist and therapist, she made it a point to dress in a way that never called attention to herself. In a room full of people, even a few people, she dressed to fade into the background. In her every-day attire, she wore a simple pullover top, a thin knit in warmer months and a heavier knit in winter. Her hair would be neatly pulled back behind her head and often, she wore a tailored pant. He remembered she wore a skirt the day she came to visit his class in the fall, and tonight, she was dressed more like an ingénue than a college psychologist. He wrote himself into a fiction writer's fantasy that she wore the dress for him.

Liv was standing with Anne Strickland, in the opposite corner of the room, as Joshua uttered his party crashing quote. He hadn't seen her until he was finished speaking. Now, she had a gleam in her eye, which Joshua interpreted as confidence. She began walking towards him with an uncharacteristic, half-controlled swagger. She held the wine glass extended just a bit too far from her body. As she approached, he turned his left side toward her, keeping his gun side to his back.

"So, is that a pistol in your pocket, or are you just happy to see me?" Liv asked.

"What?" Joshua wondered if he had flashed the grip of the gun under his jacket during his speech.

"I heard that in a movie."

It was the first provocative line Joshua had heard her say in five years.

"Liv, if I didn't know better, I would think you were flirting?"

"Dr. Stone, you don't say me like that," Liv teased.

When she first learned English as a teenager, she somehow jumbled the phrase "Don't talk to me like that" and mixed up the words. In a way, she was like Annette, playing with words and sayings. She still used the broken phrase to this day.

"Okay, I won't *say you like that*." Joshua opened his eyes widely and nodded once as he smiled at her. "And yes as a matter of fact it is a pistol in my pocket."

Joshua recalled his father's advice that sometimes the truth, told in an unconvincing manner, was the best possible lie. "And, yes I am very happy to see you." That part was the truth and very convincingly told.

Liv looked at his water glass as she brought her own wine glass to her lips and asked, "So, you're not drinking tonight?"

Thomas Moore chimed in as he reached past them for some food on the hors d'oeuvres table, quoting Chesterton again as he did, "Drink because you are happy, but never because you are miserable."

He popped a shrimp into his mouth and a small dot of red sauce landed on his white cuff.

"Oh, darn it, look at that!" He shrugged and excused himself as Liv turned back to face Joshua.

"This must be quote Chesterton night for the English department," she said to him.

Joshua smiled, a bit red in the face, "I usually do a better job in my quotes, I guess I put a damper on the evening."

He searched Liv's face for compassion or understanding or a clue that she wasn't put off by his clumsy toast.

"I would not say so. It's normal for people to not know what to say. We all know what to say at a birthday. We know how to toast at a wedding, we know how to cry at the funeral. For most people there are no words for what happened to you, so we fumble and stammer and try to change the subject."

Joshua looked away from Liv reflecting on the truth of her words. Liv continued, "But Joshua, look at me, please. How are you?"

He looked back at her.

"You're always very curious, aren't you Liv?"

"It's my job, and now you are changing the subject. Joshua how are you?"

She took another sip of her wine. Her coneflower blue eyes met his and they stared at each other, as if they were daring the other to blink first. It had taken five years, Joshua recalled, but maybe this was their moment. The small quartet hired each year by Rose began playing music and Joshua decided to take the wine glass out of her hand and take her by the other hand to the dance floor and the two of them began to dance, touching body to body, swaying to the music.

He was careful to keep his right hip and holstered pistol away as they moved across the dance floor.

"Most days, I just don't know what to feel. It's like I wasn't even there."

He thought for a moment about how a psychologist might take what he said, so he added, "I don't mean that I'm dissociative. What I mean is, one minute I was standing there with Rex in the classroom and the next minute I was in a hospital with a tube down my throat trying to figure out what happened to the lost days.

"The only thing I remember is a dream and the only reason I think I dreamed it was because it's based on Lewis Carroll. I just remember dreaming that I was falling down a hole and I couldn't wait to get to the bottom for it to stop. And I was just as afraid of being hurt when I got there."

Liv winced, ever so slightly.

"Maybe, maybe," Joshua drew a deep breath and looked around the room "maybe I heard Rex bark, I don't know. I don't know how to feel because I don't know what happened. And then this guy, Miralies? Why me? Why him? Why Rex?"

Their bodies moved closer. Alan Neal nudged Anne Strickland and gestured toward Liv and Joshua on the dance floor. Neal smiled and leaned in to whisper, "She shook my hand earlier tonight… I mean, like she really meant it. I think she's been drinking."

Perhaps it was her need to be supportive, or it was one more glass of red wine than she normally drank. Whatever the cause, Liv began to say more than she should have.

"I have been thinking about the three of you that night. My heart aches for each of you."

Joshua turned his head slightly towards her as she spoke, unsure of her meaning. He was listening over the sound of the party and the music.

"You suffered the most, if you would have — " she paused, thinking about her words.

"If you would have died, so many people would have lost someone truly special."

Joshua felt himself tense up at the word "died."

She squeezed him when she said the word "special."

182

"I also feel bad for the other two, Joshua. This does not make your suffering any less but there were three of you whose lives were forever changed that night."

"Me, Miralies, and Rex?"

"Yes, you lost Rex. I'm not thinking about Rex." She stopped dancing, turned and held both of his hands on the dance floor.

"I'm thinking about Miralies. There is no forgiving what he did, but he is also a very disturbed and sick man. Sadly, he'll never get the help he needs."

She paused to see if he was listening. Joshua had seen her compassion before. She seemed to find good in everyone.

"The other two are: you," she paused again, "and the very tall student who witnessed the attack. He came to tell me about it. Do you know Derek Underwood?"

Her cheeks, already slightly pink from the wine turned a brighter red as she brought her hand to her mouth.

"Joshua, forget his name, forget I said this." She said apologetically. She took her hand away from her face and rested it on his shoulder.

They both realized she'd said too much. He had never heard her breach confidentiality. He wanted to pretend he hadn't heard the name but instead blurted out, "Who is Derek Underwood?"

"Let's just start over," she began slowly, "there is a student who came to me. He told me what happened. What he told me was he was in the parking lot when you were beaten and he's the one who activated the emergency beacon. He's very traumatized and if not for him, you might be dead. We all owe your life to him."

Joshua tried to picture a student named Derek Underwood. He had never had him in class, and could not remember seeing his name or any mention of him on campus.

"What are you saying?" Joshua's eyes darted around as he took in her words and what they meant. "You know him? You've talked with him? This is great, I mean, I have to talk with him Liv, I have to. He maybe saw something that will help me make sense of this — of what happened."

She smiled in a therapist kind of way, understanding and directive in the same glance, "I can't, he's a client. I've already said too much. You know I can't tell you more."

"Liv, come on. Just a bit. Just tell me something. What did he tell you...what did he see?"

"Joshua," she squeezed his arm, "we can't talk about this."

"Liv, this isn't just about me, maybe I can help him and he can help me. You can't help Miralies but what about me and this Derek?"

He didn't wait for her reply and took the question a different direction, "Tell me something. How do you know for sure he is telling the truth?"

"Because. Because he told me about the fire. And Rex." Liv looked down, disturbed by the images in her mind.

Joshua tried to catch his breath. Addison assured him that no one else outside of the sheriff's department knew what happened to Rex. Stunned by the revelation and hurt by the sight of Liv's reaction, Joshua felt more confused. In his mind, he understood her pain. In his heart, he wanted more support and sympathy for his own loss. They began dancing again, closer than before and she politely smiled while his words pushed for a meeting with the witness.

"Ask him, just ask him to meet with me, I'll meet anywhere. This is such amazingly great news."

Liv nodded and suggested, "The three of you have suffered. But I don't want you to suffer, Joshua. Talk with someone. Please get some help. This won't work itself out."

Joshua made one more appeal. "Liv, what if, what if Miralies wasn't alone, what if there was another attacker? Underwood may be in just as much danger as I am. If we can talk, if there was a second attacker, we can help the sheriff find him and make the campus safe."

"Joshua, talk with someone. You're not making sense."

The music stopped and she patted him on the back with three quick pats. David Adams and his wife Ellen approached the two. David asked, "May we cut in?" And then David took Liv to dance in the far corner of the dance floor and Ellen draped her arms around Joshua's neck.

Joshua's eyes followed Adams and Liv as they moved away. He almost walked after her, but Ellen's words stopped him.

"I was so worried about you, Joshua. I was afraid we would miss our annual dance together this year," Ellen whispered in his ear.

"Ellen, I wouldn't miss the chance to be with a pretty woman..."

She noticed that he took one longer look at Liv and then returned his eyes to her.

Ellen smirked, "I figure one of these years you will actually corner her under the mistletoe."

Joshua tilted his head at her and then changed the subject, "So where is David taking you this year for Christmas break?"

Ellen looked over at David and then back to Joshua, "Snowboarding in Banff. He's entered some over-50 event."

"Really? I didn't know David knew how to snowboard."

Ellen laughed, "Neither did I."

As she danced to the salsa music played by the quartet, Joshua took a moment to appreciate Ellen's grace and style. She was tall, he thought a bit too slender, with straight long brown hair that ended near her waist. He remembered last year's party, the final time that she and Annette Demming sang *Silver Bells* together at the piano. The pair of singers always stunned the room. Their beautiful voices mixed and harmonized and everyone shared a moment of holiday bliss.

When the salsa tune ended, Liv approached Ellen and took her by the hand. Joshua watched as the two of them wandered to the piano. The band was taking a break. The two women sat on either side of the piano player who agreed to play one more song before his own break. He played a few piano riffs and then Ellen and Liv began singing a new Christmas carol tradition.

Liv and Ellen sang a pretty song, and it made Joshua's mind drift back to times with Annette. Realizing that Annette was gone also reminded him that tonight, Rex would not greet him at the door. He tried to remember if this was like losing both his mother and his father and he couldn't remember the emotions. So instead, he replaced the empty feelings with thoughts about Liv.

The night was not the homecoming he hoped for. Unlike other Christmas Galas, when faculty from across the campus surrounded him, this year, Dr. Stone and his Mele Kalikimaka tie were wallflowers, disconnected from the smiles and the laughter. As the night continued, he found his focus shifting from groups of people, to the doors, and then back to faces and hands. Since his day in the class at the Grange, he spent more time looking at people's hands and what they were holding. Peers had told the class to learn to look for elusive weapons. Now, it was becoming second nature.

When Moore caught his attention, he was motioning from across the long hallway, holding up his coat check number and suggesting they leave.

As Joshua and Moore were putting on their coats, Liv hurried towards him and leaned very close. He smelled both her perfume and the wine on her breath. The temptation to kiss her was stronger than ever. Her lips where just inches from his mouth and as he began to move, she whispered, "This is my present for your

Christmas, I make you a promise. I will bring you *semla* for *fettisdag*."

Moore was oblivious to the pending kiss and pulled him away without realizing he was interrupting. Liv, paused, then turned back to join the party and Joshua tried to understand what she had said, "Semla for fettisdag? Tom, is that a good thing?"

Moore was beaming with a happy holiday smile.

"You seriously have to ask?"

The thought of her made Joshua giddy; both with the idea that Liv could help him find the witness and that maybe she was interested in him.

CHAPTER 30

THE DOG ORNAMENT

IT WAS JUST AFTER MIDNIGHT when he and Moore pulled into his driveway. Moore put the car in PARK and turned to his colleague. Joshua turned to Moore.

"Tom...thank you. I haven't been myself. It was great to get back out among friends." Moore nodded and smiled as Joshua walked to the side door of the house.

Once inside, he exhaled a large breath and walked to his bedroom. Joshua took off his jacket and hung it on the hanger and then removed the pistol from its holster. Running his finger across the gun safe sensor, it unlocked and he secured the gun, locked the safe, and walked over and knelt by the side of his bed.

From under the bed, Joshua pulled a red and green tote box and carried it to the living room. The Stone family Christmas decorations were always put up Christmas Eve, and remained up through New Year's Day. Putting the decorations up was a favorite memory of his childhood, it was like having two Christmases: first discovering all the ornaments and decorations he had forgotten about during the rest of the year; and, second, the actual presents opened Christmas Eve night.

His parents always told him it was the family tradition to buy a tree on Christmas Eve. When he was an undergrad at the state college, he listened to his dorm mates talk about the holidays —

the rich ones bragging about ski trips in the Rockies and the poor kids talking about very slim Christmas giving. It was then Joshua figured out that his parents received bonuses on Christmas Eve, and the bonuses were counted on as the family gift and decoration money. So while he and Dad bought the Christmas tree, Mom would go out and buy the presents for the family. Most years, she also bought her own present.

Both of Joshua's parents had lived to see him earn his doctorate. They even read his first novel, *Bottle Rocket*. Its two main characters were an 18-year-old clerk at a fireworks stand and an evangelical preacher who was broken down on the side of the road. In retrospect, he tried to make too big of a book in too small of a space. It included a clumsy sex scene his mother hated and "too many big words" according to his father. Joshua smiled remembering them.

When his dad's health started to fade, he began forgetting little things. The night he got lost coming home from the hardware store scared his mother enough to call the police, and to call Joshua in Grant's Hill. It took most of the night to find Dad, half way across the county, sitting by the side of the road, trying to read a map.

It was a pretty rapid decline after that. Joshua returned home to see him in the care facility before he died. By then, his quirky forgetfulness had turned mean-spirited. Joshua never heard his father say a mean word growing up, but as the dementia took control, his father began yelling at his mother. The shouting could go on for an hour. The saddest day was the morning he shouted at her, "You ruined my life and my dream of being a pro bowler."

His dad had never set foot in a bowling alley. The confusion in his mind and the anger in his voice played out in a tragic way. Joshua and his mother laughed about the outburst, but Joshua saw the break in his mother's heart by the expression on her face. Like the saying goes, it wasn't what he said, but how he said it.

They buried him on a sunny day in April. A bugler played taps, and some men from the American Legion folded a flag and gave it to his mother.

When she died later that year, the neighbors who found her said she was holding the flag, so Joshua buried it with her. He let an auctioneer sell off most of everything, and the house, and Joshua held on to the Christmas decorations.

From the red and green box that had been under his bed, Joshua picked a few decorations, ones he had saved from the family home. There was a nativity scene his mother wrapped and packed away each New Year's Day. As Joshua unpacked the newspaper-covered figurines, he remembered some of the articles from the 1960s and 1970s.

In the box with the nativity was a children's book, a thin book with glazed linen pages, titled *The Book of Joshua.* His mother read it to him every Christmas morning. She would look him in the eye while she read verse 1:7:

"Be strong and very courageous. Be careful to obey all the law my servant Moses gave you; do not turn from it to the right or to the left, that you may be successful wherever you go."

The words took on a new light. Be strong and very courageous. His mother began his love of stories by reading the Bible. The book was worn, the pages stained. He held it close for a moment and then gently returned to the decorations.

This was the first year he didn't have a Christmas tree. In the past, he would call on a friend with a car to help him bring it home from the tree lot, but he didn't ask anyone this year and hadn't really thought about buying one. Instead, he hung a few ornaments from an improvised picture wire strung across the living room wall.

This year, the postman delivered 214 Christmas cards. He picked a few of his favorites and hung them on the wire: There was the photo of Santa on a surfboard from a former student who was now at the University of Hawaii. There was a nighttime photo of Notre Dame, and a hand drawn cross and star from another student.

There were also a few cards from former girlfriends and lovers. He had an odd track record with women: they never seemed to break up with him, they just sort of faded away. A few were married now and they sent him cards with photos of their husbands, their children, their homes. Trish Stevens sent a card, signed simply, "Trish." There wasn't much more to add. As he sifted through their cards, he gently closed his eyes and rolled his head back, thinking of Liv at the Gala, her perfume and the hint of wine on her breath. He remembered their other near misses.

She came to a summer party at his house once. At the time, he was dating Sarah Robeson-Parker, a philosophy professor at the state university. Sarah drove to see him every weekend. At first, Joshua was uncomfortable with the travel imbalance. The bicycle-riding professor didn't reciprocate the commute often, but he had visited her loft apartment a few times during the three years they dated. He called her a collector; she loved beautiful things, beautiful clothes, and beautiful jewelry. Sarah didn't come to the summer party. And Joshua, out of respect for Sarah, didn't make any attempt to return Liv's interest in him when she stood unusually close to him in the backyard.

Later that week, Sarah told him about her new love, a grad assistant who was 10 years younger. She told him an honest truth, "Joshua, you're a great guy, but you're just not so great looking."

Joshua tried to compensate and grew a beard at the beginning of the fall semester. It made his face itch and he shaved it off at the end of October.

His attention returned to the red and green tub and from it he took a gift box from a student. Her name was Shannon Brooker. He remembered Shannon frequenting his office, twice a week, the year after he found Rex by the side of the road.

In the beginning, she was like all the other students who took his course and came by to ask a question or two about the week's reading. As the semester continued, Joshua noticed that her skirts seemed to get a bit shorter and her blouse seemed to get a bit lower. The first week, he assumed she had a date, and as the last three weeks of the semester came to an end, it was more and more clear that the short skirt and glimpse of a lacy bra was a show intended for him. On her final visit, she walked into his office and began to close the door. Joshua, gracefully managed to stand up and distract her attention and pushed the door a bit wider open. He caught Mrs. Thorn's eyes and made a pleading face. Mrs. Thorn was familiar with college schoolgirl crushes, and understood she was to keep a protective eye on the two of them.

Shannon sat down and crossed her legs in a way that made her skirt ride up the top of her thigh. Joshua's mother would have said something like "it's snowing down south" an old-school euphemism the girls of his mother's generation often said to each other when their slip or petticoat was showing under the hem of their dress. But in Shannon's case, there was no "snow" to show and Joshua had the feeling there wasn't much else besides Shannon under the skirt.

She may have had a crush on her professor. She may have just wanted a better grade. But she reached down slowly, making sure to let the top of her shirt fall open as she reached into her purse, and then handed a wrapped package to Joshua.

"I just wanted to say Merry Christmas, Dr. Stone. Thank you and I hope you enjoy your new dog."

She stood up and he stood, too. They exchanged a quick hug. A watchful Mrs. Thorn eased forward in her chair, and then back as Shannon left the room. Mrs. Thorn and Joshua both looked at each other and gave a mutual shrug.

Joshua sat down, opened the box and inside was a dog bone shaped Christmas ornament. Engraved on the bone was the word *Forever.*

"Forever" was the final line of his only anthropomorphic novel, *Our Final Days.* It had been published just a few weeks earlier and was a simple, uncomplicated story of an elderly couple, doting on each other as they take a walk in the late, sunset years of life. Midway through the book, the reader discovers the couple is two old collie dogs.

Joshua was touched. He thought about the young girl's eyes. For a moment, he considered asking her to dinner when the class was concluded and she was no longer his student. She was pretty and shared her caring heart with others. Maybe he had misjudged her intentions. Maybe she was serious about him?

It was a fleeting thought at the time.

He knew her attention was a crush. Joshua concluded that he should not ask her to dinner, nor give her an A for attractive, but the B+ she deserved and by doing so, he made them both happy.

As his thoughts returned to the room, Joshua set the ornament down before he finished decorating the house for Christmas. He walked to the kitchen and noticed his reflection in the bottle of Bourbon given to him by Moore.

He walked to it and cracked the tape liquor-control seal on the top. He poured two fingers in a small glass and took it with him to the living room.

He said her name aloud, "Shannon Brooker. Where are you now?" Maybe she was nearby? Maybe she remembered him? Maybe she would like to go to dinner?

Professor Stone knew his students very well. He walked over to the sofa, picked up the pile of Christmas cards, and then sat down. David McGlone, Tennessee, was destined to be in sales. David had a gift for working a room and according to the letter his wife typed in their card, he was Vice President of International Sales for a large machinery company. Ellen Nicoll was out of place as a student and had no motivation to be in college. She left after freshman year and was now ending her second stint in the Peace Corps working with women in Syria. Her card included a photo from a party of some kind. Amy Brown was a bitch. She was aloof and never had time for her classmates. Joshua figured her for a stockbroker someday and as he looked at her card, obviously signed by an assistant, he remembered reading she was at a major brokerage house in New York. Mathew Bright was bright. He ended up a Rhodes Scholar. His card included a cheesy, grip-and-grin photo with the Prince of Wales.

There was no card in the stack from Shannon Brooker. Despite her flirtatious approach and suggestive clothing, Joshua knew the answers to his own questions. The professor figured Shannon as a good girl with high morals. He had never heard from her after she graduated, but he imagined she was married with five children, living on a farm, and doing good things for people: baking bread, serving at funeral dinners, and hosting sleepovers. Her writing was clumsy. He would coach her, telling her to read her writing aloud so she could hear the rhythm, or the lack thereof.

Now sipping from his second two-finger glass, he recalled Moore quoting Chesterton about drinking only when happy. Joshua told himself he wasn't miserable as he walked to the ornament box and picked up the Forever bone ornament.

He took the glass and bone ornament and returned to the kitchen. Through a fuzzy mind, Joshua tried to remember what Rex looked like, and realized it was hard to see him anymore. How big was the tuxedo marking on his chest? He put out his hand to feel for the dog that wasn't there. Rex would know how to make this better. Rex would turn himself in circles and Joshua would say, "Let's go for a walk," or "go run outside," or "let's go over to Annette's and bark at the squirrels."

It was enough to push him to break down. The loss of two best friends, Annette and Rex, made his heart burn with loneliness. Joshua's loneliness simmered and then built to rage.

With that Joshua hurled both the ornament and the glass across the kitchen, both colliding with the doorframe where Rex's leash had hung in happier times. Bourbon splashed the wall as the ornament fell to the floor. Joshua cried out loud. He slid his body down the face of the refrigerator and ended up sitting first, then lying on the kitchen floor.

"Why did you do this to us?" he sobbed.

"What did we ever do to you? What wrong did I do? I wasn't ready to say goodbye to him yet."

Joshua's body curled tighter into a fetal position.

"I wasn't ready to say goodbye. Why didn't you just let me say goodbye? Why? Please let me have him back so I can say goodbye. Just let me say goodbye."

Joshua Stone cried for a very long time and sometime in the tears, he fell asleep.

He woke up, cold and alone, on the kitchen floor. Christmas music was playing on the radio and his head pounded. A dribble of drool was around his mouth and on the floor. The bottle of bourbon was 2/3 empty. He had passed out.

PART SEVEN

SPRING SEMESTER

CHAPTER 31

FIRST CLASS BACK

MRS. THORN BROUGHT DR. STONE a cup of coffee and placed it on his desk. It was her way of greeting his return to campus at the beginning of spring semester. Being descended from Norwegian immigrants she was comfortable with a limited expression of emotion. The best way she knew to show him that he was missed, loved and appreciated was to bring him a cup of coffee.

The professor knew better than to make a fuss and looked at her, smiled and said, "Thank you."

He sat back in the leather office chair and felt the pressure from the pistol and holster against his body, but it was not uncomfortable.

"Welcome back, Dr. Stone," he said quietly. It felt good to be surrounded by his books and his bobble heads and sports trinkets. The professor looked around the office and thought it was as he left it in November; not realizing Adams had removed Rex's bed during his recovery. Out of the leather briefcase from home, Joshua pulled the file folder containing some notes and ideas for the first day of class. Later in the day, Mrs. Thorn would bring him the current file with the paperwork he needed for the session. But what was on his mind was the student Liv mentioned at the Gala.

Joshua opened the computer screen to the Grant's Hill College student database and typed a query for Derek Underwood.

NO FOUND RECORD was the display on the computer screen.

His fingers typed spelling variations of both Derek and Underwood. Each returned NO FOUND RECORD.

A click of the computer mouse opened a menu and a second click selected a comprehensive list of student names. Joshua leaned in and began skimming the list of all students whose name began with U. The closest name was Donna Udelman. Donna was his student. She had gone to high school as one of the Bedford Bisons. She wasn't the Derek Underwood Liv mentioned. He contemplated walking down the flight of stairs and asking Liv what his name was, but respected her enough to let it be. Liv said Derek was tall. Joshua tried to mentally picture the player rosters for 3-on-3-basketball. None of their names were similar to Derek Underwood.

Joshua muttered aloud, "The three of you," remembering Liv's statement. He never thought about Miralies' life being changed. Addison and Wiggans seemed to gloat over Miralies being deported. His mind was jumping from idea to idea. The first thought was of ways to find Derek Underwood. The next few thoughts were about Liv. Then about Miralies. Then about deportation. From deportation he jumped to courtrooms. From courtrooms, his thoughts leaped to law libraries. And then, his own collection of books. Lost in his thoughts, the professor swiveled in his chair and faced the bookcases along the west wall of his office. As he skimmed the familiar titles, his eyes paused on the second shelf. In a final fleeting thought, he wondered about the role of crime in fiction. Joshua turned back to his desk and scribbled a note to himself, "Is there a research paper topic about crime or violence?" Holding the note, he turned back to look at the second shelf. Dostoyevsky was there, *Crime and Punishment* next to Nabakov's *Lolita*. Joshua chuckled at the placement and he stood up, and took *Crime and Punishment* and slid the hand written note inside the cover and put the book in his briefcase. He noticed a note taped to his door, he had missed it on the way in. "Drinks on us tonight — welcome back." Joshua smiled, glad to be back.

At 12:50, there was no more ignoring his return to the classroom. It was the last place he and Rex were together before the assault.

Joshua picked up his soft leather briefcase and put it in his left hand and walked down to the classrooms on the ground floor. The professor scanned the hallway before he left the stairwell. The hall was empty of the students who often milled around until the beginning of the class. Joshua walked to the door, took a deep breath and stepped into the room.

The first row of chairs was empty. As were the second and third. He wondered if he had the wrong room or time and then he looked at the last row. The students had moved most of the chairs to the far wall so that all of them were sitting in the back row. A few of them were holding quarters, some had them pressed to their foreheads and they began clapping, then cheering. The noise grew to a screaming frenzy, rivaling any pep rally held on campus. In multi-colored chalk, they had written "Welcome Back Dr. Stone" across both front boards. Their praise and joy lasted several minutes. One by one, in small groups, in pairs, and trios, they approached him and handed him their quarter, his fee for sitting in the back row.

The humbled professor placed them on the podium, in orderly stacks of 4 quarters each and then the students returned to their seats.

"Wow, I don't know what to say...except..."

Several of the girls giggled.

"Lets take a pop quiz! Take out a number two pencil. And an exam book."

And the laughter resumed. The students rearranged their bodies and the chairs and moved into a traditional classroom seating arrangement.

"All right, all right, your parents didn't take out a second mortgage for us to sit around and laugh at each other. Why are we here? What is this class about?"

And around the room, the young minds began sharing their ideas around the American story.

"And what are the stories? How many can we identify?"

Dana Wilkinson was looking at the syllabus in front of her. Dr. Stone spoke to her, "Dana, I know what I wrote, I don't need you to read it back to me. What do you think? C'mon, don't be shy, wow me like you did last term in Comp."

Dana spoke softly.

"Can't hear her," came a shout from the back.

Dana began again, "It's changed. Since we were kids, the American story has changed, after Columbine and 9/11, we are a different country."

A female voice from the left side of the room objected, "No we're not. We've been at war since the moment we got here. We just change the color of the bad guys."

"Okay, great. You're starting to identify some themes." Joshua walked to the chalkboard and he erased part of his welcome back message. "So we know there is conflict in American stories. Think about books. What are some typical American stories?"

The students began suggesting titles and Dr. Stone began to scribble them on the board.

"What about *Hoop*?" a student suggested.

Stone grinned, "*Hoop*," he paused, "Tell me, what was that about again?"

About half the class responded with a giggle.

"It's the story of a senior walk-on at a NCAA Division I school, who leads the team to a playoff berth."

Stoned nodded, "Yes, and who wrote it?"

"You did, Dr. Stone."

Now, the second half of the class laughed.

"And tell me, how was it?"

"Oh, it was awesome, Dr. Stone."

The whole class laughed.

"See? That's how you earn an A."

What at first looked like a random listing of book titles started to take shape as the student suggestions began to fall into predictable story types. When they were done Dr. Stone drew line across the top of each column of titles and filled-in a descriptor for each one. The students had picked half a dozen different types:

Revenge
Metamorphosis/Transformation
Maturation/Coming of Age
Love/Forbidden Love
Sacrifice/Wretched Excess
Ascension/Descension.

This was a good class, he thought. There were many story types, and the class textbook suggested 20 popular ones; but, that this class identified these on the first day signaled a great term together.

Their work had taken most of the hour, and when they had gone as far as they could take the topic, Dr. Stone told them that the class had come to an end.

"Make sure to read the next three chapters of your textbook and come prepared with your idea of which of these story types you want to describe for your final paper.

"And please do your professor a favor. I love *Star Wars* as much as the next guy, but after 15 years of papers, please don't write about it as the Hero's Journey and identify Wookie as emotion."

Stone raised his jacket up to cover his head like a cloak and in a voice like Obi Wan said, "I don't need to see your papers; these aren't the grades you are looking for." He quickly dropped the jacket to be sure he didn't expose the weapon behind his hip.

"The trick!" several students shouted. The professor smiled, looked at several neat rows of quarters and out to the class. He hadn't been asked to do the trick since November. His mind became distracted by a flashback image of Rex, looking at him, and then walking out the classroom door. After a slight hesitation, he found the strength to push the memory from his thoughts. He took the first stack of quarters and placed it on his thumb at the top of his fist on his right hand. The class was mesmerized the moment the coins flipped in the air and reached their arc. Dr. Stone reached out with his left hand and, one by one, caught each coin and when there were no more quarters to catch, the professor slowly extended his arms out to his side, leaned forward, and took a bow.

The class applauded and cheered as they gathered up their books and headed out the door.

When the last student had left the room, Dr. Stone looked around and gathered his notes that were spread across the lectern during the class. He put them in a loose pile, then crushed the loose pile into his soft-sided case, wedging them behind the Dostoyevsky. Fastening the snap closure on the case, he looked around the room one more time and walked into the hallway. It had been a good class. Being back in the classroom was the next step in his return to routine.

Joshua turned to the left towards the men's room and stepped inside. He walked across the mosaic floor to the urinal and stood facing the wall. He unzipped his pants. The hiss of the steam radiator was punctuated every so often by the clang of pipes somewhere in the building. The first clang caused Joshua to jump, his heart pounding. Water was dripping from one of the sinks; someone had not closed the faucet. Drip. Drip. Drip. Each one sounded like a footstep. Joshua still faced the wall but had no luck urinating.

His heart beat faster as the metal pipe clanged again.

He glanced around, certain someone was behind him, but he was alone. After quickly zipping his trousers, he stepped sideways and pushed open a stall door.

The professor walked in, turned and bolted the stall shut and sat down on the toilet. Panicked, he pulled up his legs to be hidden from view. Joshua tried to catch his breath. His emotions were certain that whoever killed Rex and nearly killed him was nearby. It didn't matter that it was contrary to his logic. The killer was still out there.

Wiggans and Addison were confident Miralies had done this to him. They had arrested Miralies with Stone's credit card and wallet, and there was no other reason to suspect anyone else.

His mind was running two streams of thought: his uncertainty about his own safety, and continued curiosity about Derek Underwood. Underwood saw something. Joshua knew talking to Underwood would answer the questions and put his fears to rest. As a faculty member, Dr. Stone felt responsible for the students. It caused him to worry about Underwood. No student at Grant's Hill should have to endure the horror of an attack. But there, in the bathroom stall, there was no way to talk to Underwood, or warn him he might be in danger.

His responsibility prompted him to consider calling Addison to tell her that the evil that struck him down had returned. Both streams of thought ended as the door to the men's room opened.

From the stall, Joshua could see a reflection of a tall man in the mirror opposite the row of urinals. The man wore a full-length coat that obscured Joshua's view. Standing in front of the sink, the man looked at himself in the mirror as he washed his hands. Joshua's mouth went dry and he felt as if the endotracheal tube from the emergency room was still in his throat. The professor reached back to his right hip and wrapped his fingers around the grip of his pistol. His index finger aligned itself along the frame over the top of the holster. Joshua waited and watched. The man looked up, turned off the water and stared into the mirror looking back.

"Are you looking at me?" his voice said menacingly.

Joshua's grip tightened and he prepared to pull the pistol from the holster. The hand washing man said the phrase again, "Are you looking at me?" He then shifted emphasis in his sentence to the second word, "Are *you* looking at me?" He said it again, this time shifting the emphasis to the third word, "Are you *looking*... at me?"

The man looked in the mirror and cocked his head and then very rapidly strung all the words together "are you looking at me?"

It was only then Joshua recognized the tall man as a student. It was Eric Carnes, the sophomore drama major who landed a cameo appearance in a police series on a cable network between his freshman and sophomore years. It was a minor role, yet major enough to push the student to take his craft more seriously.

The towel holder made a ruckus as the man yanked two towels from the roll of paper. It echoed across the tiled room, causing Joshua's heart to pound again. It was only when the student tossed the damp, used paper towels into the trashcan and left through the door, that Joshua released an audible sigh. Joshua let go of the handgun's grip and folded both hands across his pulled-up knees and he sat there for the rest of the afternoon.

Dr. Stone didn't return to his office and stood-up the colleagues buying drinks for him at the F Club.

After opening the door to the bathroom, he scanned the hallway and then scanned it a second time before rushing to the outer doors and his bicycle. He carried his overcoat at first and then yanked it on before pushing the bicycle down the path and then jumping on for the pedal home.

Out of his fear came a vision of clarity. Halfway home, he thought again about publishing an article about crime in literature and Dostoyevsky. He created a mental picture of his process for beginning a new project, sketching and mapping the major sections as he had done dozens of times during his career. Liv cautioned him at the Christmas Gala, "This won't work itself out." Joshua wanted to show her he could work it out and heal. The best way to heal, he concluded, was to treat his assault like a novel. It was a familiar process: identify the characters, the plot, and the archetypes each played out. It was a path to coming to terms with what happened on the night everything changed. The process would help him find a way to overcome the uncertainty and anxiety and return to the life he enjoyed.

Joshua got to the house, rested the bicycle against the side door stair railing and walked inside the kitchen. After draping his overcoat across the chair, he opened a can of soup, dumped its contents into a small pan and turned on the stove to simmer. With a hint of confidence, his hand flipped on the light in his home office and Joshua looked at the four walls. The wall behind him had a single, framed, photographic print. It was a photo of Eastford Chapel taken by a National Geographic photographer in the 1960s for an article about Midwest colleges. The replay of Liv's words as she was standing close to him during the Christmas Gala prompted him to take the photograph down. In its place, he took four sheets of paper and wrote one word on each sheet:

THE   THREE   OF   US

He taped them in a line on the wall, symbolizing what Liv told him, that there were three lives affected by the assault.

From his desk, Joshua retrieved his smart phone and held it at arm's length to take a self-portrait. As he stared at his image, the scar on his left cheek was prominent. Joshua turned the other cheek and looked again. And then faced straight into the lens before snapping the photo. He sent the image to his computer printer, wrote the name STONE under the photo, and then wrote MIRALIES on another paper and UNDERWOOD on a third. He arranged the three men's names into a triangle on the wall, putting his own name, STONE, above the line of words that read THE THREE OF US. He placed MIRALIES under the line of words and to the left. He placed UNDERWOOD under and to the right.

Joshua turned to his desk and opened the top drawer. He closed it and opened the next drawer. He opened the third drawer and then turned to a small set of drawers behind him. Joshua searched his memory, straightened up, looked around the room, and then back at the drawers again. His hand reached for the bottom drawer, pulled it open and took out a file folder. At the back of the folder he found a copy of a billing statement from Town and Country Veterinary. During his last checkup, Sissy took a digital photo of Rex and the photo was included on his statements and reminders for annual checkups. Joshua returned to the top desk drawer, grabbed a pushpin, and walked to the wall.

He folded the statement into a tri-fold with Rex's photo visible and pinned the statement to the wall just under his own photo and name. With a step back, Joshua nodded confidently, drew in a breath and then walked into the kitchen. Somewhere in the house or garage was the collection of teaching aids created for his courses at Grant's Hill. Joshua decided to search the garage and walked out the side door and raised the garage door to look through storage boxes.

Along the back wall of the garage were a dozen stacked and arranged plastic storage totes, each with four numbers stenciled on their facing edge. The containers archived Dr. Stone's teaching, financial, and personal papers. The numbers represented the academic year. He scanned the boxes and zeroed in on the box labeled 99–00. With both hands, he pulled it from the shelf and set it on the concrete floor. He released the plastic snap locks that held the lid in place. Inside the most forward half of the plastic tub were alphabetized file folders. The back half had miscellaneous items and Joshua found what he remembered: a stack of laminated word cards secured with a rubber band. He took the cards out of the box, and left the lid and box on the garage floor. As the man pulled the garage door closed, a white dog at the end of his driveway watched his actions intently.

WHEN JOSHUA FIRST SAW THE white dog in the darkness, it was more of a shadow than a three-dimensional shape. The light from the open kitchen door reflected in the dog's eyes and it stared at Joshua and Joshua stared back. The yellow reflection of the retinas gave the dog a ghostly appearance.

"Rex? Hey, it's okay boy." The dog edged up the driveway. As the dog moved closer to the light, Joshua's hopes were dashed as he realized that while it was a Labrador, it was not Rex. Still, he hoped to get the dog close enough to see if it had a tag or collar. He called to the dog.

"I just want to help you get home."

Joshua remembered hearing a voice say "Take me home" when he discovered Rex on the side of the highway. He hoped this dog would understand the word "home."

The dog hesitated, looked around, and then back into Joshua's eyes.

"It's okay boy. Here, come here."

Just as Joshua was about to see the dog's entire body, the neighbor's outdoor light came on and Mrs. Jenkins stepped onto her porch. The dog bolted for the bushes in Mrs. Jenkins yard.

"Hello, Joshua. How are you today? Did you lose something? Do you need some help?"

"Hello, Mrs. Jenkins. There is a stray dog in your bushes. Can you see him?"

Mrs. Jenkins looked and walked partway down her steps, then turned to Joshua, "He must have run off, I don't see anything."

With that, they spoke for a few moments about the chill of the evening air.

"Did you go back to classes today?" She asked him with an optimistic lilt to her voice. "I'll bet they are happy to have you back," she added.

"It was good to be back," Joshua told her. It was then he remembered the soup on the stove. "The soup! I'm sorry, Mrs. Jenkins I think my dinner is burning," and with that he hurried into the kitchen. He reached for a hot pad and turned to the stove to see soup bubbling out the lid, down the side of the pan and over the burner elements. He switched off the knob, slid the hot pan to the side and reached into the cupboard for a soup bowl. He poured the soup into the bowl and set the pan in the sink, leaving the spill for later. He grabbed a spoon, the soup bowl, and the rubber-banded, laminated word cards and walked into his office. He set the soup on his desk, took a few bites, and then turned to face his wall.

He unfastened the rubber bands and the first of the five word cards read CHARACTER. He took the word card and walked to his desk and grabbed several pushpins from the top drawer. He walked back to the wall and pinned CHARACTER in the middle of his triangle just above THE THREE OF US. He took the other four remaining cards and spread them in a fan on the desk near the soup bowl. He sat down on the desk, eating his soup, contemplating the remaining word cards fanned out in front of him.

PLOT   CONFLICT   THEME   SETTING

"Simple, I can do this. This is what I'm good at. A great start. I know my characters. Three characters," he paused, "okay, three characters and a sidekick," when he said sidekick he remembered the stray dog in the driveway. He got up from the desk and walked to the kitchen and opened the cupboard that held Rex's food and dish. He opened the plastic tub of food and scooped the dish inside filling it. He walked to the side door, leaving both the cupboard and the plastic container open and walked down the steps and placed the dish on the driveway.

He looked around and whistled for the dog, "Here boy, come get your kibble." He looked around again, shrugged his shoulders and walked back into the house.

He returned to the office, looking at the wall as he sat at his desk and finished the soup. He considered the next unused word card: PLOT. He shook his head. This story lacked a plot.

"Boy gets girl. Boy loses girl. Boy gets girl back. That's a plot," he said aloud, almost in his teaching voice. "Man kills dog. Man tries to kill owner. Witness sounds alarm. Where's the plot in that? It's total crap."

He cast PLOT aside and picked up CONFLICT.

He tapped the edge of the card against his cheek, tapping the new scar left from the injuries and stitches he received.

"Good and evil," he said confidently and with inspiration. That was easier to work with. He took out a stack of yellow Post-it notes and a second stack of green Post-it notes. With a blue marker, he wrote the word 'good' on several green Post-its and the word 'evil' on several yellow Post-its. He pulled a yellow evil Post-it from the pad and walked to the wall placing it under Miralies' name. He returned to the desk and retrieved a green 'good' Post-it and placed it under Underwood's name on the wall. He looked at his own name and looked at the stacks of Post-it notes. He peeled off one of each. He stared at both words and his own name for several minutes and then placed a green 'good' Post-it next to Rex. The 'evil' Post-it clung to his index finger on his right hand. He returned to the desk, wrote out one more 'evil' Post-it and returned to the wall, placing an evil on Underwood's name. It made literary sense. In every character, there is good and bad. Underwood did the right thing by sounding the alarm. But...why didn't he help? Why didn't he intervene? Why didn't he save Rex?

He looked at his own last name and thought of his mother, telling him the story of John 8:7, that those without sin cast the first stone of punishment. Joshua recalled his own sins. He let Rex out of his sight. He left the dog's leash connected to his collar. He tightened the collar before class. He stuck the evil Post-it note on his own name.

The remaining cards on his desk were THEME and SETTING. SETTING was easy. He turned to his desk drawers again, opening the second drawer and finding a file folder labeled "Freshman Orientation." Inside he found a folded map of campus, opened it and refolded it to show the Quad, the Northwest parking lot and the surrounding area. He took a marker and sketched a square to represent the First Apostolic Church. He carried it to the wall along with the word card and pinned both to the left side of the diagram.

"Not to scale," Joshua said aloud and made a mental note to measure some distances the following day on campus. He returned to the desk picked up a Post-it note and scrawled on the pad:

How many steps to alarm box
How many steps to Quad door
How many steps to Rex

He paused. He'd never gone to look at the spot Addison said they found Rex. He peeled the Post-it from the pad. He walked to the kitchen found his overcoat and opened it to pull the sport coat from the inside. Inside the right breast pocket he found his wallet, opened it, and stuck the Post-it note on the brown leather face opposite his college ID.

The laminated word card that remained was THEME. He looked at the stone placard his mother had given him and read the scripture, "Be Strong and Very Courageous." Lifting the edge, he slid the THEME card underneath.

GRANT'S HILL'S COLLEGE BASKETBALL COURTS measure 84 feet long and 50 feet wide. On a fast break run, Joshua could cover the distance from end line to end line in 36 paces.

He had played the 3-on-3 games so many times that he could know his court position just by counting his steps as they shuffled through the plays. Offense or defense, he knew where to be. While he didn't count aloud, he had an innate sense of court placement.

It had only failed him once, and the result was colliding with Alan Neal and the ensuing seven stitches. He remembered Neal had said something to him just last week about a petition to get 3-on-3 as an Olympic sport. He picked up the phone and dialed him.

Alan Neal looked at his caller ID display on his office phone and answered with a sly, "Well my, my, my, the mysterious Dr. Stone on the telephone."

They exchanged some trash talk about playoffs and then Joshua brought up the petition.

"So is that Olympic petition thing still going on?"

Neal was trying not to be put off by his friend's confusion.

"Joshua, it wasn't a petition. It was a letter, co-signed by a number of coaches and players. It was due December 31. I love your follow through, but next time, a little more hustle?"

Joshua looked around the office for a calendar, unsure what month it was. The digital clock in the office was still blinking 7:19 from the power outage.

"Wow, really, Alan, I'm sorry I misunderstood. I guess I thought this was something else."

"Joshua, this is me you're talking to, I understand. I know you hit your melon really hard. We all do, we understand." The teammate changed subjects, "Hey look, the season is over, the courts are wide open. What do you say? You and me, a little one-on-one center court. How does 2:30 work for you?"

Joshua was staring at the diagram on the wall and hadn't heard what Neal was saying.

"Yeah great, that sounds right. Okay, yeah."

"2:30 then," confirmed Neal.

"Yes, look I'm late, later."

Joshua set down the phone and then walked to the shower.

After dressing for the day, and securing his holster and pistol inside his waistband, he rode his bicycle to campus and rested it in the bike rack. He changed from his shoes into running shoes and scanned around. There was no one else in sight.

Joshua stood at the door leading from the Quad to the parking lot and stared at the blue emergency beacon. He judged the distance to be about two and a half courts, and looked left and right before he started his run. He counted his steps saying each decade aloud as he sprinted the distance, "10... 20... 30... 40... 50... 60... 70... 80, one, two, three, four, five, six, seven!" He passed the emergency beacon and repeated the number again, "87."

To double-check the distance, he made a quick look back at the doorway and scanned the parking lot one more time before sprinting the reverse direction. "10... 20... 30... 40... 50... 60... 70... 80, one, two, three, four, five, six, seven!" Joshua reached into his pocket, took out his wallet, opened to the Post-it note he had placed there the night before and with a pencil wrote the number 87 and drew a circle around it. He began walking to the emergency beacon. When he got there, he stopped and looked around. Joshua picked a spot where there were no cars parked and he estimated it to be where Sophie Carr and her two paramedic preceptors found him that night. It looked to be the same distance from the emergency beacon as the Quad door and in the opposite direction. He began his sprint again, counting each stride "10... 20... 30... 40... 50... 60... 70... 80...90...100, one, two, three!" A flash of yellow on a low hanging branch caught his eye. After looking for a few moments, he guessed it was a scrap of yellow police tape blown by the wind or carried there by a bird. It was torn and only DO NOT CROSS remained. He felt a chill as he turned his body to take in a 360° view before he stopped and stared at the tree line at the end of the mowed median separating the church and the school.

He could make out a black, burned area in the otherwise brown grass of January. He was overcome with sadness and loss, and began a slow, assiduous walk. When he got there it looked like an old campfire. Rain and a brief snow had settled the disturbed ground and mellowed the appearance of horror. He began to cry. He closed his eyes and imagined Rex sitting before him, awaiting his signal that this was playtime and the two of them would go running for home or exploring the squirrel paths in the timber.

"I'm sorry Rex. I am so, so sorry." He took a deep breath, wiped his eyes, and opened them. The stray white dog was sitting in front of him. Joshua chose not to move, out of fear of spooking the dog, so the two of them stared at each other a few moments. In the light of day it was clear this dog was not Rex. It was all white and a little bit heavier and taller than his companion. The dog moved to all 4 feet and sniffed at the burned ground. Joshua took

a step back, watching, as the dog lay down then rolled its front
shoulders as if it were trying to pick up the smell that remained in
the ground. The dog rose to all four legs, shook itself, and looked
back at Joshua over its tail. It took off at a run, down a path
between the trees. Joshua began to follow then reversed course
hoping the dog would, in turn, turn around and chase him. It did
not and continued running through the trees until Joshua lost
sight of it.

With the white dog gone Joshua returned to counting paces
and kept running to the church door. "10... 20... 30... 40... 50...
60... 70... 80... 90... 100... 110... 120... 130... one, two, three,
four, five!"

Panting now with a slight wheeze from the cold air, Joshua
opened his wallet wrote down 103 and 135 for the last two
distances. He also made mental note of the distance between Rex
and the spot his own, unconscious body was found; and, wrote
that number too, 41.

He took a slow walk back to the edge of the trees to look one
more time for the white stray. He saw nothing, turned and looked
at the entry door to the Quad. It was the last leg of the alarm box
— Rex — Quad door triangle. With this final measurement, and
the others, he could estimate dimensions of all the parking lot and
surroundings. He wondered if his paces were any more or less
precise than Percy Grant's early cartography after the Louisiana
Purchase. His final sprint resulted in the number 226, which he
wrote and circled on the paper in his wallet and then tucked both
away.

As he was sitting on the curb, changing his shoes, David Adams
and Thomas Moore were walking with Liv Olsson towards the F
Club. He waved at them and they waved back. David's arm was
still in the lime green colored cast protecting the wrist fracture he
received snowboarding over Christmas break. Liv turned, and in a

rare display of self confidence said, "Joshua, please come see me. Let's catch up."

She walked backwards a few more steps, still looking at Stone. Stone smiled and waved.

On the ride home, he visualized superimposing the dimensions on a new map and adding it to the diagram on the office wall.

Later that afternoon, Alan Neal shot a few baskets and dialed Joshua's telephone number and received no answer. He gave up and left the gym around 3:45. They had been friends for a very long time but he'd never seen his friend close him out like this. He hoped he would tell him what was going on, soon. If Joshua needed help, Alan Neal wanted to give it to him.

CHAPTER 34

DEVIL IN THE DETAILS

FEBRUARY WAS A STRING OF blurred days: teaching class, scanning the hallways, hurrying to his bicycle, and returning home. He scoured the news and when he found articles about assaults or dog mutilation, he printed them and hung them; adding to his research and searching for missed connections. The office was littered with dishes, glasses, silverware and clothes. The diagram had grown to engulf the wall and was spilling across the corners on both ends

CHARACTERS was complete. SETTING was complete. CONFLICT was complete. That left him with PLOT and THEME. He researched the scientific studies of psychotics and psychopaths and trends of on-campus and off-campus crime. The articles suggested that criminals like Miralies were psychopathic because of their lack of empathy and sadistic animal torture. Joshua could not make the mental leap to that level of abuse. He wasn't sure he understood the clinical difference between a psychopath and a psychotic. That was Liv's territory, not his. But he read each article, highlighting what he thought was important.

His multi-colored highlights decorated each page and he would pin the most important sections of them around the edges of the wall. Whenever he was in the office, he would sit and stare at the diagram, re-working and re-thinking the events, trying to make sense of it all.

He looked at the papers. Each was held in place with a pushpin. He started to reflect on the patterns and his color-coding in the diagram. All of the main points, by his design, were held in place with round pushpins. The reference articles about psychopaths had square, blue pushpins, and the articles on psychotics had square, green pushpins. Articles about violence occurring on a campus had red pushpins, and the violence in the workplace articles had orange pushpins.

To show the direct relationships, Joshua used strings of green yarn that he looped around each pushpin, creating a web. The sub-text, the background linkages, he connected with yellow yarn.

He sat there, drumming his fingers on a scrap of paper. He wadded it up and tossed it into the wastebasket.

"Swish, Stone. Nothin' but net," he exclaimed and then wadded another sheet. He stood up, took a step back from the chair and made a high arcing shot into the trashcan.

He searched for another scrap paper and found a second copy of one of the articles he read. He tore the cover sheet free of the stapled stack, wadded the paper, and then did a quick fake left, then right, then a quick hop before he took his shot and sunk a third wastebasket shot.

"Stone...at the buzzer." He looked up.

A green pushpin in an article on the wall caught his eye. He moved to it and read the highlighted phrase. It was about a psychopath in Vermont. He cocked his head.

He muttered just under his breath, "This is all wrong, this is about a psychopath, it should have a blue push pin." He walked over to his desk, selected a blue pushpin and replaced the pin in the wall with the proper color. He stepped back and began looking at all the green pushpins.

"Here's another," he said out loud, and retrieved the box of push pins from the desk.

He continued to look at the papers, and found two more with the wrong color pins. As he did, he made a meticulous effort to align the tops of the sheets with each other. The collage of notes had no order, form, or symmetry, and aligning the sheet edges did nothing to alter the visual barrage of clutter he had created.

He was counting as he moved across the wall.

"114 points. 114 plot scenes," he said with confidence.

He stepped back and glanced over at the clock radio, still blinking 7:19. He pushed the power button and listened. The station was broadcasting a Grant's Hill basketball game, but he didn't hear the name of the other team. He turned the volume up a bit and sat down in his chair, listening to the game and staring at the wall. Both the wall and the game competed for his attention.

The broadcaster on the radio was describing the play by play.

"Herford at mid-court, passes to Smith...Smith, working the ball down the right side...back to Herford. Herford, at the top of the key, shoots...No good... Rebounded by Smith, Smith is up... Two points."

A second announcer joined in, "Herford has been missing those three pointers all afternoon."

The first voice resumed, "But Smith is on fire, that's 15 points just this half. Smith is truly leading this Grant's Hill team."

As he stared at the wall, Joshua began to see the push pins as representations of the players on each team and as the play by play continued, his eyes moved from push pin to push pin, as if he was watching the passing of the ball.

He turned up the volume even louder.

"Decan brings the ball down court, over to Smithfield, Grant's Hill sets up in their defensive zones."

With the words, Joshua's eyes moved over the pushpins.

A loud buzzer sounded in the broadcast, "Time out Grant's Hill."

The second announcer joined in, "They saw something they didn't like, so Grant's Hill is regrouping."

Joshua's eyes scanned the names of THE THREE OF US: Stone, Miralies, and Underwood.

The radio continued in the background, "and it looks like Underwood is coming in for the visitors."

Joshua stopped. He stared at Underwood's name, not sure if he read it or heard it on the radio.

The first announcer picked up the commentary, "Underwood has not seen much action all season. Grant's Hill has the lead by 10, end of the fourth quarter. This is a great way to end the last home game of the season"

Joshua stood up from his chair.

"Underwood plays for the opposing team? Shit."

He sprinted down his hallway and into the kitchen as he grabbed his jacket off the doorknob and left both doors open as he pushed his bicycle and ran it down the driveway before he jumped on. He had 10 minutes of riding to get to campus, and maybe another 3 or 4 to get to the gymnasium. He pedaled fast and out of the saddle and he took every short cut he could think of to get to campus quickly.

His heart was pounding and he was wheezing with each breath and he pushed the bicycle built for comfort to the limits of the gears. A smooth, fat tire ride for every day commuting was stodgy on the hills as he pushed harder.

He looked at his watch; the quarter was almost over. He didn't know how many time outs remained, but he was counting on at least one each. If they each used two, he would make it before the final buzzer.

The bicycle skidded across some loose sand at the corner turn into the college parking lot and almost spilled the bike and rider. Joshua kept pushing and kept it upright and jumped over to the sidewalk. There were a few students milling round, but the sidewalk was open and he dropped the bike into a lower gear and pressed on for the final three minutes across campus. The gymnasium was surrounded by small groups of students, parents, and fans as Joshua jumped off the bike and rested it against a railing. He sprinted up the steps and pulled open the main door into the building. It smelled like pool chlorine and popcorn, and Joshua could hear the cheers and then just as he reached the doors to the playing floor, he heard the final buzzer and huge cheer from the hometown, Grant's Hill side of the stands.

Immediately, fans began flooding out the doors, pushing and jostling Joshua back against the wall. He squirmed and worked his way against the flow as more and more fans pushed and crowded through the double-door width anteroom that separated the playing floor from the main hallway and exits.

He was nearly in the gym when he felt a hand reach across his chest, he began to forcefully push it away, but he looked up before he did and was looking into the coneflower blue eyes of Liv Olsson.

"Joshua, how good to see you. Didn't you love the game? Why didn't you come sit with us?"

Joshua began to panic. Derek Underwood was less than a basketball court away from him. He tried to see onto the court and then looked back at Liv. She was close again. Not that this was the time or place, but damn, she was within kissing distance. He looked into her eyes and smiled.

She looked back and smiled.

He looked away at the court again and then back at her then said, "I've... I've got to go, talk to you later?" and as he did, he pushed past her and pressed himself against the wall to continue to move against the exiting fans.

His view was still blocked, he couldn't see the court, or the teams, but he knew both locker rooms were on the far side of the gymnasium. He was hoping that tradition wouldn't betray him. Each team lined up and did a half-court handshake and fist bumps and then picked up their gear. He was prepared to go into the visiting team locker room, if he had to, but needed to talk with Underwood in private.

The exiting fans kept him pressed against the wall and away from the main floor. As he got close to the floor, he still lacked a clear view. He was desperate, and was running out of options so he decided it was time for the last second — at the buzzer — Hail Mary. He screamed, as loud as he could, "Underwood!"

As he pushed past the few fans that were between him and the gym floor he caught a glimpse of a player with long hair and UNDERWOOD on the singlet jersey standing at the locker room door. Joshua took a breath. Underwood turned. Now, in clear view, Joshua could see Underwood was average height and a bit stocky. And was a young woman. They all were. This was the women's game, the last home women's game of the season.

Both teams continued to the locker rooms. The stands emptied and Joshua walked along the polished plank floor until he reached the scoring table. He found a team roster for both teams, and skimmed the names. Susan Underwood listed Fremont, Nebraska as her hometown. Joshua whispered, "Fremont Tigers," and looked out at the court. He shoved both hands into the patch pockets of his jacket. She was the wrong Underwood.

A handful of student volunteers were walking through the stands, picking up debris and half empty drink cups. Joshua looked over and took a few steps and sat on the third row of the pull-out bleachers on the home team side.

He knew she was long gone, but he looked over to where Liv Olsson had stopped him. The doors were propped open and he could see out into the hallway, and other than the few remaining volunteers, the building was empty.

He watched as they worked up and down the rows, dragging large, black plastic bags, picking up the trash with their rubber-gloved hands, and then moving on. He felt like they were picking up his last hopes of finding Underwood and tossing them with the rubbish from the game. When he was home, staring at his diagram, he felt like he was getting closer to resolving everything. And when he came onto campus, he got farther from the things that mattered most. He looked back one more time at the entrance and then one more time at the locker room door. The students working his side of the stands greeted him with, "Hi, Dr. Stone."

He smiled and waved, stood up, walked back to the bicycle, and rode home.

CHAPTER 35

RUMORS

THE RUMOR MILL OF CONCERN spoke softly about
Joshua. No one had seen him at the F Club since his return. His
seat at David Adams' poker table had been empty for three
months. Mrs. Thorn noticed he ate lunch in his office every day, a
partial return to the Joshua Stone who arrived here 15 years ago,
but she also saw he was not the same as then.

Neal tried not to be angry with his friend for standing him up
on the courts. He anticipated he wouldn't be around during 3-on-3
season, but to not see him around the gym at all was so out of
character.

Liv Olsson was hoping Joshua would come see her to talk. She
started to invite him to coffee when he was in such a hurry to leave
the women's basketball game, but because of the crowd and the
small space, she didn't get a chance to ask.

She decided to go to him. On a warm afternoon, the last day of
February, she walked the few blocks from her office on campus to
his home, knocked on the door and waited for an answer.

She saw his bicycle, leaning against the side door to the house
and she knew he was at home. She looked at her reflection in the
window glass of the door and touched a wisp of hair, tucked it
behind her ear and smiled. She knocked a second time. Joshua
parted the closed blinds in the windows and seeing Liv, let the

blinds drop. She heard him unlock the door and open it to let her in.

He offered her a chair in the front room. It had been light and sunny on her prior visits. Now, with the new window blinds, the lamps painted a warm orange glow over the furniture. The room was cluttered, like he was in the middle of a project. She took that as a sign he was active and not moping around.

Liv had been here twice before. The first time was a summer party, held on the first day of the season two years ago. Joshua had invited her, lingering at her office door even after she had said, "Yes." The party was in the backyard and she managed to walk around the house, looking at the collection of things. She looked beyond the obvious superficial clean up that most people do for parties, and saw a deeper, organized, methodical approach to his life. She would later tell her sister that, "everything was just…so."

The second visit was earlier this fall, the week before the assault when they shared a cup of coffee on his front steps.

From her chair, Liv glanced around to the other rooms. She could see into the kitchen and had a clear view of the pile of dishes in the sink and on the counter.

"Oh my God, how can you live with this *ungkarl kök?*"

"Choke what?" Joshua looked confused.

"Oh, my mother used to yell that at me and my sister if we didn't do the dishes, it means…how do you say it? Bachelor's kitchen?" Liv stood up and walked into the kitchen, rolling up her sleeves.

"Let me help you. I'll clean up. You can tell me about your book."

The trashcan was overflowing, so the first thing she did was pull the plastic bag up and tie off the top. Next, she pulled the bag out of the can and carried it to the side door. She opened the door to toss it out and as she did, she saw the twin dog dish with food and fresh water. She looked around and listened, but didn't hear sounds of a dog.

"Joshua?" she called to him over her shoulder. "About Rex. How are you doing?"

He looked up from the stack of mail he was sorting for the third time, "Okay. I mean, what can I do? He's gone. I miss him every day."

"Joshua, are you still feeding him?"

"What? No, of course not. Why would you think that I was still — " he stopped and looked towards her voice. "That? Oh no, it's the oddest thing, but there is a stray dog who started coming around. I can't get close enough to it to see if he has any tags or collar, but I've seen it twice. So I put the food out to see if I could catch it and get him back home."

Liv looked around the yard through the window, but saw nothing of the stray, so she began running hot water to wash Joshua's dishes. She continued trying to draw him out over the sound of the splashing water in the sink, "If you were Scandinavian, I would tell you it's your imagination. That it's not a real dog. It's your *fylgja*. You don't have to feed her."

Joshua answered, half seriously, half skeptically, "My fylgja! Of course, that's why the dish is still full!" he laughed.

"See I knew you were like me," Liv confirmed.

Joshua liked the sound of her voice and her suggestion; it would make it easier to ask her his question.

"But I must say you something," she began.

This was a Liv thing. She often confused the word "say" with "tell" or "talk."

Joshua mimicked her, "What must you *say me*?"

"If you are seeing a fylgja, you must be Scandinavian! A fylgja is your companion, your protector. So," she smiled proudly and declared, "I have decided you are both Scandinavian and must be very special to have a protector fylgja."

Joshua pointed at the black hair that was beginning to grow out from the buzz cut he had following his injury, "I don't think I'm at all Nordic."

She smiled admitting he was right. "Is it Rex? Has he returned from the afterlife to guide you?" Liv asked, trying to be more friend than therapist. She said the word afterlife with some satire in her voice.

"It looks like it could be Rex's sister. Right? If it's a fylgja, it's a girl, right? She kind of looks like Rex, and then again, I'm not sure." He gave a long, drawn out sigh. "Some days I'm not sure I remember what Rex looked like."

Liv turned the water down and as an afterthought shared, "The old people say when you see your fylgja, it's an omen of your impending death."

Joshua didn't answer. Part of him felt as if he had already survived death, but the fear that remained inside burned at him and nagged at his thoughts. He wondered how to bring it up to her. Did their almost kiss connect them enough for him to tell her his fears? Could he just say, "It's an omen of my death because I'm afraid every day that he's coming back?" It was nonsense, especially since Miralies was locked up in some federal facility several states away. Liv wasn't afraid, so why should he be? But he was, even with his gun and new window blinds.

Liv washed away the week's stack of dirty dishes. There were dinner plates, smaller plates, and a dozen glasses in Joshua's sink. The silverware drawer was empty of forks, and most of the food scraps had begun to smell. Liv set some plates to soak before being scrubbed. The phone rang and Joshua picked it up and talked with a student about the assignment due the following week, walking him through the steps for the work. As they ended the call, Joshua walked back into the kitchen. She was finished, and draped the dishrag over the faucet. Joshua thought that, too, must be a Swedish thing.

"So I'm racking my brain, trying not to be rude, but I have a confession, I have no idea what you said to me at the Christmas Gala. You made me a promise and all I got was 'seldom falling?' Please, what did you say and what does it mean?"

She smiled with an amused grin that made him think she was enjoying having the upper hand.

"No, not seldom falling. Semla for fettisdag. What I said was a promise. 'I will bring you semla for fettisdag.' Semla is a pastry and fettisdag is Shrove Tuesday. Fat Tuesday you call it. I want to make those for you, it's a tradition. We will take *fika* and *semla*."

The two of them stood across the room from each other, smiling. She was the professional listener and he was the professional lecturer, but there were no words between them. After a few moments, she walked with him back to the front room. Their hands touched and neither let go.

"The blinds are new? Is this a new look?" she asked.

"You know whose idea this was? David Adams said I should get some; I think he's right. I'm gone so often and all day, and without Rex, there's no one here to protect the house. What do you think, do you like them?"

Liv didn't like them at all, but nodded politely. "You are lucky to have a fylgja, she is your make believe protector to keep you safe from make believe villains."

He thought silently, "my villain is not make believe."

She looked around the room before picking a chair and sitting down. He wanted to time his question to the right moment. The two of them looked at each other.

"What?"

"What what?"

"Oh, this is so silly," Liv exclaimed. "So tell me about your family?"

"What?" Joshua said back, rolling his head upward and grinning.

"Your family, I know nothing about them, are you an only child? Are your parents alive? Did you run away from home as a child? Do you have an ex-wife?" Her questions and her accent gave the mood a bit of humor.

"Let's see, yes, no, yes, and no."

There was silence as she waited for him to continue. When he didn't, she smiled and playfully tossed her hands in the air.

"Oh, now I know you so much better."

She looked around the room again. The most personal display was the stack of Christmas cards, still in piles on the floor and near the plastic box of ornaments. There were no other family pictures in sight. She remembered he had a bedroom converted to an office.

Liv looked back, "What is it? You are looking at me funny."

Joshua shifted in the sofa and then asked what he needed from her.

"Tell me about him?"

Liv nodded, "You sound like a jealous lover in a bad French movie." She half smiled, trying to be funny. She thought it was a line that he would say. His look was insistent.

"Joshua, you know I can't say anything."

"But you did. You told me his name. You told me this affected three of us. Let me know the third person. If he saw what happened, Liv, I have to talk with him."

"Joshua, no. I wish there was a way," she tried to deflect him, "maybe in a few more sessions, I can ask him if he would be willing to meet with you."

She startled as Joshua shouted, "I can't wait a few more sessions!"

Liv let the anger linger in the air before speaking again.

"Sounds like you had a rough night. I am worried, are you sleeping okay?" She crossed her legs and folded her hands across her knees.

"Sure, I'm getting a few hours every night. Some nights I just wake up, so I read."

She explored more, ""I just did your dishes. So are you eating enough?"

Joshua stood up. "Yes, but look," he pulled the waistband of his trousers and revealed a 3-inch space of excess material. "I had to tighten up my belt two full notches."

Liv began to shift her focus. Joshua was a friend. A colleague. But she was beginning to appreciate he needed more. Her professional instincts began to override her personal interest.

"Oh, I meant to tell you, I stopped over and talked with David and Tom the other day. They said you must really be working hard on your book, how is it going?"

Joshua remembered he last worked on the book in October, it was sitting since then, untouched.

"I'm hoping to start again soon, why? Are they talking about it, talking about me?"

"No, not talking about you," She tried to tell the truth without revealing their concern, "I think they just said they hadn't seen you at the F Club? And you are never in your office... I had to come find you here. We all thought you were writing away."

Again she half smiled.

Joshua snapped back, "What, so you're spying on me too? Liv just what is your problem?"

"Joshua, I'm sorry, I don't have a problem. I was just saying that we — "

"We? Who's we? Who? Or is it just you? You want to know what my problem is? My problem is you not letting me talk with Underwood, or whatever his name is."

"Joshua — ."

"Just tell me, let me talk to Underwood," he pounded his fist on the sofa cushion.

"Joshua, stop it, you are frightening me."

"Frightened? You are frightened? How the hell do you think I feel?" He looked to his left and to his right to find the words to help her understand.

"Every day, every hour, he is out there trying to get me again and Underwood is the only one who can help and you won't even give me the decency of letting me talk with him. Do you want me killed?" You said three of us were wrapped up in this. You'll help Underwood but you won't help me?"

They were stinging words. Her face betrayed her years of training as a psychologist. Her eyes grew big, her cheeks withdrew slightly, she cowered and shifted slightly.

"No, Joshua, no."

"Oh, the hell with you," and he threw the glass he was holding against the far wall and it broke into dozens of shards that scattered across the floor.

Liv screamed. It reminded her of her childhood fears. As a teenager, she had gone to Gröna Lund to ride the Jetline roller coaster. The ride scared her so much, that she screamed as it reached top speed and didn't stop until the ride was over. Her lungs ached for the rest of the afternoon once the ride stopped. She felt the same urge to keep screaming seeing the rage in his eyes.

"Liv wait," Joshua jerked out and grabbed her by the wrist. He felt her try and pull away. His hold was much stronger and more aggressive than he intended, she pulled her hand back a second time, this time able to break free of his grasp, and retreated towards the front door.

"Get help. Joshua, get some help. You need help!"

She left the front door open as she hurried down the drive and across the sidewalk. She was rubbing her wrist where he had gripped her.

Joshua ran to the door yelling loudly, "Why won't you help me? You help him if he needs help, why won't you do this" he yelled and pounded his fist hard into the solid core door. The pain shot through his hand and up his arm. "There's three of us. Why won't you help me? I should be the first one you help, not the last."

He stood at the door for several minutes before realizing Mrs. Jenkins had been watching the end of his shouting tirade.

"What are you staring at?" he said to her and slammed the door, sitting down in the living room. He sat there most of the afternoon, replaying the conversation and trying to imagine a different outcome.

That hadn't gone well at all, he told himself.

The sun was low in the sky and it was dark in the house, so he got up and moved to his office. He stared at the wall, and then at a blank pad in front of him. He picked up a pencil and looked back at the wall, and then began writing a set of instructions. When he finished, he walked over to get his pistol. He opened the safe and removed the firearm. He racked the slide. The pistol was empty. He then opened the drawer where he kept the supplies and ammunition he purchased at Johnson's. He grabbed a magazine and then carried the note and the pistol with him as he crossed the house to the side door and walked out into the night air. He looked over at the garage exterior. There was enough light to still see, so he walked all the way around the outside of the garage, and then, entered through the side door and closed it behind him. He flipped on the light and a bare bulb lit up the floor and walls. He looked at the note and carefully read the instructions he had written one more time and then placed the sheet in the lighted part of the garage, so it could be easily seen.

He drew a deep breath, and then blew it out. He faced the far wall and began to focus on his breathing. After three breaths, he said, "I'm ready," and raised the pistol. His finger was along the frame, just as he had been taught, and he moved it to the trigger. He took in one more breath and let it out slowly and pressed the trigger.

Click.

The striker of the pistol hit the plastic dummy ammunition Stan Johnson sold him to use for practice.

"Dry fire drills are the best way to reinforce skills," Johnson told him. He looked over at his instructions.

20 times, raise pistol and fire one time
20 times, draw pistol and fire one time
20 times, draw pistol and fire two times
20 times, draw pistol, switch hands, fire one time

It had become his meditation. He had done this daily now since he purchased the handgun. Every day he carried. Every night he drilled. And in between, he cultivated the complex relationships displayed on his office wall.

THE NEXT DAY, LIV LOOKED up, surprised to see the man visiting her, wearing a sheepish and apologetic expression.

He walked in and stood near a chair.

"I almost didn't come."

Liv noted his demeanor and lack of eye contact.

"I'm glad you did. I'd like us to talk."

Derek sat down in the chair, and nodded, "I'd like to talk, too."

Liv noticed he was cleaner than the first visit and looked like he had slept. His general appearance was healthier.

"How are things going, how are classes, are you getting along okay?"

Derek shifted in his chair and looked down in his lap. He was fidgeting with the fingernails on his left hand.

"I need to know if I did something bad if it would get me in trouble."

Liv set down her pen and looked at him.

"Like what, Derek?"

"What if what I told you wasn't the truth?"

"You can tell me the truth now." Her voice expressed no judgment. Derek took that as a sign of approval.

"I'm not, really." He paused before he began again, "I'm not a student, yet."

"What do you mean?"

"I'm applying. I mean, I should hear next week, right? I hope to start classes this fall."

The story began to fill in the blanks for Liv, and his evasiveness was more understandable. After his first visit, when she returned from Christmas break, she searched the computer and, like Joshua, found no record for "Derek Underwood" in the Grant's Hill student database. Because of that, she was limited in her counseling options. As a student, there were many things she could do on his behalf, but as an unknown, until today, she didn't know if he was real or just some kind of attention seeker.

"I applied twice before, and they turned me down, but now, now that I helped rescue that professor, that ought to work in my favor, right, I mean, I saved his life, right?"

"What you did was a very good thing. Did you tell them that in your admission interview?"

"No, I didn't bring it up, I didn't go to the interview, but they have all my papers and forms. That should get me in, won't it?"

Liv made a few notes, "Derek, I am sure you have wonderful gifts and would do well at anything you try."

She was being encouraging. He took her comment to mean he was assured a place in the freshman class.

"So what about your family, do they know where you are? Where are you living?"

Underwood looked up at her.

"I have a new place. It is a little further out, but it's nice."

Something was not quite right. He wasn't telling her enough to know if he was depressed, or just lonely, or confused.

She asked some questions, which he didn't answer consistently enough for her to settle on a diagnosis. She made a note that if he was admitted, he would be an at-risk student and that she would plan on working with him during his first year on campus. Dorm life would stabilize his living situation and maybe help him face whatever his true problems were. She made a note to contact the admissions office to get their take on him. She wanted him to take an assessment, so she asked him if he had some time.

"Now? Sure, yeah, I guess. How long will it take?"

Liv looked at her watch, "Maybe a little bit, just a couple of hours, there are no right or wrong answers, and I will be right here when you are finished."

Derek agreed and she stood up to go to another room to get the papers. She was looking over the forms and talking as she came back into her office.

"The test is called the MMPI" she began. She looked over the top of the pages and saw an empty chair where he had been sitting. She looked out in the hallway and saw no sign of him. She waited a few minutes to see if he had left for the bathroom, but he did not return.

Liv made a few more notes in his file and returned it to her cabinet. She did a quick search online to see if he had a phone listing or address in Grant's Hill and found nothing. Liv shook her head and mused that between the three of them, Miralies, speaking only Spanish, would tell her more she would understand than the other two. Stone and Underwood were telling her nothing. It was a long road to recovery for them all.

PART EIGHT

PILOT'S DAY

THE WEEK BEFORE SPRING BREAK, President Rose circulated a memo to all the faculty, staff and students. Pilot's Day would be Friday, making spring break officially one day longer. The music started blasting from the dormitory windows Thursday evening, and Murphy Z's delivery cars were supplying a continuous flow of pizza to the dorms. Joshua planned to spend the day on campus enjoying Pilot's Day and also scouting to find Derek Underwood. The tall student would be easy to spot. He wasn't sure what he would say when he met him, but Joshua knew they could help each other, that Underwood held the key, even if Underwood himself didn't understand what it was.

In the morning, before riding his bicycle to campus, Joshua turned towards town to stop at Royal's grocery and pick up some food. The Royal's parking lot was filled with cars and students were making a long line in and out the doors buying snacks, drinks, and bags of ice. Joshua looked at each student's hands as they came out the door, watching what they were carrying and what direction they were walking. The tallest men received his closest attention, looking at each one to see if he recognized them or if they could be Underwood. After watching for nearly an hour, he decided to buy the week's groceries. As he crossed the parking lot, someone to his left slammed the lid of the trunk deck of their car as they struggled to get their keys from their pocket. The sound was very familiar to Joshua, but he didn't make the conscious connection to his assault and his own head being pounded. He reacted by spinning and dropping to the ground, protecting his head.

"Dr. Stone, are you okay?" came the voice of Emily Owen, his student from first semester.

Joshua looked around and then rose to his feet, wiping the dirt from his hands.

"Yes, I slipped. Looked pretty goofy I bet, must have twisted my foot or something."

Emily looked at him, a bit unsure of what to say.

"Thank you, enjoy Pilot's Day," Joshua said and continued across the parking lot.

Joshua cautiously walked up and down each aisle. Once his list was complete, he checked out at Tina's register and struck up a conversation.

"Do you ever get tired of all this?" he inquired.

"They're just kids having fun," she shrugged, "kind of makes me feel young again."

Stone looked at Tina's nametag, it read TINA and underneath 21 YEARS. He guessed that she started working there when she was his current age. It suited Joshua to imagine working 21 more years at Grant's Hill.

Joshua finished putting the groceries in his carry bags, said thanks to Tina, and walked out to the front of the store. When he got to his bike, a pickup truck rolled up and Sergeant Addison rolled down her window.

"Dr. Stone, hello."

Joshua had seen the truck coming and as it approached, turned slightly to have his body bladed with his right hip behind him with the bicycle between his body and the approaching truck.

"Sergeant Addison, are you going to campus to join in the festivities?"

"Not this year," she said and pointed at Larry in the driver's seat, "we're going south to look at a new tractor."

Joshua nodded and looked out at the parking lot.

"You're starting to act the part. Your situational awareness is good. You must have learned something from Peers," the Sheriff's Sergeant said, and then lowered her voice, "hey Doc, gear check?"

Joshua looked at her puzzled, and then understood her question. He brushed his jacket and stopped just above his holster.

"Good man. I like that you are serious about this."

"Everyday."

"Really, everyday? Good for you, Doc," Addison looked at the professor and then decided to ask her next question.

"Hey Doc, you're on break next week at the college, aren't you?"

Joshua nodded, "Yes, until the 17th."

"I need a favor, but I will make it worth your while. The department has a big tactical training exercise next week, it lasts three days. The third day is a scenario drill, and we need vict-" she stopped herself from saying victims, "we need actors for a bunch of role playing. It's totally safe."

Joshua looked at her in the passenger seat.

"So here's what I can do, if you can be an actor for a day, the next two days, this training group is doing a defensive pistol class. I think you would like it. So we can swap, a day of acting for the class fee."

Joshua shrugged, "How hard can it be? Where is it?"

Larry Addison piped up, "This is why you never marry a cop — it's at our place. They're taking over my old barn for the week."

Jessica slugged her husband with a playful grin.

Joshua smiled. "Sure, I guess I can. So what day? Wednesday?"

Addison handed him a flyer with a picture of a group of overweight guys in tactical garb and a hideous logo with a handgun.

"Okay, here's the details. Don't judge a book by its cover, this guy is one of the best. You won't regret a minute of it."

Joshua waved as they drove off and read the brochure. The thing about logos, he said to himself, is no matter how hideous, some spouse lay in bed and told the artist, "It's really good, I'm proud of you honey."

Professor Stone suppressed the urge to rewrite and edit the language in the brochure but the course looked interesting. He folded the flyer in half and stuck it in his rear pocket. He mounted the bicycle and headed to his house to drop off the groceries.

Once there, Joshua opened the side door, set the cold groceries inside the refrigerator and left the rest on the kitchen counter to be put away later. Joshua got back on his bicycle and headed north out of his driveway to campus and the Pilot's Day activities. The white dog caught up to him at the end of the driveway and ran along side on the sidewalk. Joshua looked over and the dog looked back at the house for a moment, and then continued the rest of the way to campus. As they approached the Quad, the dog darted in and out of the parked cars and when Joshua looked back, she was gone. He scanned the parking lot again, but she was nowhere to be seen.

JOSHUA SPENT THE EARLY PART of the morning sitting at his office window, looking at the people crossing the Quad and their comings and goings. He realized that even if he saw Underwood, it would take too long to get down the steps and cross the courtyard, so he got up to move to the outside. As he left, he grabbed his black and white, Grant's Hill varsity jacket from the coat hook on the back of his office door.

The jacket was a classic and fit loosely on his body, allowing him to conceal his handgun. Its black wool body was adorned with contrasting white leather sleeves that had the patina of both Stone's wear and care. He received it as a gift from the Grant's Hill men's basketball team the year their assistant coach was sidelined with a heart attack. It was Joshua's second year on campus and the only season he worked with the team. The head coach had asked for some help during drills practice. Joshua worked out with them a couple nights a week and traveled with the team through the second half of the season.

The scanning began again once he was in the courtyard. It was becoming habitual. He evaluated every person: first their hands and then their faces. His eyes tracked their movement for any hint of gun, or a knife or a package that looked out of place. A sophomore girl screamed from the far side of the fountain and three large sophomore men picked her up. Joshua turned, beginning to move his hand to his belt line to sweep his varsity jacket back. The girl continued to scream and they dangled her above the water, just touching her long hair in the spraying jet and then lifted her back and put her feet on the ground. She wrapped her arms around one of the men and planted a kiss on his lips. In the far corner, one of the college rock bands was beginning to play and the crowd shifted closer to listen.

The only tall men Dr. Stone saw were the ones he played against in 3-on-3 last year and a few incoming freshmen. But he knew them all and none of them had names even close to Derek Underwood.

His attention shifted when a familiar woman's voice spoke his name, "Joshua Stone, what have you done to your hair?"

Joshua was sitting on the North side of the fountain in the middle of the Quad when he heard the long absent voice of Annette Demming taunting him.

Annette. The sound of her voice was enough to recognize her, even though she had been off campus since her retirement last year. He turned, putting the plastic spoon in the small cup of chocolate ice cream and shielded his eyes from the mid day sun.

"Annette? Is it you? Annette, how are you?" The two embraced and held each other close. Neither was in a hurry to let go, but Annette let go first and Joshua lingered for a moment longer. "Oh, I've missed you."

Annette ran her hand over Joshua's short hair, "Does it still hurt?"

"Hurt? No, I have a few headaches now and then. Why are you here? You retired, I moved into your office. The End. Shouldn't you be with your grandchildren or in the south of France or anywhere? Somewhere?"

"I am somewhere, I'm here. It's Pilot's Day. Where else on Earth should I be?"

The two former colleagues turned towards the F Club as they spoke.

Joshua began telling her about his American Story class, "It's a great group, above average, even in a Grant's Hill kind of way. We've worked quickly through archetypes and I'm starting to see some good stuff, one or two potential writers in the group."

He held the door to the F Club open as Annette walked inside. The rooms were brimming with groups of faculty talking and laughing. "Maybe we should get coffee for outside?"

Joshua approached the coffee bar, making sure to keep his eyes on Annette and the rest of the room. He pressed his back against a portion of wall. Annette was surrounded by well wishing faculty with shrieks of recognition and congratulations. By the time Annette had worked the room, Joshua had the coffees in hand and was waiting for her outside.

"First time," Joshua began.

"My first time? It was 1969! In the back seat," Annette said in a voice that was half whisper and half boast.

"No, not *that* first time," Joshua said, shaking his head. "First time for me, being back in the F Club since..." His voice trailed off and the two of them sat at an outdoor table set up for the day.

"Joshua," Annette began, "tell me about it. What happened?"

"I got the living crap knocked out of me. I was blindsided. I don't know. I was teaching Freshman Comp — the late afternoon section, we had a great class. Rex came to campus with me, he almost never comes on Friday's but he insisted..." Joshua looked over the top of his coffee cup and away into the bushes behind them both. He scanned around the area and then continued.

"Rex was just not himself that day, maybe he was feeling ill, but he wandered off at the end of class. I went upstairs to my office —

well your office. By the way, do you need your copy of Dostoyevsky? I found it when I moved in."

Annette smiled, "No, you keep it. So tell me, what happened?"

Joshua took a sip and looked down at the table, then back to her eyes. "Annette, he wasn't in the building, he was just...gone. So I went outside, looking for him and I called him and I called him and I called him... And then." Joshua stopped and looked at her.

"Well don't leave me hanging in suspense, and then?"

"That's just it. I have no idea. I remember hitting my head — or more likely, Miralies — that's the name of the guy they think did this — hit me and I was out cold. I came to once in the ER with a tube in my throat. Then again a second time a few days later. I had a very small head bleed, about 6 mm, and normally they treat those with a burr hole. Like I really need a hole in the head."

Annette furrowed her brow, she noticed the lack of the typical lilt in Joshua's voice when he said his punch line, "Go on."

Joshua took another sip. "So I woke up 73 hours later. A lady sheriff's deputy interviewed me. That day, they arrested this guy Miralies, while he was using my credit card in town at Royal's. He's in federal prison waiting to be deported. I came back to work this term. All through December, they had me on very low activity and some follow up head scans. And I got a new smile." He opened his mouth to show off the dental reconstruction.

Annette breathed in a deep breath. "Joshua, I wanted to come, right when I heard. But I couldn't stand the thought of knowing you were hurt here. It broke my heart. I should have been here to protect you."

Joshua looked at her robust, retired body and shook his head.

"I appreciate the thought, but this was a very tough animal. It would have taken three or four of you...and me."

Annette took his hand. "I need to tell you a story. Something you probably don't know about me. I deplore violence. It has no place on a college campus. This is our sanctuary. I saw violence one time...one time...and I vowed to never let it ever happen on my campus again. And I fear I let you down." She drew a deep breath and continued.

"Do you know when I started teaching here?"

Joshua thought, "Yes, 1971, the year I turned one."

"You were only one? Oh, you are just a baby. Yes, and do you know why?"

"Well, I imagine you were like me: new grad, new horizons, Grant's Hill was looking."

Annette drew another breath and began again, her voice grew softer.

"I had a tenure track position at another school. In Ohio. My first year teaching was 1970. It was a very different time in our country and campuses were quite unsettled. There were protests, sit-ins, everything was about — " she sat straighter and jostled her shoulders like a soldier, "challenging authority!"

She fiddled with her coffee cup, moving it from hand to hand.

"In May of '71, the protests grew and colleges were confused and clueless. They didn't know how to handle the unrest.

"So when the students started fires and throwing rocks, they told the students they could not protest. And then the local police and the college called in the National Guard."

Joshua interrupted, "Oh my God, you're talking about Kent State? You were there?"

"I said 'never again' Joshua." He had never seen Annette cry, but now saw a small tear glisten in each eye.

"I was just walking. I was just walking. I heard the chanting and the yelling and I saw the soldiers. There were some near me and some a long way off..."

251

She drew in a breath and looked down in her coffee and then back at him.

"Joshua they were so far away...why did they shoot so far? I was walking by Prentice Hall when I heard thunder. It sounded like thunder and I saw Allison just fall to the ground. I thought it was thunder but it was shooting." Annette stopped talking. Her lip quivered and she and Joshua stared at each other.

"67 bullets in 13 seconds, Joshua," Annette stopped again. The silence hung in the air between them.

"Now, after 42 years... now... This old professor can look back and see that *everyone* was wrong that day. The students lit fires, and threw rocks, the administration over reacted, the police... the National Guard... everyone did wrong. But Joshua, four dead students, nine others wounded, and all of us. All of us, scarred for life. On a college campus sanctuary!"

She drew one more breath and ended with, "And I vowed never again." Annette stared down on the ground, as if she was seeing Allison Krause's lifeless body before her.

"When I came here, students had been on strike in the spring, and in the fall, I was asked to join a committee to make recommendations to the Board of Trustees. We made sure that there would never be any uniformed guards on campus, never any guns, never any displays of military, no ROTC, no soldiers, ever. No one would ever die here.

"When I heard what happened to you, I felt guilty. I felt that if I had been here, like I have for the last 42 years, that I could have protected you. I could have spared Rex's life."

The wind caught the corner of Joshua's jacket and he crossed his arm across himself so his holster would remain concealed. Joshua considered telling her about his gun, reassuring her that he could now protect himself. Instead he shared his fears.

"The world has changed. Or at least, our view of the world needs to change. We can't just ignore the threats. It's not just Miralies. There is someone else. This is not a safe place," He told her.

"Of course it is safe. The police arrested the man who did this to you and he's on his way out of the country."

"But what if?" Joshua began timidly, "what if he wasn't alone? What if there is someone else, waiting to kill again...maybe this time kill a student like Allison and the others?"

"Joshua you're talking nonsense. I wish I could have stopped it. I felt guilty for so so long. But I know now that it was one in a million. It can't happen twice. Didn't you say the police caught this man with your wallet? Was there a witness?"

"There was a witness, a student. He talked to Liv about it, but of course, she can't tell me what he said. But what if he saw something that proves the other guy is still out there?"

"Joshua, use that head of yours. They caught the man who did this to you and Rex. I came here to see you and to have some closure on my own silly fears and rationalizations. Now it's your turn. Find some closure. It won't help you heal by dwelling on what never happened. For years I wondered what might have happened if I had been friends with Allison Krause, if I had talked to her, if I could have changed history so that she and I would have been walking somewhere else. But I can't change what happened. She was in a parking lot at the wrong time...and so were you and Rex."

Joshua knew this wasn't the time to talk about his gun. Or the wall in his home office that diagrammed his story about the attack. She wanted to heal him, and they did not share the same view of the danger at Grant's Hill. So he changed the subject.

"So you really don't like my new hair cut?"

She smiled, "I miss those beautiful black locks... Promise me you will grow it out, promise me?"

Joshua promised and they both stood to hug and say their goodbyes. Joshua held her and feared this was the last time he would see her.

JOSHUA WAS DREAMING. IT WASN'T pleasant. Joshua was being punished and beaten and as only happens in dreams, he was both in and out of his body in the same moment. He could see himself being kicked and slugged, and he could feel each blow. This time, he wasn't unconscious and it hurt.

His attacker was dressed as an Ohio National Guardsman in military gear. While he was beating Joshua, the guardsman brought a long gun to his shoulder. When the guardsman pulled the trigger, a canister of tear gas exploded. The gas and smoke filled the air making it hard for Joshua to breathe and see. The soldier slung the long gun behind his back and began shooting a group of dogs with a pistol. Dog after dog died. The dogs turned into students screaming, some being pulled away by other soldiers, dragged by their hair, by their arms.

In the dream, Joshua was struggling to draw his pistol and couldn't get it out of the holster. He pulled and pulled and nothing moved. The smoke and the dying dogs were all moving in slow motion. Joshua struggled to do something, to intervene, to stop the killing, but his arms and legs would not move at all.

Joshua woke up with a flinch. As he became aware, he felt his right arm pinned under his body. Still fighting the battle in his dream, he struggled to pull his arm free when he flipped to his back. Short of breath and panting, he lay on the damp sheets, catching his breath and rubbing the paresthesia from his tingling arm.

PART NINE

SPRING BREAK IN

CHAPTER 40

OFFICER DOWN

AS JOSHUA ROLLED HIS BICYCLE up the lane at the
Addison farm, he passed fields of grazing cows, a hen house and
stopped in a farmyard that was filled with close to a dozen police
cars and a handful of dark vans. Wandering around the yard and
mingling among the cars were several groups of men and women,
partially dressed like soldiers and SWAT teams with body armor,
helmets, some face masks and lots of rifles and shotguns.

Joshua leaned the Skeppshult against a post and was greeted
by Larry Addison. Larry was the most civilian looking person
there, sporting a Carhartt jacket and overalls, a Grant's Hill High
stocking cap and holding a coffee cup that read:

THE ORIGINAL BIO-FUEL.

"I think it would be a good day to rob a bank, every cop in the
county is here," Larry said.

"I wish I had the donut concession." Joshua replied back.

Just then, two cops in reflective sunglasses with thick,
muscular bodies strolled past, each with a donut in their gloved
hands and a carbine in the other.

Larry and Joshua nodded, sharing the inside joke about the
donuts.

Jessica Addison approached with a man at her side.

"Doc, welcome. This is Dwight Evans. Dwight is the lead trainer. Dwight, this is Dr. Joshua Stone. He's a professor at our local college and one of the best handgun shooters I've ever trained as a first-time shooter."

Joshua was surprised that Addison gave the compliment so openly.

"Dr. Stone, the pleasure is all mine; and, I look forward to having you in our course tomorrow, too. I'm hoping you'll feel free to give me a critique. I'm sort of self-taught when it comes to teaching. Today, you'll be with me."

With that, the two men walked over to the old barn and Evans walked Joshua into a small corner of the barn loft. It was barricaded with OSB particle board on two sides and was bare inside the 'room.'

"Dr. Stone," Evans began and Joshua interrupted.

"Josh is fine."

"Okay Josh, this will be the most boring day of your life, but you are teaching these officers some incredible skills. And you'll do that," he paused, "by doing nothing." Evans walked to the center of the room.

"Have you ever had any tactical training?"

Stone shook his head.

"Okay, well, you know what an entry team is, right?"

"The guys who kick in the doors on the SWAT teams?"

"Well, yes, we call them response units, but yes. Here's the deal. Our scenario is called 'Officer Down.' You are going to lay on the floor right about here." Evans produced a bright flashlight out of a hidden pocket and lighted a space on the deck of the loft.

"I want you to lay on your hands and face toward this corner — so the entry team can't see your hands or your face." He moved the light to the entry and then back to the corner of the room. "Here's the thing, no matter what they say or do, don't react. Pretend you are unconscious. We're telling them you are a law enforcement officer who has come to serve an arrest warrant and all they know is you are down and the shooter is still somewhere up here."

Joshua nodded.

"Okay, are you armed?"

Stone's memory flashed to his concealed weapon class and remembered how to approach the situation when an officer asked about his firearm.

"I have a legal permit to carry a concealed firearm," he said slowly and calmly.

Evans interrupted, "I know that, are you armed now?" Joshua wondered what it was with all the gear checks and figured it to be a cop thing.

"Yes."

Evans picked up his walkie-talkie and keyed the button, "Command to Safety, I need one checked in the loft."

"Roger that," answered the radio.

"Josh, one of my guys will be by in a minute and he'll safety check your firearm and then we'll wrap the barrel and the grip with orange safety tape. Just a precaution. There are no live rounds in this exercise and we need to be sure that everything happens as planned."

In a moment, a large officer entered the room and asked for Joshua's firearm. He unholstered and the officer asked him his name.

"Stone, S T O N E."

The officer wrote on white masking tape and then asked Joshua to unload the pistol. Joshua dropped the magazine and handed it to the safety officer who wrapped it with the masking tape with his name on it and then placed the magazine in a carry bag with a dozen others. Joshua racked the slide, ejected a round and the safety officer took that as well.

The safety officer asked Joshua to show the pistol was clear and unloaded, and then took it from him. Joshua looked on as the officer wrapped orange tape around the muzzle and then a second wrap around the grip. The officer handed the pistol back to Joshua.

Evans picked up the conversation with more instructions. "Every firearm you see should have orange tape on it. At any time, if you see a firearm without it, yell — "

Joshua interrupted "Gun!"

"Jesus, no. Don't yell 'gun,' yell 'safety!'. We don't yell 'gun' unless it is a threat. Yell 'safety' and the exercise will stop immediately."

Joshua holstered his safety-checked weapon and Evans came back into the corner. "Okay, any questions?"

Joshua shook his head.

Evans looked at his watch. "We'll start in about three minutes, so go ahead and lie down."

Joshua got first to his knees, then faced the wall and rolled down to the ground. The floor was cold even through his Grant's Hill varsity jacket and he tucked his hands under his torso.

"Nice, that's great." Evans complimented, "Now, here's what's going to happen: these guys work in a four man team. They will evaluate the room, make a decision about what to do about you, and then act on their decision. They will yell and give you lots of orders. Just lay there. You are unconscious; don't move, don't help them move you, go limp and stay limp. Got it?"

Joshua said yes, and then turned his face to the wall.

He wondered about the rest of the day. It seemed to be an easy task to just lie there for the next several hours. He heard some bustling a few yards away from him and some whispering.

"Show me your hands!" came the order in a deep husky voice. Joshua flinched and almost thrust his hands to his side, but did nothing.

"Sheriff's department! Show me your hands now!"

Again, Joshua remained motionless.

In softer voices, a second and third voice chimed in "I don't see movement."

"I can't see his hands."

There was silence and the shuffling of feet near him.

As if in a surround sound movie, three different voices echoed around his body.

"Clear!"

"Clear!"

"Clear!"

And then he felt the weight of a knee between his shoulder blades and felt a leather-gloved hand cross his face. The leather smelled like aftershave, gun oil and sweat. He felt his hands being thrust behind his back. The cold steel of handcuffs wrapped around his wrists with a distinctive ratchet sound.

"Ready to move!"

"Withdraw!"

In a sweeping thrust, he was being dragged by the legs across the loft floor and through the particleboard opening that simulated a doorway.

Once they had dragged Joshua's limp body clear of the door, Evan's voice shouted, "Stop! Stand by."

There was a pause as Evans made some notes and looked at his chronograph on his wrist.

"2:15. Nice work."

A face leaned down and through the facemask and goggles, made eye contact with Joshua.

"You okay?" At the same time, Joshua could feel the handcuffs being loosened and his hands being released. As he rolled over, all the tactical teammates were taking down their goggles and facemasks and turning towards Evans.

"Okay, what was your concern with this situation?"

The officer with the husky voice began his debrief.

"We knew we had a hot zone, and at least one shooter, and one officer down." He paused. As he did, Joshua realized he was breathing as fast as when he climbed Grant's Hill in too high of a gear. His heart was pounding. He looked at the response team and they were not breathing hard at all.

Officer Husky Voice continued, "From the door, we couldn't make out who this individual was. He failed to respond to our commands, so we secured the room, secured him, and upon identifying him as an officer, we withdrew him to the hallway and then we would take him down to a yellow zone."

"Okay, nice work, what went wrong?"

The officer who had been on Joshua's left spoke first, "I crossed John's line of fire when we first came in."

"How do you solve that?" Evans asked.

"I need to be responsible for my sector and ignore the rest of the room"

"Exactly. Team work, trust your team. Your life depends on your ability to trust your team. Okay, on to your next scenario and let the next team know we are ready."

Joshua got up, brushed the dirt off his front and returned to the place he began, lying down, and facing the back wall.

"Welcome to police work, Josh."

Each team performed the same steps. Joshua got to the point were he could visualize their moves as they worked in and out of the room with him lying on the floor, refusing to comply with their orders.

He wondered why Addison was part of this training. After being jostled and drug around by several teams, he realized he was quickly assuming a sexist opinion. This was serious physical work and probably no place for a woman. Addison seemed tough enough to be a cop, Joshua thought, but these guys play at a much higher level.

Joshua's thoughts were interrupted by the most aggressive command of the day.

"Show me your hands! Do it now!" Joshua's heart pounded and he felt his throat tighten in reaction. The voice had a wrath, a teacher voice overdosed on steroids. For the first time, he was intimidated.

"Do as I tell you! Show me your hands, do it now."

The mood in the room was tense, and the movement of this team was precise. Joshua remembered watching a drill team at the college performing with flags and rifles. Each movement, each hand slap done in a perfect cadence. This entry team moved as one, synchronized machine.

Snap, swish, swish.

"Clear!"

"Clear!"

"Clear!"

He felt the weight of the officer on top of him, with a knee in his shoulders. The now familiar smell of leather, gun oil, was mixed this time with a hint of something fresh. She was much more forceful, much more sure of her moves than the previous teams. Joshua felt that at any moment, she could make any part of his body hurt, just by applying more force. Two officers swooped his arms out to his side and then with the same fluidity of motion, they took control of his body. As if they had levitated him, they picked him up and he was glided into the open space outside the room.

"Stop! Stand by... 92 seconds."

The team high-fived each other.

"Sista cop owns the house," came a muffled shout from behind a facemask.

Joshua had the bottomless stomach feeling in the same way the first drop of a roller coaster is terrifying. His mind reasoned with his body, assuring him he was safe, but his body was in free fall panic. He struggled to catch his breath, and the color drained from his face. Evans walked over.

"You okay? Need a break?"

Joshua was trying to hide his shivering. Some from fear, some from lying on the cold floor.

"Yeah, I'm fine. What a ride." He shouted to make the others think he was having fun. Addison flipped down her goggles and looked at Joshua. Then past him, "Simmons, nice entry, smoothest one yet."

Evans commented on the aggressive Sergeant's forcefulness, "Where does that come from?"

She smiled, "You don't help your husband push cows into a stock trailer in a thunderstorm by being dainty. If you want girly-girl, you better knock down some other door."

Joshua made a mental note of her line for his novel. It was the kind of line that might have a place in a fight.

Just before lunch, a team assembled for the simulation room and instead of making entry, they began a whispered argument outside the opening.

"It's a trap, don't make entry."

"It's not a trap, lets go."

He heard them shuffling into the room and yet, they made no verbal commands to him.

He felt the weight on his back and someone reaching for his arm.

"What are you doing?"

"I'm handcuffing him"

"Why? He's an officer. He's one of the good guys. Let's get him out of here."

"No, he's in a hot zone, everyone in a hot zone is a threat."

"He's a downed cop. Let's scoot and move!"

The officer working the handcuffs did a quick pat down and felt Joshua's pistol and holster, he lifted the varsity jacket and saw the orange safety tape.

"Gun!"

Now, the entire team was in a dog pile on top of Joshua.

An officer fumbled to get Joshua's pistol and then stuck it in his tactical vest; the other officers released their hold as they realized Joshua was still motionless on the ground. Each one grabbed an extremity and picked Joshua up, slinging him across their shoulders and working toward the opening. They struggled, as it was not wide enough for them all to get through. They lay Joshua back down, rolled him to his side and slid his body out the door.

Evans was shaking his head. "Stop. Stand by."

The tension and frustration in the team was palpable. One of the team jerked off their goggles and tossed them to the floor. Joshua rolled and sat up.

"Okay, what happened?" Evans asked.

The team leader began. "We made entry without a plan. We couldn't decide if he was hostile or friendly. We didn't execute the move and we were on scene too long."

"4:15," Evans said as he looked at his chronograph.

Groans from the team.

Evans knelt down and faced the team leader in a private conversation. "If you want to lead, you have to lead. These guys will follow you, not the other way around."

"Yeah, but what about the handcuffs, did we need to handcuff him?"

Evans looked him in the eyes. Joshua admired the patience in his critique of the team. "Handcuff him, don't handcuff him, it doesn't matter. Make a plan and run it. What did you know?"

"He was non-responsive in a hot zone"

"Exactly. Get in, secure him, and get him out. Arrest or assess, doesn't matter. Get in and get off scene. Just have a plan."

The officer who confiscated Joshua's pistol handed it back to him. "Nice piece, what department are you with?"

Joshua smiled, "The English Department."

Evans rolled his eyes with a smirk.

"Joshua, we're actually through with the drills here so if you want to leave, you are free to go. Tomorrow we start at 8:30 and we'll run until about 6:00. That way we can do a little bit of night shooting and flashlight work."

Joshua walked down the ladder of the barn and crossed the farmyard to a group of officers standing outside and found the safety officer who taped his pistol talking with Addison.

"Hi, I'm Joshua Stone, I'm heading out. I was the actor up in the barn?" The safety officer reached into his bag, sorted through the pistol magazines and found the one with white masking tape and S T O N E on it. He handed it to Joshua.

Joshua turned to Addison.

She was holding a cup of coffee and looking around the pasture just over his left side, "What did you think, Doc?"

Joshua smiled. "Kind of fun, like playing cops and robbers as a kid. I don't mind telling you, you scared the shit out of me when you started yelling."

She laughed, "Now you know how the cows feel."

Joshua decided to ask the question he had been wondering as he lay on the floor all morning.

"So why do you do all this?"

"No, not the, 'what's a pretty girl like you doing in a place like this?' question. Remember Doc, you can't spell sheriff without she."

Joshua looked back into her sunglass covered eyes, "Well, that's a good question, too, but what I mean is, why does Grant's Hill need to know all this tactical stuff? When will you ever use it? Why is this necessary?"

Addison looked at him, "Doc, last year, our multi-county task force did 17 armed entries on drug dealers and labs. On every one of those we found weapons and usually, we found bad guys ready to use them. Every entry.

"Let's take you for instance. We won. We got Miralies and he's gone and off the street. But for every Miralies who attacked you, there are 5 more lying in the bushes.

"Someone in my department has a subject with a knife or a gun at least once every month.

"I was on campus, I heard your President Rose brag about the statistics, but you live in this town. You need to know what the real world is like. And we're mild compared to Chicago, or Louisville, or Little Rock. Every single person in your concealed carry class has a good reason to carry a gun. Everyday. So you do your part and I do mine by getting this training." She began to turn away and then turned back to face him.

"Here's what's scary to me," she told him as she lifted her sunglasses and stared into his doubting eyes. "Every single badass who threatens me as a deputy got their practice by threatening people like you.

"By the time they face off with me, it ain't their first rodeo. They've practiced against you and now they are not fooling around."

Joshua felt like a cow being corralled and brought back in line with the herd. But instead of feeling put down, it felt more like being included. He felt he had a place in this herd. That carrying for his own protection was important. She was counting on him to keep doing it. With magazine in one hand, and pistol still in the other, he brought the two together, seated the magazine, racked the slide, pushing a live round into the chamber.

"Way to go Doc, way to stay off that slide." She told him, and then turned to walk towards the barn and the other officers.

CHAPTER 41

THE SECOND DREAM

JOSHUA WAS DREAMING. HE WAS in what they called the stack, a line of officers in a tight tactical formation used to make entry into a room. He was the last person in the stack, moving towards Officer Down. At first, they were in Larry Addison's barn, but then, in that odd, time-space shift of dreams, the stack was at Grant's Hill, in the parking lot.

He knew Officer Down was dying.

He tried to get the stack to speed up. But the team moved slowly, shuffling their feet and whispering something he couldn't understand. With him in the stack were Sergeant Addison and Sergeant Wiggans and Dwight Evans. Joshua called out a command and Addison moved to cover the left side of their field of fire. Wiggans moved past Officer Down and covered center, Dwight Evans moved to the right field of fire. Each of them told Joshua, "Clear" and Joshua moved in to help Officer Down.

As he rolled over the motionless body he looked and saw himself. He was Officer Down. He didn't know what to do, he panicked.

Officer Down was dying.

So he called to Evans.

Evans turned and took off his face shield. When his face was no longer hidden, Joshua saw that Evans was now David Adams.

Wiggans turned and under his face shield was Thomas Moore, and Addison turned around and was Annette Demming.

In the dream, Joshua was now laying on the ground, looking up at the forth officer in the stack. Joshua watched as this fourth officer took off his mask and revealed he was Miralies and now Joshua was going to die. Adams and Moore and Demming stood there as Miralies kicked Joshua over and over again. Miralies splashed gasoline all over his body and around him and then flames jumped to life, dancing on his skin.

CHAPTER 42

NOT DEAD YET

THE SCENE AT THE ADDISON farm Thursday was different from the collection of police cars on Wednesday. There were only seven cars in the farmyard when Joshua rolled up and leaned the Skeppshult against the flagpole.

He walked inside the barn and saw a dozen people in the room besides Evans. Most of the students were holding foam coffee cups and there was a box of donuts from Royal's on the front table. Evans nodded at Joshua and then clapped his hands to grab the room's attention.

"If you don't mind, let's all get a seat and we'll get started. If you haven't done so already, please sign in on the clipboard that's going around the room and verify for me your concealed permit number. If you do not have a professional or civilian concealed permit, please let me know now."

Everyone looked around at the other, Joshua felt old as he calculated the average age in the room was in the early 20s. Several of the men wore some form of tactical clothing mixed with work jackets or farm clothes. There were two women, both with military style haircuts and khaki tactical pants.

"Let's start off with introductions and a little bit of why you are here. How about you?" suggested Evans.

He pointed at one of the women and she spoke in a crisp, assertive voice. "I'm Officer Laura Hampton. I work in the state Office of Drug Enforcement."

"My name is Tina Rogers. I'm Laura's roommate and I just left the Navy and am looking to get into law enforcement."

"I'm Mike Moon. I own the Pale Blue Moon tavern and I want to know how to better use a pistol. I keep a shotgun behind the bar, but I can't take a shotgun with me to make the bank deposit."

A man with a chiseled face made the next self-introduction, "I'm Dennis Holden. I work for the weather service so I have to carry a gun." The people in the room snickered.

"Okay, technically I work for NOAA and the Fisheries Office of Law Enforcement, but we're also in the same department as the National Weather Service. I'm a training officer and I'm here to learn some things to take back to my guys."

As each told their story, Joshua wondered what he would say. When his turn came, he spoke up.

"Hi, I'm Joshua Stone. I live in town and just started concealed carry. I shot some guns when I was a kid, but as you can probably see, that was a long time ago."

"Welcome back, Doc!"

"Okay, what 'bout me? I'm Dwight Evans. I'm a firearms trainer and I work about 75 percent of the time with law enforcement agencies and the rest of the time with private citizens. I prefer private citizens because," he pointed out the donut box, "usually you leave the sprinkle kind for me."

Everyone laughed.

"I got my start working for a very large government agency that most of you *have* heard of but don't know what we really do."

Holden chimed in, "I know that feeling."

"After 20 years in that three letter agency, I joined another large company you probably have *never* heard of. We provide personal protection services to some of the most at risk individuals in the world. You might say we run the top ten list that no celebrity ever wants to be on. I'm based out of Nashville and I work on our special events details when I'm not teaching classes.

"What makes me different as a teacher is that we will not be in this classroom very long or very often. In fact, when I talk, I set a timer for 15 minutes, and if it goes off, I shut up. I'm here to work with you on pistol manipulation. Skills. But I want to be very clear about something. What I teach you will not save your life."

The students in the room looked at each other.

"There is only one thing that will save your life."

Evans scanned the room with what Joshua would come to recognize as his trademark pause and assess. Evans used the same look when he stopped shooting and before he holstered his firearm.

"You. Your mind, your commitment, your decision to survive. I can outfit you with all the best guns and training in the world, and if you won't practice, if you won't decide and commit to your personal survival, it's all for nothing. I can open the door, but you have to decide to walk through and practice the skills I share with you.

"We don't teach tactics here. I can't teach you what will save your life at 3 a.m. in..." He looked at the side of the grocery store donut box to read the name of the store, "I can't teach you what will save your life at 3 a.m. in Royal's grocery...When some badass with a shotgun walks down the aisle. I can't say, move here, do this twice, and then bang bang, problem solved.

"What I can do is give you some skills. And if you commit to practicing them, if you focus your mind, you can win."

His self-set timer began beeping in his shirt pocket

"Remember this key, you are the weapon. Your gun is just a tool."

For two days, Joshua and the others started from the basics and moved through more challenging manipulations. Evans' approach to the pistol seemed more like yoga or dance. His focus and coaching was on smooth fluid motion, and surprisingly to Joshua, never speed. But it made sense to him. The quarter trick was never about speed, it was about consistency: performing the toss and then smoothly catching each coin. To his English students, he seemed to move like a samurai, swiping the quarters from the air. In reality, he moved his catching hand ever so slightly, and let each coin fall into his grasp.

As they finished working in the twilight, Dwight asked a question. "Joshua, what is it you do for work again? You teach, right?"

Joshua nodded.

"Let's talk about the worst possible situation. You are in your parking lot and you hear a woman scream, you look up and a row of cars away, you see a man with a gun with one of your students with a stranglehold around her throat and pulling her toward a van with open back doors."

Laura Hampton and Mike from the Pale Blue Moon both nodded. Joshua pictured the situation and ran his tongue over his replacement teeth, remembering his recovery time from his attack. He pictured the scene from his dream when the students were being dragged by their hair.

"I can't tell you what to do. And I can't predict what you will choose to do," Evans looked at all of them. "What I can do is give you a skill, based on my years of experience, and if you practice this skill, you, and only you, can decide if that is the time to use it. I for one could never retreat in that situation, but I would never hold you, as a civilian, accountable if you did retreat. Self-preservation is critical. There is no easy answer and anyone who tells you there is, is stupid — or lying — or both."

They ended the first night there and Evans gave them a handout. It was single spaced, both sides of the paper, and had a list of drills, broken down into weekly installments. It outlined twelve weeks.

"This is a set of dry fire drills, you do this at home, with an unloaded gun you have checked, and rechecked and checked again. Do this in a room with no live ammunition," Evans instructed. The group nodded.

"Think of this as your homework. Do these drills for twelve weeks, then just like it says on the shampoo bottle: lather, rinse, repeat. Go through these 4 times a year in addition to your live fire practice."

Joshua looked at the list; he was ready to add to his daily drilling with some new practice. He felt like his dry fire work in the garage had reached a plateau.

The second day, Friday, was spent reviewing the prior day and some final instructions before beginning the live, force-on-force training. Live fire, force on force training sounded intimidating to Joshua. In place of traditional ammunition, the guns were swapped and loaded with a special simulated bullet that was more like a paintball. It marked where the round struck and when it hit, according to Evans, "You will feel it." He called it penalty pain. At the distances they would be firing, there was minimal risk, but everyone participating or observing wore a helmet and full protective face shield.

The scenario was straightforward. The participants had to move down a simulated hallway to a pair of fake rooms and if they identified a threat, they were to shoot two times, assess their situation and shoot again if necessary. The challenge: unlike the paper targets from yesterday, this time the threats would be shooting back.

Mike from the Pale Blue Moon had gone before Joshua and was just walking back, winded and howling. "Ohhh man, you will not believe it! Whoooo!" He was smiling, with large eyes and sweat covered his forehead and face. He had two colored splotches of paint on his jacket.

"That is a rush. That is nothing like anything we've done. Whoooo!"

Joshua was both intimidated and eager to give this a go. He was the final student and walked over to the area set up by Evans. Evans gave him simple instructions.

"Josh, there are two threats in the house. Here's what I want you to do: you walk through the space, holding your pistol at a high ready position. Watch your doorways, watch your muzzle. Don't sweep your muzzle across your body or any of the observers and work your way through the rooms like we practiced. Keep your finger off that trigger until you are ready to shoot with your firearm sights on the threat. If you identify a threat, shoot. And don't you get shot."

Joshua thought back to the drawings Evans had shared and the un-armed practice moves through the simulated rooms yesterday. He had shown them how to move and look carefully, visually dividing the room before entering and exposing themselves to a threat.

Joshua nodded from inside the protective helmet. He was beginning to sweat under his varsity jacket and began working through the first room, when he exposed himself in the doorway, he heard two shots and felt the sting of two impacts on his right chest. He stopped, grinning sheepishly, acknowledging he had been beaten and turned to surrender to Evans who was behind him, as he shrugged his shoulders.

"What are you doing?" Evans was upset with the situation.

Joshua replied through the face shield, "He shot me, I'm dead."

"You're what?" Evan was agitated. "You're what? You are not dead, do you hear me? You are not dead yet."

The other students turned as they heard Evans yelling.

"You are not dead until I say you are dead, do you understand me? Do you hear me? You stay in the fight until you are dead and you are not dead until I say you are dead."

Joshua stepped back.

"Set it up again!"

From behind Evans, the rest of the class looked down and away, relieved they weren't the ones being yelled at.

Joshua began again, this time, going slower as he moved through the door, and again, the threat shooter identified him first and fired two rounds, both striking Joshua in the pelvis. The idea of penalty pain was much more real than imaginary. The paint ball rounds hurt and Joshua ignored the shots, extended the pistol and pressed the trigger. He stopped after he had fired 7 times, each one landing in the center of the threat.

Evans pointed at the threat and said, "You." He paused with a smirk. "You...are dead." Joshua continued through the house, this time engaging the next threat with three rounds before the threat fired a first shot.

"That's it, that's how you shoot. Way to stay in the fight."

Joshua took off his helmet and the others all stood around. Evans made a full circle as he spoke.

"This is just a beginning — and for you civilians, I hope you are never in this situation, but if you are, I hope you continue to practice and prepare. Carry every day. Train, every day or at least every week. Find my courses or other courses and go at least once a year. Do that, and you'll be way ahead of everyone else and in reality, you will be way ahead of most police officers."

The group stood around talking a few minutes before each walked off to begin their trips home.

Jessica and Larry Addison were standing near the gate as Joshua was pushing the Skeppshult out the driveway.

"What did you think?"

"Wow, so much to take in. I think I held my own, thanks for inviting me, I learned a lot."

"You need to watch out for Simmons, did you see his chest?"

Joshua was unsure what she meant.

"Simmons and I were your threats. You nailed me three times, but Simmons took all seven rounds. His chest is beet red."

Joshua smirked, "I didn't have any idea. I wondered where you went." She smiled, "Part of the job, hopefully you learned something useful and thank you for lying on the floor Wednesday and letting us drag you around."

Joshua looked at Addison. "Which reminds me, now I need a favor." He paused and then slung his leg over the bicycle seat.

"I'm writing again, which is good news. Actually, I'm working through a new angle on a novel," Joshua looked away and down at the handlebars of the bike. As a fiction writer, he was used to making things up, but telling a sheriff's deputy about a novel that didn't exist seemed more like lying than fiction.

"I have this scene that involves the police. My two main characters are in a nasty divorce case and there is some deception about assets and property. There is a police report that the insurance company is trying to get a copy of. So to be able to write about it, I'd like to look at a real police file."

Addison smiled with a flattered look. "Doc, gee I'd love to help, but all our files are confidential."

"Well...yes, I know that. But one file isn't confidential — at least, the victim won't mind. My file. Sergeant, I want to read my case file."

Addison mentally flipped through the file. There were certain photos she didn't want anyone to see, especially Stone: the dog's carcass and the burned out remains. She mentally went through the rest of the file contents and figured she could sanitize it enough to share with him. She assessed his recovery. He seemed a little shaken and unsure of himself, but she didn't see anything that concerned her.

"Sure Doc, but no red pencils. I can't have you correcting my work, you'll give me a complex."

"Great. Well, can I come by tomorrow? Do you work Saturdays?"

"Sure Doc, come on by. You can't take it with you but I'd be glad to let you look it over. It's a closed case, not a problem."

"Great, and Sergeant, thanks."

"Sure, Doc." She smiled at Larry and then turned back to watch him ride the bicycle down the lane and out to the highway back to Grant's Hill.

Larry Addison turned to his wife. "He's not too bad for a college boy."

She smiled, and reached her arm around her husband and slid her hand into his back jeans pocket. "But what does he actually...do? I mean, you and I have jobs and we work. What can they possibly do all day?"

ON HIS WAY UP THE sidewalk of the Grant's Hill Sheriff's Department, a uniformed deputy was walking in the main door and turned and gave a look of recognition to Joshua.

"Hey, you're Officer Down."

Joshua thought he was mistaken and began to say his name, "No I'm Dr. — oh yes, from the tactical class, yes. I'm Dr. Joshua Stone."

"Hey, Doc, I'm Steven Shroder. I'm on the response team here at Grant's Hill. I work with Addison and Wiggans and those guys. You here on business?"

Joshua looked inside at the metal detector and remembered he was carrying his pistol and hesitated.

"Yes, I'm here to see Sergeant Addison."

They entered the building and Shroder waived off the guard manning the metal detector, "Step here, Doc," and Shroder reached behind the partition and pulled out a red ID badge. It read VISITOR just like the badge he was given before, but reversed out of a red stripe at the top of the badge were the words VISITING AGENCY.

"I'll walk you down there. I need to drop off some payroll paperwork over there."

Addison was on the phone as Joshua and Shroder walked into the squad room. The room was pretty much as Joshua remembered. It was crowded. It was hot. It smelled like Chinese food and pizza. He waited a few moments to approach Addison. As he did he noticed her hand on a stack of photographs next to a file folder. She looked over and caught his eye, then looked down at the stack of photos, pick them up and turn them face down. She raised her hand and motioned for him to come over and pointed at the metal chair adjacent to her desk. He sat down and waited for her to finish her call. Once again his eyes shifted to her belt line. She was wearing a bulky sweater that hung over her belt and again he was unable to see the shape or outline of her service pistol stuck inside her jeans. She finished her call, pushed the stack of photographs to the opposite side of the desk and sat down in her chair.

She looked at his visitor badge and smiled, "I see you've been deputized." Joshua looked back puzzled and uncertain.

"Your visitor badge. You got a red one. That tells us you are armed. One of the good guys."

Joshua remembered his own uncertainty over the 'good' and 'evil' Post-it notes when he first made his wall diagram. Joshua smiled and then nodded in the direction of a stack of file folders. "Is one of those mine?"

Addison let out a big sigh, "Yes, and a dozen others that I need to work on this afternoon. But you have to promise me something?"

Joshua prepared himself for the worst and asked, "And that is?"

"Promise me you don't have a red pen and I'm not going to get this back filled with grammatical corrections and edits," she said to him almost in a pleading voice.

"What do you take me for, a book editor?" Joshua asked.

"No, I have no idea about book editors because I've never had one. You are a teacher and I've had plenty of those... so no red ink."

Joshua nodded in agreement.

"Doc, here's the deal. Some of the crime scene photos I can't let you see. I can't and wouldn't let anyone see these who didn't have to," she paused for a second, looking him straight in the eye, "and you don't have to."

Joshua nodded, taking in the seriousness of her voice.

"This file," she handed him a file folder with codes, numbers and imprints from a rubber stamp or two on the face, "this is your case file. You can sit at Wiggans' desk and read it. You can't take it with you but I won't stop you if you want to take a few pictures or notes. I think you're okay with this. I'm not a shrink and I don't know where your head is at. But if you think you're up to this, I trust you."

Joshua gave a slight bow with his head and said, "thank you." He stood up, walked to the desk opposite her and sat down. He looked at the closed file folder. None of the markings made sense. He pretended to have an interest in the markings, making some notes as if his make-believe book was a police procedural. He didn't really care, he wasn't interested in police procedure or the process of archiving a police record. He opened the file folder and reviewed its contents. The first report was from Deputy Bill Simmons who had responded with the ambulance to the automated emergency call. The second report was from Addison and had an addendum describing his interview in the hospital and a notation about Simmons' call from Royal's grocery. Another document was several pages long and appeared to be a transcription of an interview with Miralies. At the back were half a dozen photographs that included the back of the car where he had been hit repeatedly, a wide view of the car and crime scene tape and the college parking lot. The photo was a view from the car towards the emergency beacon on campus and a very wide shot that showed the spatial relationship between the car and the area where Rex was burned.

Joshua spent two hours with the folder. He read, reread and read again the words written by Simmons and Addison describing the crime scene. Their writing lacked emotion. It gave him facts but told him nothing. He tried to keep his professor head out of reading, but he kept coming back to reading it for a grade. The report gave him no feeling for either the author or the victim. It made him wonder why he thought it might.

He took out his cell phone and took pictures of the diagram drawn by Simmons the night of the attack. He took pictures of the photographs at the back of the file. He looked at the transcript as he snapped photos with his phone. It read a little bit like interrogations he'd seen in movies. It told him nothing about Miralies. The notes indicated that he only said phrases in Spanish that translated approximately into "I have to save the dog" and "I have to feed the dog." The only other understandable portion of the interview was Miralies' insistence that he found the wallet. Every time Addison or Wiggans asked or accused him of taking the wallet he remained consistent and said he "found it." As Joshua finished with the file folder he looked up to see Addison crossing the squad room. As she was pulling on a windbreaker she stopped midway in the room and looked at him.

"Are you still here? Tell me you are not still reading my report," she looked at him.

He stood up, "I was just finishing, Sergeant." And he started walking with her. When they got to the metal detector, he took off his visitor badge and handed it to the polyester coated guard who was doing a crossword puzzle.

"So why did Miralies say he found my wallet?"

Addison looked at him and shook her head with a sly smile. "Of course he *found* your wallet. They all *find* the wallet. He *found* it in your coat pocket after he beat your head into the trunk of a car and left you to die."

She looked around the lobby and back into his face. "Don't go all soft on me. He's not worth your sympathy. The sonovabitch wanted to light you on fire, too. Real criminals are nothing like what you see on TV, or what you write in your books. No offense, Doc, but have you ever read a book that accurately describes what you felt in the hospital when you and I talked? Have you ever read anything that comes close to what it felt like to learn about what he did to your dog?"

She angled her head, searching for a look of agreement in his face. "Just don't feel sorry for the guy who did this to you."

Addison turned and continued walking across the lobby, swiped her ID card to open a locked door and Joshua walked down the steps got on his bicycle and rode home.

When he arrived at his house, he opened the side door and stepped over the three plastic bags filled with trash that he'd taken out of the wastebasket, but had not carried outside to the trashcan. As he closed the door, it caught on one of the plastic bags in the pile. It ripped open and spilled used coffee grounds on the kitchen floor. He brushed the coffee grounds away with his shoe and shut the door. He walked into the office and connected his cell phone to his computer, and as the images of the police file downloaded, he opened the screen and selected three or four of the phone images and printed them on the printer.

Joshua stood up and walked around the house. With all the blinds drawn, he turned on a few lights. The front room had several new piles of mail to be sorted along with the others that had been there since the first of the year. The red and green

Christmas decoration box was pushed in a corner. Piled on it were the ornaments and cards from the holiday.

When he went to the kitchen, he grinned, thinking of Liv and her *ungkarl kok* statement. The trashcan was overflowing, so he pulled out the liner bag and gave it a twist, setting it in the pile next to the other three. He shoved a new plastic bag in the can and then saw the calendar on the wall near the refrigerator. It was still turned to February, so he lifted the page and looked at Spring Break week. He touched his index finger on the coming Monday and resolved to find Liv at the end of break and apologize to her.

Joshua opened the refrigerator door. Earlier in the week, he had a pizza delivered from Murphy Z's and he moved the last two remaining pieces, dried out from the cold air, to a paper plate and poured a glass of water. He took a few bites, on and off, through the rest of the evening and he re-read the stack of articles, looking for new sections to highlight and pin to the wall.

SUNDAY MORNING, JOSHUA WOKE UP in his home office chair, thinking about Bob Thornton, the maintenance foreman at Grant's Hill. Thornton may have been the college troubleshooter and Mr. Fix-it, but Joshua didn't think he could do much to fix up his current problem. Joshua woke up hot, and dialed down the thermostat and that made him think of their first meeting. The heat in Joshua's campus office had soared to 86 degrees. Thornton showed up with a small set of tools and as he worked, Joshua noticed the tiny patch that resembled a military service ribbon on the tool bag. It had a field of tan with red, white, blue, green and black vertical stripes. Joshua opened the conversation, "Desert Storm?" and gestured to the ribbon.

Thornton nodded.

"Thanks for your service. I don't see many military insignia around here."

"Can't wear 'em, it's not part of the college image," Thornton spoke in a mocking voice, "There shall be no display of insignia of war."

At the time, Joshua knew nothing about Annette coming to Grant's Hill from Kent State, or her committee work when she first arrived that banned displays of military insignia.

Thornton had told Joshua his story when they first met.

Seventeen-year-old Thornton enlisted in the Army in the late 1980s during a time when few in civilian life gave the military a second thought. Thornton was hoping to get out of the Army in December of 1990 and celebrate his 21st birthday stateside. His plans were put on hold in August when Iraqi troops began to spill over the border into neighboring Kuwait; and by February, Thornton and half a million other US troops were on the ground and on cable news fighting a televised war for viewers around the world.

When it was over, Thornton came home and was greeted by a ride on a hay wagon, pulled behind a big red tractor in a small parade. Thornton told Joshua that the hand painted sign that read "Hero" still hangs in his garage. Thornton picked up odd jobs around town before signing on with the facilities crew at the college. He had worked there a handful of years when he became foreman and has held that job ever since.

Now, reflecting back on both the conversations with Annette and Thornton, Thornton's hiding of his military patch made more sense. In a way, Joshua now felt he and Thornton shared the same sort of secret. Thornton's military service and Joshua's concealed handgun. He wondered if Thornton carried a firearm. He wondered if Thornton knew Joshua was carrying. He suspected Thornton knew — that even post military, he still had a watchful eye and situational awareness. He thought again to that first long conversation.

"So were you Guard or active duty?"

"2nd Armored" Thornton mumbled.

"Hell on Wheels, interesting."

Thornton lay down his tools. "Dr. Stone, you know your Armored. Did you serve?"

"No, no I didn't. But my dad did. Shame they disbanded the unit." Joshua knew enough from his dad to know the unit had been reorganized.

Thornton looked at the professor with a new respect. "You're alright Doc."

Joshua smiled and then brought up the question that bugged him since he arrived on campus.

"So how do you keep this place up? I never see anyone doing anything." Joshua realized that came out entirely wrong. "I mean, obviously you do lots of things, but I never *see* any work being done — no heavy equipment, no loud tools, loose ladders, caution signs…but things get fixed?"

"The tunnels." Thornton replied

"Tunnels? What tunnels?"

With that, Thornton got a devilish look. "Do you really want to see?"

He looked up with the twinkle in his eye that Joshua always felt made him look like a department store Santa.

Joshua stood up, "We have *tunnels*? Sure, show me," and the two men walked down the hall to the far west stairwell and walked down to the first floor. Thornton extended a ring of keys from a retractable keeper on his belt. They jingled as he unlocked an access panel door marked MAINTENANCE. Behind the panel was a space that a led to a second stairwell down. As they turned, Joshua could see a large storeroom with high ceilings below the ground level. The two walked down and found an array of grounds keeping tools, small powered tools and workbenches. Thornton flicked on the lights and revealed a corridor tunnel that ran in two directions.

"If you go that way, you go under the Quad and it connects to Eastford Chapel. They built these during the Depression, between the two wars. Mostly as a bomb shelter. But it connects the buildings and contains the underground power and water supply lines and the main steam tubes that heat some of the buildings."

Joshua looked down the row of lights that were spaced out every 15 feet. He counted a dozen or more lights before he could not see any farther. The space was muggy and smelled a bit musty, but not offensive.

"And this way, takes us to the other shop."

"Where's that?"

"C'mon" and the two men walked west. They walked for a few hundred feet and came to another large room equal in size to the one under the Quad.

"And up here," he pointed to a ladder that led to a steel door in the ceiling. "Open that and you are at the northwest corner of campus, right near the parking lot next to the church."

Joshua repeated the phrase, "northwest corner of campus" aloud as he returned to the present. When his eyes reopened, he was staring at the ceiling of his home office; he now understood why he remembered Thornton.

The tunnels were his best way on and off campus without being seen. And if he could get on and off campus, he could get to Liv's office. And if he could get there, he could read Underwood's file. Liv could keep her client-counselor confidentiality and he would know what Underwood knows. Now, more than a dozen years later, Joshua wondered if he could find his way back in through the underground maze.

His preparations for the break in began by rummaging around the house, digging through the plastic storage tubs, looking for a dark colored rugby shirt. Both the rugby shirt and a navy blue pullover were in a plastic tub and Joshua yanked them from the tub.

He went to the kitchen and dug through the drawers, looking for the flashlights. There were two; neither was very bright. He unscrewed the end of one and dumped the batteries on the floor, and rummaged through the drawer for replacements. When he found them, he dropped them in and the light shined about twice as bright.

In the second bedroom closet, he found some blue jeans and pulled them from the hanger. He stripped down and then pulled the jeans on. They were as loose as his dress pants, so he fastened a belt and snugged it tight.

Joshua pulled shoes from the shoe racks, searching for the hiking boots he had worn in college. He stopped, trying to imagine why he had kept them all this time and never worn them. He pulled them on and they were stiff, but still fit. Lastly, he went to the front closet of the house and found a wool watch cap. With clothing for the night picked, he waited for the sun to go down.

When it did, Joshua unlocked the gun safe, retrieved the pistol and fastened the holster to his belt. He switched off the light in the bedroom, walked out to the garage and climbed on his bicycle. It would be easiest to just walk in the building, but he didn't want to be seen or risk being recorded on any of the campus security cameras. The only way to access the notes Liv kept on her meetings with Derek Underwood was to take them from her office. If he was wrong, he could simply leave them there and no one would be wiser. If he was right, he could gain her help and take them to Addison and Wiggans.

As he rode down the driveway, the white dog began barking. It barked and then chased after him and darted across the street between some cars. Joshua considered going back, but pushed on without her.

When he got to the parking lot, he rode in circles, looking for the metal access door. When he found it, he was more than 100 feet from where he remembered it being. He rested the bicycle against a tree and bent over the access door in the ground. There was no padlock on the latch, so he raised it up slowly. The metal hinge made a scream-like creak and the door slammed as it slipped from his hand and fell open. He looked around and waited, but no one heard the noise or was curious enough to come see, so he shined the flashlight into the hole and located the ladder rungs.

Once at the bottom, he moved the flashlight to look around the remote maintenance room that had been at the end of Bob Thornton's tour. Joshua expected change, it had been a dozen years since his visit, but nothing looked at all like he remembered. It was messy — there were empty food containers in a pile in one corner and what looked like a makeshift bed in another corner.

His light crept across each wall. Gone were the tools, shelves, and maintenance equipment he remembered. He shined the light on the next wall, first highlighting a photo calendar complete with a photo of Miss June 2003 who was eating an ice cream cone. The cone in the photo was dribbling white ice cream down her very tan skin. She was nude, prompting Joshua to say aloud, "At least it won't leave a stain." He laughed at himself. It was the first funny thing he had heard himself say in weeks. It was sophomoric, but he enjoyed it just the same.

The room smelled like sewer gas and death, and a little like stale urine. Joshua dismissed the odor as a decaying mouse.

His flashlight faded in a short distance along the lengthy corridor to the maintenance room under the Quad. The overhead lights that lit up the passage during his visit with Thornton were dark. Ten steps down the passage, the flashlight slipped from his hand, fell to the concrete floor, and blinked off. As it hit, Joshua heard several pieces spinning across the floor. The light had come apart on impact. He stopped, and stood still, waiting for his eyes to adjust to the total darkness, then he knelt down and began to feel along the cold concrete. It was hot inside his layers of clothing, and the wool cap made his head itch. The stench was strong. He was closer to whatever had died in the tunnel. There was no putting it out of his mind as he methodically moved his hand.

The first piece of the flashlight he found was the body, and he could tell from touch that the head and reflector were still attached. At the tail end, the end cap was missing, as were both batteries. Joshua began moving his fingers in sweeping S shapes, moving from side wall, across the floor, to opposite side wall. He found the tailpiece first, and near it, one battery.

He widened his search, moving first three, then five, then seven feet from where he stopped. Without the flashlight, Joshua could only make out some dim structure to the tunnel. There was no way to see well enough to walk and he didn't want to feel his way blindly along a wall. He was about to turn around and climb back to his bicycle when he took a final sweep down the edge of the wall on his left and found the second battery. He inserted both batteries into the light, secured the tailpiece, and the light turned on again.

Joshua pushed on, down the tunnel, until he came to a stud frame wall with a metal exterior door. He hadn't remembered this door. As he moved the light around its frame, he saw an exposed 2 x 4 stud wall with drywall sheets on the opposite sides of the studs. Some of the studs had dates from the lumber mill: August 2003. He looked at the tunnel surrounding the wall and door and shook his head. He had no tools to pry open the door or cut a hole in the drywall.

Once more, he considered giving up and turning back, then looked closer at the lock on the door. The knob on his side had a key lock, but as he shined his light around the doorframe, he realized the door trim was missing. He knelt down, bringing himself to knob level, and peered at the latch. Joshua could see the faceplate and the strike plate, with the latch pushed through both.

He searched around on the floor for a piece of wire or scrap metal, retracing his steps until he noticed a small 5-inch piece of wire about the diameter of a coat hanger.

He walked back, and shaped the wire into a crude J and then passing it through the gap in the door, managed to snag the latch. As he pulled forward, the latch moved free of the strike plate and the door opened.

He drew a big breath and blew it out again, and made his way through and continued to follow the tunnel wall until he came to the maintenance room under the Quad.

This room was more familiar. He saw the workbench and tools reminiscent of his first visit down the tunnels with Thornton. He found the stairway to the Maintenance hatch that led to the building stairs. He pressed hard against the hatch and it popped open.

He stopped and listened on the first floor. The only sound was his own breathing and his footsteps as he moved to the stairs and took each step, one at a time, to reach the second floor. He stopped again, listening. Hearing nothing, Joshua climbed the final flight.

Once on the third floor, he stopped to listen for any sounds of activity or late night workers. He didn't expect anyone in the building during spring break, but waited to be sure. His breathing was faster and, out of habit, Joshua felt to be sure his pistol was secure in his holster, and then walked down the hallway to Mrs. Thorn's desk, just outside his office.

Mrs. Thorn was also the back-up secretary to the some of the administrative offices, a role left over from her days as secretary to the president. Joshua was optimistic that her back-up role included Academic Counseling and was hoping she had an extra set of keys to Liv's office and files.

He walked to her desk and sat down in her chair. He opened the center drawer and found plenty of office supplies, but no keys.

He searched from drawer to drawer, stopping on the bottom drawer. He smelled the dog biscuits first, then lit up the inside of the drawer with his light. He hadn't smelled those biscuits since November, but he knew the smell instantly. He stopped and drew in a breath, wanting to savor the moment and remember Rex. She hadn't thrown them out, even after nearly six months. A tear filled his eye as he shined the light at the back of the drawer and found a divider with hooks and several sets of keys, all labeled neatly and professionally, as he would expect.

DR. OLSSON, 2nd FLOOR, OFFICE, read the tag.

Joshua reached in and removed the keys. He paused. Took one more breath, and closed the drawer. He then crossed the hall, reached the stairwell, and walked down one flight of stairs to the second floor and the Academic and Psychological Counseling Center. Liv's key opened the main door and her office door and the only other key fit the file cabinets. He took a step towards the file cabinets and then stopped, leaning against the wall.

"What am I doing here? I've lost it." Joshua slumped to the floor. Sweat soaked his cap. He took it off and moved it back and forth in a fanning motion, but it did little to take away the heat. He tried to imagine how he had come to this. He was prowling in her office at midnight, stealing from her work files.

Liv told him he needed help. Addison urged him to call the Rape Crisis Center. Now, he had been getting less than a few hours sleep each night and had resorted to breaking into her office to read what? The file of a mixed up kid who was as traumatized as he was. Joshua got up. He spoke, but he wasn't sure if he spoke aloud, "Just a quick skim of the file, if it all looks okay, then put it back and close the door. And get help."

Joshua unlocked the file cabinet and located current year files. Inside, there were three groups of folders, the third was identified by numbers, not names. There were 20 – 30 file folders, with six digit number labels. Joshua took them to be dates and started working through the drawer.

Joshua skimmed the first file 090911. Whoever the student was had severe test anxiety and recurrent fears of failing exams. There was nothing in the file to suggest this was Derek Underwood.

After skimming a few more files, Joshua figured out the numbering was the date of the student's first visit with Liv. That led him to filter most of the files to the few that began in November or December. He opened a file with an 11 and another with a 12 as the first two digits. It didn't fit. Some of the notes were from March. The next file began with a 15 and after that was 21.

"Liv, there aren't 21 months in a year," so Joshua looked again at the file patterns. He was confused. He rubbed his eyes and looked at all the files in the drawer en masse. Then, he returned his attention to the stack he was working with. It occurred to him that the numbers were dates. They were European dates, Liv's Swedish secret code. He returned to the files and looked at middle digits.

The next file caught his eye.

The client states he has difficulty sleeping and has not slept in 3 weeks due to recurring nightmares of being beaten up in parking lot. Patient self identifies as person who sounded emergency beacon after assault on Professor S.

"Yes, this is him."

Joshua's pulse raced and he felt tightness in his throat. Heat flushed across his face. He took the file and slammed the drawer shut, eager to get away from the office. He locked the doors behind himself and ran the length of the hallway to the building stairwell.

A phone rang and he froze in place. It rang a second time. His heart pounded. He waited three more rings before it fell silent. He stood there, counting silently to 60, a number he arbitrarily chose and then continued on down the stairs.

He pushed open the hatch that lead to Thornton's workshop, the tunnel, the newly constructed door, and the final workspace under the parking lot. He formed the mental checklist and map in his mind and then once through the hatch, he pulled it shut, and descended the final steps. He moved through the maintenance shop.

Check.

Then into the tunnel where he sprinted its length, his steps illuminated by the flashlight, to the newly constructed door.

Check.

He was panting now, exhilarated and anxious. It was the same feeling he had as a child, when his father would send him into the dark basement of their home to retrieve a tool or a jar of canned goods. Going down was always easy, but Joshua, fearing the unknown things that lurk in an 8-year-old's dark basement, ran as fast as he could up the stairs, and back to the safety of his father.

Reaching the newly constructed passage door was the half way point.

Check.

He pushed it open, turned, and latched it, returning it to its 2003 state. His flashlight bounced as it lit the way to the final room and the ladder that lead up to fresh air and his bicycle.

Check.

As he began to climb the ladder, something blue caught his attention. He stepped back down and walked over to the rubbish and picked up the item. The blue braided webbing ended in a black melted end. Black soot stains were smeared on both sides, and as he held it close to the flashlight, he made out what was left of a blue dog collar. At the burnt end, he could read "Rex." He was filled with rage and confusion.

He shined the light around the room once more. Thornton would never harm Rex and would never leave the shop like this. The doorframe lumber and the girlie calendar were nearly ten years old. He picked up one of the food wrappers and found a cash register receipt from October. Miralies must have hidden here. He looked around, it all fit. Miralies found this place and was hiding out, that's how he caught Rex and that's how he snuck up and hit him. Joshua was chilled and unconsciously drew his hands in close to his chest. He had to leave, now.

Check.

He climbed, got out, closed the steel plate hatch, pushed his bike with a running start and flung his leg over the saddle. He stood up out of the bike saddle, working the pedals as fast as he could. When he got back to his home, the white dog was sitting there, waiting for him. He rested the bike against the side door stairs and knelt down facing the white dog in the driveway.

"Do you talk, too? What do you know about this?" he held the charred blue collar for the white dog to see.

"You're my fylgja, tell me. Guide me, help me."

The dog looked down as if she had been scolded and turned and walked away.

Joshua sped up the steps, flung open the door and then locked it behind himself.

He took the pullover and tossed it across the arm of a chair. As he did, his wallet fell out of the center pocket and landed on the floor upside down, partially opened like a pup tent in a camping diorama. He looked around at the chaos that was once his organized home office. He looked at the office wall and the increasingly complex diagram. If this were a student's project he would tell them to stop, take out a clean page and start new. But he wasn't ready to let go.

Joshua opened the file from Liv's office and read the notes she made during her sessions with Underwood. He tried to learn his real name or student number, it made no sense to him that Underwood was not listed in the college database. He scoured the file to find his real name, certain he had misheard it when Liv revealed it at the Christmas Gala. He found some notes from their second meeting.

Client tells me he is applying for admission at Grant's Hill again this fall and that his previous two applications have been denied. While services are restricted to students only, will continue to see client as he works towards admission.

"Damn it. I knew something was wrong," Joshua said. He felt a bit surer of himself.

He picked up Rex's collar and held it, remembering the first time he placed a collar around the dog's neck. This wasn't that same first collar; Rex had worn out two others. In their time together, the dog always seemed more content with his collar on than off.

He walked to the wall and hung the collar buckle on the pushpin that held up the sheet of paper with Miralies' name. The collar's weight was too much and the collar, pin and name paper all fell to the floor. Joshua picked them up. He rested the collar on the pin that was holding Underwood's name as he used both hands to hold Miralies' name paper and he pressed the pushpin into the wall, making a new hole.

This was the new plot. Joshua picked up the PLOT card. Miralies was living in the old underground maintenance shop.

Miralies killed Rex, attacked him and then took his wallet.

"Yes!" Joshua looked over the wall. He hung the PLOT card on the wall and turned to walk to his chair and sat down.

He looked at the diagram and whispered the three names: Miralies, Underwood, Stone, and nodded off to sleep, sitting in the office chair.

He only dozed. When he woke again, he wiped his face and mouth, and licked his repaired smile.

Joshua studied the wall and then moved his eyes across the hardwood floor until they paused on his wallet. Six months ago he would've picked it up the moment it fell. He cocked his head and looked at the way it rested. Somehow it looked familiar to him, yet he didn't remember dropping it earlier today or any time this week.

He shifted his focus to the desk and the photographs taken by Simmons. His eyes came to rest on the wide-angle photo. It showed the scene from the back of the car toward the emergency beacon in the college parking lot. The parking lot was clean and empty. There was no trash, litter or debris. Bob Thornton's crew hard at work, even if invisible. Joshua stopped and looked at the picture closer. He couldn't tell if the small dark shape was a shadow so he picked up the paper and looked even closer. There was something at the base of the beacon. He turned to his computer and brought the image up larger until the item at the base filled the screen. He stood up and crossed the room and looked back at his desk and the monitor. And then to the floor. The thing at the base of the beacon had the same shape as his upside down wallet on the hardwood floor. He went back to the computer screen and looked again and could make out something blue. He looked at the charred collar hanging on the pushpin and back at the photo.

"Why did Miralies leave my wallet there? He stole it, why put it back down and why there? And why didn't Underwood pick it up when he activated the alarm?"

Why did he take Rex's collar and leave it there, too? He knew that two people could answer that question, Miralies and Underwood. Underwood told Liv he saw it all, and so Joshua had to find him soon. Underwood could explain the wallet. He sat down and dozed a second short nap.

CHAPTER 45

THE THIRD DREAM

JOSHUA WAS DREAMING. HIS PISTOL was extended out from his body and his sights were aligned on the first target in the line of paper targets. They were in a straight-line row, at the edge of an outdoor shooting range. The paper targets were poster-sized photos of pretend villains. But the photos in the dream were not villains, they were his students. All of them. They were in a line that stretched as far as Joshua could see, as if they were waiting their turn. Joshua was dressed as a soldier. Instead of shooting the paper targets from the tactical course, now he was shooting photographs of his students, they were frozen in time. As he shot each one, they became a live person and fell to the ground, screaming.

STARTLED AWAKE FROM THE DREAM, Joshua was unsure if it was day or night. The house was dark and the blinds closed. He looked at the clock, still blinking 7:19. As the fuzzy mind of sleep left and he became more alert, he realized Spring Break was over. It was Monday morning and he had classes later that day. His pistol was tucked into the holster between his body and his belt. His bed was still made, unused all break. He began to think about classes. He opened his calendar and looked at his schedule and saw Friday night blocked out with the department dinner at the F Club.

"Damn," he exclaimed, "the Joke!" He searched around in the piles on his desk and found the photo album with pictures from the years of faculty telling the Joke. He opened it and flipped to last year. Annette, as her final two parting shots did this: she passed the photo album to Joshua, meaning he had to do the follow-up and then, as only Annette could do, she told the Joke like it had never been told.

Last year, on the Friday following spring break, the group of them was assembled in the F Club, dining on some lamb chops and cous cous. And despite the fact that it's nearly a 100-year tradition, the thing Joshua noticed about the Joke was it can be told at any time during the evening, and while everyone knows it is coming, it always manages to take everyone in the department by surprise.

Joshua remembered Annette was sitting at the table. She was wearing a loose, navy blue blouse, but that was not uncommon. Annette was never flashy. She dressed conservatively, but men couldn't help but notice she had very large breasts. None of this would even be worth mentioning except that in the middle of the salad course, Annette suddenly stood up at the table and unbuttoned.

She stripped off her shirt and it fell to the floor, revealing some kind of leotard underneath. But on top of the leotard, was the largest brassiere anyone in the room had ever seen. Annette had taken pipe cleaners and doll clothes, and attached them to the cups of the bra, so that her breasts became bizarre, abstract puppets, one with a sombrero and googly eyes and the other with a handlebar mustache and a cowboy hat.

She clasped each breast, one in each hand, and that's when she started the Joke.

She told the story of a small county, deep in the Southwest, so far away from civilization, that the only people who knew it was there were the people who lived there. A hot, nameless desert.

"One day, the local rancher hears a donkey ride up from over the hill, and he spots a lone man, wearing a sombrero. The rancher paused, and the rider was stunned." She jiggled her breast and the googly eyes spun in opposite circles. Everyone began to laugh loudly. Adams laughed loudest above the rest of the crowd.

Joshua remembered Annette telling the joke. Her breast puppets acted out the scene: the visitor in the sombrero describing the card playing, singing, dancing, cussing, fighting, and sex. With each line of the joke, Annette became more animated, as did the googly eyes on the breast-puppet wearing the sombrero.

Annette built to the punch line by saying, "The rancher looked down at his boots" and when she did this, she bent over almost touching her breasts to the table…she waited there. The other faculty were howling in laughter, Thomas Moore's face was so red Joshua wondered if he had stopped breathing. Adams had knocked over a glass of water and the others in the room were hooting. Even the reserved spouses were beside themselves with laughter.

Annette stood up, holding the rancher breast-puppet in her hand, making it bob up and down with each word, and said, "It sounds like fun, what can I bring?"

The sombrero breast puppet jiggled, "You don't have to bring nothing, it's just gonna be the two of us!"

Joshua grinned as he looked at the photo of Annette in her body suit and brassiere-turned-puppets. He practiced his punch line, sounding like Eric Carnes in the mirror of the men's room his first day back. Instead of saying, "are you looking at me?" Joshua delivered the punch line of the Joke.

"It's just gonna be the two of us." Joshua stood taller and changed his emphasis of the line. He emphasized the second word.

"It's *just* gonna be the two of us." He shook his head.

"It's just gonna *be* the two of us." He didn't like the sound of that one either.

"It's just gonna be the two of *us*." No, that wasn't right; it had to be the "two." So he said it again.

"It's just gonna be the *two* of us."

It was now 6:30 a.m. He forced a chuckle and looked back at the mosaic filled wall. In the center was his initial idea.

The three name cards of Miralies, Stone and Underwood connected by yarn.

And the words THE THREE OF US.

He stood up and unfastened the string from Miralies in the middle.

He took his marker and drew through the word THREE on the wall and wrote TWO.

THE ~~THREE~~ TWO OF US

"What if there was just the two of us? What if Miralies wasn't there? Underwood saw it all because…he wasn't just a witness. Underwood witnessed what he did himself."

Joshua grabbed the police file photo of the emergency beacon and placed it on the wall. The wallet was there, on the ground, after the attack. If Miralies beat him and stole it, it wouldn't be in this photo.

Joshua found the transcription of the police interview with Miralies, took a highlighter and marked the phrases that said he found the wallet. Miralies said it 17 times in a 46 minute interview. The castle Miralies lived under was Grant's Hill, he lived in the tunnel. Underwood dropped the wallet when he hit the emergency beacon.

Underwood dropped the wallet because he found it in my jacket. He repeated what Addison told him, "They all *find* it."

Joshua read the notes from the day Underwood told Liv about the attack. He says he was standing near the emergency beacon and he saw Miralies standing on the leash. No way. Joshua had paced off the distances; it was too far to see that kind of detail.

Joshua had had similar rushes of clarity before, most often when he was at a standstill with a character or plot in his writing. But now, everything was clear to him.

Underwood killed Rex, then attacked me from behind. He stole my wallet. He freaked out when he saw my college ID because he feared it would hurt his chance at admission. Then, he panicked and hit the emergency beacon. Miralies must have come out and found my wallet after the officers had left the scene. He must have seen Rex's remains and taken his collar, and then decided he needed to *feed the dog*.

Joshua Stone began to put together his plan.

Liv. First, he had to go to Liv; to tell her the truth, about stealing her file. To help her see that with what she knew and what he knew, together, it was proof Underwood attacked him and killed Rex.

No. First, he had to apologize to Liv. To make this right with her; to tell her how sorry he was for everything he said and for hurting her, and then he could tell her the truth.

Next, Liv had to come with him to talk to Addison. He knew she would refuse, even as his friend she would never violate patient confidentiality. But he had to find a way. Addison had to find and arrest Underwood.

Joshua looked at his watch. It was 7:30. If he hurried, he could catch Liv before her 8:00 presentation. He counted on her being late after the long spring break.

PART TEN

DEAN'S LIST

CHAPTER 47

911

WHEN JOSHUA GOT TO CAMPUS, it was 7:50 and he climbed the stairs to Liv's second floor office, two at a time.

Mrs. Thorn was sitting at the reception desk for Academic Counseling. She ignored his unwashed hair and the wrinkled shirt. She didn't say anything about the bicycle chain grease on his pant leg.

"Dr. Stone, good morning sir. Did you have a pleasant spring break?" Then as an afterthought adding, "My niece is selling cookies again; would you like one?" as she pointed at a box on the corner of her desk.

"I had a nice break and thank you, Mrs. Thorn." He ignored the cookies and continued, "Is Dr. Olsson in yet today?"

"She was in at 7:30 and has her presentation in Eastford Chapel today from 8 until 9:15"

As Mrs. Thorn sorted through the stack of mail that had accumulated over the break period, Joshua paced back and forth, unsure what to do. He wanted to interrupt the presentation. He debated between waiting in his office and waiting here, in the reception, with Mrs. Thorn.

Mrs. Thorn took a very large manila envelope out of the pile. The backside was covered with hand drawn icons and in large red letters was scrawled CONFIDENTIAL. She made a face and set it to the side in Liv Olsson's in-basket.

"What's that?" Joshua asked.

Mrs. Thorn gestured with a finger in circles around her ear to suggest "he has a screw loose" and then said, "There is something not right about that young man."

Joshua looked at the return address: Derek Underwood. He picked up the envelope and tore it open. Mrs. Thorn objected loudly, "Dr. Stone! That is privileged and confidential information, you may not open that. Stop, stop it now."

Joshua nodded to reassure her, "Dr. Olsson and I have spoken about this student." It wasn't a lie, and it wasn't the truth. The professor tilted the envelope and poured the contents out onto the desktop. The first item was a red, spiral bound sketchbook with a linen cover and an embossed GH on the front. The pages were interspersed with some photographs and had a few sheets of loose paper tucked in between the bound pages. The other item was a note, written on college ruled paper, with a frayed edge from where it was ripped from a notebook. The note read, "Dr. Olsson, I like you, maybe this will help explain it all. Don't go anywhere today."

Joshua looked at the note and shook his head, then turned it around to show Mrs. Thorn. She leaned in and read the words and then read them again and shrugged. Joshua concluded it meant Underwood would stop by her office today.

Joshua thought about how to best apologize to Liv. If Underwood was coming to see her, Joshua had to persuade her to let the two men meet. Maybe they could sort this all out together, before going to Addison.

Joshua set the note to the side. He glanced up at the clock on the wall, 7:54. He looked into Liv's office and around the reception area and decided to begin looking through the notebook while standing next to Mrs. Thorn's desk.

The opening page had a sketch of a skyline. It was pretty good, with some reasonable detail and artistic expression. In the far edge was an arch, Joshua thought it looked like the city of St. Louis.

The next page was something entirely different. A photo of a small animal about the size of a chipmunk. In the picture, the chipmunk was mounted to a foam board like a science project. The animal was cut open, in a crude dissection, and on the opposite page, was a sketch of the photo. Joshua made a thoughtful "huh," he didn't understand Derek Underwood's art.

With each turn of the page, Joshua found similar sketches. A few of the animals were skinned, and there were photos of the carcass and photos of the removed fur.

Joshua shook his head and considered closing the book and leaving it for Liv to discuss with her client. He looked up at the clock, it was now 8:01, and he looked at Mrs. Thorn who had returned to sorting mail and reviewing her computer screen. Joshua sighed and turned another page of the sketchbook.

The next set of sketches was quite good. There was a postcard photo of Eastford Chapel and the accompanying sketches were rich with detail and precision, as if a different artist drew them. Joshua flipped back a page, the quality and the details were quite different, but the ink and the handwriting used for the dates written on the pages was the same.

He flipped another page and stopped. A chill swept over his body. He knew the place in the sketch; it looked like one of the evidence photos from his sheriff's department case file. It wasn't a copy, like the other sketches, but it was clearly the same place. He saw the car, the median, the emergency beacon. The detail on the car was precise, but around it were child-like flames and scribbles.

Joshua took a small step back. Mrs. Thorn looked up from her computer screen and Joshua turned the book at a slight angle to show her the image.

He turned the next page and revealed a sketch of the emergency beacon. The beacon was drawn with intricate detail, like the other inanimate objects in the book: the car, the chapel. But next to the beacon was a crudely drawn person, with oversize hands and feet, towering over the beacon. There were squiggles coming from the beacon, like a comic book, suggesting it had been activated. Mrs. Thorn looked up at Joshua and he looked back at her. Neither knew what to say.

Joshua looked again at Liv's office and then the clock: 8:06. The professor returned his attention to the book and leafed through the remaining pages. They were blank and near the final page, Joshua found three, tri-folded letters.

He unfolded the first letter. It was addressed to Derek Underwood at a Missouri address. It was a letter from the Grant's Hill admission office, dated two years ago, saying that Underwood would not be admitted to the next year's freshman class. Mrs. Thorn recognized the letter, she had typed similar letters hundreds of times back in the day before the campus adopted personal computers.

Joshua set the letter aside and unfolded the second letter. It was identical, except it was dated last year and was mailed to Underwood at a different address. Mrs. Thorn rolled her eyes and shrugged. Joshua unfolded the last of the three letters.

It was dated the day before spring break. Again, it was a letter saying Underwood would not be admitted to the next year's freshman class.

Joshua turned the letter over and found a sketch. It depicted the man with giant hands and oversized feet. In this sketch, he was holding a gun. He was shooting a crowd of people who were on fire. It looked like something drawn by a child. The shooter was twice the size of the people in the crowd. Both hands in the sketch were clenched. One, wrapped around the gun. The other formed in a fist, ready to punch. The eyes were red and the shooter was frowning with exaggerated lips out of proportion to the face.

He showed it to Mrs. Thorn who first looked at it oddly, and then gasped as she understood its meaning. "Is this make-believe?" she asked aloud. Joshua looked at the sketch.

"I need to tell Liv. I need to warn her that he is dangerous."

With his cell phone in his left hand, Joshua rushed the length of the hallway of the second floor towards the stairway closest to the Quad courtyard. He would need to cross the courtyard, pass the building on the opposite side and sprint to make it to Eastford Chapel. A woman's voice answered on the phone.

"9-1-1 what is the nature of your emergency?"

"I need the sheriff and ambulance at Grant's Hill College in Eastford Chapel, we have an active shooter. This is Professor Joshua Stone."

Stone listened and heard some electronic tones, followed by the operator speaking.

"Stay on the line with me, sir," her voice shifted as she pressed the red button on the dispatch console, "6-30 and all units, caller is reporting active shooter at Grant's Hill in the Eastford Chapel," she returned her focus to the phone caller, "Sir, can you identify the shooter, can you see him?"

"The shooter is a student. Derek Underwood, he's about 20 years old and tall. Taller than six foot."

The dispatcher was typing Stone's words and Underwood's description to update the data terminals in the patrol cars. Multiple cars were acknowledging the call on her computer screen, she had two cars near the college: 6-30 Deputy Bill Simmons, and the School Resource Officer car at the high school;

the others were at least 10 minutes away. She pressed another set of buttons that activated a pager alert to the countywide EMS system. As she gave the dispatch for both ambulances in the county, she advised them to use the church parking lot as a staging area.

Monday morning following spring break was not an active time in the courtyard. Joshua did a quick scan and counted 13 students. He pushed the door with his right hand and still pressing the receiver to his left ear, began a new sprint across the grass. Bob Thornton had groomed the green space in the courtyard with diagonal passes of his mower. At a dead run, Joshua crossed each line marked by the tire tracks. As he passed the fountain he took the phone away from his head, "Get down, get out of here — get inside the Quad" he yelled.

The students looked up curiously and most laughed as the professor ran screaming at them while holding his cell phone.

Jack Reading had his own cell phone in his hand and made a quick movie of Joshua running across the quad that went viral on the Internet later in the day.

Joshua was running through the east Quad building when the operator spoke again, "Can you see the shooter? What is he wearing? Where is he standing?"

Frustrated, and slightly winded from his sprint, Joshua spoke in short bursts, "I can't see him... I'm running there now... He sent us a warning... He sent it to our offices... He's going to... shoot everyone... And burn... the place to... the ground."

As the dispatcher typed his words, the responding officers were updated:

"CALLER NOT WITH SHOOTER RECEIVED THREAT. NO DESCRIPTION OF CLOTHING AT THIS TIME. POSSIBLE FIRE." The dispatcher activated a second set of pagers for the fire department.

Joshua made the final dash to Eastford Chapel and then paused at the steps. He began a slower cadence up each one before reaching the doors. Just as Evans had instructed in the tactical course, the professor slipped the still connected cell phone into his shirt pocket.

Chapter 48

When you see your fylgja

ONCE AT THE WOODEN EXTERIOR double doors that opened into Eastford Chapel, Joshua stopped to catch his breath and look around him. His breathing fogged the glass as he peered through the small sidelight next to the doors. Inside, Liv was standing at the front of the room, just to the side of the wooden lectern. He counted 52 students in the chapel.

He strained to see the entire room and could not. With his left hand on the door latch, Joshua took one more deep breath, and pulled the door open. Inside, as he stepped through the doors, Liv stopped and all eyes turned to look at him. The room was silent.

It was a long, uncomfortable silence. The seated students looked half shocked and half amused. Joshua realized he hadn't slept, hadn't showered in two days, and hadn't shaved. Joshua looked at Liv, and then around the room at the familiar faces. He recognized them all, having taught most of them. Shelley Parmar, Connor Westwood, Tamara Banner were closest to him, sitting in the middle of Eastford Chapel in the last pew occupied by students.

He knew a story about each of them. Tamara Banner was leaving classes a week early to meet her birth father for the first time. She had made friends in her high school computer club and got their help as she searched for him. The group scoured online records and social media looking for any clue. They found him this fall and she called him at the end of September. She had written about it in Freshman Comp, saying the man sobbed when she first called him "daddy."

Connor Westwood was the first in his family to go to college. And one of the few to finish high school.

Shelley Parmar wrote a very funny essay about coming home for Christmas with two piercings: one in the eyebrow and one through the tongue and her parent's reactions. Joshua had laughed aloud while he graded it. He had urged her to find an agent and launch a career as a writer. He told her she had a gift.

Now, they were all looking back at their former professor. His heart fell, his stomach knotted. Perspiration ran down the small of his back. He stepped from the carpeted aisle and onto the stone tile floor between the pews. He sank into the pew in the back row, gradually, everyone turned his or her attention back to Liv, and she continued with her presentation.

The cell phone was still in Joshua's pocket. He stared at his feet, and then imagined sheriff's deputies bursting through the doors. It was time to admit paranoia had taken control of his imagination. At the same time, the drawings from Liv's office were very vivid; it was difficult to know if they were fantasy or therapy. He was certain Underwood killed Rex. He wondered if his rage had distorted everything else.

He imagined this was the feeling his father had on the side of the road the night he didn't find his way home from the hardware store. How years of living with a good mind could erode into something where reality and make-believe were confused as one. And instead of thinking he was a professional bowler, like his father's dementia, Joshua was playing make-believe cops and robbers. It was just a matter of moments before the sheriff's deputies would come in through the doors and he would just have to explain it all to them. He would take them back to look at the package Underwood sent and they could sort out what Underwood knew or didn't know about his attack.

As he expected, a large commotion rattled the back doors and the first of the men in tactical clothing entered the room. "Great," Joshua thought and he slumped his shoulders lower and leaned forward. "I called 9-1-1 for help and I traumatize a bunch of kids in the process."

The figure crouched and tossed a metal container that clanked as it skidded across the floor. Joshua wondered why the officer had decided to deploy a smoke canister and he prepared himself for the soon to follow pop and cloud of spray. The students looked up, perplexed at the sight of the soldier in their chapel.

Joshua felt his entire body stuck in a fear-filled logic loop. He struggled to move, he struggled to shout. He struggled to do anything as he realized the man in tactical clothing was not Simmons, or Wiggans or any responding officer. They were still minutes away. The person at the back of Eastford Chapel was Derek Underwood, just as he had drawn on the papers he sent in the package to Liv Olsson. Joshua saw the flash of the shotgun in the man's hands and he broke the grip fear held on his voice.

"Oh my God, this can't be happening," he said in a normal voice, followed by a louder outburst, "Oh shit!"

All the heads in the room turned in reaction to the profanity. Joshua yelled louder, "Gun! Everybody down, gun! Gun! Gun!"

It was then the man fired the first shot.

The 9-1-1 dispatcher heard the shotgun blast and Joshua's shouts over the cell phone in his shirt pocket. The dispatcher typed "SHOTS FIRED – CHAPEL" on her dispatch console and the message flashed across the screens of the patrol cars as the first two cars arrived on campus. Addison leaped from her car as it stopped and dashed to the trunk as Wiggans, who had been driving, popped the lid open from inside and joined her at the back. They strapped on ballistic vests, snugged down the Velcro, and sprinted to the exterior lower doors of Eastford Chapel. Wiggans and Addison made final eye contact and simultaneously cautioned each other, "Watch cross fire," and went to separate entries about 100 feet apart.

Bill Simmons drove over the curb and the patrol car's tires tore two trenches in the manicured lawn as it skidded to a stop at the far end of Eastford Chapel. Simmons sprinted towards the back doors.

Inside, the flash and sudden explosion of Underwood's first shot echoed through the back empty pews and the tall ceilings. Joshua turned his head to follow the blast back to Underwood.

The students, who had all been frozen with fear by the sight of their attacker, now scrambled, some up and running for the far doors, others diving to hide. Joshua watched as their faces, stricken with panic, began to vanish. Joshua's ears were ringing from the discharge of the shotgun; he heard his students' screams. He felt their fright. Some were moving behind pews, diving to the floor, hiding behind each other. Others seemed frozen in place, unable to move to safety.

Underwood pointed the shotgun at the closest row of students and pulled the trigger a second time. The blast from the shot struck the pew, splintering the thinnest sections and sending wood and lead shrapnel in several directions. Shelley Parmar and Connor Westwood had just dropped to hide behind the wooden backs.

The smoke from the canister filled the space quickly with a thin bluish veil.

Joshua's mind began to see impossible things in the melee. In some ways, it seemed very familiar. This was the active shooter scenario Evans told them about. The shock, the daze, the freeze of fear. Just three days ago, he was with Laura, Tina, Mike and the others, doing pretend versions of what was unfolding in front of him. With Evans, it wasn't real and it was fun to play along. Now that it was real, Joshua didn't want to play at all. He wanted to be out of the room, but he couldn't move.

In the drills, he was able to move, focus, and react. Now he was stiff and immobile. Each shot became more muffled and his vision began to narrow. The only movement he saw was Underwood. A second, small metal container spun across the floor and wedged against the middle pew, halfway up the aisle. When the final investigation was complete, the container would be identified as a one-pound propane cylinder rigged as a bomb. Its failure to detonate saved their lives that day. But in the moment, Joshua knew for sure was Derek Underwood was still determined to kill them all.

Joshua's attention moved from Underwood to the front lectern. Liv was standing, with her hands firmly gripping the sides of the lectern as she pushed her shoulders back and head up, assuming a commanding posture and defiantly staring at Underwood.

"Derek put down that gun, we can talk about this," she said calmly as she began to step sideways around the lectern to approach Underwood with arms outstretched in a more open and inviting manner.

Joshua looked at her with a pleading look, as if to force her to take cover behind anything that would keep her from being hurt. She shifted her focus from the student to the professor, and gave him a look of professional confidence, as if to say, "I know how to handle this."

Underwood racked the pump on the shotgun and fired again. Joshua first looked back to Underwood and then back to Liv. She had moved and was behind the podium on the floor.

There was a hollow sound of metal and Joshua turned his head back to see Underwood struggling with the gun. In his haste, he had jammed the pump action of the shotgun. Joshua had a final desperate thought of self-preservation, "Do something!" and struggled to get out of the pew.

There was no grace to his movement. It felt like a beginner basketball player's attempt to guard an experienced forward. He danced a clumsy, crouching half shuffle that mimicked a chimpanzee. He finally straightened to a half stand — half crouch and faced the shooter.

Joshua Stone was in the same room with the man who left him for dead in the parking lot and killed his dog. Underwood's expression wasn't human. He wasn't focusing at any one, even as he turned and faced Joshua. It was as if he was looking through the things and people around him and into some other time and place. Underwood's mouth was shaped into a chilling partial smirk, partial grin. It was unlike any expression Joshua had seen in his years standing before hundreds of students. The professor studied his attacker's face and was stunned. Underwood's face lacked any emotional connection to the mayhem he was creating.

Underwood flipped the jammed shotgun to his back. It clung close to his body, suspended by a sling draped around his shoulder. He yanked a pistol strapped to his leg and turned his attention to the only man standing: Joshua. He pointed the pistol at Stone and squeezed the trigger.

Ballistics testing and police reports would identify the pistol in Underwood's hand as a 9mm. A 9mm bullet travels roughly 1250 feet per second. The fraction of a second it took Underwood's bullet to travel the length of the aisle stopped in a bizarre, freeze-frame of Joshua's mind, as if it were a high speed movie or trick of the supernatural. Joshua's left hand went up on instinct to protect his body and in the millisecond of impact, Joshua's brain saw everything as if he were performing his classroom stunt: catching the stack of coins for amused freshmen. He saw the bullet and felt his hand close around the smooth hot shape, as if he could keep it in the palm of his hand and stop it from continuing. It was a split second of denial, his last denial, as it entered the flesh. With a new reality he watch the hole appear on the back of his hand as the bullet passed through and continued on its trajectory to the plaster and stone wall behind him. A small splash of blood spattered his face. Joshua continued staring at his hand.

Then Joshua Stone saw the white dog.

The dog was just at his feet and looked up at him with eyes that rapidly changed from curiosity to obedience. The two stared at each other, feeling the intensity of their bond and the stronger intensity of their impending separation. Both dog and the man knew this was their final walk together. Joshua stared at the dog's eyes, brown and clear. The dog stared back. He had seen the same look in Rex's eyes so many times. He wanted to hug the dog. To let it lick his face. To run his injured hand across its fur. Instead, he understood the dog had an important job to do.

The dog sprang from the floor and began running as the shooter's next 9mm bullet entered Joshua's left shirt sleeve and tore out the flesh on its exit. Joshua had turned his body to blade his position against the attacker who was beginning to move from the protection of the chapel pews toward the open aisle. Joshua's good hand was moving down to grasp his own pistol. In the few moments, the white dog covered the distance separating him from the shooter.

From his memory, and at the same time, Joshua Stone heard two voices talking to him. The first voice was Liv, telling him, "Seeing your fylgja is an omen of your impending death."

The other voice was Evans, screaming at him, "You're not dead until I say you are dead."

Joshua's inner voice responded with, "I've let you both down."

Joshua drew his pistol using one hand and as he brought it up and toward the center of his body, he took a step forward and pushed the handgun out into his field of vision.

His next emotion was rage. He'd been blindsided once by Underwood in the November assault. He had to do this, right now. 52 students placed their trust and minds in the hands of the college. Underwood had no right to take that from them. Liv was in this room. Connor, Shelley, and Tamara were in the room, too. The fiber optic front sight glowed as it captured the light from the windows and Joshua centered it on Underwood. The rear sights merged to form his sight picture, aligned squarely on the center of Underwood's chest. Joshua had practiced this over and over with Evans and the others for two days in the tactical course.

Underwood was ready to shoot again. Joshua feared that they were all going to die. This was awful. There was no way out. Joshua moved his finger from along the frame to the trigger as he saw the white dog leap and push Underwood's gun hand outward and away from his body.

Joshua pressed the trigger but the sound of the .40 caliber shot didn't register in his mind. He didn't hear his own gun firing. It was only the recoil pressure pushing his hand slightly up and mostly to the rear that gave him any hint the gun had discharged. He regained his sight alignment on the center of Underwood's chest and pressed the trigger a second time. Joshua half stepped and half hopped forward during the recoil, realigning his sight picture one more time. While he hadn't heard his own gunshots, his ears isolated and amplified his footsteps as they moved across the floor, with a sound that mimicked sandpaper on a coarse surface. Over that, the sound of his loud and deep breaths from breathing smoke-filled air remained constant, raspy, and rushed. Joshua now only cared about one thing: Underwood was still standing. Joshua found the sight picture he needed and pressed the trigger a third time.

Underwood's gun hand quivered and his pistol dropped with a thud on the carpeted aisle. Underwood's head twitched as if he were looking to the side and then his body collapsed.

Joshua stood still. It was the same firing sequence he had done with Evans. Before he lowered the handgun and just as in the drills, he looked left and then right and then behind him. He saw no one else in the room. There were no faces looking back at him. The white dog was gone. The smoke from Underwood's canister curled through the air. In the pause, he thought, "what next?"

He flashed back to the day he spent as Officer Down. Knowing that the sheriff's deputies were still coming, and he was the only one standing in Eastford Chapel holding a gun, he guided the handgun to his holster. Once it was secure, he drew another big breath and clasped his hands behind his head, unaware of the blood dripping from his injured left hand. He stood there, in the quiet, surrendered to the emptiness.

The cell phone in his pocket had transmitted it all to the dispatch center. The earlier shotgun blasts were recorded, followed by the newer sound of pistol shots. The three responders had made their assault plan while driving to the scene. They opted to enter from three doors instead of a single-door assault. Between radio talk and hand signals, they put their plan into play. Addison reached her door first, Wiggans, and Simmons were reaching the upper and lower doors just a few moments behind her. They knew she was ahead of them, and they knew her well enough to know she would rush the door and not wait for them. They ran faster, trying to catch up to her pace, even though both had a farther distance to cover. They wanted to be sure she had the backup she needed.

The experienced deputies, who had each spent hundreds of hours on a shooting range, were picturing the action in their minds. The shotgun blasts had stopped, and they identified the first pistol rounds being fired individually: bang...bang. As Wiggans and Simmons approached their own doors, they heard the louder .40 caliber rounds in rapid succession: bam bam bam.

ADDISON WAS RELYING ON INSTINCT. Part cowgirl, part cop. As she opened the door and was the first to cross the threshold, she sized up the crisis in the room. Ever since age 9 or 10, she had been walking into the unknown. As a child, it was walking into a dark barn in the middle of the night. She learned to use her hearing and smell to isolate the calf in trouble, or the goat with a breech delivery gone wrong. She had walked pastures for miles to find cows in the middle of snowdrifts.

As part of her tactical team making entry into a drug house, she could smell the adrenaline and predict which suspect was going to move, and which one was going to stay in place.

She moved through her door as soon as she got to the threshold. Standing in a vestibule, with the outer doors behind her, her view of the chapel in front of her was obscured. The Eastford Chapel scene brought all her senses to full alert. She could smell the gunpowder and smoke from the canister, and she could smell the blood. From the vestibule, she heard the same three rapid, .40 caliber gun shots Wiggans and Simmons heard from outside. She moved forward, trying to see through the smoke, and moved clear of the corner. She took an aggressive stance, planted her feet, and scanned the room, evaluating the things she could see through the haze. As her eyes swept the room, she saw the outline of a dead man with severe head trauma on the floor and made out the form of another man standing. She took it all in and acted quickly. She didn't see a pistol. Her sights were aligned in the high center of his back and she moved her finger from the frame of the pistol to the trigger. She knew her duty. She was prepared to kill at the slightest provocation. He was moving both hands up behind his head. His left hand was bleeding; she concluded he was hit. From behind her gun sights, she identified Joshua by the general shape of his body and his black hair.

"Down on the ground, do it now!" she ordered. With her concentration on Stone, she watched her periphery to be sure Wiggans or Simmons didn't cross into her line of fire if they entered the room. But for now, it was just the sergeant and the professor standing in Eastford Chapel.

Joshua dropped to one knee and rolled to the side. His arm was oozing blood through his shirt as he got down on the floor. She stepped close and slammed him face forward onto the carpet. Still holding her gun in her strong hand, she pressed Joshua down hard to the floor.

"Stay down, let me see your hands." She took each arm, brought it behind his back, and handcuffed him. He recognized both her scent and her commanding tone. There was a hint of fear in the woman's voice. No one else would notice it. Both of his hands were now behind his back, one oozing blood into a small puddle on the floor. Her knee pressed on the base of Joshua's neck and she continued to scan the situation around her. The dispatcher had updated her almost continuously for the last five to seven minutes so Addison knew it had been Joshua on the 9-1-1 call with the dispatcher.

She saw the shape of the gun grip under his jacket. Addison put the shooting scene together in her mind. She had heard the shots: The student came in shooting the shotgun and then switched to the pistol. Stone was hit, and the other guy was down. She looked over at the dead body. His pistol was on the floor, shotgun slung on his shoulder. Stone's gun was holstered.

"Damn, Doc, you stopped him," she said with shock and awe. Her mind raced as she considered the implications of the college professor killing an armed assailant. It would not turn out well for Joshua, the college, or the town.

Addison remembered they both carried the same gun model and the same caliber.

In the only moment of indiscretion in her career, Addison took her own pistol and placed it in the center pocket of her ballistic vest. She raised Joshua's jacket and reached into the holster between his body and the inside of his pants. She took hold of his pistol and pulled it free. She looked at it and looked at him handcuffed, lying face down on the floor in front of her with his head turned away. She paused and exhaled audibly, letting herself relax momentarily then put the barrel of his gun into her empty holster, and pushed it home. With his gun secure, she slipped his holster from his waist and into the cargo pocket of her pants.

At that moment, she assumed the public responsibility for his actions. The shooting was now a law enforcement intervention.

"Doc," Addison whispered, "don't say anything, don't talk to anyone. Stay down and don't move until I tell you to." Joshua could barely breathe, he was panting hard, his heart pounding to the point it ached. He felt like he had the strength of a dozen men. He knew something was odd about his hand, he had no comprehension that he had been shot twice. Addison said one more thing to him, "I'll get you home safe."

She heard the other two doors open as Wiggans and Simmons entered from opposite sides. Simmons looked around and saw Addison on top of Stone on the floor of the chapel. From his vantage, he could see several students cowering in fear and several others injured.

"Down, down, everyone stay down," he yelled. He exchanged a look and raised his eyebrows in a questioning manner at Addison who nodded in reply.

Simmons's tense voice spoke in the chapel and was echoed through the walkie-talkies

"Dispatch. Shots fired. Tango down, all deputies safe."

"Did you see him? Did you see what he was doing? He had so many guns. Why?" Joshua whispered to her, "Why did he do this to us? Why?" The adrenaline dump in Joshua's body continued to affect him. He began to shake, a tremor at first, it gradually grew in intensity to a near seizure. Joshua started to gag on his own vomit and Addison rolled him to the side. When he was done, she slid him back and rolled him back to his stomach. The shaking continued for several minutes.

As other responding officers entered Eastford Chapel, they kept their guns pointed in the general direction of the students scattered on the floor. In the next 30 minutes, more than 36 law enforcement officers from the Grant's Hill Sheriff's Department, highway patrol, game and fish department and neighboring towns arrived on the scene.

"Listen to me very carefully, everyone," Wiggans shouted. "Do not move, do not speak. A deputy will come to your side and do exactly as he tells you to do. Stay on the ground with your hands out to your side. Do not move."

One by one, a pair of officers approached each student, searched them for weapons, and then told them to stand up and exit the chapel.

Three of the student's faces were covered in blood and the officers quickly searched them and left them in place.

Other responding officers met each exiting student and took them to a grassy area between the chapel and the Quad. Wiggans keyed the switch on his hand-held walkie-talkie "Dispatch, we need 10-52 for gunshot wounds to multiple victims."

"10-52" was all Paramedic Sophie Carr needed to hear from the parked ambulance stationed in the designated staging area just off campus in the church parking lot. She nodded to Eric and her senior paramedic started the truck and they made their way towards Eastford Chapel. Sophie looked over her shoulder to the green median space, remembering her first intubation and the college professor who would have died without her help and the dog, mutilated and burned. Now she was going to a shooting. She smiled, thinking she had the coolest job in the world. She and Eric were met by Deputy Simmons and guided to the chapel interior.

"Be careful what you touch or move," Simmons instructed as they stepped along the outside of the pews, not walking down the center aisle.

They began to seek surviving patients. Sophie took charge. She scanned the room and first saw Underwood's head trauma and obvious lack of life. She began calling out audible triage color codes to her partner.

"Black."

Black was the designation for a dead patient. The remaining colors assigned a treatment priority. Green patients were the walking wounded, patients whose care could be delayed until last and were not critical. Yellow patients were more severe. Red patients would be the first into ambulances.

She next turned her attention to three students left in place by the officers. Their faces were covered with blood and tears. Sophie was at first confused by the amount of blood and their apparent signs of life. She expected they would be dead. She regained control. She looked at all three from across the room and gave them a command, a diagnostic test to see their general level of consciousness. "Tell me your names." All three looked back at her and two of the three spoke. The third moved her mouth, but her severe facial wounds and bleeding made it difficult for her to make a sound. "Two green, one yellow."

She then turned and scanned the room, seeing Addison standing and pointing down at Stone. She moved and saw the puddle of vomit and blood.

"Is he?"

"He's alert and responsive," Addison said back.

"Green."

Near the front of the room, Eric found a victim with obvious fatal head injuries. He caught Sophie's eye and said, "Black."

Sophie picked up her radio and connected with the dispatch center.

"Dispatch, we have two Black, one Yellow and three Green at this time."

Eric nodded at her and the two paramedics began taking care of their patients, and directing other responders to care and transport the wounded to Jefferson County Hospital.

CHAPTER 50

DEAN'S LIST

DEAN EGGARS RELEASED A LIST of names late in the day.
The names were:

Tamara Banner, age 20, injured
Shelley Parmar, age 20, injured
Connor Westwood, age 19, injured
Dr. Joshua Stone, age 42, injured
Dr. Olivia Olsson, age 39, deceased

The news media and informal Internet media scrambled to find
details, striving to be first with news and then hoping to backfill
any inaccuracies. The first two names they had were Joshua Stone
and Derek Underwood and half the media confused who was alive
and who was dead. Several wire services misreported which of the
two was the attacker. By mid afternoon, most were unofficially
identifying Stone as the hero calling 9-1-1.

While the stories were reversed and corrected, it fueled the
conspiracy theories and confusion. As the news spread into the
afternoon, media trucks and reporters began to flood Grant's Hill.
It would take several days for a consistent chain of events to be
reported.

When asked for the video recordings from the cameras in Eastford Chapel, Grant's Hill provided the recordings for review by investigators, and then, with their consent, the college approved their released to the public.

In the days that followed, the most replayed witness statement came from Tamara Banner, the girl who was weeks away from meeting her father for the first time. Her version described the shooting and the events in a way that best matched videotape security footage.

In the middle of Tamara's statement, the media pool grows remarkably quiet when she begins to weep as she says the words, "Dr. Stone saved everyone's life." In the moment that every photographer should have snapped a frame, they were uniformly silent. Then, the barrage of shutters drowns out her next word.

The video footage was very clear and sharp until the smoke blurred the view. In the footage, Derek Underwood is seen walking in the back door, tossing the smoke canister and pulling his shotgun up to aim. The video shows his first shot across the pews striking their wooden back. His second shot also strikes a pew, but the video does not show the injured students being struck.

Liv Olsson stands up and defiantly faces the intruder. Underwood's third shot strikes her violently and she collapses to the floor behind the lectern. The video shows his struggle with the shotgun as it apparently jams. Next, Underwood draws his pistol. Joshua's jerky side-shuffle-hop as he moves off camera is followed by Underwood's next two shots aimed directly at Joshua. The video does not show Joshua firing the three deadly shots from his pistol.

There is no white dog visible in the video or reported by any of the students or the responding officers. In the footage, Underwood's arm clearly flies to the side. The investigating deputies and coroner's conclusion is it was the impact of the first shot that caused the spasm.

The coroner's report would later say that all three shots that struck Derek Underwood were fatal shots, the original shot bifurcated the heart and the second shot severed his descending aorta. The third shot traversed the brain. The video also showed the entire exchange of bullets between Underwood and Joshua lasted 6.4 seconds. The entire rampage lasted 57 seconds.

In her pre-hospital report of emergency medical treatment, Sophie Carr reported she found Shelley Parmar, Connor Westwood, and Tamara Banner sitting, slumped on the floor, covered with blood. She identified each had severe lacerations over their faces from the wooden pew as it exploded from being shot by Underwood's shotgun. Later in the day, Jefferson County Hospital doctors would report that while not life threatening, all three students' injuries were severe enough to require dozens of stitches and reconstructive surgery to minimize scarring.

Tamara was struck by the empty, plastic shot cup from the shotgun cartridge and lost most of her left external ear as a result.

Wood splinters from the pew lodged in Connor's right eye and despite their efforts, doctors in the state capital ultimately removed the eye and fit him with a prosthesis.

Shelley, who's parents were enraged when she returned home for Christmas break with pierced tongue and eyebrow was struck in the cheek by a shotgun pellet. The through and through wound began where the shot pellet entered her left cheek crossed her oral cavity and exited her right cheek. The fact that she was screaming minimized the damage or the need for an oral surgeon. Her facial bleeding made her look to be the most seriously wounded, however, once the bleeding was under control, the resulting damage was minimal, leaving her with piercings that later healed to resemble dominant dimples.

One of the first photojournalists on the scene captured an image of Shelley, blood covered and in pain. She was strapped on an ambulance cot, being raised into the back of Sophie Carr's ambulance. It became the iconic image of the attack.

CHAPTER 51

THE PRESS CONFERENCE

ONCE AGAIN, PUTTING ALL THE pieces together was no easy task for the sheriff or the campus.

While Joshua was on his run to Eastford Chapel, Mrs. Thorn got up from her desk and calmly walked down the hallway to the president's office. She walked inside and informed President Rose and Dean Eggars that Dr. Stone was racing to warn Dr. Olsson of a disturbed student and they ought to come to Dr. Olsson's office.

The three of them walked down the hallway and when they got to a window, saw the sheriff cars arriving and then heard the shots.

"Oh my God," said Mrs. Thorn as she put her hand to her mouth and sat down. Brian Eggars turned to face the wall and Mathew Rose pressed his cell phone speed dial and connected with the president of the Board of Trustees. While Rose stepped out of the room to speak, Eggars turned to Mrs. Thorn's desk and looked down at the notebook.

The sketches confused then disturbed Eggars as much as they had Mrs. Thorn and Joshua. When he reached the last item in the sketchbook, Eggars unfolded the admission's department letter of denial. The dean looked at the drawing on the backside of the sheet with a stoic expression.

"Mrs. Thorn, ask my secretary to find Dr. Olsson, have her come here now." Hours later they all learned that Liv Olsson would never return.

By mid afternoon, the college, the sheriff, and the media had coordinated the first press conference. Dozens of cables were stretched across the courtyard in the Quad, and the podium was set up just south of the fountain. The mid afternoon light gave the cameras and video crews a cliché collegiate image. The major networks and several Internet sites fed either the live video or just audio. Standing near the podium were Rose, Eggars and Sheriff JB Jardine.

Jardine, who was known to everyone as JB, was a fixture in Grant's Hill. He controlled the politics and processes in local and many state elections. Jardine managed to be reelected for 8 terms, often with 65% of the votes. His no-nonsense approach attracted a few deep-pocket donors. Anyone running for public office in the county made sure to take two meetings: one with President Matthew Rose and the other with Sheriff JB Jardine.

Matthew Rose stepped to the microphones first.

"Good afternoon, everyone, I want to welcome you to Grant's Hill College. We understand you have a difficult job to do and we wish we were welcoming you under much different circumstances. My name is Matthew Rose. I am President of Grant's Hill College and I'm here to tell you what we know about the events on campus and the heroic acts of the faculty, students, and the Grant's Hill Sheriff's Department in containing a very dangerous situation.

"At approximately 8 a.m. this morning, a troubled individual attempted to harm a number of students and faculty in our chapel during a presentation. A faculty member identified the potential for danger, and called 9-1-1. His 9-1-1 call alerted the quick and timely response of the Grant's Hill Sheriff's Department who were able to immediately take control of the situation. As you know, two individuals died and four were injured. I am not able to discuss the criminal aspects of this case, but I am able to talk about the support our Grant's Hill Community is providing the students, faculty and great team of support staff we have at our college.

"We have sought counselors from neighboring colleges to meet with our students and faculty throughout the week. We will be suspending classes today and tomorrow and will resume our schedule Wednesday.

"At this time, we will take any questions you have."

Question: have you identified the shooter?

Jardine stepped to the podium to address the question, "We have positively identified the shooter as Derek Matthew Underwood, age 19 of St Louis, Missouri. His family has been notified. He is the single suspect in this incident."

Question: President Rose, is he a student?

Eggars stood closer to the center of the podium and leaned into the microphone.

"Good afternoon everyone. Welcome. My name is Brian Eggars, E G G A R S, and I am the dean of Grant's Hill College, Student records are confidential, and at this time, we are fully cooperating with the Grant's Hill Sheriff's Department. Mr. Underwood is not enrolled as a student on our campus and has not been a previous student."

Question: was the shooter targeting anyone specifically?

Jardine looked at Eggars and waited for a slight nod before stepping closer to the microphones.

"At this time, we believe his intent was to shoot anyone in the chapel and we have not identified any single target. We may learn more in the coming days about his intent. We have a thorough investigation ahead of us. We are the lead agency at this time, and we are requesting the assistance of the state crime lab and state investigators."

Question: what about the victims, what can you tell us?

From his papers, Jardine pulled the list authored by his department and the college. "The injured victims are: Shelley Parmar, age 20, Connor Westwood, age 19, Tamara Banner, age 20. All three are stable at this time and being treated in hospitals in the capital city. The final injury is Joshua Stone, age 42 of Grant's Hill. He is Professor of English at Grant's Hill College. The two fatalities are Dr. Olivia Olsson, age 39, and the shooter, Mr. Underwood."

Question: what is Professor Stone's condition?

The sheriff skimmed his notes again and answered, "We do not have his condition at this time."

Question: who made the call to 9-1-1?

Jardine was looking around at the cameras, lights and reporters. His focused shifted, not being sure who was asking the questions or where to look. On the video screen, his eyes appeared to shift from side to side.

"The 9-1-1 tape will be available to all media by 1530 hours today; please contact my office. The caller was Professor Stone, who called us while he was running to the scene."

Question: how did he know there was trouble? Did the shooter know Professor Stone?

Eggars sensed the sheriffs overload with the press queries and stepped forward.

"Grant's Hill is a small community and every one of our students and faculty know each other. As Mr. Underwood was not a student on our campus, I can say categorically they did not know each other in the context of our college. Any contact they may have had off campus is unknown to us at this time."

Question: we've heard reports of Underwood sending a notebook to the school. Can you confirm and if so, what did it contain?

Jardine looked at Rose and Eggars. "We are in possession of the notebook at this time. It is evidence. I cannot reveal its contents."

Question: how many shots were fired? What guns were used in the attack?

Jardine recognized the reporter from the network news channel she worked for. Hoping to impress her, he jumped in to answer the question.

"Our investigation is ongoing. We believe, based on the injuries to the students and early forensic evidence, that a shotgun was used and, based on shell casings found at the scene, that a 9mm pistol was also used in the attack. Multiple shots were fired. Underwood did throw an object which our bomb unit —

correction — our hazardous material team is investigating to determine if it is a threat or dangerous object."

Question: you said bomb, did he have a bomb?

The sly country politician smirk returned to Jardine's face and both Rose and Eggars grinned, knowing that if Jardine could charm the cameras, it would take some of the negative focus from the two of them.

"Whoa, take it easy on this small town sheriff, please. I know you do this every day, but this kind of thing doesn't happen here in Grant's Hill. Back in the day, we called it a bomb squad, because that's what we called it in the service." Jardine shrugged, took a breath and continued.

"After 9/11, these are the folks who look at everything from white powder in an envelope to a couple of road flares by the side of the highway. If our deputies see anything out of the ordinary, we ask our hazardous material team to analyze it." The reporters and photojournalists nodded, knowing they had a potential sound bite for the 6 o'clock news tease. The sheriff continued, "At this time, we are continuing our investigation and working to look at all angles of this case."

Jardine then delivered his best sound bite of the day,

"We are making available the security footage from inside Eastford Chapel. I need to urge you to warn your viewers. This footage does show the shooting of Dr. Olsson and of the suspect and it is graphic. We will release it with the strongest of warnings." That sound bite would be the lead in every local TV broadcast across the nation.

Question: another media outlet is reporting that a student claims a faculty member shot the suspect, is this true?

Jardine smiled, "When you work with witnesses, we know the fear and stress of an assault can make a confusing situation. I am not making fun of any witness, but when you've been Sheriff in a rural county as long as I have, you learn that witnesses see all kinds of things. Our job is to take everything everyone says, take it at face value, and let the facts combine to show us the likely truth. We do know a few facts and I can share them with you at this time.

"The coroner has confirmed the suspect was struck by three bullets and that any of them may have been fatal. The bullets were confirmed to be .40-caliber ammunition. In the video sequence, you can see each of the shots as it hits the suspect; his arm flies out to the side on the first shot, and the second and third shots are also fatal. The shooting was done exactly how we train our deputies to respond. With all due respect to my colleagues at Grant's Hill College, if you think a college professor can shoot like that under stress, send me his name. I'd like to hire him on my department."

Eggars seized the opportunity and added, "We are pleased Professor Stone was able to warn everyone and wish him a speedy recovery."

Jardine decided to have the final word, "Thank you all very much, we will have another press conference at 1530 tomorrow. That should be in time for you to make your evening news feeds and deadlines."

CHAPTER 52

UNOFFICIAL VISIT

JOSHUA WAS LOOKING OUT THE window at the horde of news vans in the circular driveway of Jefferson County Hospital. The medical staff had isolated him from any news on the radio or television. Joshua wasn't sure if he wanted to know the outcome. He tried to block the images of the faces looking back at him when he interrupted the presentation. And the lack of faces in the chapel when the shooting was over. The memories taunted him, urging him to wonder how many made it to safety. It was dusk and in the far distance he could see the light of Eastford Chapel, undimmed by the events of the day.

Silently, a woman stepped in through the partially open hospital room door, past the uniformed sheriff's deputy standing watch to limit media access. It was Jessica Addison and she broke the silence after watching him for a few moments, "I think you should know that was a damn good shoot."

Joshua turned, surprised to see her.

"Hi."

"Hi, how's your hand? Arm?" She looked concerned.

"You know, it burns, but it doesn't feel like I thought it would." Joshua answered.

"How did you think it would feel?"

"I don't know. I have no idea," Joshua smiled a half smile, "I like to think this is a social call, but I'm guessing you're here on official business. I need a lawyer, right?"

"Lawyer, why? Are you going to sue me for police brutality?"

"No, not sue you."

"Then no, you don't need a lawyer. Why would you need one?" Addison asked.

"Because of what I did. In the chapel, before you got there."

Addison looked out into the hallway and then closed the door.

"Um, about that. See, the official version is you didn't actually do anything, and in the official version, I'm not here."

Their eyes met.

"You're a terrible liar," he told her.

"Okay, I know. It goes with the badge. So this isn't a lie: Doc, you and I have the same gun. So let's just say that when I took my service pistol out of my holster and gave it to the sheriff, the gun I gave him had 3 rounds fired.

"What went on in Eastford Chapel, stays in Eastford Chapel. No one needs to know anything more than you did the right thing."

"But Sergeant — "

Addison stopped him. "Jesus, are you always like this? You are such a college boy. It's Jessica. It's time you started acting like you live here with us in Grant's Hill and call me Jessica."

"We need to do the right thing..."

"You did the right thing. Take your red pencil and make a period. You did the right thing, period. Now let me do the right thing."

He took a deep breath. Then another. She was always Sergeant Addison, it was right to call her that. And then from deep inside, he saw her as the only person who was close enough to understand what happened in the final seconds of Derek Underwood's life.

"Jessica," he looked into her eyes and found the strength to say, "I killed a man."

The words left his lips and hung in the air between them. It was his confession, both to her as officer of the law and to himself.

The finality of his words showed on Addison's face. Her eyes widened only slightly, but Joshua sensed their connection in the moment. They both knew that fractions of a second and the slightest change in actions could have resulted in his death, her death, and the deaths of dozens of students. But it didn't change the facts.

"Joshua, you did what you had to do."

He drew another big breath in and looked down at the bed sheets. There was a long silence before he turned to her again.

"Did I? Wasn't there another way? How will I know? I killed him. He's dead. Maybe I could have reasoned with him, maybe I didn't have to shoot."

"Doc. I'm going to say this now and I want you to remember it. You won't understand yet, but someday, there will be a time when you will. You should have died last November with your dog."

She shook her head, "I saw the crime scene, I saw you. I have no idea how you survived, but you lived. I never understood the reason.

"And today, hell, I still don't know...God, fate, luck? Underwood was shooting people and you stopped him. And you saved dozens of lives. The truth is you saved lives. But I know it comes at a heavy, heavy cost. I'm sorry Doc. What you will come to know, someday, is that you did the right thing." She pursed her lips and tilted her head slightly up and to the left.

"I've seen you. I've met dozens of victims. You are so strong — strong enough to work this through. The questions may never go away completely, but in time, you'll find the place for it and move on."

Joshua looked at her and saw her as a person for the first time. Her badge, her gun, her role, her title all fell away from his thoughts. He felt both vulnerable and protected. In her face, he saw that she shared the same feelings. They had just sealed a secret pact. This lie bonded them as blood brothers in bizarre, unspoken intimacy. In the moment, he remembered what trust felt like.

"The public doesn't have to know how you did it. You'll live in your own private hell long enough. You don't need their judgment, too. You're a hero for calling us and the world will always know you as the man who saved the day. It's a consolation prize, but it's better than the truth."

She leaned in closer to him.

"If the media thinks anyone other than the police stopped this, it just makes everyone's life worse. The only two people in the world who will ever know any different are you and me. You did what you had to do. I did what I had to do."

She smiled, rocked back on her heels, and folded her arms across her chest.

"So for now, I'm a desk monkey until the investigation is over — which it already is for the most part, except for the waiting.

"This is the official story, you called us, you ran to the Eastford Chapel — nice sprint by the way, some student posted you on the Internet, you've gone viral." She waited to see if her remark made him smile. The corner of his mouth turned, just slightly.

She continued, "You interrupted the class and you warned them about the shooter. No one will know you were carrying a gun on campus. That's our secret. Your gun is locked away, at the farm. When you're ready to have it back, let me know."

Joshua let what she was saying sink in. As it did, he asked the question he had avoided asking everyone else.

"Tell me, how bad is it? How many? I didn't save everyone, did I? A few are hurt?"

Addison looked over and pulled a chair up to the side of his bed. She sat down. She reached into her jacket and pulled out a paper copy of the dean's list of names. She unfolded it and looked up at Joshua.

"Three students were injured by Underwood, Doc. Tamara Banner, age 20, Shelley Parmar, age 20, and Connor Westwood, age 19."

Joshua rolled his eyes upward and exclaimed, "Oh dear God. I had every one of them in class. They were sitting right in the back row, I watched him shoot them."

He tried to rationalize the confusion in his head.

"I should have yelled faster, I should have tried to tackle him. How bad are they hurt?"

"Not bad, they went to the capital after being treated here. Everyone says they will live."

He took in what she was saying.

"Three..." his hand smoothed a wrinkle in the sheet as he repeated her words.

"They will all live? Good..." he thought a moment more and did a word play in his head.

"Oh wait, live — Liv? Does Liv know? Has someone told her? She'll want to go see them."

Addison set her jaw. Joshua felt a chill as he recognized her expression. He had seen it only once, when she told him about Rex. He never forgot how she looked.

The silence hung.

"No." He paused. "No." Slowly his body began to tremble as he brought his cast-covered left hand to his mouth. He looked everywhere in the room but at Addison. His right hand formed a fist around a clump of bed sheet.

"No, no no. Liv? No no no no. Not Liv."

His eyes finally came to rest on her face and they both sat looking at each other. Slowly breathing, listening.

In her academy days, she studied critical incident stress. She knew what was next; that after his body's initial adrenalin dump, the following energy crash would push him to sleep. She stayed at his side, shrouded in silence, until he nodded off. As he did, she slid the chair back, took the cell phone from her pocket, and nodded to the deputy at the door as she walked towards the elevator with the phone to her ear.

"Hi babe. I'm on my way home."

JOSHUA SLEPT FOR MOST OF the evening and woke around 10 p.m. Sophie Carr was sitting in the room.

"Hi, I was just going off my shift, and I wanted to see if you were still here."

Joshua nodded.

"So yeah, I just came by to say that we have got to stop meeting like this." She smiled and looked at him. "So …yeah."

"Thank you," Joshua said, "for the first time…and today."

She nodded and said, "I'm sorry for all you went through. I just came by to say thank you for being a great teacher."

Joshua looked at her face, not recognizing her from his classes.

"Are you at the college?" he asked.

"No, I just finished my paramedic school. It's just that, taking care of you taught me a lot and I just…want to tell you thanks."

"You're welcome," Joshua said.

As she left the room, Joshua saw a uniformed sheriff accompanying President Rose and Dean Eggars. They let the young paramedic move past them, then walked into his room and closed and latched the door.

"Dr. Stone, I'm Sheriff Jardine." Joshua shook his hand and the hands of the president and the dean with his good hand.

"Dr. Stone, my deputies tell me you were instrumental in stopping the attack, that you called 9-1-1 and disrupted the shooter long enough for our deputies to get there."

Joshua looked down, "Is this where you read me my rights?"

All three of the visitors gave a short, nervous laugh.

"Joshua, we have a major event here and you seem to be the one with all the answers."

Rose interrupted, "Joshua, we are so appreciative of what you have done. But tell us what happened?"

Joshua struggled with where to begin. As a storyteller, he debated starting at the beginning, but instead, picked up from the discovery of Underwood's notebook in the mail.

"I found a notebook Derek Underwood sent to the college, to Dr. Liv Olsson, and it showed disturbing images and drawings that just concerned me."

"So I called 9-1-1 and ran to Eastford Chapel, thinking he might be there. I just had a feeling he was going to do something bad. When I got there," Joshua paused to re-create the events.

"I heard the metal clunk, and then he shot me. That's when I..." he stopped, realizing that to go on would incriminate his role in Underwood's death, he was not sure what to say.

Jardine interrupted and boasted to Eggars and Rose, "That must be when my Sergeant Addison shot the suspect. We're very proud of her. It was a tough situation. We've got two heroes here."

Joshua stopped, Jardine didn't know? Addison didn't get there until after Underwood was dead on the chapel floor. He remembered her ordering him to the ground. Now as he thought about what he had done, he became disgusted. The rush of having survived was gone. His body shuddered as he pictured Underwood's lifeless form.

Jardine turned to Eggars, "Brian, I'd like to see any files you have on Underwood."

Eggars smiled, "You have our full cooperation and transparency, Sheriff."

Rose spoke up. "Joshua, we are truly fortunate to have you on our faculty. Is that all, Sheriff?"

Jardine nodded and left the room.

Eggars turned to Rose and then to Joshua. "Joshua, you've been through a lot this year, that tragic event off campus, and now this. And you lost your dog. Joshua, we would fully understand if you wanted to take an early retirement."

"Retire? I'm only 42. I'm in the middle of a book. I can come back."

Eggars continued, "Well that's just it Joshua, you can't really come back, can you?"

Rose began speaking, "I've met with the trustees, Joshua, and in recognition of your service, we'd like to offer you a retirement package at half your salary until age 62 and then you can access your retirement accounts."

Joshua stopped, did some quick mental math and expressed his disbelief, "This isn't about retirement. You think I'm going to sue you. A million dollars? You're buying my silence for a million dollars?"

Eggars said, "Well, yes, we would like you to sign a non-disclosure agreement and—"

"I've been beat up and shot and now you want to fire me and buy my silence?"

Rose sounded conciliatory, "Joshua, no, you are a valuable faculty member, we are just..."

Eggars resumed, "Concerned for your well being." Just then Moore and his beaming smile walked in the door.

"So, Joshua, they tell me you are gonna retire, whoa, what a deal, now you can write all day."

Rose looked at Eggars, Eggars looked at Joshua and Moore. Joshua recalled Moore's advice when he accepted his job offer and looked back at Eggars:

"Full salary, no less, to age 62." Eggars didn't blink, Rose nodded. Eggars jotted on some papers he pulled from his briefcase and handed them to Joshua to sign. Rose signed when he was done. And the two men left.

Moore smiled, "So I guess this means you won't be telling the Joke Friday, huh?"

CHAPTER 54

THE CALL

THE BRIGHT LIGHTS FROM THE media trucks shined through the window most of the night as Joshua lay in bed, staring at the ceiling. At 55 minutes past each hour, the lights would brighten for about five minutes, he guessed that a media reporter did a live-from-the-scene update, and then the lights would dim until the next hour.

Annette was off on retirement. Rex was dead. Liv was dead. Moore, Adams, and Neal were good friends; but he assumed that outside of college, they would seldom meet. He considered traveling, maybe enjoying his new retirement by couch surfing in the homes of his Christmas card list. If he stayed with a different one each a week, he could surf for nearly four years. Had David Adams already done that very thing? If not, David knew someone who had done it for five years. Alan Neal was always bragging about his summer place out west. Maybe this was the year to go see it. Joshua Stone reflected back on his life. He started kindergarten at age five and now, at age 42, was leaving school for the first time. This was the first fall he wouldn't to return to a campus.

Joshua reached across to the rolling bedside table and slid out the drawer. He found his wallet and opened it, looking for the card given to him by Sergeant Addison when they met. He picked up his cell phone and stared at the card, then looked at the phone and dialed the number.

He almost hung up after the second ring, but as he pulled it away from his ear, the call connected and he heard a woman's voice on the other end of the line.

"Good afternoon County Victims Services - Rape Crisis Center, my name is Diane how may I help you?"

Joshua winced as he heard the words "victim" and "rape crisis." And then he began to tell his story to the stranger on the other end.

"My name is Joshua Stone and in November, I was assaulted and it happened again this week. I..."

He paused. It would be easier to hang up, and then, he remembered he had told her his name.

"I'm calling today," tears began to fill his eyes. He drew a deep breath to find the words.

"I'm calling you because, I need some help. And I've lost everyone who matters to me and everything I cared about..."

"Joshua, I'm here to help and to listen. Are you in a safe place now? Are you in any danger?"

Joshua looked around the hospital room.

"No, I mean, yes. I mean, yes I am safe and no I'm not in any danger I'm in the hospital."

"Thank you for sharing that with me. Joshua, tell me what happened?"

He started in November, and walked her through the details of his assault, the recovery, his fear and suspicions and ended with the shooting scene on campus. It was the first time he had actually said some of the details aloud. It was the first time he heard his voice say 'my friend Liv is dead.'"

He wanted to confess, too. He needed to tell the story of killing Underwood. But he was bound to keep it concealed. He listened as she shared some ideas about talking and coping, and near the end, she suggested he come to a victim's group meeting the next day.

"Come visit us, talk with the group. You are not alone," she told him, and then continued, "we're located in the same building you are, we're at Jefferson County Hospital. Just come and listen. You are not alone."

Joshua nodded as he held the phone. Diane could not see the nod, or know the appreciation Joshua had as he began to tell his story.

He met the group for the first of many weekly sessions the following morning. Joshua listened to their stories, and often cried with them, and for them, as together, they all tried to come to terms with how violence had changed their lives.

They only used first names, and Joshua sometimes wondered if the names were real, but it didn't matter. Tina, a woman in her thirties, was there because her live-in boyfriend shot himself on the deck of their doublewide trailer. Patti, slightly older, had a broken arm after her husband threw her down a flight of stairs. Alycia, who looked to be college age, had been raped and beaten after a night of underage drinking at a party.

What stunned Joshua was their collective sense that they had each done something to deserve what happened to them. He told each one that they were not to blame.

When it was his turn to speak, he told his story. They knew parts of it from the news reports. What was different about the group was their interest. The media was most interested in Underwood, who he was and why he shot up a chapel filled with students. Tina, Patti, and Alycia and were interested in hearing Joshua's pain and feelings. It helped him when they repeated his own caring words back to him, "Joshua, it wasn't your fault."

PART ELEVEN

AFTERMATH

CHAPTER 55

THE CIRCUS LEAVES

FOR THE SECOND TIME IN less than half a year, Joshua was taking a discharge ride in a wheelchair down the hallway of Jefferson County Hospital. As they approached the long corridor that led to the front lobby doors, Deputy Simmons came alongside him and turned him down a side hallway.

"Doc, there's about five news trucks outside in the parking lot and about seven in front of your house. If you don't mind, why don't you ride with me?" When they got to the end of the hallway, they met Wiggans and Addison.

"Hey Doc. I get to be you today," Wiggans said taking the corduroy jacket from Joshua's hands. He held it up in front of his face "See, I look like you" and with that, he and Addison headed for the front door. When they got there, there was an instant commotion as Addison put Wiggans, holding the jacket in front of his face, into the back of a squad car and drove off.

Simmons and Joshua strolled out to Simmons' car.

"Here's how this will go, I'll pull up in your alley behind your garage. They'll pull up to the front and just beyond your door. They will get out, you walk into your house, by the time the news folks all figure out it's a bait and switch, you'll be inside. Stay there or talk to them, that's up to you."

Joshua looked at Simmons and reached out to shake his hand. "Thanks."

Simmons grinned, "Just remember, Doc, this is twice you owe me."

"Twice? Why?"

Simmons flipped his sunglasses onto his face and turned the ignition on the car. "Today is two. The first time is when you planted those seven paint ball rounds on my chest in the tactical house."

Joshua remembered Evans telling him he wasn't dead and then firing at the unidentified threat in the helmet.

"Oh jeez, yeah, sorry about that." Joshua said sheepishly.

Simmons looked over. "I'm still pissed." He said then smirked, "But there's about 50 lucky kids who are alive because of it. You keeping us informed until Addison could drop him saved a lot of lives." Simmons pulled the car out of the hospital parking lot and drove to Grant's Hill.

As planned, Addison drove just beyond the driveway and made a big show of getting out of the car, and ordering some media folks to step back.

She took a long, slow, intentional look around, with her hand on her hip, and then walked around the front of the car. She got to the rear door on the curb side and then paused as she reached for the handle. The photographers pressed close to get a photo of 'Professor Stone' in the back seat, the tinted windows and cage made it impossible to see inside.

While the distraction was going on in front of the house, Joshua walked along the garage, hobbled up the side steps, and into the kitchen where he closed and locked the door. Through the front shades, he watched as Wiggans stepped out of the back seat of the car, acting as if nothing was unusual and he and Addison then walked up and down the sidewalk, asking the media to be sure they were not blocking sidewalks and driveways and reminding them to be courteous to the neighbors.

The media circus camped in front of Joshua's house for 3 more days. By Saturday, a woman in Phoenix was admitted to the hospital to give birth to quintuplets, and the circus packed its vans and antennas and moved on, taking the story of Grant's Hill off page one.

While they were camped outside his home, Joshua took down the diagram from his office wall, and began putting weeks of trash into plastic bags. It was a slow, one-handed process.

He shook his head at the chaos of articles, sketches, web pages and notes, along with the color-coded pushpins and yarn strands. He understood what each paper said, and its literal meaning, but now, in his present mind, he saw the real story it told: confusion and anger.

The Monday after the media trucks left, he carried the trash bags out to the large container and pushed it to the curb. He waited there in the morning light for the garbage truck to come by and he waved as the truck's arm lifted the container up and into the back of the compactor, listening as the hydraulics compressed it all into a mass destined for the landfill.

He walked into the house, and raised each of the window blinds in the main room, looked around, and then walked to his office bedroom where he opened the closet, retrieved the winter and spring garment bags, and rearranged his wardrobe for the season. As he spread the clothes across the bed, he moved the disconnected telephone cord out of the way, wrapping it into a loop and setting it on the floor. He had unplugged his phone after the first night of strangers calling. They wanted to ridicule him, pray for him, sell his life story, or borrow money.

He asked the telephone and the cell phone companies to change his numbers, and he was looking forward to sending the new numbers out to his friends.

When he did, the conversations felt forced and brief. Even the normally supportive David and Ellen Adams said less than usual. When he brought this up in his group counseling, the others in the group said the same thing about their friends. He remembered Liv telling him people didn't know what to say. There would come a time when he and David and Ellen could talk about the pain they all shared. David had already told him he'd secured a book contract to write about the rampage on campus.

He knew David would ask him about what went on inside the chapel. Joshua hated the idea of lying to his friend. Even more, he hated that his friend would never be able to know or write the whole story. For now, he consoled himself with Ellen's words, "Let us know if you need anything."

Anything? Mostly, he needed time. He found his mind drifted off and many times each day he would realize he had been sitting, just sitting. Every time that happened, he made it a point to call someone to talk. The short conversations began to grow longer. He picked up the piles of mail, sorted and filed the necessary bills, and returned the Christmas ornaments to their plastic box and slid it under his bed. He met once each week with Dianne, and once each week with the group. He told them everything he could say, and what he couldn't say, he wrote about. At the suggestion of the group, he began writing his emotions in a journal.

He thought about Patti, the woman in group with the broken arm, as he was cleaning his bedroom. He smiled because she was the kind of person who spoke it like she saw it, "You're the damn writer, write." She made it sound so easy.

He was on his hands and knees, using the suction tube of his vacuum with his good hand when it picked up an object that rattled in the flexible tubing. He shut the vacuum off and let the noisemaker fall out onto the hardwood floor. It was the ammunition cartridge he had taken out of the gun the first night he carried his pistol, the night of the Christmas Gala.

Joshua held the cartridge in his hand and flashed back to the visual and word montage he had created that night on his dresser and in his mind.

He spoke aloud as he held the cartridge up to his face, "Holster, magazine, cartridge, gun."

Addison had offered to return his pistol when he was ready. He looked at the cartridge and thought about the events of the last few weeks. He set it down and found his wallet, took out her business card, and dialed the number. He did a quick gut check and waited. Her voicemail picked up, and he waited for the beep.

"Sergeant, er, Jessica. Hi, it's Joshua. I'm ready. Whenever works for you."

Later that day she showed up in his driveway. She nodded and handed him a box. Neither of them spoke, but just looked at each other with a confident, connected nod. She put the patrol car into reverse and Joshua spoke up as she neared the end of the driveway, "Hey Addison?"

She looked up at him.

"Gear check?" he said, mimicking her.

She grinned, "Everyday."

He nodded and smiled back, "Everyday."

It was Friday night when Alan Neal came to Joshua's house with a six-pack of beer and two cigars. Neither of the men were habitual cigar enthusiasts, but both accepted the gesture of sharing a smoke together as a metaphoric peace pipe, acknowledging that all had been forgiven. They were sitting on the front step, talking about basketball when Alan brought up the idea.

"Come with me this summer. Hang out at my place in the Rockies. It's big enough. You can crash on the foldout bed. You can meet my neighbor. But don't get any ideas, she's sweet on me."

Joshua scoffed at his friend, "Are you kidding me, she'll forget you the moment she meets me," he turned his left cheek towards Neal "chicks dig scars, she'll be all over me."

"Oh Joshua, that's no scar. That's a dang razor burn. You're gonna make a big deal out of this, just like your damn nose." Neal puffed his cigar and Joshua took a swig of beer, both men laughing.

The following week, Joshua was standing in Tina's checkout at Royal's waiting for the woman in front of him to move her cart ahead. He was looking at the chewing gum, candies and impulse-buy items, trying to figure out what was missing. When he stepped up to Tina at the register, he realized what was gone.

"Tina, what's up with the tabloids? Did you finally decide to stop selling them? How will I know who's having my love child?" he said as a joke.

Tina blanched for a moment and glanced over at Howard the manager. Howard walked over to the two of them.

"Hi Dr. Stone. I guess you noticed."

"Noticed? I was just teasing, you know, I never know who any of those people are."

Howard reached under the conveyor belt and pulled up a stack of tabloids. "You might as well see these."

The manager fanned out a stack of magazines and tabloid papers. Joshua looked at half a dozen newsprint photos of himself, Grant's Hill, and Derek Underwood. The most common cover photo was of Shelley Parmar, reclined on the ambulance cot. One of the tabloids had highlighted the image of a plain clothed state police officer holding a rifle, with the caption, "Second gunman! What do we really know about Grant's Hill?"

The embarrassed professor read the headlines:

"Once Bitten, Twice 'Bye! Assaulted Professor Retires"

"Which Teen Idol Most Wants Private Tutoring from Sexy Prof?"

"Stone Cold Dead - Shooter Killed on Campus"

"College Professor Saves Students, is Looking for Bigfoot"

"Hear no Evil, See no Evil, Speak no Evil, Injured Students Speak Out on College Violence."

"The Joshua Stone Diet: From this to *this* in 6 weeks"

"Where do they find all these pictures?" he was half laughing, half shocked.

Tina blushed and looked at her register keys. Joshua studied at the "before" and "after" photos of himself and concluded they were digitally enhanced. He confessed to the two of them, "I haven't talked to any reporters."

"Well, Dr. Stone, now you know how these things get here. You're one of the celebrity set now."

He flipped one more tabloid over and saw Liv's coneflower blue eyes staring back at him. She was in a photo with her sister in Sweden. They were on a sailboat with a red boathouse in the background. Joshua had never seen it, but it looked like the boathouse Liv described once at his summer party. She looked confident, soulful, alive.

He took the index finger of his cast-covered, left hand and traced the edge of her cheek in the photo.

"She was pretty, did you know her?" Tina asked.

Joshua continued looking at the photo.

"She wasn't from this country, was she? Shame such a pretty girl dies so young," then Tina added, "and single, too."

Joshua smiled, "You know what she would say about all these stories?" He turned the magazine away and looked at the two of them.

"You don't say me like that."

Chapter 56

The van

WHEN HE ROLLED INTO HIS driveway, he put the bicycle in the garage and carried the groceries in the house, taking time to put each item away in the cupboard and refrigerator. He took care folding the reusable canvas grocery bags, and then walked out to the garage and placed them in their shelf next to the trash container. The sun was setting; the amber glow made the neighborhood look pristine and warm. He drew a breath. Mrs. Jenkins opened her side door and smiled and waved, but didn't say anything. He smiled and waived back.

Down the street, he noticed a dark van slowing down in front of the houses at the corner and then moving forward before it came to a stop at the base of his driveway.

A man in his 70s got out of the driver's seat, walked around the front of the van, looked at a piece of paper and the address on Joshua's house. Joshua approached him with caution, stopping at the halfway point of the driveway. The visitor wore a pale blue jumpsuit, with a fabric belt and some patches on his sleeves and across the back. It reminded him of something his dad would wear.

"Can I help you?"

"I bet you can. Beautiful day, isn't it? I'm looking for Stone." The man's voice was crisp. "Are you Stone? Joshua Stone?"

"Yes, I am, but I'm not giving interviews, sorry."

"Good," the older man continued walking around the front of the van, taking slow, measured steps.

"Neither am I." He waved his hand and moved to the back of the van and fiddled with the latch.

"Can I ask who you are and what you want?"

"Me? I'm Darrel. I'm a volunteer with Rescue America." He pointed at one of the patches on his sleeve.

"Look, I'm not interested in your pitch, okay? I'm not in the mood." Joshua began to turn back to the house.

"Pitch? No, no. Don't you know who we are?"

The man squinted through thick glasses and then said, "Here."

He patted a few of the pockets on the jumpsuit, then walked up to Joshua and handed him an envelope that was hand addressed with a woman's handwriting. The return address was Ohio. As Joshua opened the letter, the man went back to the rear of the van.

"Dear Dr. Stone,

"I don't know if you remember me, but I am Shannon Lewis (well you knew me as Shannon Brooker). I was a student of yours the year you found Rex. I wasn't a very good student and, well, I think you knew I had a tiny crush on you.

Anyway, I'm married now and I have 5 beautiful children and I am living my dream. I run a dog rescue with my loving husband — he's the greatest man in the world — and I live on 30 acres in southern Ohio.

When I heard what happened to your beautiful Rex, I was heartbroken, but every dog is a gift, we just don't know how long they will be with us. Rex was so blessed to have you in his world, and that you gave him a second life. You are my hero and my inspiration.

I know time heals all wounds, and I hoped maybe enough time had passed that you would be ready. Please welcome this beautiful puppy into your life..."

As he read that line, Darrel opened the back of the van and retrieved a German Shepherd puppy on a leash. The dog jumped, turning left and right, looking down at the ground and then playfully turned to snap its jaws at the leash connected to his collar. The puppy strutted to Joshua's side and sat, as if on command.

"Well look at that?" Darrel said.

Joshua knelt down and the dog gave a quick lick to his face and then remained focused on his surroundings.

Darrel shook his hand. "Good luck to both of you. She's a lucky dog."

"Did you drive this dog all the way from Ohio?"

"Nope, somebody got him as far as the capital, I drove him down from there, that's where I live. I go all over, helping these guys get to their new homes."

Joshua looked down and then watched as Darrel got back in the van and drove away. The dog looked up at Joshua and Joshua looked down at the dog. "Come" and the two turned and walked towards the house.

When they got inside, Joshua took off the leash and renewed an old habit by hanging it on the hook by the door. Joshua felt the Stone house beginning to feel like a home again. The dog roamed from room to room, stopping to smell the corners and look around at its new surroundings.

The sunlight streamed in the windows as Joshua sat down on the office chair and the dog walked the perimeter of the room and then lay down next to Joshua.

He looked at the dog's classic German Shepherd markings and large paws. In the time he owned Rex, he learned more about dogs and knew that this dog would be much bigger than Rex. He had no idea of the dog's age but he could tell that the puppy was too big to ride on the bicycle and too small to run along side, so after rummaging through the collection of boxes in the garage and finding some of Rex's toys and his bed, he decide to take the dog on a walk. The two of them walked to the end of the driveway and turned down the sidewalk.

As the spring sunset faded in the sky, Joshua whispered to the dog, "There's someone you have to meet," the dog turned upon hearing the sound of his voice.

They cut across the grass, stopping every few trees for the puppy to sniff or mark his territory, and at last they came across a large area of fresh sod. Bob Thornton and his crew had worked invisibly in the weeks following the rampage to erase the tire tracks from Simmons' patrol car and the trampled footpaths of investigators and media. Joshua stood at the edge of the sod, looking at the lush green color and breathing in the night air.

In the middle of the sod was a polished, round granite sphere, about the circumference of one of his bicycle tires. It had a flat rectangular face, chiseled with the name: Olivia Olsson and her birth and death dates. A small blue flag with a gold Scandinavian cross was moving in the gentle breeze, stuck in the ground at the base of the memorial. On both sides were a mound of flowers, cards and stuffed toys. The dog sniffed at the mementos and then sat, looking at Joshua.

"This...this...is in memory of my friend Liv. Liv Olsson." The dog looked at the man as his voice quivered slightly.

"Liv, I am so, so, sorry. Every day I wish I could take back what I said to you. Every day I wish I had done more to save you."

He sat down in the grass, propping himself with his good hand and resting the cast-covered left hand in his lap. The dog licked his face.

Joshua turned to the puppy. "You're a licking thing, aren't you?" The dog batted at the man's face with his paws, wagging its tail.

"Liv tried to get me help." The dog slipped and rolled to his side and then sprang up. It spotted a stuffed tiger in the pile of toys and began to growl protectively.

"She was going to make me semla for Fat Tuesday. It's some kind of pastry, I guess." Joshua looked around and stared up at the stars. He lay down on the grass and the dog curled up in the bend of his elbow.

"I uh," he paused and drew a breath, "I scared her once. I was out of control and mean and hurt and angry," he stopped. "I never got a chance to say 'I'm sorry' and 'I was wrong.'"

He blew out a breath of air through pursed lips. The dog cocked its head, looking at his new master.

"So I brought you here to meet her. This is Liv Olsson."

He scratched the dog's head several times.

"Liv, did you ever work with a student named Shannon Brooker? She sent me this puppy and I wanted you to see her."

The light from the spire of Eastford Chapel made it possible for Joshua to see his face, reflected in her name on the polished stone. He sat quietly for a few minutes before he spoke again.

"Liv?" he paused, listening for her accent. He waited a moment more. With another sigh from deep within his heart, he accepted the feeling she was gone.

"I heard what you told me…about getting help. That it wouldn't go away without help. I'm getting some. I should have listened sooner. I am so, so sorry this happened."

Joshua folded his arms, bracing his cast with his right hand.

"So…" he looked at the dog, "This is Liv and Liv, this is…"

Joshua realized he hadn't given the dog a name.

"Liv, I want you to meet…Fylgja, my new protector."

ACKNOWLEDGEMENTS

Cover photo courtesy of ATK Federal Premium ammunition. Used with permission.

Excerpt from *Call of the Wild* by Jack London, originally published 1903. The work is now considered public domain.

Excerpt from *Pride and Prejudice* by Jane Austin first published in the United States in August 1832 as *Elizabeth Bennet or, Pride and Prejudice*. The work is now considered public domain.

Excerpts from G.K. Chesterton *The Man Who Knew Too Much*, originally published 1922. The work is now considered public domain. *Heretics* copyrighted 1905 by the John Lane Company. The work is now considered public domain.

Post-it® is a registered trademark of 3M Company

Skeppshult is a trademark owned by Skeppshultcykeln AB

Carhartt® is a registered trademark of Carhartt, Inc.

S&W® is a registered trademark of Smith & Wesson

Tupperware® is a registered trademark of Tupperware Brands Corporation

Taser® is a registered trademark of Taser International, Inc.

KYDEX® Sheet is a registered trademark of KYDEX, LLC.

MMPI® is a registered trademark of the University of Minnesota, Minneapolis, MN

VELCRO® is a registered trademark of Velcro Industries, BV

ABOUT THE AUTHOR

F.R. "Fritz" Nordengren writes, farms and cooks at Two Mile Ranch, a small, heritage breed poultry farm and home to the Iowa Writer's Retreat. Online at www.twomileranch.com

www.ingramcontent.com/pod-product-compliance
Lightning Source LLC
Chambersburg PA
CBHW071153020726
47502CB00002B/393